Alfred J. Church

Callias

A tale of the fall of Athens

Alfred J. Church

Callias
A tale of the fall of Athens

ISBN/EAN: 9783743318212

Manufactured in Europe, USA, Canada, Australia, Japa

Cover: Foto ©Andreas Hilbeck / pixelio.de

Manufactured and distributed by brebook publishing software
(www.brebook.com)

Alfred J. Church

Callias

SOCRATES AND ALCIBIADES.

CALLIAS

A Tale of the Fall of Athens

"Athenae Lysandro superfuerunt: occiso Socrate tum demum civitas eversa est."

BY

REV. ALFRED J. CHURCH, M. A.

Professor of Latin in University College, London

MEADVILLE PENNA
FLOOD AND VINCENT
The Chautauqua-Century Press
1891

The Chautauqua-Century Press, Meadville, Pa., U. S. A.
Electrotyped, Printed **and Bound by Flood** & Vincent.

CONTENTS

CALLIAS

A Tale of the Fall of Athens.

CHAPTER I.

A NEW PLAY.

IT is the second year of the ninety-third Olympiad *
and the Theatre at Athens is full, for the great dramatic
season is at its height, and to-day there is to be performed
a new play by Aristophanes, the special favorite of the
Athenian public. It is a brilliant scene, but a keen observer.
who happened to see the same gathering some five
and twenty years ago, must now notice a certain falling off in its splendor. For these five and twenty years
have been years of war, and latterly, years of disaster.
Eleven years ago, the City wild with the pride of power
and wealth, embarked on the mad scheme of conquering Sicily, and lost the finest fleet and army that it
ever possessed. Since then it has been a struggle for life
with it, and year by year it has been growing weaker and
weaker. This has told sadly on the glories of its great festivals. The furnishing of the stage, indeed, is as perfect as

* According to our reckoning B. C. 406.

ever, and the building itself has been pushed on several stages towards completion. * However scarce money may be in the public treasury, the theatre must not be starved. But elsewhere there are manifest signs of falling off. The strangers' gallery is almost empty. All the Greek world from Massilia in Gaul to Cyrene among the sands of Africa used to throng it in happier days. Now more than half that world is hostile, and the rest has little to hope or fear from the dispossessed mistress of the seas. Dionysius of Syracuse, has sent an embassy, and the democracy, which once would have treated with scant courtesy the representatives of a tyrant, is fain to flatter so powerful a prince. There are some Persian Envoys too, for the Persians are still following their old game of playing off one great state against another. A few Greeks from Sinope and from one of the Italian cities, persons of no importance, who would hardly have found a place in the gallery during the palmy times of Athens, make up the company of visitors. Look at the body of the theatre, where the citizens sit, and the spectacle is deplorable indeed. The flower of Athens' sons has perished, and their successors are puny and degenerate. Examine too the crowd that throngs the benches, and you will see that the slaves, distinguished by their unsleeved tunics, fill up no small portion of space. And boys form an unusually large proportion of the audience. Altogether the theatre is a dispiriting sight to a patriotic Athenian.

To-day, however, all is gaiety, for, as has been said, there is a new play to be brought out, and an Athenian must be

---

* It was not actually finished till twenty-three years later.

in desperate straits indeed, if he cannot forget his sorrows
at a new play.

When the curtain rises, or rather, is withdrawn, as the
Greek arrangement was, into an opening in the floor of the
stage, a murmur of recognition runs through the audience.
The scene is the market place of Thebes, and a familiar
figure occupies the foreground.

The portly figure, the ruddy face, the vine-leaf crown,
and the buskins show him to be Bacchus, the patron-god,
it will be remembered, of the Drama. But why this lion's
skin and club? The god gives a lordly kick at the door of
the house which was one of the familiar stage-properties,
and Hercules appears. He roars with laughter to see his
own emblems in such strange company. Bacchus explains.
"The tragic poets grow worse and worse. There is not one
who can write a decent line. I am going down to the
regions of the dead to fetch Euripides, * and thought that
I had better dress myself up in your fashion, for you, I
know, made this same journey very successfully. Perhaps
you will tell me something about the way, and what inns
you can recommend, where they are free from fleas, you
know."

" Are you really going ? "

" Yes, yes. Don't try to dissuade me; but tell me the
way, which must not be either too hot or too cold."

" Well there is the Hanging way, by the sign of the Rope
and Noose."

" Too stifling."

" There is a very short cut by the Mortar and Pestle."

* Euripides had died a few months before.

"The Hemlock road, * you mean?"

"Exactly so."

"Too cold and wintry for me."

"Well; I'll tell you of a quick road and all downhill."

"Excellent! for I am not a good walker."

"You know the tower in the Cemetery? Well; climb up to the top when the Torch race is going to begin; and when the people cry out 'start,' start yourself."

"How do you mean 'start'? Start from where?"

"Why, start down from the top."

"What, and dash my brains out? No, not for me, thank you."

So it is settled that Bacchus and his slave, for he has a slave with him to carry his baggage, shall take the usual route by the Styx.

To the Styx, accordingly, they make their way. Charon the ferryman is plying for hire, "Any one for Rest-from-toil-and-labor Land? For No-Mansland? For the Isle of Dogs? †"

Bacchus steps in, and by Charon's order, takes an oar which he handles very helplessly. The slave has to go round: Charon does not carry slaves, he says. As they slowly make their way across, the frogs from the marsh raise the song of their kind, ending with the burden which is supposed to represent their note, *Brekekekex, coax, coax.*

It is pitch dark on the further side. When the slave turns up, he advises his master to go on at once. "'Tis the

---

* The Athenians used to inflict the penalty of death by a draught of hemlock.

† For the "Crows" in the original. "Going to the crows" was the first equivalent for our "Going to the dogs." The "Isle of Dogs" is a wellknown spot near London.

very spot," he says, "where Hercules told us those terrible wild beasts were." Bacchus is very valiant.

> "A curse upon him! 'twas an idle tale,
> He feigned to frighten me, for well he knew,
> How brave I am, the envious braggart soul!
> Grant, fortune, I may meet some perilous chance
> Meet for so bold a journey."

"O Master, I hear a noise."

"Where, where?"

"It is behind us."

"Get behind then."

"No—it is in front."

"Why don't you go in front?"

"O Master, I see such a Monster."

"What is it like?"

"Why! it keeps on changing—now it's a bull, now it's a stag, and now it's a woman; and its face is all fire. What shall we do? O Hercules, Hercules help."

"Hold your tongue. Don't call me Hercules."

"Bacchus, then."

"No, no; Bacchus is worse than Hercules."

The travellers pass these dangers, and reach the palace of Pluto. Bacchus knocks at the door. "Who's there?" cries Æacus the porter. "The valiant Hercules," says Bacchus. The name calls forth a torrent of reproaches, and threats. Hercules was only too well remembered there.

> "O villain, villain, doubly, trebly dyed!
> 'Twas thou didst take our dog, our guardian dog,
> Sweet Cerberus, my charge. But, villain, now
> We have thee on the hip. For thee the rocks
> Of Styx, and Acheron's dripping well of blood,
> And Hell's swift hounds encompass."

"Did you hear that dreadful voice?" says Bacchus to the slave. "Didn't it frighten you?"

"Frighten me? No, I didn't give it a thought."

"Well, you are a bold fellow. I say; suppose you become me, and I become you. Take the club and the lion skin, and I'll carry the baggage."

"As you please."

They change parts accordingly. No sooner is this done, than a waiting maid of Queen Proserpine appears. "My dear Hercules," she says, "come with me. As soon as my mistress heard of your being here she had a grand baking, made four or five gallons of soup, and roasted an ox whole."

"Excellent," cries the false Hercules.

"She won't take a refusal. And, hark you! there's *such* wine!"

"I shall be delighted. Boy, bring along the baggage with you."

"Hold," cries the "boy." "Don't you see it was a joke of mine, dressing you up as Hercules? Come, hand over the club and the skin."

"You are not going to take the things away when you gave me them yourself."

"Yes, but I am: a pretty Hercules you would be. Come, hand them over."

"Well; if I must, I must. But I shouldn't wonder if you were sorry for it sooner or later."

It turns out to be sooner rather than later. As soon as the exchange is made, two landladies appear on the scene. Hercules had committed other misdemeanors besides stealing the dog.

First Landlady. "This is the villain. He came to **my** house, and ate sixteen loaves."

The Slave (aside). "Some one is getting into trouble."

First Landlady. "Yes, and twenty fried cutlets at three-half-pence apiece."

The Slave **(aside).** "Some one will suffer for this."

First Landlady. "Yes, and any quantity of garlic."

Bacchus. "Woman this is **all rubbish. I don't know** what you are talking about."

First Landlady. "Ah! you villain, **because you have** buskins on, you thought I should not know **you—and then** there was the salt-fish."

Second Landlady. "Yes, and the fresh cheeses which he ate, baskets and all; and when I asked him for the money he drew his sword, and we ran **up,** you remember, into **the** attic."

The **Slave.** "That is just the **man. That's how he goes** on everywhere."

The angry women run **off to fetch their** lawyers; and Bacchus begins again.

"My dear boy, I am very fond of you."

"I know what you are after. Say no more; **I'm not going** to be Hercules; 'A pretty Hercules I should make,' you say."

"I don't wonder that you're angry. **But do** take the **things again. The gods** destroy me and mine, root and branch, **if I rob you of them again.**"

"**Very well; I'll take them, but mind, you** have sworn." So the exchange is **made again.**

Then Æacus with his infernal policemen appears on the scene.

"That's the fellow who stole the dog," he cries to his men, "seize him," while the false slave murmurs aside, "Some one is getting into trouble."

"I steal your dog!" says the false Hercules. "I have never been here, much less stolen the worth of a cent. But come. I'll make you a fair offer. Here's my slave. Take him, and put him to the torture, and if you get anything out of him against me, then cut my head off."

"Very fair," says Æacus; "and of course, if I do him any damage, I shall pay for it."

"Never mind about the damage; torture away."

"Hold," shouts Bacchus, as the policemen lay hold of him, "I warn you not to torture me, I'm a god."

Æacus. "What do you say?"

Bacchus. "I am Bacchus, son of Zeus, and that fellow there is my slave."

Æacus (to the false Bacchus) "What do you say to that?"

The false Bacchus. "Say? Lay on the lash; if he's a god, of course he can't feel."

Bacchus. "And you're a god too, you say. So you won't mind taking blow for blow with me."

The false Bacchus. "Quite right." (To Æacus) "Lay on, and the first that cries out, you may be sure he's not the real god."

So the trial takes place. Both bear it bravely, till at last Æacus cries in perplexity. "I can't make it out. I don't know which is which. Well, you shall both come to my master and Queen Proserpine. They're gods, and they ought to know their own kind."

Bacchus. "An excellent idea; I only wish that you had thought of it before you gave me that beating."

Things are now supposed to be set right. Bacchus goes to dine with Pluto and Proserpine; the slave is entertained by Æacus in the servants' hall. While they are talking a tremendous uproar is heard outside; and Æacus explains to his guest that it is a rule in their country that the best poet or writer or artist should have a seat at the King's table and a place at the King's right hand. This honor Æschylus had held as the first of the tragic poets, but when Euripides came, all the crowd of pick-pockets and burglars and murderers, who were pretty numerous in these parts, had been so delighted with his twists and turns, that they were for giving him the first place; and on the strength of their support he had claimed the tragic throne."

"But had not Æschylus any friends?"

"O yes, among the respectable people; but respectable people are scarce down here, as they are up above."

"What about Sophocles?"

"Oh! as soon as he came, he went up to Æschylus and kissed him on the cheek, and took him by the hand. He yielded the throne, he said, to Æschylus; but if Euripides came off best, he should contest it with him."

"Well, what is going to be done?"

"There will be a trial."

"Who is to be judge?"

"Ah! there's the difficulty. Wise men, you see, are not so plenty. Even with the Athenians Æschylus didn't get on very well. However they have made your master judge. He is supposed to know all about it."

I have tried to give some idea of the first, the farcical half of the play. It is possible to appreciate the fun, though much of **its flavor has** evaporated, and **there are** many strokes of humor which, for one reason or another, it has **not been** possible to reproduce. The second half is a series of subtle literary criticisms on the language, style, **dramatic construction, and** ruling sentiment of the two poets. **No** one can appreciate it who is not familiar **with** their works; no version **is** possible that **would give any that** idea of it. **One specimen I** shall attempt. Æschylus finds fault with **the prosaic** matter-of-fact **character of his rival's opening** scenes. " I'll **spoil them** all with a **flask,**" he says. " Go **on and repeat whichever** you **please."** Euripides begins **with the opening lines of the** Danaides (a play now lost).

> " Aegyptus—so the common story runs—
> **Crossed** with his fifty sons the ocean plains,
> **And reaching** Argos — "

> " **Lost a** little flask."

puts in Æschylus.

He begins again with the opening **lines of another**

> " Cadmus, Agenor's offspring, setting sail
> From Sidon's city — "

> " Lost a little flask."

Then he tries with the **first lines of a third**

> " Great Bacchus, who with wand and fawn-skin decked,
> In pine-groves of Parnassus, plies the dance,
> And leads the revel— "

> " Lost a little flask."

The reader may have had enough. **It will suffice to give** the result of the contest. All the tests **have been applied.** Euripides, as a last resource, reminds the judge that he has **sworn to take** him back with **him.**

Bacchus replies:

"My tongue hath sworn; yet Æschylus I choose."

A cruel cut, for it is an adaptation of one of the poet's own lines (from the **Hippolytus**) when the hero, taunted with the oath that he had taken and is about to violate, replies:

"My tongue hath sworn it, but my mind's unsworn."

When the curtain rose from the floor and hid the last scene, it was manifest that the "Frogs" of Aristophanes, son of Philippus, of the tribe Pandionis, and the township Cydathenæa, was a success. Of course there were malcontents among the audience. Euripides had a good many partisans in young Athens. They admired his ingenuity, his rhetoric, and the artistic quality of his verse, in which beauty for beauty's sake, quite apart from any moral purpose, seemed to be aimed at. They were captivated by the boldness and novelty of his treatment of things moral and religious. Æschylus they considered to be old-fashioned and bigoted. Hence among the seats allotted to the young men there had been some murmurs of dissent while the performance was going on, and now there was a good deal of adverse criticism. And there were some among the older men who were scarcely satisfied. The fact was that Comedy was undergoing a change, the change which before twenty more years had passed was to turn the Old Comedy into the Middle and the New, or to put the matter briefly, to change the Comedy of Politics into the Comedy of Manners.

"This is poor stuff," said an old aristocrat of this school, "poor stuff indeed, after what I remember in my younger days. Why can't the man leave Euripides alone, especially now he is dead, and won't bother us with any more of his plays? There are plenty of scoundrel politicians who might to much more purpose come in for a few strokes of the lash. But he daren't touch the fellows. Ah! it was not always so. I remember the play he brought out eighteen years ago. The 'Knights' he called it. That was something like a Comedy! Cleon was at the very height of his power, for he had just made that lucky stroke at Pylos *. But Aristophanes did not spare him one bit for that. He could not get any one to take the part; he could not even get a mask made to imitate the great man's face. So he took the part himself, and smeared his face with the lees of wine. Cleon was there in the Magistrates' seats. I think we all looked at him as much as we looked at the stage. Whenever there was a hard hit—and, by Bacchus, how hard the hits were!—all the theatre turned to see how he bore it. He laughed at first. Then we saw him turn red and pale—I was close by him and I heard him grind his teeth. Good heavens! what a rage he was in! Well, that is the sort of a play I like to see, not this splitting words, and picking verses to pieces, just as some schoolmaster might do."

But, in spite of these criticisms, the greater part of the audience were highly delighted with what they had seen and heard. The comic business, with its broad and laughable effects, pleased them, and they were flattered by being treated as judges of literary questions. And the curious thing was that they were not unfit to be judges of such matters. There never was such a well-educated and keen-witted audience in the world. They knew it, and they

* When he captured the Spartan garrison of the Island of Sphacteria, B. C. 425.

dearly liked to be treated accordingly. The judges only echoed the popular voice when at the end of the festival they bestowed the first prize upon Aristophanes.

One criticism, strange to say, no one ever thought of making—and yet, to us, it seems the first, the most obvious of all criticisms, and that is that the play was horribly profane. This cowardly, drunken, sensual Bacchus—and he is ten times worse in the original than I have ventured to make him here—this despicable wretch was one of the gods whom every one in the audience was supposed to worship. The festival which was the occasion of the theatrical exhibition was held in his honor, his altar was the centre round which the whole action of every piece revolved. And yet he was caricatured in this audacious manner, and it did not occur to anyone to object ! Verily the religion of the Greeks sat very lightly on their consciences, and we cannot wonder if it had but small effect on their lives.

CHAPTER II.

I ANTICIPATED the course of my story when I spoke of the first prize being adjudged to the comedy exhibited by Aristophanes. There were various competing plays—how many we do not know, but the titles and authors of two that won the second and third prizes have been preserved—and all those had of course to be performed before a decision could be made. Two or three days at least must have passed before the exhibition was at an end.

The next competitor had certainly reason to complain of his ill-luck. Just before the curtain fell for the opening scene of his comedy an incident occurred which made the people little disposed to listen to anything more that day. The spectators had just settled themselves in their places, when a young officer hastily made his way up to the bench where the magistrates were seated, and handed a roll to the president. The occurrence was very unusual. It was reckoned almost an impiety to disturb the festival of Bacchus with anything of business; only matters of the very gravest importance could be allowed to do it. The entrance of the young man, happening as it did, just in the pause of expectation before the new play began, had been generally observed. Every one could see from his dress that he was a naval officer, and many knew him as one of the most promising young men in Athens. "News from the fleet," was the whisper that ran through the theatre, and there were few among the thousands there assembled to whom news from the fleet did not mean the life or death of father, brother, or son. The president glanced at the document put into his hands, and whispering a few words to the messenger, pointed to a seat by his side. All eyes were fastened upon him. (The magistrates, it may be explained, occupied one of the front or lowest rows of seats, and were therefore more or less in view of the whole theater, which was arranged in the form of a semicircle, with tier upon tier of benches rising upon the slope of the hill on the side of which the building was constructed.) When a moment afterwards, the curtain was withdrawn, scarcely a glance was directed to the stage. The action and the dialogue of the new piece were absolutely lost upon what should have been an audience, but was a crowd of anxious citizens, suddenly recalled from the shows of the stage to the realities of life.

The president now carefully read the document and passed it on to his colleagues. Some whispered consultations passed between them. When at the end of the first act a change of scenery caused a longer pause than usual the president quietly left the theatre, taking the bearer of the despatch with him. Some of the other magistrates followed him, the rest remaining behind because it would have been unseemly to leave the official seats wholly untenanted while the festival was still going on. This proceeding increased the agitation of the people, because it emphasized the importance of the news that had arrived. Some slipped away, unable to sit quietly in their places and endure the suspense, and vaguely hoping to hear something more outside. Among those that remained the buzz of conversation grew louder and louder. Only a few very determined play-goers even pretended to listen to what was going on upon the stage. Meanwhile the unfortunate author, to whom, after all, the fate of his play was not less urgent a matter than the fate of the city, sat upon his prompter's stool—the author not uncomonly did the duty of prompter—and heartily cursed the bad luck which had distracted in so disastrous a way the attention of his audience.

When at last, to the great relief of everyone concerned, the performance was brought to a conclusion, the young officer told his story, supplementing the meagre contents of the despatch which he had brought, to a full conclave of magistrates, assembled in one of the senate-rooms of the Prytaneum or Town-hall of Athens. I may introduce him to my readers as Callias, the hero of my story.

Many of the details that follow had already been given by Callias, but as he had to repeat them for the benefit of the magistrates who had stopped behind in the theatre, I may as well put them all together.

"We know," said the president, "that Conon was beaten in a battle in the harbor of Mitylene. So much we heard from Hippocles, a very patriotic person by the way, though he is an alien. He has a very swift yacht that can outstrip any war-ship in Greece, and often gives us very valuable intelligence. Do you know him?"

"Yes," said Callias, flushing with pleasure, for indeed he

THE THEATER OF DIONYSUS AT THE PRESENT DAY.

knew and respected Hippocles greatly, " I know him very well."

"Well, to go on," resumed the president.   " So much we know, but no more. Tell us exactly how Conon fared in the battle."

" Sir," answered the young man, " he lost thirty ships."

" And the crews," asked the president.

" They escaped; happily they were able to get to land."

"Thank Athene for that;" and a murmur of relief ran round the meeting. " And the other forty—he had seventy, I think, in all? " Callias nodded assent.

" What happened to the forty? "

" They were hauled up under the walls when the day went against us."

" Now tell us exactly what has been going on since."

"The Spartans blockaded the harbor, having some of their ships within, and some without. Our general saw that it was only a matter of time when he should have to surrender. The Spartans had four times as many ships, the ships not, perhaps, quite as good as his, but the crews, I am afraid, somewhat better."

"Shade of Themistocles," murmured one of the magistrates, "that it should come to this—the Spartan crews 'somewhat better' than ours. But I am afraid that it is only too true."

" He could not break through; and could not stand a long siege. Mitylene was fairly well provisioned for its ordinary garrison, but here were seventy crews added all of a sudden to the number. He sent some officers—I had the honor of being one of them—and we found that by sparing everything to the very utmost, we might hold out for **five** weeks. **The only** chance was to send news to Athens. **You** might help us, we thought."

"**We might;** we *must,* **I say.** But how it **is to be** done is another **matter.** Tell us **how you got here?**"

"**The** general took **the** two fastest ships in his squadron, manned **them** with the very best rowers that he could find, practised the crews for four days in the inner harbor, and then **set** about running the blockade with **them.** The Spartans, **you see, had** grown a little careless. **We** hadn't made any attempt to **get** out, **and Conon** got a Lesbian **freedman to** desert to the Spartans **with a story that we were meaning to surrender.** This **put them off their** guard **still more.** They got into a way of leaving their ships at noon, **to take** their meal and their siesta afterwards on shore. **We** made a dart **at an** unguarded place between two of their **block-** ading ships and we got through. I don't think **that we** lost a single man. By **the** time **that the crews of the** blockading galleys regained **their vessels we** were well **out** of bow-shot. Our instructions **were to** separate, when we got outside **the harbor. We did not** do this at once because **we had** planned **a little trick which might,** we hoped, **help to** put the enemy off the scent. **The ship** that I was in was really the swifter of the two. **This was,** of course, **the reason why I** was put into it. **But as long as we** kept together we **made believe that** we **were the slower. When** they came out after us—they had manned **half-a-dozen** ships or so as quickly **as** they could—we **separated. My ship,** which you will understand, was **really the faster of the two, was** put **about the north as** if making for Hellespont; the other kept on its course, straight for Athens. The Spartans told off their best ships to follow the latter which they thought that they had the better chance of catching. And of course, as it was headed this way, it seemed the more important of the two."

"I suppose that they overtook it," said the president, "or it would have been here before this."

"Well, we soon outstripped the two galleys that were told to look after us. When we were well out of sight, we headed westward again, took a circuit round the north side of Lemnos, and got here without seeing another enemy."

" How long is it since you left Mitylene ? "

" About five days."

" But how long did Conon think he could hold out ? "

" About forty days; perhaps more, if the men were put on short rations."

" You have done well, my son," said the president kindly, "and Athens will not forget it. We will consult together, though there is small need of consulting, I take it. The relief *must* be sent. Is it not so gentlemen ? "

His colleagues nodded assent.

"But there are things to be talked over. We must decide how much we can send, and that cannot be done upon the spot. But there is a matter that can be settled at once. Conon must be told that he is going to be relieved. Now, who will tell him? Will you?"

"Certainly, if you see fit to give me the order."

" And how ? "

" I would consult with Hippocles."

"Excellent!" cried the president. "He is just the man

to help us. You will go and see him, and then report to me. Come to me to-night; it will not matter how late it is; I shall be waiting for you."

Callias saluted, and withdrew.

CHAPTER III.

HIPPOCLES has been described as an alien. An "alien," then at Athens, as in the other Greek cities, was a resident foreigner. He might be an enfranchised slave, he might be a barbarian (as all persons not Greek were described), or he might be a Greek of the purest descent, but if he had not the rights of Athenian citizenship, he was an "alien." He could not hold any landed or house property: he was obliged to appear in any law suit in which he might be concerned in the person of an Athenian citizen who was described as his "patron," and he was heavily taxed. A special impost that went under the name of an "alien-tax" was only a slight matter, some twelve drachmas * a year, but all the imposts were made specially heavy for them. And though they had no share in directing the policy of the State, they were required to serve in its fleets and armies. This treatment however, did not keep aliens from settling in Athens. On the contrary they were to be found there in great numbers, and as almost all the trade of the place was in their hands, some of them were among its richest inhabitants.

* This would amount to about $2.25—a drachma being equal to about 20c or 9½d. in English money.

At the time of which I am writing Hippocles had **the** reputation, which we may say was by **no means unde-served**, of being the **richest resident** in Athens. **And more than** that, he **was one of** the most patriotic. **He,** loved the city as if it had **been his native** place, and did the **duty and more than the duty of a son to** her. The special **contributions which as a wealthy man he was** called upon **to make to the** public service * were made with a princely **liberality. He** even voluntarily **undertook services** which were not required of him by law. Every **year he** had come **forward to furnish** the crew and munitions of a ship-of-war, a charge **to which citizens only** were **properly liable.** And of the **fleet of which such** gloomy tidings **had just** reached Athens, **he had** equipped **no** less than three.

Hippocles had a curious history. He was born in **the** Greek **colony of** Poseidonia.† He was just entering **on manhood when** his native city fell **into** the hands **of its Lucanian** neighbors. The barbarians **did not abuse** their victory. They did **not** treat the conquered **city, as the Greeks of** Croton **some** ninety **years** before **had** treated **Sybaris, reducing it to an absolute ruin. On** the contrary **they contented themselves with** imposing a tribute, and **leaving a governor, with a** garrison **to support** him, to see **that their new subjects did not** forget **their duty.** But **the**

---

* These "liturgies," as they were called, were charges imposed upon all residents in Athens whose property was assessed at more than a certain amount (three talents, which, as a talent contained 6,000 drachmæ, may be roughly estimated at $3,500, equivalent, it is probable, to much more in actual value). These were originally equivalents for special privileges and powers which the wealthy enjoyed under the earlier constitution, but they were continued in force after the democratic changes which put all citizens on an equality. The Aliens were not liable to all.

† Better known **by** its Latin name **of Paestum.**

presence of the foreigner was a grievous burden to the proud
Greeks. For ages afterwards their descendants were accustomed to assemble once a·year and to bewail their fate, as
the Sons of Jacob at the Vale of Weeping, the Gentile
domination over their city. The disaster broke the heart
of Hippocles' father Cimon who was one of Pacidoninus'
most distinguished citizens and had actually held the office
of Tagus or chief magistrate in the year of its fall. He survived the event scarcely a year, recommending his son with
his last breath to leave the place for some city where he
could live in a way more worthy of a Greek. His son spent
the next two years in quietly realizing his property, nor did
he meet with any interference from the Lucanian masters
of the place. His house he had to sacrifice; to sell it might
have attracted too much notice; but everything else that he
had was converted into money. When this was safely in-
vested at Athens—Athens having been for various reasons
the city of his choice—he secretly departed. But he did not
depart alone. He took with him a companion, who, he declared, more than made up to him for all that as a Posei-
donian citizen he had lost. Pontia, the daughter of the
Lucanian governor, was a girl of singular beauty. The
Lucanian, in common with the other Italian tribes, gave to
their women a liberty which was unknown in Greek house-
holds. Under the circumstances of life in which he had
been brought up, Hippocles though a frequent visitor at
the governor's house, would never, except by the merest
accident, have seen the governor's daughter. As it was he
had many opportunities of making her acquaintance. Instead of being shut up, after the Greek fashion in the women's

apartments, she shared the common life of the family. At first the novelty of the situation almost shocked the young man; before long it pleased him; it ended by conquering his heart. The young Greek, who was leaving his native land because it did not suit his pride of race to live under the rule of a barbarian, did not submit without an effort. Again and again he reproached himself with the monstrous inconsistency of which he was guilty. "Madman that I am," he said to himself, "I cannot endure to live with barbarians for neighbors and yet I think of taking a barbarian to wife." Again and again he resolved to break free from the influence that was enthralling him. But love was too strong for him. Nor indeed, were there wanting arguments on the other side. "Actually," he said to himself, "I am a Greek no more; a Greek without a city is only not a barbarian in name." This argument, of little weight, perhaps, in itself, gained force from the loveliness and mental charms of the young Pontia. She had long felt a distaste for the rough, uncultured life into which she had been born. The culture and refinement of her father's young Greek guest charmed her. The sadness of his mien touched the chord of pity in her heart, and admiration and pity together soon grew into love.

Hippocles had just completed the settlement of his affairs, and was ruefully contemplating the curious dilemma in which he found himself—everything ready for his departure from Poseidonia, but Poseidonia holding him from such departure by ties which he could break only by breaking his heart—when circumstances suggested a way of escape.

The governor was a widower, and had more than the

usual incapacity of busy men in middle life for discerning the symptoms of love. It was accordingly, with a cheerful unconsciousness of his guest's feelings that he said to him one morning:—" I have good news about my dear Pontia. The girl is growing up, and should be settled in life, and I have had a most eligible proposal for her. I have told you, I think, that I am getting tired of this life, and want to get back to my farm among the hills. So I have asked to be relieved, and I hear from the Senate that they have chosen a successor, Hostius of Vulsi, a cousin, I should say, of my own, and a most respectable man. Hostius has come to announce the fact in person, and at the same time to ask for my daughter in marriage. A most eligible proposal, I say. Perhaps he is a little old, about five years younger than myself. But that's of no consequence. I mentioned the matter to her. She did not say much, but, of course, a girl must seem to hold back. I suggested that the marriage should take place next week—for I should dearly like to be at home in time for the barley harvest. That roused her. Of course she said that she had no clothes. I don't know about that—she always seems to me to look very nice—but I should not like to annoy her, for she is a dear, good girl, and I gave her another month. It's an excellent arrangement—don't you think so?"

Hippocles muttered a few words of assent; but long before the month was out, he and his Pontia were on their way to Athens.

The marriage and the settlement in Athens had taken place twenty-one years before the time of which I am writing. Two children had been born, a son and a daughter. The son had fallen, not many mouths before, at the battle of Notium * and the death of the mother, who had been in feeble health, had soon followed. The daughter, to whom her parents had given the name of Hermione, had just completed her sixteenth year.

Hermione united in herself some of the happiest characteristics of the two races from which she sprang. Her father was a Greek of the Greeks. Poseidonia had been founded by Dorian settlers from Sybaris, who could not contrive to live on good terms with the Achaean Greeks that had become the predominant element in that city; and Hippocles, who claimed descent from the Messenian kings, yielded to none in nobility of birth. A purer type of the genuine Hellenes it would have been impossible to find. Pontia brought from the Lucanian hills, among which she had been reared, some of the best qualities, moral and physical, of the Italian race. The simplicity, frugality, and temperance which then and long after distinguished rural Italy, were to be seen in her united with a singular feminine charm not so often found among that somewhat rude population; until the close air of the Piraeus, ill-suited to a daughter of the hills, sapped her constitution, she had had a frame magnificently healthy and strong. To the daughter the climate which had shortened her mother's days, happily did no harm. It was in fact her native air, and she throve in it. She was still undeveloped, for she had only just completed her sixteenth year; but she gave promise of remarkable beauty, and indeed, the promise was

* Fought in 407. Notium was the harbor of Colophon a city of Asia Minor, about nine miles north of Ephesus, and about fifteen miles from the sea.

already more than half fulfilled. When she had performed the duty, sometimes imposed on the daughters of resident aliens,—it might be called, rather, privilege conceded to them—and walked **in the great procession of** the patron-goddess, holding a sunshade over some high-born Athenian **maiden, *** all the spectators agreed that the prize of beauty belonged to the stranger. Her **stature reached the very ut**-most height that the canons **of beauty** conceded to **women**; so far **she was more of an** Athene than an **Aphrodite. But** her face and her whole bearing were exquisitely feminine. The sapphire-colored eyes, **shaded by** long drooping lashes the forehead, broad and low with the clustering ringlets **of** light **chesnut on either side,** perfectly rounded cheeks, firm, delicate mouth, showing a glimpse, but only a glimpse of pearly teeth, and **a** faultlessly **clear** complexion, just tinted with the brown caught from Ægæan suns and winds **—for she was** dearly fond of a cruise in her father's yatcht—made up together a remarkable combination of charms.

Callias had seen her but once before, and that was on a melancholy occasion. **He had been commissioned by the** general in command **to break to her** father the death of her brother, killed **as has been said, in the un**-lucky conflict at Notium. He had behaved there with **con**-**spicuous gallantry,** having led the boarding party which captured the only Lacedaemonian galley that the Athenians had to set off against their own fifteen **losses,** and had fallen in the **moment of victory. It** was not the first **time** that he had **shown distinguished** valor, and it was for this reason, as

* Noble Athenian damsels were the "basket-bearers" (*Canephoroi*), daughters of aliens "Sunshade-bearers" (*Skiaphoroi*) in the Paratheraea, or Great Procession of Athens.

well as on account of the high reputation of his father, **that**
Alcibiades had sent Callias with a special message of condo-
lence. The blow, which could not be softened by any **deli-**
cacy in the telling, and for which the praises of the general
were **but** a slight consolation, broke Hippocles down **com-**
pletely. **It was then that** Hermione showed the strength
of her character. **Tenderly** attached herself to her brother
she had **come forward to support her** broken-hearted father.
With a patient endurance **that was beyond** all praise, she
had battled with her **own grief in the** effort to help a
sorrow even more agonizing **than her own, till** for very
shame Hippocles had raised **himself to bear his loss with
resignation.** The effort saved his life; for **even the** physi-
cians **had at** one time been greatly alarmed. Callias, **accus-**
tomed to think of women as encumbrances rather **than**
helps in time of need **was** profoundly impressed **by the**
girl's demeanor. If he had been inclined, for a moment,
to think that her singular self-possession indicated a want
of womanly feeling, he would have been soon undeceived.
Paying a visit of inquiry to the house next day, he found
that Hermione's endurance had not lasted beyond the occasion for which it was wanted. Her father received him,
and told him that his daughter had broken down under the
strain. **"I was cowardly enough,"** he said, "yesterday to
rest upon her strength when I should have summoned up
my own. The gods grant that I may not **have taxed it**
overmuch, and that I may not lose both my children. **I**
have learned that I ought not to have grudged my son to the
city which has been a second mother to me; if only **I** have
not learnt **it at too terrible a price."** Callias had to leave

Athens on the next day to rejoin the fleet, **but he had the** satisfaction of hearing before his departure that Hermione was on a fair way to recovery. Since then he had not been in Athens.

CHAPTER IV.

THE house of Hippocles was on a smaller scale than might have seemed suitable to his vast wealth. The fact was that both he and his daughter had simple tastes. They had a special dislike to the enormous establishments of slaves which it was the fashion for rich Athenians, whether of native or of foreign birth, to maintain. In each division of the house—for, it was divided after the usual Greek fashion, into two "apartments," to use that word in its proper sense, belonging respectively to the men and the women *—there were but three or four inmates besides the master and mistress. Hippocles had his house steward and his personal attendant, both older than himself, long since emancipated, who had accompanied him from his Italian home, and a lad of seventeen, who was still a slave, but who, if he conducted himself well, would certainly earn his freedom by the time that he had reached the age of thirty. Hermione's establishment, on the other hand, consisted of a lady who had just exchanged the post of governess, now no longer necessary, for that of companion or duenna, a housekeeper, and two domestics who may be described by the modern terms of

* The Andronitis and Gynaekonitis, as they were called.

lady's-maid and house-maid. Stephanion, the companion, was of pure Athenian descent. She belonged to one of the many families which had been reduced to poverty by the war, and she had been glad to take employment in the house of the wealthy alien. She had more education than was commonly given to Athenian ladies, but this is not to say much, and Hermione would have fared but ill for teaching, according at least to our standard if her father had not always found time even in his busiest days, to supplement her education. The housekeeper was a Laconian woman. She, too, had found her way into the family through circumstances connected with the war. She had been nurse in a wealthy Athenian household. Before the war it had been the fashion, my readers should know, for the upper classes at Athens to get their nurses from Sparta. A true Spartan, a daughter that is, of the military aristocracy that ruled Laconia and its dependencies, it was, of course, impossible to obtain, but girls from the farmer class that cultivated the lands of their soldier masters often sought situations in other countries. This was the case with Milanion, who as the youngest of the five daughters of a Laconian farmer, had been delighted to find a place with an Athenian lady, Melissa, wife of Demochares, at a salary which almost equalled her father's income. This was just before the commencement of the long war. She had been nurse to Melissa's five children when the disastrous expedition to Sicily brought irretrievable ruin upon her employer's family. Demochares was one of the army that surrendered with Nicias, was thrown with his comrades into that most dreadful of prisons, the stone-quarries of Syracuse, and died of a fever before the end of the year. His property had consisted, for the most part, of farms in the island of Chios, and when Chios revolted from Athens, the widow and her children were reduced to something very like poverty. Nothing was left to them but a small farm at Marathon, and as it so happened, the rent of the house which Hippocles unable, as has been said, to own real property in Attica, had been accustomed to hire. The establishment had to be broken up, the slaves being sold and the free persons looking for employment elsewhere. Milanion was about to return, much against her will, to Laconia, where her long residence at Athens would have rendered her an object of suspicion and dislike, when an opening suddenly presented itself in the family of Hippocles. Pontia's long illness had come to a fatal end, and the widower was looking for an experienced woman to take charge of the young Hermione. Milanion seemed to him exactly the person that he wanted, and she, on the other hand, was delighted to come to him. As her charge grew older, her duties as nurse gradually changed into the duties of a housekeeper. She had come to her new situation accompanied by a middle-aged woman, a Marian by birth, Manto by name, whom Hippocles had bought, at her suggestion, at the sale of Demochares' slaves. Manto had steadily refused the emancipation which her master had several times offered to her.

"No, sir," she said, "I thank you very much, but I am better as I am. I desire nothing more than to live in your house, and, when my time comes, to die in it."

"What if I should die first," suggested the merchant.

"The gods know, my master, the gods know," cried the

poor woman in an agony. But it is impossible; the gods would not do anything so cruel, so unjust. But, if you wish, you may put what you please into your will. As long as you live you are my master, and I am your slave." So matters stood when my story opens. Perhaps it may be added that Manto's condition did not prevent her tongue from being truthful; but affectionate, faithful, and honest she allowed herself and was allowed—no unusual circumstance, yet she was under a system of slavery—a liberty of speech which in one free born would certainly have been impossible. Finally, to complete my account of the household, Hermione had for her maid a girl about a year older than herself. She too had come into the family along with Milanion and Manto. Demochares had bought her at the sale of the prisoners taken by the Athenians when a little Sicilian town was captured. She was then a singularly pretty child about seven years old, and Demochares had meant her to be a playfellow or plaything, as the case might be, of a daughter of his own of about the same age. She was of mixed race; her mother was a Sicanian, that is, one of the so-called aboriginal inhabitants of Sicily, her father a Carthaginian trader. She was now grown up into a handsome maiden, who with her raven-black hair, dark piercing eyes, and deep brunette complexion, made a remarkable contrast to the fair beauty of her mistress.

When Callias reached the house the hour was late, later than etiquette allowed for a visit, except from an intimate friend, or on a matter of urgent business. His business, however, was urgent, and he did not hesitate to knock, that

is to strike the door sharply with a brass ring which was
attached to it by a staple. The day-porter had gone home
for the night, and the door was opened by the young slave
mentioned above. He explained that his master was just
about to sit down to his evening meal. "Take him **my**
name," said Callias, "and say that I come from the magistrates on an important matter of business." The lad invited
him to enter, and to take a seat **in** a small chamber which
looked upon the central court of the andronitis, a grass plot,
bordered on all sides by myrtle and **orange.** In a few minutes he returned, and invited the **visitor** to follow him.
Callias crossed the court and passed through **the door** which
led into the women's apartment. Hippocles, it should be
said, was accustomed to see visitors on business in the front
or men's portion of the dwelling, but spent his leisure time
in the **rooms** assigned to his daughter. The two had **just**
taken their places at the table, Hippocles reclining on a
couch, Hermione sitting on a chair by his right hand, **so**
that his face was turned towards her.* The steward had
placed the first dish on **the table,** and was standing in front,
with Hippocles' personal attendant behind him. The latter
at a sign from his master, prepared a place for the new-comer.

Hippocles saluted his guest in a most friendly fashion,
and Hermione gave him her hand with a charming smile,
though the moment afterwards tears gathered in her eyes,
when she remembered the last occasion on which they had
met.

---

* A Greek at table, after it became the fashion **to** recline instead of
sit (as had been the practice in the heroic ages) lay on his left side, sup-
porting his head by his left arm, the other arm being left free to help
himself from the dishes when they were placed before him. Women
and children always sat at table.

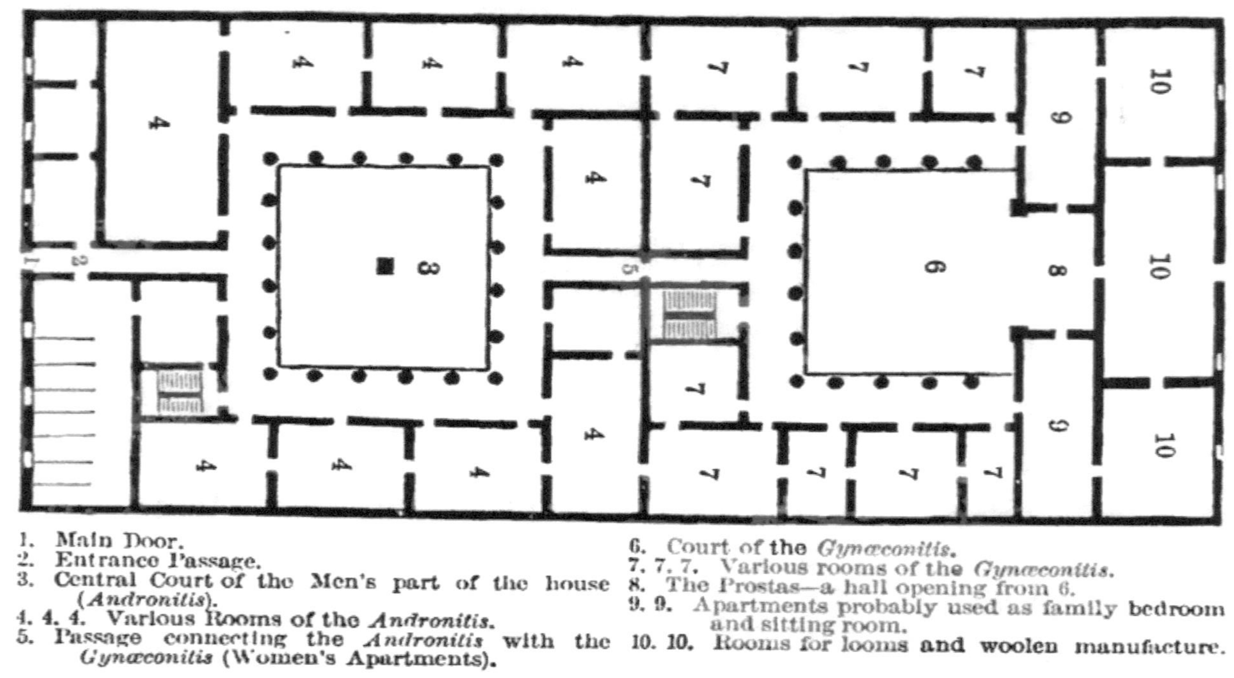

Plan of a large Grecian House, probably more pretentious than the House of Hippocles.

"If the business will wait for half-an-hour," said the host, "postpone it for so long. I have had a long day's work, and shall be scarcely myself till I have eaten. And you—doubtless you have dined before this; but you will take a cup with us."

As a matter of fact Callias had not dined, though in the excitement of the day's business he had almost forgotten food. A hasty meal snatched on board the trireme which had brought him to Athens had been his only refreshment since the morning.

"Nay, sir, but I have not dined; unless you call some five or six dried anchovies and a hunk of barley bread, washed down with some very sharp Hymettus, a dinner; and that was rather before noon than after it."

The meal was simple. It consisted of some fresh anchovies, a piece of roast pork, a hare brought from Eubœa, for Attica swept as it had been again and again by hostile armies, had almost ceased to supply this favorite food, and a pudding of wheat flour, seasoned with spices. This last had been made by Hermione herself. The rest of the dinner had been cooked by a man who came in daily for the purpose. When the viands had been cleared away, Hippocles proposed the usual toast, "To our Good Fortune," the toast not being drank, but honored by pouring some drops from the goblet. A second libation followed, this time to "Athene the Keeper of the City." The host then pledged his guest in a cup of Chian wine. His daughter followed the rule of the best Grecian families, and drank no wine.

"We can dispense, I think, with these," he said, when

the steward was about to put some apples, nuts and olives on the table.

"Just so," replied his guest, "and this excellent cup of Chian will be all the wine that I shall want."

"Now then for business," said Hippocles. "Let us hope that the city will pardon us for postponing it so long. But we must eat. Shall my daughter leave us? For my part, I find her a very Athene for counsel."

"As you will, sir," replied Callias, "I have nothing to say but what all may know, and indeed will know before a day is past."

The young man then proceeded to tell the story with which my readers are already acquainted. The question was briefly this: How was Conon to be told that relief was coming?

"I see," said Hippocles, "that he must be told. He is a brave fellow, and a good general, too, though perhaps a little rash. But he must make terms for himself and his men, unless he has a project of relief. He would not be doing his duty to the state if he did not. But if he capitulates before the relief comes—how many ships has he?"

"Forty," said Callias.

"And we can have a hundred, or possibly, a hundred and ten here, by straining every nerve. The Spartans have a hundred and forty, I think."

"A few may have been disabled in the battle; but it would not be safe to reckon on less, for very likely others have been dropping in since then."

"Then Conon's party will turn the scale, and they will be better manned, I take it, than any that we shall be able to send out from here.   They must not be lost to us.   If they are, we shall do better not to send out the fleet at all, but to stand on our defence."

"Is the *Skylark* in harbor now?" asked Callias.

My readers must know that the *Skylark* was Hippocles' fast sailing yacht.

"Yes," was the reply, "she is in harbor and very much at the service of the state."

"Trust me with her," said Callias, "and I will run the blockade."

"I don't think it is possible," answered Hippocles. "I gathered from what you said that the Spartans are inside the harbor. Now you may give the slip to a blockading squadron when it is watching a harbor from the outside. They always keep close to the mouth you see; and a really good craft, smartly handled, that can sail in the eye of the wind, and does not draw much water, has always a good chance. I'll warrant the *Skylark* to do it, if it is to be done. But with the blockade *inside* the harbor, the case is different, and I must own that I don't see my way."

"May I speak, father?" said Hermione.

"Since when have you begun to ask leave to use your tongue, my darling?" replied her father with a smile. "You should hear her lecturing me when we are alone," he went on, turning to his guest. "But our counsellor is not used to speaking in an assembly."

"Would it be of any use," said the girl, "to disguise the *Skylark*, by painting her another color and altering the cut of her rigging?"

"A good thought, my darling," replied her father, "and

one that I shall certainly make use of. Now let me think; just for the present, things do not seem to piece themselves together."

He rose from the couch on which he had been reclining, and paced up and down the room in profound thought. Fully half an hour had passed when he suddenly stopped short in his walk, and turned to his daughter.

"My darling," he said, "I see that you are getting sleepy."

"Sleepy, father?" cried the girl, who indeed was as wide awake as possible, "sleepy? what can you mean? how could I possibly feel sleepy, when we are talking about such things?"

"Nevertheless your father says it," replied Hippocles, "and fathers are never mistaken." And he laid his hand upon her shoulder.

Without another word Hermione rose from her chair, kissed her father, held out her hand again to Callias, and left the room.

Hippocles waited for a few minutes, and then sat down on the couch by Callias' side.

"You will have guessed," he said, "that I wanted the girl away. I wish that I had never let her stay; now she will suspect something; but it cannot be helped. Now, listen. What the girl said about disguising the *Skylark* set me thinking. That will be useful another time; indeed I shall do it now. But it won't do all that we want. Disguised or not disguised, I don't see how she is to get past the Spartan ships in Mitylene harbor. Now we must try a bolder play. I shall disguise myself, and go."

"You, sir," cried Callias in astonishment. "But think of the danger."

"Well," replied Hippocles, "we cannot expect to get anything really valuable without danger. And I am something of a fatalist. What will be will be. Now listen: I shall disguise myself as a trader of Cos. I am a Dorian by birth, you know, and I can use the broad vowels and the lisps to perfection I flatter myself. I say Cos,* because I happen to be particularly well acquainted with its dialect. I shall go to Callicratidas † and tell him my story—what the story shall be I have not yet made up my mind, but it is not hard to impose upon a Spartan. However leave all that to me. Go and tell the magistrates that I undertake to tell Conon that he will be relieved. And, mind—not a word to my daughter. I shall tell her that I am called away on important business. Very likely she will guess something of the truth; but it would only trouble her to tell her more."

"And the magistrates, sir?" asked Callias, "how much are they to know?"

"Nothing more, I think, than what I said, that Hippocles the Alien undertakes to communicate with Conon. I don't doubt the good faith and discretion of our friends; but the fewer there are in the secret of such a plan, the better. Keep a thing in your own mind, I say. If you whisper a secret even unto the earth, when the reed grows up it will repeat it.‡

---

* Cos was one of the cities belonging to the Dorian Pentapolis.

† Callicratidas was the admiral in command of the Spartan fleet.

‡ Hippocles is alluding to a well known story. Midas deciding in favor of Pan as a better musician than Apollo was punished by being given the long ears of an ass. He hid them under his Thurgian cap from all men except the barber who cut his hair. This man, oppressed with the secret, dug a hole in the earth, whispered into it, "King Midas has asses' ears," and filling it up again, so found relief from his burden. But a reed grew from the spot, and as it was moved by the wind whispered the secret to the world.

You **will say simply that it is a** matter which it is **well for the state to** conceal. **If I succeed, I** justify my-self; if not—well, I take it, no man's **anger here will concern** me much. **And now** farewell! Don't vex yourself about me. All will turn out well; and if not—how can a man die better **than in saving** Athens. **All my** affairs are arranged, **if I** should not return. My patron Melesippus will, of course, **be** my executor, and **I have** ventured to join your **name with** his in the trust? **Have I** your permission?"

Callias pressed his hand in silence.

"That is well, and now my mind is easy. And now," he went on in a cheerful tone, "farewell again; **but** before you **go,** we must have a libation to Hermione **who for the next ten** days must be my special patron. If I come back **safe, I** will regild this temple from roof to basement."

The libation was duly **poured, and** the vow repeated as **the drops fell upon the ground.**

CHAPTER V.

RUNNING THE BLOCKADE.

HIPPOCLES, who was a ship builder as well as a merchant, put all available hands to work on the alterations which he proposed to make in the *Skylark*. To disguise her effectually was a more difficult thing than Hermione had imagined when she had suggested this idea. To disguise her beyond all risk of discovery was probably impossible, a landsman might be deceived by different colored paint, and a nautical observer, if he did not give more than a casual glance, by an altered rigging. But the lines of the ship would remain. These Hippocles endeavored to conceal by a false and much broader bow which was ingeniously fitted on to the true hull, and which made her look anything but the fast sailer that she really was. Heavy bulwarks were substituted for the light ones that had been a familiar feature of the *Skylark*. Altogether she was metamorphosed in a fairly satisfactory way from a smart yacht into a clumsy merchantman. As the venturous owner intended to time his arrival for the night, and to do his errand before day-break, he hoped that the disguise would save her as long as it should be wanted.

So much energy did the workmen, stimulated by their master's presence and by his liberal promises of renumeration, throw into their work, that by the evening of the seventh day the *Skylark* was ready for sea in her new dress, disguised beyond recognition, except by very skilful eyes indeed. The dockyard had been strictly closed against all visitors while the work was in progress, and the men had been lodged within its walls, so that no hint of what was going on might leak out. Hippocles had paid a daily visit to his home, and did not conceal from his daughter that he was busy in carrying out her suggestions. So frank, indeed, was he, and so cheerful in manner, that the girl was fairly thrown off her guard. Not a suspicion crossed her mind, that her father was meditating a desperate enterprise in which the chances were certainly rather against his life than otherwise, nor did she realize the extraordinary haste with which the work was being pressed on, though she was generally aware that a good deal of expedition was being used. Hence she was taken by surprise, when on the eighth day instead of her father's usual visit, timed so that he might share her noon-day meal, a written message was delivered to her, to the effect that her father was suddenly called away from Athens on business of importance, and that he could not be certain of the day of his return. The surprise almost overwhelmed her, chiefly because she felt that this unusual hurry on the part of her father was significant of the perilous nature of the enterprise. It was only her unusual fortitude, backed by the feeling that she herself must not deviate from doing her duty, that enabled her to bear up at all.

Meanwhile Hippocles was on his way to the scene of action. The *Skylark* crossed the Ægean without meeting with any misadventure. She was overhauled, indeed, when about half her journey was accomplished by an Athenian cruiser, and her owner had the satisfaction of finding that so far his disguise was successful. The Athenian captain was an acquaintance of his own (indeed there were few prominent people in the city to whom he was not known) and had actually been on board the *Skylark* more than once; but he did not recognize either Hippocles or his vessel. In fact he was about to carry her off as a prize when Hippocles, still without discovering himself, produced the pass with which he had been provided under the seal of the Athenian authorities. His arrival at Mitylene was happily timed in more ways than one. By a stroke of that good fortune which is proverbially said to help the bold it so happened that there was a violent north-east wind blowing. This was a wind from which the harbor of Mitylene afforded little or no shelter. In fact, when it was blowing, most sailors preferred to be out on the open sea. Hippocles accordingly found everything in commotion. The blockading ships, which moored as they were across the mouth of the harbor, felt the full force of the wind, were anxious about their moorings, and had little attention to give to any strange ship. The *Skylark* was in fact hardly noticed in the darkness and confusion, and actually got beyond the line of the blockading galleys, and as far as the admiral's ship, without being challenged. For a few moments he thought of boldly pushing on to the inner part of the harbor, where, as has been said, the remainder of the Athenian fleet was lying hauled up under the walls; but when he was hailed by a voice from a Spartan ship, one of two that lay almost directly in his way, he abandoned the idea. "Anaxilaus, merchant of Cos, to see the admiral, on business of importance," was his reply to the challenge. At the last moment he dropped his anchor. A few minutes afterward, he came on board the admiral's galley and reported himself to that officer.

It would be unjust to Callicratidas—for this was the admiral's name—to describe him as a model Spartan. He was rather a model Greek. The Spartans had great virtues which however, it is curious to observe, seldom survived transplantation from their native soil. * They were frugal, temperate, and just; but they were narrow in their habits of thought and their conceptions of duty. A good soldier whose efficiency was not diminished by any vice was their ideal man. They could not enter into any large and liberal views of life. And their views of statesmanship whether as regarded their own city or the whole race in general were as narrow as were their notions of private virtue. They sometimes showed a great amount of diplomatic skill, a strange contrast with the bluntness which was their traditional characteristic, but of wide and general views they seem to have been incapable. Yet Callicratidas seems to have been an exception. We know comparatively little about him. He emerges from absolute obscurity at the beginning of the year with which my story opens, and it is only for a few months that he plays a conspicuous part in history, but

* The instances in which a Spartan general sent to fill some office abroad seemed to lose all self-restraint and all sense of shame are deplorably numerous. Pausanias, the Spartan who commanded at Platæa, and was afterwards banished for treacherous dealings with the Persians, was the first conspicuous example of this national failing, as it may be called; but it was an example often followed. The Spartan governors in allied or conquered cities were almost proverbial for profligacy, tyranny and corruption.

from now up to the hour when we see him for the last time, all his words and acts are marked with a rare nobility.

It was not difficult for Hippocles to invent a story which should account for his presence at Mitylene. The domestic polities of almost every Greek state were mixed up with the great struggle that was going on between Athens and Sparta. Everywhere the democratic party looked to Athens as its champion, the aristocratic to Sparta. This was especially true of the states which were called the allies but were really the subjects or tributaries of Athens. A turn of the political wheels that brought the aristocrats to the top was commonly followed by a revolt from the sovereign state; when, as was usually the case, they remained underneath, they busied themselves in plotting for a change, and their first step was to open communications with the Spartan general or admiral in command.

In Cos the popular or pro-Athenian party was in the ascendant, and their opponents were weak. The fact was that the Spartans were not in good repute there. Six years before their admiral Astyochus had plundered the island laying hands impartially on the property of friends and of foes. Still there was a party which remained faithful to Sparta, and Hippocles preferred to speak as their representative. His wide-spread connections as a merchant—and Cos had a large trade with its famous vintages and equally famous woven stuffs—gave him a knowledge of details and persons that would have deceived a far more acute and suspicious person than Callicratidas.

The merchant began the conversation by offering the admiral a present of wine, and one of those almost transparent robes of silk that were a specialty of the island.

"I will not be so churlish as to refuse what you have the good will to offer me," said Callicratidas, "but you must understand that I do not accept these things for myself. I accept no personal gifts; it is a dangerous practice, and has given rise to much scandal. I shall send them to Sparta, and the magistrates will dispose of them as they think fit. What is this?" he went on, taking up the robe and holding it between his eyes and the lamp. "What do you use it for? for straining the wine?"

Hippocles explained that it was a material for garments.

"Garments!" exclaimed the Spartan, "why, we might as well wear a spider's web. It is not clothing at all. It neither warms nor covers. Is it possible that there are people so foolish as to spend their money on it? It is costly, I suppose?"

"As you ask me," replied Hippocles, "I may say that it costs about two minas a yard."

"Two minas a yard!" cried Callicratidas, whose Spartan frugality was scandalized at such a price. "Why," he added after a short calculation, "it is very nearly a seaman's pay for a year,* are there many who buy such costly stuff?"

"A dress of this material is the top of the fashion for ladies in Athens and Corinth."

"What?" said the Spartan, "do women wear such things? It is incredible. I have always thought that things had changed for the worse at home, but we have not got as far as that. And now for your business.

* A seaman was paid four obols a day, the rate having been increased by the liberality of Cyrus from three to four. Five obols went to the drachma, and a hundred drachmas to the mina.

Hippocles explained that there was a dissatisfied party in Cos which was very anxious to get rid of Athenian rule. "We are not strong enough," he went on, "to do it of ourselves, but send on a force and we will open the gates to you. Cos is a strong place now, since the Athenians fortified it, and, I should think, quite worth having."

"And if we put you in power," said the admiral, "you would begin, I suppose, by putting all your opponents to death."

Callicratidas was quite a different person from what Hippocles, with his former experience of Spartans in command, had expected to find. His disinterestedness, simplicity and directness were embarrassing, and made him not a little ashamed of the part that he was playing. He would have dearly liked to speak out of his own heart to a man who was transparently honest and well-meaning, but in his position it was impossible.

"We have, as you may suppose, sir," he said in answer to this last suggestion, "a great many injuries to avenge, but we should not wish to do anything that does not meet with your approval."

"The whole thing does not meet with my approval," said the Spartan, "I hate these perpetual plots; I hate to see every city divided against itself, and see the big persons in Greece hounding them on to bloody deeds, and making our own gain out of them. I wish to all the gods that I could do something to bring this wretched war to an end. Why should not Athens and Sparta be friends as they were in the old days? Surely that would be better than our going on flying at each others' throats as we have been doing for now nearly twenty years past, while the Persian stands by, and laughs to see us play his game. Where should we be—you seem an honest man, by your face, though I cannot say that I particularly like the errand on which you have come —where should we be, I ask, if we had shown this accursed folly twenty-odd years ago, when Xerxes brought up all Asia against us? As it was we stood shoulder to shoulder, and Greece was saved. And now we have to go cap in hand, and beg of the very Persians who are only biding their time to make slaves of us. I tell you, sir, I feel hot with shame at the thought of what I have had myself to put up with in this way. When I came here I found the pay-chest empty; I don't want to complain of anybody, so I won't say how this came about; but that was the fact, it was empty; the men had had no wages for some time, and they would very soon have had no food. I asked my officers for advice.

'You must go to Cyrus,' they said, 'Cyrus is pay-master.'* It was a bitter draught to swallow, but I managed to get it down. I went to his palace at Sardis. 'Tell your master,' I said to the slave who came to the door, a gorgeous creature whose dress I am sure I could not afford to buy, 'tell your master that Callicratidas, admiral of the Spartan fleet, is here, and wishes to speak with him.' The fellow left me standing outside, and went to deliver his message.

* This was the prince commonly called the younger Cyrus, the second of the two sons of Darius Nothus, King of Persia, by his Queen Parysatis. He had come down about a year and a half before the time of which I am writing to take the government of a large portion of Asia Minor, viz: Lydia, Phrygia, and Cappadocia. He was strongly pro-Spartan in his views, and as has been explained in a previous note, had increased the rate furnished by the Persian treasury to the Spartan fleet. But Lysander, in his anger at being suspended in the command, had, with the selfishness characteristic of Spartan officers, paid back to Cyrus all the money that had been furnished for the pay of the sailors.

After I had waited till my patience was almost exhausted, the man came back, and said 'Cyrus is not at leisure to see you. He is drinking.' Well, I put up with that. 'Very good,' I said, 'I will wait till he has done drinking.' I thought that I would go earlier the next day, though even then it was scarcely an hour after noon. So I went at a time when I thought that he could not possibly have taken to his cups, and asked again to see him. This time they had not the grace even to make an excuse. 'Cyrus is not at leisure to see you,' was the answer, and nothing more. That was more than I could stand, and I went away. I vowed that day, and believe me it was not only because I had myself been insulted, that if I lived to go home, I would do my very best to bring Sparta and Athens together again. And now, sir, as to your business. I will send home a report of what you say. If the authorities direct me to take any action in the matter, I shall do my best to take it with effect, but I tell you frankly that this idea does not commend itself to me, and let me give you a bit of advice: do your best to make peace in your city, as I shall do my best to make peace in Greece. Depend upon it, that if we don't, we shall have some one coming down upon us from outside. It may be the Persian, though he does not seem to me to have improved as a soldier; it may be the Macedonian, who is a sturdy fellow, and helps us already to fight our battles. Whoever it is he will find us helpless with an endless quarrel and will make short work with us. And now good night."

Hippocles left the Spartan admiral full of admiration for his manly and patriotic temper, and not at all pleased that he had been obliged to play a false part with a man so transparently honest.

About an hour after midnight the harbor was alarmed by the cry that the ship from Cos had parted from her moorings. Hippocles had taken advantage of a temporary increase in the force of the wind to cut his cables, and to drift toward the Athenian part of the harbor. Nobody was able to answer the cry for help, even if it had not been purposely raised too late. The *Skylark* had run the blockade, and Conon knew that he was to be relieved.

CHAPTER VI.

ARGINUSÆ.

AT Athens, meanwhile, the relieving fleet was being fitted out with a feverish energy such as had never been witnessed within the memory of man. Nine years before, indeed, preparations on a larger scale, if cost and magnificence are to be taken into account, had been made for the disastrous expedition against Syracuse; but there was all the difference in the world between the temper of the city at the one time and at the other. Athens was at the height of her strength and her wealth when she sent out her armament, splendid, so to speak, with silver and gold, against Syracuse. It was a mighty effort, but she did it, one may almost say, out of the superfluity of her strength. Now she was sadly reduced in population and in revenue; she was struggling not for conquest but for life; she was making her last effort, and spending on it her last talent, her last man. To find a juster parallel it would have been necessary to go back a life-time, to the day when the Athenians gave up their homes and the temples of their gods to the Persian invaders, falling back on their last defences, the "wooden walls" of their ships. Many men had heard from father or grandfather, it was just possible that one or two tottering veterans may have seen with their own eyes, how on that day a band of youths, the very flower of the Athenian aristocracy, headed by Cimon, the son of Miltiades, had marched with a gay alacrity through the weeping multitude, to hang up their bridles in the temple of Athene. **For the** time the **goddess needed not horsemen but** seamen, and they gave her the service that **she asked for.** Now the same sight was seen again. **Again** the knights, the well-born and wealthy **citizens of Athens,** dedicated their bridles to the patron goddess, and went to serve as **mariners on** board the fleet. Every ship that could **float was hastily** repaired and equipped. Old hulks that had been **lying in dock** since the palmy days when the veteran Phormion* led the fleet of Athens to certain victory, were launched again and manned. In this way the almost unprecedented number † of one hundred and ten triremes were got ready. To man these a general levy of the population **was made. Every one within the** age of service not actually disabled by sickness, was taken to form the crews, and not a few who **had** passed the limit volunteered. Even then the quota had **to** be made up by slaves, **who** were promised their freedom in return for their services. It was a stupendous effort, **and** one which Athens made with **her own** strength. **These were not mercenaries,** but her own sons whom she was sending out to make their last struggle for life. Night and day the preparations were carried on, and before a month **was out from the day on which the tidings of the disaster** at Mitylene reached

---

* Phormion won some brilliant victories in the Corinthian gulf in the early years of the war. He died prematurely, it would seem about 429 B. C.

† The number of triremes contributed **by** Athens to the Greek fleet of Salamis was one hundred and eighty, **but** this comprised, of course, literally every ship that they possessed. In the expedition against Syracuse, the triremes numbered one hundred and thirty-four.

the city, the fleet was ready to sail. Its destination was
Samos, an island that had remained faithful to Athens
even after the disastrous end of the war in Sicily. Here it
was joined by a contingent of forty ships, made up of the
same squadron scattered about the Ægean, the two triremes
of Diomedon * being among them. Diomedon was related
to Callias, and the young man asked and obtained leave
from the captain with whom he had sailed from Athens to
transfer himself to his ship.

A battle was imminent. The Spartan admiral had left
fifty ships to maintain the blockade of Mitylene, and sailed
to meet the relieving force. His numbers were inferior, but
pride, and perhaps policy, forbade him to decline the combat. He had made a haughty boast to Conon, and he had
to make it good. "The sea is Sparta's bride," he had said.
"I will stop your insults to her." His fleet was now off
Cape Malta, the south-eastern promontory of Lesbos. The
Athenians had taken up their position at some little islands
between it and the mainland, the Arginusæ, or White Cliffs,
as the name may be translated, a name destined to become
notable as the scene of the great city's last victory.

Callicratidas had watched the arrival of the Athenians,
and had concluded that, according to the usual custom of
Greek sailors, they would take their evening meal on shore.
Before long the fires lighted over all the group of islets

* Diomedon was the officer in command of Samos, and had already
attempted with the twelve ships that composed his squadron, to relieve
Conon. His force was so inferior to that of the Spartans that he could
only have hoped to succeed by eluding their observations. Accordingly
he had avoided the harbors and endeavored to make his way up a narrow channel, known by the common name of " Euripus " (a channel
with a swift current) by which Mitylene could be approached. Callicratidas, however, had discovered the manœuver and captured ten out
of the twelve ships.

showed that he was right. His own men had supped, and they were ordered to embark in all haste and make an attack which would probably be a surprise. What success his bold and energetic action would have had we can only guess. The stars in their courses fought against him. A violent thunderstorm with heavy rain came on, and prevented him from putting to sea.

The next day was fine and calm and the two fleets were early afloat. Their arrangement and plan of action showed a curious contrast, a contrast such as was almost enough to make one of the great Athenian seamen of the past turn in his grave. The Athenian ships were massed together; the Spartans and their allies were formed in a single line. Callias, who had never before been present at a great sea-fight, but who had taken pains to acquire as much professional knowledge as he could, expressed his surprise to Diomedon. "How is this, sir?" he said, "how can our ships maneuver when they are packed together in this fashion?"

Diomedon, an old sailor who had been afloat for nearly forty years, smiled somewhat bitterly as he answered.

"Maneuver, my dear boy! That is exactly what we want to avoid. We can't do it ourselves, and we don't mean to let our enemies do it, if it can be helped. The generation that could manoeuver is gone. Five and twenty years of fighting have used it up. But, happily, we can still fight, at least such a fleet as we have got to-day, the real Athenian grit, can fight. If the weather holds fine, and I think it will for the day, though I don't quite like the looks of the sky, we shall do well, because we shall be able to keep together."

The arrangement of the Athenian line may be very briefly described. It had two strong wings, each consisting of sixty ships, formed in four squadrons of fifteen. These wings consisted wholly of Athenian galleys; the contingents of the allies were posted in the centre, and were in single line, either because they were better sailors, or because, as being directly in front of the group of islets, they were protected by their position.

The policy of the Athenian commander was successful. Arginusæ was not a battle of skillful maneuvers, but of hard fighting. Such battles are often determined by the fate of the general, and so it was that day. Callicratidas, had that pride of valor which had often done such great things for Sparta and for Greece, but which some times resulted in immediate disaster. His sailing master, a man of Megara, had advised him to decline a battle. A rapid survey of the position, of the numbers of the enemy and of the tactics which they were evidently intending to pursue, had convinced this skillful, experienced seaman, that the chances were against him. Callicratidas would not listen to him. "If I perish," he said, "Sparta will not be one whit the worse off." It was the answer of a man who was as modest as he was brave; but it was not to the point. Sparta would be a great deal worse off if she lost not only him—and he was worth considering—but, as actually happened, nearly the half of her fleet.

The signal to advance was passed along the line, and the admiral himself took up his place in the foremost ship. The whole fleet could see him as he stood a conspicuous figure in the lead. His stately and chivalrous presence, the feeling that a man whom it was a privilege to follow anywhere, gave, for a time, an effective encouragement. But the loss was proportionately great when that presence was removed. Early in the day his ship endeavored to ram that which carried the Athenian admiral Diomedon, itself in the van of the opposing force. Diomedon himself was at the rudder and managed his galley with remarkable skill. He avoided or rather half avoided the blow of the enemy's boat, and this in such a way that the Spartan admiral lost his balance, and fell into the water. Callias, who was standing on the rear of the Athenian galley, at the head of a detachment of men ready either to board or to repel boarders, endeavored to save him; but the weight of his armor was fatal. He sank almost instantaneously. His death, it is easy to believe, cost Athens even more than it cost Sparta. It would have been infinitely better for her to fall into his hands than to have to sue for terms, as she did not many months afterwards, to the less generous Lysander.

The battle lasted for several hours. About noon the weather became threatening. The wind changed to the south-west and the sea began to rise. By general consent the struggle was suspended. Both sides had fought with conspicuous valor, but there could be no doubt that the victory remained with the Athenians. Their losses were serious, nearly a fifth of their force, or to give the numbers exactly, twenty-nine ships out of one hundred and fifty. But they had inflicted much more damage than they had suffered. Out of the small squadron of Spartan ships, ten in number, nine had been destroyed; and more than sixty belonging to the various allied contingents were either sunk or taken.

The fifty that remained—and there were barely fifty of them—made the best of their way either to the friendly island of Chios, or to Phocæa on the mainland. Without doubt the Athenians had won a great victory. Whether the opportunity could have been used to restore permanently the fortunes of the city, is doubtful; but it is certain that it was lamentably wasted.

CHAPTER VII.

AFTER THE FIGHT.

A COUNCIL of war was held by the Athenian admirals on one of the Arginusæ islets as soon as they could meet after the fighting had come to an end. Callias, by Diomedon's desire, waited outside the tent in which the deliberations were being held, and could not help hearing, so high were the voices of the speakers raised, that there was an angry argument about the course to be pursued. The intolerably clumsy system of having ten generals of equal authority was on its trial, if indeed any trial was needed, and was once more found wanting. * Even if the right decision should be reached, time was being wasted, time that, as we shall see, was of a value absolutely incalculable.

When at last the council broke up—its deliberations had lasted for more than an hour—and Diomedon rejoined the young officer, he wore a gloomy and anxious look.

" I am afraid," he said, " that mischief will come of this. I feel it so strongly that, though I ought not, perhaps, to tell outside the council what has been going on within, I

* I may refer my readers to a signal instance in earlier Greek history where the same system almost led to disaster. It was only by the unusual personal influence of Miltiades, a personal influence almost unparalleled in Athenian history, that thus the ten generals were induced to fight at Marathon. There can be little doubt that, if the conflict had been delayed the pro-Persian party might have seriously hampered, if it did not altogether defeat the efforts of the patriots.

must call you to witness. I did my very best to persuade my colleagues. 'Our first business,' I said, 'is to save our friends. There were twenty-six ships, I said, disabled. A few were sunk on the spot; others, I am afraid, have gone down since; but more than half, I hope, are still afloat. Even where the ship is gone already, there are sure to be some of the crew who have been **able to keep** themselves afloat **either by** swimming or by holding on **to** floating stuff. For the sake of the gods, gentlemen,'—I give you my very words—'don't **lose** another moment. We have **lost too many already. Send every seaworthy ship that you** have got **to** the **rescue** of the shipwrecked. **It is better to** let ten enemies escape, than lose a **single friend.' They** would **not listen to** me. They were bent, they said, on following up their victory, an excellent thing, I allow; but only when the first duty of making all that you have got quite safe has been performed. One of them—I will mention no names—positively insulted **me.** 'Diomedon,' he said, 'has doubtless had enough **fighting for the day.'** Why, in the name of Athene, do they put **such** lowbred villains into office. The fellow has a long tongue, and so the **people elect him. I** 'tired of fighting' **indeed? I** might have **some excuse if I** were, for I was hard at it, when **he** was a thievish boy, picking up unconsidered trifles in the **market-place. Well;** the end of it was that we came to a sort of compromise. Forty-odd ships are to go and save what can be saved from the wrecks—the gods only know how many will be left by this time—while the rest are to make the best of their **way to Mitylene, and cut off the** blockading squadron."

"And you, sir?" asked Callias, "with which squadron are you to be?"

"I am to go to Mitylene, of course, after what that fellow said, I could not ask to have the other duty; but I feel that it is what I ought to be doing."

"Who is to have it, sir," said Callias.

"No one, if you will believe it," answered the admiral, with an angry stamp of the foot. "I mean no one of ourselves, of the Ten. They are all so anxious to follow up the victory, as they put it, and make a great show of taking Spartan ships, that they will not take the trouble. Theramenes and Thrasybulus are to do it. I know that they have been in command in former years and may be supposed to be competent. Thrasybulus, too, is trustworthy; but Theramenes—to put it plainly—is a scoundrel. You know that I don't care about politics; I am a plain sailor and leave such things to others; but I say this, politics or no politics, a man who turns against his friends is a scoundrel.* I don't know what trick he is not capable of playing. Anyhow, whether these two do the business ill or well, one of the Ten ought to go. It would be better; and I am sure trouble will come of our not going. Mind this is all in confidence. You are never to breathe a word of it, till I give you leave."

"And am I to go with you, sir?" said Callias.

"No," was the answer; "I forgot to tell you; the worry of all this put it out of my mind. You are to take the despatch to Athens."

* Theramenes had taken a prominent part four years before this date in the establishment of the oligarchy of the Four Hundred; finding that his own position was not such as he conceived to be suited to his merits, and having reason also to believe that the oligarchy would soon be overthrown—the fleet had declared against them—he changed sides, and was the means of bringing up the condemnation of two of his own intimate friends, Antiphon and Archeptolemus.

" But the shipwrecked men "—exclaimed **Callias.**

" We must obey orders."

An hour afterward Callias was on his way to Athens; the storm had now increased **to** something like **a gale.** As the waves came from the south it was impossible to **take** a straight course **for** the **point in view, lying as** it did almost due **west. Few ships in those days** could keep **a** straight **line with the** wind on the quarter.* Indeed it **was soon impossible** to keep up any sail at all, nor was it safe, even if the strength of the rowers already wearied by the labors of the day, had permitted it to keep the ship broadside to the waves. Nothing remained but to put her about and drive before the wind, a sail being now hoisted again and the rowers exerting themselves to the utmost to avoid being " pooped " by the heavy waves. Toward morning the wind moderated, but by that **time the** *Swallow*, for that was the name of the despatch-boat which had been told off for the service, **had** been driven as much as fifty miles out of her course. This would not have been of much consequence, but that the timber of the *Swallow* had been so strained by her battle with the sea that she began to leak inconveniently, if not **dangerously. Her crew, too,** were now in urgent need **of rest.** Under ordinary circumstances, Chios, which could be seen, as the day broke, about ten miles **on the right bow,** would have afforded **a** con-

---

* Catullus mentions it as a special excellence of his yacht that it could

> " Carry its load o'er stormy seas
> Whether from right or left the breeze
> Call o'er the main, as safe and fleet
> Over course, as when, on either sheet
> With equal strength blew fair behind,
> With level keel the following wind."

venient shelter; but Chios was in the hands of the enemy. The little island of Vara, lying some ten miles to the north-west, was the only alternative. Here Callias, much against his will, for he feared that his news would be anticipated, was compelled to stop, the captains of the despatch-boat refusing to proceed, until vessel and men were better able to face the weather.

As it turned out, the delay did no harm. In fact it was the means of his reaching Athens with more speed and safety than he might otherwise have done. A day indeed was lost in doing such repairs as the imperfect resources of the little island permitted, but on the morrow, Callias set out again, and was groaning over the day that had been lost, and the very little good that the clumsy boat-builders had been able to do for him, when he found himself being rapidly overhauled by a vessel which had not long before hove in sight. Before noon he recognized the cut of the disguised *Skylark*, and at once ran up a signal which Hippocles whom he supposed to be on board would, he knew, recognize. The signal was immediately answered, and before another half-hour had passed the *Skylark* was along-side. After a brief colloquy it was arranged that the *Swallow* should make the best of her way to Samos, where there was an arsenal in which she could be properly repaired and that Callias with his dispatches should take his passage to Athens in the yacht.

Hippocles was acquainted with the general fact that the Athenian fleet had won a great victory ; but he knew no de-tails, and was eager to hear from the lips of one who had taken a part in the action. And he had much that was interesting to say **to his** young friend. The three weeks **which** he had spent in Mitylene with the blockaded squadron had not made him hopeful about **the first issue** of **the war.** He had found that Conon was not hopeful, and Conon was as able and intelligent an officer as Athens had in her service.

"**This** has been a stupendous effort **on the part of the city,**" he said, "and it has saved us for a time, but **it can't** be kept, and it can't be repeated. Athens is like a gambler **reduced** to his last stake. He wins it; very good. But then he has to throw again; and as often as he throws, it is the same—if he loses, he loses all. And, sooner or later, lose he must. In the long run the chances are against us. We have lost our *morale.* I saw a good deal of Conon's men when I was shut up, and I thought very badly of them; **and he** thinks badly, too, I know. It is only a question **of time.** Do you know," he went on, sinking his voice to a whisper —"and mark you, this is a thing that I should not venture to say to anyone in the **world but** you—I am half inclined to wish that we had been beaten in **the** last battle—that is, **if** Callicratidas had lived. A noble fellow indeed! Do you know that he let the Athenians whom he took at Methymna go on their *parole?* **Any** one else would have sold them for slaves."

"Well," said Callias, who was a little staggered by his friend's view **of affairs, "as your** hero is drowned—mind that I quite agree **in** what you say of him—perhaps it is better that things have turned out as they have. And I can't believe that our chances are as bad as you make out. Anyhow **we are better** off than when I saw you last."

"**I hope so;** I hope so;" said Hippocles **in** a despondent tone, "But they might have done better. For instance, we have let the blockading squadron at Mitylene escape."

"How was that?" asked Callias. "Did you see nothing of our fleet. It was to sail northward at once."

"No—I never saw or heard of it. Now listen to what happened. On the day after the battle—though of course I knew nothing of what happened—*two* despatch-boats came into the harbor—so at least everyone thought—and the second had wreaths on mast and stern, as if it had brought good news. And Eteonicus—he was in command of the blockading squadron—was good enough to send us a herald with the intelligence that Callicratidas had won a great sea fight, and that the whole of the Athenian fleet had been destroyed. Of course we did not quite believe that, but if only a quarter of it was true, it was not pleasant hearing. My old sailing master, who has as sharp eyes as any man I know, said to me. 'My belief, sir, is that it is all nonsense about this great victory, and that the second boat was only the first *dressed up*. I observed them both particularly, and they were amazingly alike. In both the bow sides oars were just a little behind the stroke, and one of the oars, I noticed, was a new one, and not painted like the rest. And why should the man take the trouble to tell us about the victory as he calls it. If it is true, he has us safe, and can cut us up at his leisure. No, sir, I don't believe a word of it.' Well, I was not certain that the old man was right, but I strongly suspected that he was. Anyhow I was so convinced of it that I spent the whole night in getting ready; and, sure enough, the next morning the blockading squadron had slipped off, with nobody to hinder them."

"That was a very smart trick for a Spartan," said Callias.

CHAPTER VIII.

THE NEWS AT ATHENS.

THE *Skylark* excelled herself in the display of her sailing qualities. Thanks to this, Callias, in spite of the untoward delays which had occurred on his journey, was the first to bring intelligence of the victory to Athens. The news ran like wild fire through the city, gathering, as may be supposed, a vast number of imaginary details, as it passed from mouth to mouth, and the assembly which was called by proclamation for the next day, to hear the reading of the despatches, was, considering the empty condition of the city, most unusually crowded. No one who could crawl to the market-place was absent, and all the entrances and approaches were thronged by women, children, and slaves. The first stress of fear had been relieved, for it was known that a victory had been won; but there was still much room for anxiety. The victory had not been gained without cost —no victories ever were—and it was only too probable that in this case the cost had been heavy. The despatch was brief and formal. It told the numbers engaged, and the order of formation, with the number of hostile vessels captured or sunk. It mentioned the fact that there had been losses on the side of the conquerors, and promised details when there should have been time to ascertain the facts.

After the assembly had been dismissed, Callias **was overwhelmed with** enquiries. **To** these he thought it well **to** return very vague answers. The fact was that **there was** much that he knew and **much** that he did not **know.** He knew the name of more than one of the ships that had been sunk or disabled. **Two or three** had been run down before his eyes. About others **he had** information almost equally certain. He could have told some of his questioners what would have confirmed their worst fears. On the other hand he could not give anything like a complete list of the losses. Some enquirers he could reassure. He had seen or even talked to their friends after the battle. **All** the admirals, he **knew, were safe.** And steps, he was sure, had **been taken** to rescue the shipwrecked crews. On the subject of **Diomedon's** fears he preserved absolute silence. **If any** disaster **had** happened, it was only too sure **to be heard** of before **long.**

On the evening of the day of assembly **a** great banquet was held in the Prytaneum, or Town-hall of Athens. Such a banquet was always an interesting sight, and on this occasion Callias, as he witnessed it for the first **time, also saw** it to the very greatest advantage. All the public guests * of the city that were not absent on active service or were not positively hindered from coming by age or infirmity were **present.** The ranks of these veterans were indeed sadly **thinned.** The war **had been** curiously deadly to officers high in command. **The fatal** expedition to Sicily had

---

* Persons who had rendered distinguished services to their country in peace or war received, among other rewards, the privilege, lasting for life, of dining in the Town hall. The city had no greater honor to bestow.

swept off many of the most distinguished. Others had fallen in the "little wars" in which Athens like all states that have wid dominions had been perpetually involved. One famous survivor of a generation that had long since passed away was there, Myronides, the victor of Œnophyta. The old man had been born in the Marathon year, and was therefore now eighty-four. His life, it will be seen, embraced with remarkable exactitude the period of the greatness of Athens. The victory that had made him famous had been won fifty-one years before, and had been, so to speak, the "high water mark" of Athenian dominion.* He had lived to see almost its lowest ebb, though happily for himself as he died before the year was out, he was spared from seeing the absolute ruin of his country. Callias was distantly related to him and was on terms of as close a friendship as the difference of age permitted with his son Eteonicus, one of the ablest and most patriotic statesmen of the time. After the libation which was the usual signal for the wine drinking, had been poured, the old man rose from his place, as his habit was, and walked down the hall, touching our hero on his shoulder as he passed.

"Come," he said, as Callias looked up, "if you can spare half an hour from the wine cup to bear an old man company."

The young man immediately left his place and accompanied the veteran to one of the small chambers leading from the hall.

"And now tell me all about it," he said, when they were seated.

* It had brought about for a time the subjection of all the Bœotian towns (Thebes only excepted) and of Phocis to Athens.

Callias gave him as full an account as he could of all that he had seen during the campaign. Myronides plied him with questions that showed an intelligence of unabated vigor. The armament and sailing qualities of the ships, the *morale* and *physique* of the crews, every detail, in fact, that concerned the efficiency of the force that Athens had in the field, were subjects of liveliest interest to the old man. When he had heard all that his young kinsman had to say, he heaved a deep sigh. "Ah! my dear boy," he said, "things have come to a pretty pass with Athens. As an old soldier I know what some of the things that you tell me mean better than you do yourself. We are near the beginning of the end, and I can only hope that I shall be gone when the end itself comes. I don't mean that this is not a great victory that Diomedon and the rest of them have won; but it is a victory that will never be won again. In the very nature of things it can not. Do you think that the old men and boys that I won the day with at Œnophyta * would have sufficed for a regular force, a force that the city could rely on? Of course not. I could not even have afforded to risk the chance if they had not had something strong behind them. But now what is there? Old men and boys, and nothing behind them. The slaves, you say? Very good; they fought very well, I hear. And of course they will get their freedom. Do you think that they will fight as well again after they have got it? Why should they? A man may as well die as be a slave, and so they

* Myronides marched out with the citizens above and under the military age—all the available force that was left at Athens at the time—and won two victories, the first at Megara, the second and most famous of the two at Œnophyta in Bœotia.

might very well risk their lives to get free. But, once free, why should they risk them again?"

"What!" cried Callias, "not to keep the Spartans out of Athens?"

"You talk as an Athenian," said the old man, "and they are not Athenians. You and I, I allow, would sooner die than see Spartans within the walls: but what would it matter to them? They could eat and drink, buy and sell just as comfortably whoever might be their masters. Yes, my son; it is all over with a city that has to fall back on its slaves. There is only one chance, and that is to make peace *now*, before we lose all that we have gained. But what chance is there of that? Is there any one who would even dare to propose such a thing?"

"You would, sir," said the young man.

"Yes, I might; but to what profit? I don't suppose they would do me any harm. 'Poor old man!' they would say, 'he dotes.' But as for listening to me—I know better than that. Is there one of the responsible statesmen who would venture to give such advice? Would my son Eteonicus venture? Not he; and yet he is a sensible and honest young man, and knows that I am right. But it would be as much as his life, or, what he values more, his whole career is worth, to hint at such thing. Oh! what opportunities I have seen lost in this way. Unfortunately a victory makes the Athenians quite impracticable.* They don't

---

* The old man was thinking of the Spartan offer to make peace after the capture of the five hundred and ninety-two prisoners at Pylos (B. C. 425). Terms much more favorable might have been secured than were obtained four years afterwards by the Peace of Nicias. Again, after the defeat and death of the Spartan admiral Mindarus in B. C. 410 peace might have been made, and the ruin of Athens probably postponed for many years; but the people refused to enter into negotiations.

seem capable of realizing **that the wheel is certain to take a turn. But you have** had enough of an old man's croakings. The gods grant that these things may turn out better than **my fears!** And now give me your arm to **the gate, where** my people will be waiting for **me."**

Callias conducted the old man to the door, and saw him put safely into the litter which was waiting for him. He then stood meditating how he should dispose of himself for the rest of the evening. He was unwilling to return to the banquet. Questions would **be put to him, he knew, by** many of the guests to which **it would be** difficult either to **give or to refuse an** answer. He would gladly, indeed, have hidden himself altogether till the fuller despatches should **have arrived,** which would relieve him of the necessity of **playing any** longer **the** difficult part which **had been im-** posed upon him. **His** thoughts naturally turned to Hip- **pocles and Hermione, and** he had already taken some steps in the direction of the Peiraeus, when the thought occurred to him that he was scarcely on terms of such intimacy with the family as would warrant a visit at so late an hour. **As** he stood irresolute, the door of a neighboring house opened, **and a** party of four **young men** issued from it into the **street.**

"Ah!" cried one of them, "'tis the sober Callias. Seize him, Glaucus and Eudaemon, and make him come with us."

The two men addressed ran up to our hero, **and** laid hold **each of an arm.**

"**You are** a prisoner of my spear," said the first speaker, whose name, **I may** say, was Ctesiphon, "and may as well **submit to** your fate with as much grace as possible. You shall not suffer anything unendurable, and shall be released at the proper time.   Meanwhile you must join our expedition."

"I submit," said **Callias,** willing, perhaps, to have the question that had been puzzling him settled for him. "But tell me, if I have to follow you, whither you are bound."

"We are going to the **house of Euctemon, where there** will be something, I know, worth seeing and hearing."

"But I am a stranger," said Callias.

"A stranger!" cried Ctesiphon, "you are no such thing. The man who brings good news to Athens is the friend of everybody.   Besides Euctemon is my first cousin, and he is always pleased to see my friends.   You should have been at his dinner, but that there was no room on his couches for more guests.   But now when the tables are removed * we shall easily find places.   But come along or we shall lose something."

There was no want of heartiness in Euctemon's greeting to his new guests.   To Callias he was especially polite, making room for him on his own couch.   When the new arrivals were settled in their places, the host clapped his hands.   A white-haired freedman, who acted as major-domo, appeared.

"We are ready for Stephanos," said Euctemon.

A few minutes afterwards a figure appeared, so curiously like the traditional representations of Homer that every one was startled.   Stephanos was a rhapsodist, or professional writer, and he had made it one of the aims of his life to imitate as closely as he could the most distinguished member that his profession could boast.   In early life he had been a school master, and an accident, if we may so describe a blow

---

* When the meal was ended the tables were not cleared, but removed.

from the staff of a haughty young aristocrat, whom he had ventured to chastise, had deprived him of sight. His professional education had included the knowledge of the authors whom the Greeks looked upon as classics, Homer holding the first place among them, and he was glad to turn this knowledge to account, when he was no longer able to teach. In this occupation too his blindness could be utilized. It had its usual effect of strengthening the memory, and it helped him to look the part, which, as has been said, he aspired to play.

The blind minstrel was guided to the seat which had been reserved for him in the middle of the company by an attendant, who also carried his harp.

"What shall we have, gentlemen?" asked the host. "You will hardly find anything worth learning that Stephanos does not know."

The guests had various tastes, so various that it seemed very difficult to make a choice. One wanted the story of the Cyclops, another the tale as told by Demodocus to Alcinous and the Phæacian princes, of the loves of Ares and Aphrodite. A third, of a more sober turn of mind, called for one of the didactic poems of Solon, and a fourth would have one of the martial elegies with which the old Athenian bard Tyrtaeus stirred, as was said, the spirits of the Spartan warriors.

"Let Callias, the bringer of good news, name it," said Euctemon, after some dozen suggestions had been made.

The proposal was received with a murmur of approval.

The young man thought for a moment. Then a happy idea struck him. About a year before there had occurred an incident which had roused the deepest feeling in Athens.

The aged Sophocles, accused by his son Iophon before a court of his clansmen, of imbecility and incapacity for managing his affairs, had recited as a sufficient vindication of his powers, a noble chorus from a play which he was then composing, the last and ripest fruit of his genius—the "Œdipus in Colonus." The verses had had a singular success, as indeed they deserved to have, in catching the popular fancy. They were exquisitely beautiful, and they were full of patriotic pride. Every one had them on his lips; and before they had time to grow hackneyed, the interest in them had been revived by the death of the veteran poet himself.

"Let us have the 'Praises of Athens' by Sophocles the son of Sophilus of Colonus."

The choice met with a shout of applause. The minstrel played a brief prelude on his harp in the Dorian or martial mood,* and then began:

---

* There were three original moods in Greek music, the Dorian, Phrygian, and Lydian. The last of these was in a major scale, and was reckoned to be plaintive and effeminate. So Milton writes in *L'Allegro*.

> " And ever against eating cares
> Lap one in soft Lydian airs
> Married to immortal verse ;
> Such as the melting soul may pierce
> In notes with many a winding bout
> Of linked sweetness long drawn out."

The Dorian was in a minor scale, and was considered to be manly and vigorous. Martial music was of this kind. So, to quote Milton again, we have :

> " Anon they move
> In perfect phalanx to the Dorian mood
> Of flutes and soft melodies; such as raised
> To heights of noblest temper heroes old
> Coming to battle."

The third, or Phrygian, was also minor, and was considered to be suitable for sacrifices and other religious functions as being of an ecstatic kind. There were combinations and modifications of these moods. Readers who may desire to know more of the subject, should consult Professor Mahaffy's *Rambles and Studies in Greece*, pp. 424-444 (3rd edition). A more elaborate account may be found in Mr. Chappell's History of Music.

"Swell the song of praise again;
  Other boons demand my strain,
  Other blessings **we** inherit,
  Granted by the mighty spirit;
  On the sea and on the shore,
  Ours the bridle and the oar.
  Son of Chronos old whose sway
  Stormy winds and waves obey,
  Thine be heaven's well-earned meed,
  Tamer of the champing steed;
  First he wore on Attic plain
  Bit of steel and curbing rein.
  Oft too, o'er the water blue,
  Athens strains thy laboring crew;
  Practiced hands the barks are plying,
  Oars are bending, **spray is flying,**
  Sunny waves beneath them glancing.
  Sportive myriads round them dancing,
  With their hundred feet in **motion,**
  Twinkling 'mid **the foam of ocean.**"

He concluded amidst thunders of applause, the **reference** to the fleet being especially rewarded with a purse from the host and a shower of gold pieces from the guests.

Other recitations followed, not **all, it** must be confessed, **in** so elevated a strain; each was produced with a few bars **of** music appropriate to its character.

The next entertainment was of a less intellectual kind. Now dancers were introduced into the room by the trainer who had taught them, and whose slaves in fact they **were. The** man was a red-faced, bloated looking **creature, who, how-** ever, had been very active in his time, **and could still dis-** play a wonderful amount of agility when he was engaged in teaching his pupils. The dancers were brother and sister, twins, and curiously alike, though the boy was nearly **a** half-head taller, and generally on a larger scale than the girl. The performance commenced with a duet of the harps

and the flute. The harp, a small instrument not larger than a violin was played by the boy, the flute by a female player, who had come into the room along with the dancers. After a while the harp became silent, **the** flute continuing to give out a very marked measure. To this the girl began to dance, whirling hoops into the air as she moved, and catching them as they fell. Many were in the air at once, and the girl neither made a single step out **of time nor let a single hoop** fall to the ground.

A more difficult and exciting performance followed. The flute-player changed the character of her music. The Lydian measure which had been admirably suited to the graceful steps of the dance gave place to the swift Phrygian scale, wild and fantastic music such **as** might move the devotees of Cybele or Dionysus to the mysterious duties of **their worship. At** the same **time** an attendant **of the** trainer brought in **a large hoop,** studded round its inner **circle** with pointed **blades.** The girl commenced to dance again with steps that **grew** quicker and quicker with the music, till, as it reached a climax of sound, she leapt through the hoop. The flute-player paused for a moment, as the dancer turned to recover her breath, her **bosom** rising and falling rapidly, **and her eyes** flashing with excitement. Then the music and the dance began again, **with** the same *crescendo* of sound and motion, till the same culminating point was **reached, and** the same perilous leap repeated.

The spectators watched the scene with breathless interest; but it was an exhibition that was scarcely suited **to Greek taste. A Greek could** be even horribly cruel on occasions, **but** a cruel spectacle—and **spectacles** that depend for their attraction on the danger to the performer are critically cruel—offended their artistic taste. The company began to feel a little uneasy, and Euctemon finally interrupted the festival when after the second leap had been sucessfully accomplished he signed to the flute-player to cease her music.

"Child," he said to the dancer, "Aphrodite and the graces would never forgive me, if you were to come to any harm in my house. It is enough; you have shown us that no one could be more skilful or more graceful than you."

The boy and girl now performed together in what was called the Pyrrhic or war dance. Each carried a light shield and spear, made of silvered tin. They represented two warriors engaged in single combat. Each took in turn the part of the assailant and the assailed, the one darting forward the spear which had been carefully made incapable of doing any harm, the other either receiving the blow upon his shield or avoiding it with agile movements of the body.* The flute-player accompanied the dance with a very lovely and spirited tune, while the company looked on with the greatest admiration, so agile, so dexterous, and so invariably graceful were the motions of the two dancers.

When the boy and girl had retired, and while the guests were again devoting themselves to the wine, Callias was accosted by a neighbor with whose handsome features, characterized as they were by a gravity not often seen in young Athenians, he was familiar, though he did not happen ever to have made his acquaintance.

"I am about to retire," said the stranger, "and if I may

* So Hector in the single combat with Ajax.

presume so far, I would recommend you to do the same. Our host is hospitable and generous, and has other virtues which I need not enumerate; but his entertainments are apt to become after a certain hour in the night such as no modest young man—and such from your face I judge you to be—would willingly be present at. So far we have had an excellent and blameless entertainment; but why not depart. What say you?"

"That I am ready to go with you," answered Callias. "My friend Ctesiphon brought me hither, and I know nothing of our host except the report of his riches and liberality." "What! are you going?" cried the host, as the two young men rose from their places. "Nay, but you are losing the best part of the entertainment. It is but a short time to the first watch when Lyricles will come with his troop of dancers. He says that they are quite incomparable."

"Nay, sir," said the young man who had spoken to Callias, "you must excuse us."

"Ah!" cried one of the guests, a young dandy, whose flushed face and flower-garland set awry on his forehead seemed to show that he had been indulging too freely in his host's strong Chian wine, "'Tis old Silverside. He pretends to be a young man; but I believe that he is really older than my father. At least I know that the old gentleman is far more lively. Come, Philip and Hermogenes," he went on addressing two of his neighbors, "don't let us permit our pleasant party to be broken up in this way."

The three revellers started up from their places, and were ready to stop the departing guests by force. But the host,

who was still sober, and was too much of a gentleman to
allow annoyances of the kind to be inflicted upon anyone in
his house, interfered.

" Nay, gentlemen," he cried, " I will put force on no man
for if our friends think that they can be better or more
pleasantly employed elsewhere, I can only wish them good
night, and thank them for so much of their company as
they have been pleased to bestow upon us."

The two, accordingly, made their escape without any
further interference.

" Will you walk with me as far as my house," said Callias'
companion to him. "It lies in the Agræ.*   The night is
fine and I shall be glad of your company."

Callias cheerfully consented, and was glad that he had
done'so, so witty and varied was his companions conversation.

When they had reached their destination his new friend
invited him to enter. This he declined to do for the hour
was late, and he wished to be at home.

" Well then," said the other, "we can at least meet again.
This, you see, is my house, and my name is Xenophon, the
son of Gryllus."

* A quarter of Athens south of the city on the Ilissus.

CHAPTER IX.

SOCRATES.

CALLIAS lost no time in cultivating the acquaintance of his new friend. The very next day he called upon him at as early an hour as etiquette permitted, and was lucky enough to find him at home. He had lately returned, indeed, from drilling with the troop of Knights to which he belonged, and was just finishing his breakfast, which had been delayed till his military duties had been performed.

" Will you drink a cup to our new friendship—if you will allow me to call it so ? " said Xenophon, to the young man as he entered the room.

" Excuse me," replied Callias, " if I decline."

" You are right," said Xenophon, " this is one of the offers which formality commands us to make—whether rightly or wrongly, I cannot say—but which I always myself refuse, and am glad to see refused by others. But what will you? A game of koltabos, or a walk to the springs of the Ilissus ?

"Either," replied Callias, " would be agreeable, but first now I have set my heart on something else. You are a disciple of Socrates, I am told. Can you manage that I may have the privilege of hearing him ? I have never had the chance of doing so before."

Xenophon's face brightened with pleasure when he heard the request. "Excellent, my dear sir, you could not have suggested anything that would have pleased me better. We shall certainly be good friends. I always judge a man by what he thinks of Socrates. You are ready, I know, to admire and love him, and I offer you my friendship in advance. Now let us go and find him. It will not be difficult, for I know his ways pretty well. There is a sacrifice in the Temple of Theseus, and he will probably be there. There is no more diligent attendant at such functions, and yet the fools and knaves say that he is an atheist. We shall catch him just as he is leaving.

The subject of conversation between the two young men as they walked along was naturally the character of this philosopher whom they were about to see. Callias had much to ask, and Xenophon had still more to tell.

"As you are going to see this man for the first time," said the latter, "you will be interested in hearing how I first came to make his acquaintance. It was about nine years ago, very soon, I remember, after the first expedition sailed for Syracuse. I had been hearing a course of lectures by Prodicus of Ceos, who was then all the fashion in Athens, and was hurrying home to be in time for the midday meal. Socrates met us in a narrow alley, and put his staff across it to bar the way. What a strange figure he was, I thought. I had never seen him before, you must know; for we had been living for some years on my father's estate in Eubœa. Certainly he looked more like a Silenus than an Apollo. 'Well,' my son, he said, looking at me with a smile that made him look quite beautiful, 'can you tell me where a

THE TEMPLE OF THESEUS.

good tunic is to be bought?' I thought it was an odd question, though certainly he might want a tunic for himself, for his own was exceedingly shabby. However I answered it to the best of my ability. ' And a good sword—where may that be purchased?' That I told him also as well as I could. Some half-dozen more things he asked me about, and I did my best to reply. At last he said, 'Tell me then, my son, since you know so well where so many good things are to be procured, tell me where the true gentleman * is to be found? That puzzled me exceedingly, and I could only lift my eyebrows and shrug my shoulders. How could I answer such a question? Then he said, "follow me my son, and be taught.' I never went near Prodicus again, you may be sure. My father was somewhat vexed, for he had paid a quarter of a talent as fee for the course of lectures. However it did not cost him anything, for Socrates will never take a fee. From that day to this I have never missed an opportunity when I was not campaigning of hearing him. But see there he is!"

Socrates was standing in the open space in front of the Temple of Poseidon, with the customary group of listeners round him. As the two young men came up the discussion which had been going on came to an end, and the philosopher turned to greet the new comers. " Hail! Xenophon," he cried, " and you, too, sir, for the friends of Xenophon are always welcome." " You, sir," he went on addressing Callias, " are recently back from the war; now tell me this." And he asked questions which showed that military de-

* The " Kalokagathos " (literally handsome and good), combining the two Greek ideals, beauty of mind and beauty of body.

tails were perfectly well known to him, better known to him in fact than they were to Callias himself. These questions were becoming a little perplexing, for **Socrates** had an inveterate habit of driving **into a** corner, it may be said, every one with **whom he** conversed. Luckily for Callias, another friend came up at the moment, and the great examiner's attention **was diverted.**

"Ho! Aristarchus," he **cried to the** new comer, "how fare you?"

"But **poorly, Socrates,"** was the reply. "Things are going **very ill with me."**

"And indeed," said the philosopher, "I thought **that** you **had a somewhat** gloomy look. But tell me—what is your trouble? Xenophon here **is** your kinsman, I know, and you **will** not mind speaking **before** him, and he will answer for the discretion of his friend. Or would you prefer that we should go apart and **talk,** for **to** that too, I doubt not, **these two** gentlemen will consent?"

"Nay," said the man who had been addressed as Aristarchus, **"I am not ashamed or** unwilling to speak before **Xenophon and** his friend Callias, in whom I have the pleasure **of recognizing a** kinsman of my **own. For that from which I am suffering,** though it troubles **me, has** nothing shameful in **it."**

"Speak on then," said Socrates, "and, perhaps, among us we shall be able to find some remedy for your trouble. **For sure-** ly it is of some use to share a burden if it be too heavy for one."

"Listen then, Socrates," said Aristarchus, "I have **been** compelled for kindred's **sake to** take into **my home** not a few ladies, sisters, and nieces, and **cousins,**

whose husbands or fathers, or other lawful protectors, have either perished in the war, or have been banished. There are fourteen of them in all. Now, as you know, nothing comes in from my country estate, for who will farm that which at any time the enemy may ravage? And from my houses in the city there comes but very little, for how few are they who are able to pay rent? And no business is being done in the city, nor can I borrow any money. Verily there is more chance of finding money in the street, than of borrowing. O, Socrates, 'tis a grievous thing to see my own flesh and blood perish of hunger, and yet, when things are as they are, I cannot find food for so many."

" 'Tis grievous indeed," said Socrates. "But tell me—how comes it to pass that Keramon feeds many persons in his name, and yet can not only provide what is needful for himself and his inmates, but has so much over that he grows rich while you are afraid of perishing of hunger?"

"Nay, Socrates, why ask such a question? The many persons whom he so keeps are slaves, while the inmates of my house are free."

"Which then, think you, are the worthier, your free persons, or Keramon's slaves?"

"Doubtless my free persons."

"But, surely, it is a shame, that he having the less worthy should prosper, and you with the more worthy, be in poverty."

"Doubtless 'tis because his folk are artisans while mine have been liberally educated."

"By artisans you mean such as know how to make useful things."

"Certainly."   .

"Barley meal is a useful thing, for instance?"

"Very much so."

"**And** bread?"

"Very much so.**"**

"And men's and **women's cloaks,** and short frocks, **and** mantles, and vests?**"**

"Very much so."

"But your folk **don't know how to make any of these things.   Is it so?"**

"**Nay, but they know how** to make them **all.**"

"**Do you not** know then, how Nausicydes not only supports himself and his household by making barley **meal,** and has become so rich that he is often called upon to make special contributions to the **State*** and how Corœlus, the **baker,** lives in fine style on the profits of bread-making, and **Demias on** mantle-making, **and** Menon on cloak-making, **and nearly every one in** Megara on the making of vests?**"**

"**That is very true,** Socrates. But all these buy barbarians **for** slaves, and **make them** work; **but my** people are free by birth and kinsfolk of my own."

"**And because** they **are** free and kinsfolk of yours must they **do** nothing but eat and sleep? Do you suppose that other **free people** are happier when they live in this indolent **fashion,** or when they employ themselves in useful occupa**tions? What about** your kinsfolk, my friend? At present **I** take it, you do **not love them, and they** do not love you, **for you** think them **a great trouble and loss** to you, and they **see** that you feel **them to be a burden.**   It is only too likely

* See **note** page 22.

that all natural affection will turn under these circumstances to positive dislike. But if you will put them in the way of making their own livelihood, every thing will go right; you will have a kindly feeling for them because they will be helping you, and they will have as much regard for you, because they will see that you are pleased with them. They know, you say, how to do the things that are a woman's becoming work; don't hesitate therefore to set them in the way of doing it. I am sure that they will be glad enough to follow."

"By all the gods, Socrates, you are right. I dare say I could borrow a little money to set the thing going; but to tell you the truth, I did not like to run into debt, when all the money would simply be eaten. It is a different thing, now that there will be a chance of paying it back, and I have no doubt that there will be some way of managing it."

Just at this point a little boy came up with a message for Socrates. "My mistress bids me say," he cried in a somewhat undertone, "that the dinner is waiting, and that you must come at once." "There are commands which all must obey," said the philosopher with a smile, "and this is one of them. And indeed it would be ungrateful to the excellent Xanthippe, if after hearing she has taken so much pains to prepare one's dinner, one was to refuse the very easy return of eating it. Farewell, my friends."

And the philosopher went his way.

To Callias the conversation which he had just heard was peculiarly interesting, because the theory in his family was that which was probably accepted in almost every upper class house in Athens, that it was a disgrace for a free-born woman to work for her living, and that all handicrafts, even in those who constantly exercised them, were degrading and lowering to the character. Xenophon already knew what his master thought upon these points, but to his younger friend this "gospel of work," as it may be called, was a positive revelation. He did not value it even when, a few days later, he heard from Aristarchus that the experiment had succeeded to admiration. "I only had to buy a few pounds of wool," he said; "the women are as happy as queens, and I have not got to think all day and night, but never find out, how to make both ends meet."

CHAPTER X.

THE MURDER OF THE GENERALS.

ALL this time a gloom had been settling down over the Athenian people. The official despatch, which, as giving details of the loss in the late engagement, was so anxiously expected, did not arrive; but quite enough information to cause a very general anxiety came to hand in various ways. Private letters from men serving with the fleet began to be brought by merchantships; and not a few persons were found who had talked or who professed to have talked with sailors and marines who had taken part in the action. These written and oral accounts were indeed far from being consistent with each other. Some were obviously impossible; more were presumably exaggerated. But they were all agreed in one point. Not only had there been a serious loss of ships and men during the battle, but this loss had been grievously aggravated by the casualties that had taken place after the battle. It was pretty clear, unless the whole of these stories were fictitious, that the second loss had been more fatal than the first.

At last the long expected despatch arrived. It ran somewhat in this fashion:

"The victory which, by the favor of the gods and the good fortune of the Athenian people, we lately won over the

Spartans and their allies at the Islands of Arginusæ has turned out to be no less important and beneficial to the state than we had hoped it would be. The squadron of the enemy that was blockading the harbor of Mitylene has disappeared; nor indeed are any of his ships anywhere to be seen. Our fleet, on the contrary, is stronger than it has been for some years past; and we are daily receiving overtures of friendship from cities that have hitherto been indifferent or hostile. But this success has not been achieved without loss. The late battle was long and obstinately contested, and, as has been mentioned in a former despatch, not a few of our ships were either disabled or sunk. We did not neglect the duty of succoring the crews of the vessels that had met with this ill-fortune, committing to officers whom we knew to be competent, the task of giving such help and assigning to them a sufficient number of ships. At the same time we did not omit to make provision for a pursuit of the enemy. But unluckily when the battle was but just finished, a storm arose so severe that we could not either rescue our friends or pursue our enemy. These then escaped, and those, or the greater part of them perished, having behaved as brave men toward their country. Lists of those that have so died, so far as their names are at present known, are sent herewith."

In this official communication, it will be seen, no blame was laid on any person. The weather, and the weather alone, was given as the cause of the disaster that had occurred. But in their private communications with friends at home the generals were not so reticent. They had commissioned, they said, Theramenes and Thrasybulus to save the shipwrecked men. If all that was possible had not been done to execute this commission it was they and they only who were to be blamed. Such words, even if they are intended only for the private reading of the people to whom they are written, seldom fail sooner or later to get out. In this case so many people were profoundly and personally interested in the matter that they got out very soon. And, of course, among the first persons whom they reached were the two incriminated officers, Theramenes and Thrasybulus. It was a charge, hinted at if not exactly made, which no man would allow to be made against him without at least an attempt to refute it. Theramenes, who had come back on leave not many days after the battle, at once bestirred himself in his own defense. He was an able speaker, all the more able because he was utterly unscrupulous; and he had a large following of personal friends and partisans. On the present occasion he was reinforced by the many citizens who had lost relatives or friends in the late engagement. These were furious and not without some cause. What had been at first represented as a great victory had at length turned out to be as fatal as a great defeat. They loudly demanded a victim. Somebody, they said, must be punished for so scandalous, so deadly a neglect. Theramenes had the advantage of being on the spot, and of being able to guide these feelings in a way that suited his own personal interests. "I was commissioned," he said, "to do the work; I do not deny it. But the charge was given me when it was almost too late to execute it, and I hadn't the proper means at hand. I could not get hold of the ships that were told off for this task, or of the crews who should have manned them. **If one of the ten had come himself to help me,** things might have been different. **As it was,** the men either could not be found, or refused to come. A subordinate **must not** be blamed for failing in what ought to **have been** undertaken by a chief in command."

These representations, in which, **as** has been seen, there was a certain measure of truth, had a great effect. An **assembly** was held to consider **the** contents of the second despatch, and **at this it was resolved, with scarcely an op**posing voice, that the generals should **be recalled.** They were publicly thanked for the **victory** which they had **won,** but they were suspended, at least **for the** present, in their command, and successors were sent **out to** replace them. **Conon, as** having been shut up **at the** time in Mitylene, and being therefore manifestly clear of all blame in **the matter, was continued in office, and** another of **the ten had died.** Eight, therefore, **were left to** be affected by the decree. **Of** these eight two determined not to run the risk of returning; the other six sailed at once for home. Of these **six Diome**don, **about** whom something has been said already, was one.

As soon as was practicable after their arrival at Athens, an assembly was held and they were called upon **for their** defence. The chief speaker against them **was Theramenes.** His colleague, Thrasybulus, stood by apparently approving **by his** presence **the** charge that was **brought** but not opening his mouth. One man among the accused men might **have** easily secured his own safety **at the** expense of his **colleagues. If** Diomedon **had stood** up and recapitulated **the** advice which he had given **in the** council held after the battle; if he had affirmed what none of his fellows **would** have been able to deny, "I urged you to make the rescue of the imperilled crews your first business, to use for it all the means at your disposal, and to undertake it yourselves," he must have been triumphantly acquitted, but he was of too generous a temper thus to save himself. He chose to stand or fall with his fellows. All, accordingly, put forward the same defence, and it was in substance this: "We did what seemed best in our judgment. We detailed for the duty of saving the crews what we considered to be an adequate force, and put over it men whom we knew to be competent. If Theramenes accuses us, we do not accuse him. We believe that he was hindered from doing the duty intrusted to him by the storm, and that if he had had double the number of ships, even the whole fleet, at his disposal, he would have been no less powerless to give the shipwrecked men any effectual help."

There was a sincerity of tone about their defense which was just the thing to win favor of such an audience as the Athenian assembly. There were murmurs indeed. The friends and kinsfolk of the drowned men could not endure to think that no one would be punished for what they believed to be a shameful neglect. But the general applause drowned the dissenting voices, and the friends of the accused began to hope that they were safe. If there had been only a few more minutes of daylight, such might have been the result. A show of hands was taken by the presiding magistrate, and it was believed to be in favor of the accused, but it was too dark to count; no regular decision could be made; and the matter had to be adjourned to another meeting of the assembly.

But now came another change in the impulsive, passionate temper of the people. The next day or the next day but one was the first of the great family festival of Athens, the Apaturia, a celebration something like the Christmas Day or the New Year's Day of the modern world. It was one of the most cherished, as it was one of the most ancient of the national festivals. All the great Ionic race, with scarcely an exception, kept it, and had kept it from times running back far beyond history. The family annals were now, so to speak, made up, and consecrated by a solemn association with the past. If a marriage had been celebrated in the family during the year it was now formally registered; if a son of the house had reached his majority his name was now entered upon the roll. These formalities were duly marked by customary sacrificing and sacrifices were accompanied, as always in the ancient world, by festivities. But family festivites are apt, as most of us know only too well, to be marred by melancholy associations. It is delightful to greet those that remain, but what of those who are gone? And so it had been year after year, since the day when Athens embarked on the fatal war which for nearly thirty years drained her resources. So it was, in a special way, in the year of which I am writing. The men whom Athens had lost were not hired servants but sons. Every one, the slaves only excepted, left an empty place in some family gathering. And now for the first time the city realized the greatness of her loss. The numbers had been known before; but numbers, however startling, do not impress the mind like visible facts, and now the visible facts were before the 'eyes of all. The streets were filled with men and women in mourning garb, **for the families which** had suffered indi-vidually assumed it.   It seemed as if almost every passer by had lost a kinsman.   **There could scarcely have been** any such proportion of mourners, but any uniform garb renders the impression of being much more numerously worn than **is** really the case.

And there can be but little doubt that **the demonstration** was purposely exaggerated. For now came in the sinister in-fluence of political strife, which **since the** oligarchical revolution of five years before had **grown** more than ever bitter and intense.   The accused leaders belonged **to the** party of moderate aristocrats; a party loyal to the democrat-ic constitution of Athens, but disposed to interpret its provisions in **a** conservative **sense.**   The oligarchy hated them, and Theramenes had been an oligarchical conspirator before, and **was about to be** again.   And **the** extremists on the **other** side hated them.   Between the two a plot was concocted. **Men who had** no kinsfolk among the **lost** soldiers **and sailors** were bribed or otherwise persuaded **to** behave as if they had, * **to** come into the streets with black clothes and shaven heads, and to swell the numbers **of the** mourners, thus increasing the popular excitement.

Strangely enough it was the senate, the upper chamber of the Athenian constitution that first gave this excitement an expression. **At** the first meeting after the festival, Callix-enus, a creature of Theramenes—the man himself was prob-ably too notorious to take an **active** part—proposed a reso-lution which ran as **follows:**

* Xenophon, who was probably in Athens at the time, positively as-serts that this was done, and I cannot think that the arguments of Mr. Grote countervail his authority.

" **For as much as** both the parties **in this** case, to wit, the prosecutor, on the one hand, and the accused, on the other were heard in the late assembly, **it seems good to us that** the Athenian people now vote on the matter by their tribes, there being provided for each tribe two urns, and that the public crier make proclamation **as** follows in the hearing of each tribe: ' Let every one who finds the generals guilty of not rescuing the heroes of the late sea fight deposit his vote in **Urn No. 1. Let him** who is **of the contrary** opinion deposit his vote in Urn No. 2.' Furthermore it seems good **to** us, that, if the aforesaid generals be found guilty, death should be the penalty; that they should be handed over to **the** Eleven,* and their property confiscated to the state, excepting a tenth part, which falls **to the** goddess [Athene]."

The Senate passed this resolution, though there was a strong minority that **protested** against it. The assembly was held **next** day, and Callixenus came forward again and proposed his resolution as having received the senate's sanction.

It was received with a roar of approval from the majority. But there were some honest men who were not inclined to sanction a proceeding so grossly illegal, for such indeed it was. One of them, Euryptolemus by name, rose in his place, and spoke:

" There is an enactment which for many **years** has been observed by the people of Athens for the due protection of persons accused of crime. By this enactment it is provided that every person **so accused** shall be tried **separately**, and shall have proper time allowed him for the

---

* The " Eleven " were commissioners of police who had, besides the charge of the guardians of public order, the care of the prisoners, and the custody of criminals.

preparation of his **defence.** Seeing then that the resolution just proposed to the assembly contravenes this enactment by providing that **the accused persons should be tried** altogether and without such allowance of **due time, I** hereby give notice that I shall **indict Callixenus its proposer** for unconstitutional action."

A tremendous **uproar followed** the utterance of **these** words. "Who shall hinder us from avenging the dead?" **cried one man. "Shall this pedant** with his indictment stand between the Athenian people and their desire to do justice?" shouted another. But the excitement rose **to its** height when a man clad **as a mariner forced his way** through the crowded meeting, and struggled by the help of **his companions into the** *Bema*, **the platform or** hustings **of the place** of assembly.

It was a strange figure to stand in that place from which some of the famous orators and statesmen of **the** world **had** addressed their countrymen. He was evidently of the lowest rank. His dress was ragged and soiled. His voice, when he spoke, was rough and uncultured. Yet not Pericles himself who so often speaking from that place

> "Had swayed at will that fierce democracy,'

ever spoke with more effect.

"**Men** of Athens," he cried, "**I was on** the *Cheiron*. **I was** run down by a Corinthian ship **just before the battle came to an end.** The *Cheiron* sank immediately; **I went down** with **her, but** managed to get free, **and came up again to the** surface of the water. I saw a meal-tub floating **by me,** and caught hold of it. Some ten or twelve men **were near me.** They kept themselves up for a time by swimming, **but sank** one by one. I spoke to several of them, and bade them keep up their spirits, because the admirals would be sure to rescue us. No help came. At last only one was left. He was my brother-in-law. I made him lay hold of the other side of the meal-tub; but it was not big enough to keep us both up. He let go of it again. He said to me 'Agathon'— that is my name—'you have a wife and children; I am alone. Bid them remember me; and tell the men of Athens that we have done our best in fighting for our country, and that the admirals have left us to perish."

Was the man telling the truth, or was he one of those historic liars that have made themselves famous or infamous for all time by the magnitude of the fictions that they have invented just at the critical time when men were most ready to accept them.*

Whether it was true or false, the story roused the people to absolute fury. Thousands stood up in their places and shook their fists at the accused, and at the orators who had spoken in their favor, while they screamed at the top of their voices, " Death to the generals ! death to the murderers ! "

A momentary silence fell upon the excited crowd when a well-known orator of the intense democratic party threw himself into the hustings.

" I propose that the names of Euryptolemus and of all those who have given notice of the indicting Callixenus be added to the names of the accused generals, and be voted upon in the same way for life and death."

* One of the most notorious instances in modern times was that of the Tartar who after the battle of the Alma invented the news that Sebastopol was taken. The report was almost universally believed in England for some days, and the contradiction of it caused the bitterest disappointment.

The speaker added no arguments; and the **roars of approval** that went up **from** the assembly showed sufficiently **that no** arguments were needed. **The advocates of constitutional** practice were cowed. It was only too plain that **to persist** would surely be to meet **themselves the fate of the accused.** Euryptolemus was a brave man, **and as** we shall **soon** see, did not intend to desert his **friends; but** for **the** present **he gave way.** "I withdraw my notice," he cried, reflecting doubtless that he could renew it when the people should become more ready to listen to reason and justice. **But** there was still another constitutional bulwark **to be** thrown **down.** The presiding magistrates refused **to put the motion to the assembly.** Their chief (or chairman **as we** should call him) **rose in his place.** He was pale and agitated, **and his voice could not be heard beyond the** benches **nearest to** him when **he said, "The** motion of Callixenus is against the laws, and **we** cannot put it to the assembly."

"They refuse **! they refuse !"** was the cry that went from **mouth** to mouth. Again the rage of the multitude rose to boiling point, and again the popular orator saw his opportunity.

"I propose," **he said, appearing** again in the hustings, "that the names of the **presiding** magistrates be added to those of the accused in the **voting** for life and death."

A shout of approval more vehement than ever greeted this announcement. **Once** more **the** policy **of** concession, **or** shall we say of cowardice **prevailed.** The magistrates conversed **a** few **moments in hurried** whispers, and then advanced to the railings in front of their seats. It was immediately seen that they had yielded, and loud applause followed.

"Hail to the popular magistrates! Hail to the friends of the people!" was the universal cry. But one was still sitting in his place. His colleagues turned back to bring him. They talked, they gesticulated, they laid hold of him by the arms; they were trying to force him out of his seat. He heeded them not; to all persuasion he returned the same answer: "I am set to administer the laws, and will do nothing that is contrary to them." The most of the house could, of course, hear nothing of what was being said; but they could see plainly what had happened. "Socrates refuses! Socrates refuses!" was now the cry, followed by shouts of "Death to Socrates!" "Death to the blasphemer! death to the atheist!"

The philosopher sat unmoved, and his colleagues made no further attempt to persuade him. They took what was, perhaps, the only possible course under the circumstances —for they had not all the martyr-like temper of Socrates— and put the question without him. It was carried by a large majority.

The presiding magistrate, having announced the result of the vote, went on: "Seeing that it has seemed good to the Athenian people to try the generals accused of negligence in saving the lives of citizens, the said generals are hereby put upon their trial. If they, or any citizen on their behalf, wish to address the assembly, let them or him speak."

It might have been thought that the furious crowd which had been ready to overpower with violence the advocates of constitutional practice would have howled down any who dared to advocate so unpopular a cause. But it was not so. The majority, having swept away, as they thought, the trammels of technicality, in their **eagerness for justice, had no** wish to disregard justice by refusing a hearing to persons on their defense. Whatever the faults of the Athenian **democracy, it was at** least ready **to** hear both sides. When therefore Euryptolemus rose to address the assembly on behalf of the generals, an instantaneous silence followed; nor was he interrupted during the delivery of his speech except, it may be, by occasional murmurs of approval. He spoke as follows :

"Men of Athens, I have three things **to do** now that I address you. First, I have to blame in some degree my dear friend and kinsman Pericles, **and** my friend Diomedon; second, I have to plead somewhat on their behalf; third, **I** have to give you such advice as will **in my** judgment **best** advantage Athens. I blame them **because they,** through their generous temper, have **taken upon** themselves the fault which, if it exists, **lies** upon **others.** For indeed what happened after the **battle** was this : Diomedon advised that the whole fleet should proceed to the relief of the disabled ships **and their crews.** Herasinides counselled **that** the whole fleet **should be sent in** pursuit of the enemy. Meranylus declared that both duties might be discharged together, part **being** sent against the enemy, and part **to** help the shipwrecked men. And **this last** course was **actu**ally taken. Forty-seven ships **were told off for** this duty. Three, that is, from each of the eight divisions, ten belongto private captains, ten that **were from Samos, and** three **that belonged to the** commander-in-chief. And three ships **were committed to the charge** of Thrasybulus and **Thera**menes, the very men who **now bring these** charges against

the accused.　Yet these men I do not even now, on behalf of
the generals, myself accuse.　I allow that the violence of
the storm prevented them from executing this order which
had been given them.

"So far then, men of Athens, do I blame the accused, and
I do plead for them.　And now let me venture to give you
some advice.　Give these men time, if it be but one day
only, to make their defence.　You know that there is yet a
form of law by which it is enacted: ' If any person hath
aggrieved the people of Athens, he shall be imprisoned and
brought to a trial before the people; and in case he be convicted, he shall be put to death and thrown into the pit, h's
goods and chattels to be confiscated to the state, reserving a
tenth part for the goddess.'　By this law try the accused.　Give to each a separate day and try them in due
order.　So will you judge them according to the law, and
not seem, as verily you will seem if you adopt the resolution of
Callixenus, to be allies of the Lacedæmonians, by putting
to death the very men who have taken twenty of their ships.

"Why indeed are you in such vehement haste?　Are you
afraid to lose your hold of life and death?　That right no
one doubts or threatens.　Should you not rather be afraid
lest you put an innocent man to death?　One man do I say,
nay many innocent men?　And lest, afterwards repenting of your deed, you shall reflect how ill and unjustly you
have acted?　Forbid it, ye gods, that the Athenians should do
any such thing.　Take care, therefore, I implore you, that
you, being successful, do not act as they often act, who are
on the brink of despair and ruin.　Only those who are
without hope insult the gods; yet somehow you will insult

them, if instead of submitting to them on points that are subject to their will alone, you condem those men who failed because it was the **pleasure of the gods** that they should fail. You would do more justly if you honor these men with crowns of victory **rather** than visit them with this punishment **of death."**

A visible effect was produced **by this speech. That the** republic should put to **death its successful** generals **almost** in the moment of victory seemed to many to be **the very** height of folly, **even of** impiety. The gods had favored these men. To lay hands upon them would **be an** insult **to** heaven. But supposing they had erred, would **it be well** for the state **to deprive itself of the** services of its most skillful servants? This seemed the common sense view. The question was: would it **prevail against the sticklers for law, those who were** hardened **by the sense of personal** loss, **and the** unscrupulous partisans who **were** ready to seize any pretext for destroying political opponents? The voters filed **past the** balloting **urns,** and **dropped** their votes as they **passed. No one could guess what the result** would be, for no one could **watch** more than one of the ten pairs of urns—a **pair to each** tribe—which **were placed to receive the suffrages. The process took** no little time, **and** then when **it was** finished, **there** was the counting, also **a** long and tedious **process. It was** almost dark when the **tables were finished.**

In the midst **of a profound silence** the presiding magistrate stood up. **It was now** dark, and his figure was thrown into striking relief by the **lamps** with the help of which the **votes** had **been counted. He read the numbers from a** small slip of paper.* "There **have** voted," he said, "**for** condemnation 3254, for acquittal 3102."

The sensation produced **by** the announcement was intense. Not a few who had voted 'guilty' already **half re**pented of what they had done. Indeed the reaction which ended in the banishment and ultimately the death by starvation of the author **of** the proposal may be said to have begun at that moment. **The** general excitement rose to a still higher pitch when the officers **of** the Eleven, **the** magistrates to whose custody condemned criminals **were** handed, were seen making their **way,** lighted **by** slaves holding torches, to the place where the accused were sitting. There was not one of the six whose features were not famil**iar to** many **in** the assembly. More than one had tendered distinguished service to Athens; and one, Pericles, son of **the** great statesman by **Aspasia,** bore a name which no Athenian could pronounce without some emotion of pride and gratitude. It so happened that it was he on whom the officers laid hands. Something like a groan went up from the crowd; but it was to late to **undo** what they had done, and it was too early for the repentance that had already begun to work to have **any** practical effect. **The six were** led off to immediate execution.

Callias anxious **to say a few words of** farewell to his friend **and** kinsman **Diomedon had** hurried round, as soon as he heard the announcement of the numbers, to the door **by** which **he** knew the condemned would be taken from **the**

* Paper made from the rind of the *papyrus*, a reed which grew in the Nile and which the Egyptians knew by the name of *Byblos* (hence our 'bible'). Parchment in its present form did not become common till much later than this time (even B. C. 150), though skin seems to have been used for writing. For ordinary purposes paper was used.

place of assembly. The president of the Eleven who was conducting the matter in person, as became an occasion so important, allowed a brief interview.

The young man was so overcome with grief that he could only throw himself into the arms of his friend and cling to him in speechless agony. Diomedon, on the contrary, was perfectly calm and collected. "My son," he said, "this has ended as badly as I thought that it would—you will remember what I said to you after the battle. For myself, this that I am about to suffer is scarcely a thing to be lamented. It is hard indeed to have such a return for my services to Athens; and I would gladly have served her again. It has not so seemed good to the Athenians. Let it be so. I am delivered from trouble to come. I would not have fled from them willingly, but if my countrymen compel me, why should I complain? That at least Socrates has taught me not to do. And this day has at least brought this good, that no one can doubt hereafter that he believes what he says. For you, my son, I have but one word. Do not despair of your country. A grateful child pays his dues of nurture even to an impassive mother. And now farewell!"

An hour afterwards he and his colleagues were lying mangled corpses at the bottom of the pit.*

* Mr. Grote says that the condemned generals drank hemlock but it is evident from the report of Euryptolemus which is substantially taken from Xenophon's report that the mode of execution for persons condemned under such charges as that brought against the generals was by being thrown into the Pit. This place was called the *Barathron* and was within the city walls and was a deep pit with hooks fastened into the walls. The officer in charge of it was called "The Man of the Pit."

CHAPTER XI.

THE execution of the generals was a blow of such severity that Callias was absolutely prostrated by it. As a patriotic Athenian he felt overwhelmed both with shame and with despair. That his country should be capable of such ingratitude and folly, should allow private revenge or party spite to deprive her of the generals who could lead her troops to victory made it impossible to hope. The end must be near, for the gods must have smitten her with the madness which they send upon those whom they are determined to destroy. And then he had loved Diomedon almost as a son loves a father. Left an orphan at an early age he had found in this kinsman an affectionate and loyal guardian; and he had made his first acquaintance with war under his auspices. He had in him a friend whom he felt it would be quite impossible to replace.

For some days Callias remained in strict seclusion at home, refusing all visitors, and, in fact, seeing no one, except the aged house-steward, who had been now the faithful servant and friend of three generations of his family. Even when Hippocles himself, on the fifth day after the disastrous meeting of the assembly, sent in an urgent request that he might be allowed to see him, the steward was directed to meet him with the same refusal. The old man contrary to his custom of prompt and unhesitating obedience, lingered in the room after he had received this answer, and was obviously anxious to speak. "Well! Lycides," said the young man, his attention attracted even in the midst of his preoccupation by this unusual circumstance, "What is it? What do you want?"

"It would be well, sir," replied the man, "if you would see the worthy Hippocles. He declares that the affair of which he is come is one of the very highest importance."

Callias simply shook his head.

The steward began again, "Oh! sir—"

Callius interrupted him. "You are an old man, and a friend whom my father and my grandfather trusted, and I would not say a harsh word to you. But if you will not leave the room, I must."

The old man's eyes filled with tears. He had never heard his young master speak in such a tone before. Still he would not go, without making another effort.

He rapidly advanced to where his master was sitting, his face buried in his hands, and throwing himself on the ground, caught the young man by the knees.

"Listen, sir," he cried, "I implore you, by the gods, and by the memory of your father and your grandfather, who both died in my arms."

"Speak on," cried Callias. "It seems I am not my own master any longer."

"Oh! sir," the old man continued, "your liberty, your life is in danger."

These words, uttered as they were in a tone of conviction

that could not be mistaken, startled the young man out of the indifference which his profound depression had hardened.

"What do you mean?" he cried.

"I have known it since yesterday at noon," the steward replied, "and have been anxiously thinking over with myself how I could best make it known to you. And now Hippocles has come to say the same thing. For the sake of all the gods, trust and listen to what he has to tell you."

"Bring him in, if you will have it so," said Callias.

Hippocles came into the room with outstretched hands and caught the young man in a close embrace. The warmth and tenderness of this greeting had the happiest result. Callias was moved from the stupor of grief which had overwhelmed him. Bowing his head on his friend's shoulder, he burst into a passion of tears,—for tears were a relief which the most heroic souls of the ancient world did not refuse to themselves. His friend allowed his feelings to express themselves without restraint, and then as the violence of the young man's emotion began to subside, he put in a few words, instinct with heartfelt sympathy, about the friend whom they had lost. Thus, with his usual tact, he waited for Callias himself to open the subject in which he now felt sure his interest had been aroused. It was soon after that the young man asked: "What is this that old Lycides has been saying about my liberty and life being in danger? He has known it, he says, since yesterday, and you know it too. What can he mean?"

"He is quite right," replied Hippocles. "He knows something and I know something. Now listen. Your parting with Diomedon was observed. The men who murdered him—and by all the gods! there never was a fouler murder done in Athens—cannot but look for vengeance to come upon them. To avoid it or to postpone it they will stick at nothing. No near friend or relative of their victims is safe. I know—for I have friends in places you would not think—mark you, I *know* that your name is among those who will be accused in the next assembly."

"Accused," cried Callias, "accused of what? Of being bound by kindred and affection to one of the noblest of men. By heavens! let them accuse me. I should glory to stand and defend myself on such a charge. If I could only tell that villain Theramenes what I think of him I should be afraid of nothing."

"That is exactly what I thought you would say," replied Hippocles, "nor can I blame you. But have patience. Theramenes will get his deserts if there are gods in heaven and furies in hell. But have patience. Leave his punishment to them. But meanwhile don't give him the chance of burdening his soul with another crime."

"What would you have me do then?" asked Callias.

"Fly from Athens," replied his older friend.

"What! fly, and leave these traitors and murderers to enjoy their triumph! Not so; not if I were to die to-morrow."

"My dear young friend, you will help your country, which, in spite of all her faults, you wish, I presume, to serve, and avenge your friends all the more surely if you will yield to the necessities of the time."

"Don't press me any further: it would be a dishonor to me to leave Athens now."

The argument was continued for some time longer; but Hippocles could not flatter himself with the idea that he had made any impression. At last he seemed to abandon the attempt.

"Well," he said, "a willful man must have his way. I can only hope that you will never live to repent it. But you will not refuse to come and see us—my daughter adds her invitation to mine—you will not be so ungallant as to refuse."

"No, I should not think of refusing" said Callias. "You have called me back to life. I thought that my heart would have burnt with grief and rage. You can't imagine what your sympathy is to me."

"Well," said Hippocles, "show your gratitude by dining with us to-night."

Callias promised that he would, and accordingly at the time appointed presented himself at the merchant's house.

After dinner the discussion was resumed. Hippocles and Hermione urged all the arguments that they knew to persuade the young man to think of his own safety, but they urged in vain.

"No!" said the young man, as he rose to take his leave, "no, I thank you for your care for me, but your advice I may not follow. I refuse to believe that the Athenian people can keep the the base and ungrateful temper which they showed the other day. It was the madness of an hour, and they must have repented of it long ago. If they have not, then an honest man who happens to be born into this citizenship had best die. Athens is no place for him. Anyhow, I shall try, at the very next assembly, unless I can get some other and abler man than I am to do it for me, to indict Callixenus for unconstitutional practices. Did I pass by this occasion of vengeance, the blood of Diomedon and his brave colleagues might well cry out of the ground against me.

Several days passed without any disturbing incident. Callias had warnings indeed. Mysterious letters were brought to him, bidding him beware of dangers that were imminent; more than one stranger who found him in the streets let fall, it seemed by the merest accident, words that could not but be meant to give a warning; friends spoke openly to the same effect; but the young man remained unmoved. At the table of Hippocles, where he was a frequent guest, the subject was dropped. It seemed to be conceded by common consent that Callias was to have his own way.

He was returning to his home in the upper city from the Piraeus on a dark and stormy night, picking his way under the shelter of one of the Long Walls* when he felt himself suddenly seized from behind. So suddenly and so skilfully made was the attack that in an instant the young man, though sufficiently active and vigorous, was reduced to absolute helplessness. His arms were fastened to his side; his legs pinioned; his eyes blindfolded, and a gag thrust into his mouth. All this was done without any unnecessary violence, but with a firmness that made resistance impossible. The young man then felt himself lifted on to some conveyance which had been waiting, it seemed, in the neighborhood, and driven rapidly in a northerly direction. So

* The "Long Walls" ran from Athens down to its chief harbor the Piraeus.

much the prisoner could guess from feeling **the wind which he** knew had been coming from the east, blowing upon his right cheek. After being driven rapidly for a few minutes the gag **was** removed with an apology **for the necessity** that had compelled **its use. The** journey **was continued** with unabated **and even** increased rapidity, the lash, as Callias' ear told him, being freely used to urge the animals to their full speed. Before long the sound of the waves breaking upon the shore could be distinctly heard above the clatter of the horses' hoofs and the grinding of the chariot wheels upon the road. Then came a stoppage. The prisoner was lifted from his seat and put on board what **he guessed** to be a small boat. **He** felt that this was pushed out from the land, that it began **by** making fair progress, and that not long after starting, when it had **passed,** as he conjectured beyond the shelter of some bay or promontory, it began to meet bad weather. The waves were breaking, it was **easy** to tell, over the boat, in which the water was rising in spite of the efforts of the men **who** were busy bailing to keep it under. It was time for our hero to speak; so busy were the sailors in struggling with their difficulties, that they might easily have forgotten their prisoner, and let him go to the bottom like a stone.

" Friends," he cried, **" you** had best let me help you and **myself."**

" By Poseidon ! I had forgotten him," he heard one of the men cry. **If he** drowns there will be no profit to us in floating." A consultation carried on in low, rapid whispers followed. **It ended in** the prisoner's bonds being severed, **and the bandage being** removed from his eyes.

When the situation became visible to the young Athenian it was certainly **far** from encouraging. The boat was low in the water, and was getting **lower. It was evident** that it could not live more than a few minutes more. **The night** was dark, and the **sea** so high **that even the most expert** swimmer could **not expect** to survive very long. **The only** hope seemed to lie in **the chance of being blown ashore.** But obviously the first **thing to be done was to** prepare for a swim. Callias, accordingly, **threw off his upper garment** and untied his sandals. **This done he waited for the end.**

It was not long in coming. The boat was too low in the water to rise to **the waves, and one of unusual size now** broke **over and swamped it, immersing the crew, who num**bered nine persons **including Callias. Happily they were good swimmers, and if speedy help were to come, might hope to escape. And, luckily, help was nearer than any of** them had **hoped. A** light became visible **in the darkness;** and the swimmers **shouted in concert to let the new** comers **know** of their whereabouts. **An answering shout came from** the galley, for as may **be supposed, it was a** galley that **car**ried the light. **"Be of good cheer," shouted a voice which** Callias thought that **he** recognized. **The swimmers** shouted **in answer, and felt new** hope **and new life infused** into them. **But the rescue was no easy task. Each man in** turn had **to fasten under his armpits a rope with a noose at** the end **which was thrown to him, and was then drawn** up the side **of the galley. This took time. Some of the men** found it hard **to do their part of the work, and so delayed** the rescue of **the others. By the time that Callias was** reached, and he was the last of **the nine, he was almost**

beyond **the reach of help.** By one supreme effort, however, he managed to slip the rope about him. **As he was** dragged on to the deck the last conscious impression that he had—and so strange was it that he thought it **must be a** dream—was the face of Hermione bent over him with an expression of intense anxiety.

CHAPTER XII.

It was not long before Callias recovered his consciousness; but he was so worn out by excitement and fatigue, coming as they did after the exhausting emotions through which he had passed since the death of the generals, that he found it impossible to rouse himself to any exertion. The yacht, which as my readers will have guessed was that excellent sea-boat the *Skylark*, had never been in any danger, though she had had to be very skillfully handled while she was engaged in picking up the swimmers. This task accomplished, her head was put northward, and before very long she had gained the shelter of Euboea. Callias guessed as much when he found that she ceased to roll, and gladly resigned himself to the slumber against which he had hitherto done his best to struggle. He slept late into the morning; indeed it wanted only an hour of noon when at last he opened his eyes. The first object that they fell upon was the figure of Hippocles, who was sitting by the side of his berth.

"Then it was not a dream," said the young man. "I thought I saw your daughter on board last night, but could not believe my eyes."

"Yes, she is on board," said Hippocles, with a slight smile playing about the corners of his mouth.

"But tell me what it all means. I was seized in the streets of Athens, pinioned, blindfolded, and gagged. I was carried off I know not where, thrown into a boat, as nearly as possible drowned, and now, when I come to myself, I see you. Surely I have a right to ask what it means."

"My dear Callias," replied Hippocles, "I have always tried to be your friend, as it was my priviledge to be your father's before you. You will allow so much?"

"Certainly," said the young man. "I shall never forget how much I owe you."

"Well, then, trust me for an hour. I will not ask you to do anything more. If you are not fully satisfied then, I will make you any redress that you may demand. I know that you have a right to ask for it. I know," he added with an air of proud humility that sat very well upon him, "that Hippocles the Alien is asking a great favor when he makes such a request of Callias the Eupatrid,* but believe me I do not ask it without a reason."

The young Athenian could do nothing else than consent to a request so reasonable. Some irritation he felt, for there was no doubt in his mind that Hippocles had had something to do with the violence to which he had been subjected. The intention, however, had been manifestly friendly, and there might be something to tell which would change annoyance into gratitude.

A sailor now brought him some refreshment, and when this had been disposed of, another furnished him with some clothing. His own, it will be remembered, he had thrown

* The Eupatridae were the old aristocracy of Athens. Under the early constitution they were the ruling castæ, and they always retained the monopoly of certain religious offices.

away, when preparing to swim for his life. His toilet completed, he came up on deck and found Hippocles and his daughter seated near the stern. Both rose to greet him. He could not fail to observe that Hermione was pale and agitated. The frank friendliness of her old manner, which, blended as it had been with a perfect maidenly modesty, had been inexpressibly charming, had disappeared. She was now timid and hesitating. She could not lift her eyes when she acknowleged his greeting. He could even see that she trembled.

The young man stood astonished and perplexed. What was this strange reserve of which he had never before seen a trace? Was there anything in himself that had caused it? Had he—so he asked himself, being a modest young fellow and ready to lay the blame on his own shoulders—had he given any offence?

"Tell him the story, father," she said, after an anxious pause during which her agitation manifestly increased, "tell him the story. I feel that I cannot speak."

"My little girl has a confession to make. In a word, it is her doing that you are here to-day."

"Her doing that I am here to-day," echoed Callias, his astonishment giving a certain harshness to his voice.

The girl burst into tears. Callias stepped forward, and would have caught her hand. She drew back.

"Tell him, father, tell him all," she whispered again in an agitated voice.

"Well then," said her father, "if I must confess your misdeeds, I will speak. You know," he went on addressing himself to the young Athenian, "you know how we vainly

sought to persuade you to leave Athens. I had a better and
stronger reason for speaking as I did than I could tell you.
From private information, the source of which I could not
divulge, if you had asked it, as you probably would have
done, I had found out that you were in the most serious
danger. Not only were you to be arrested—so much you
know—but having been arrested, you were to be put out of
the way. You talked of answering for yourself before the
assembly, even of accusing your enemies and the men who
murdered your friends. You never would have had the
chance. There are diseases strangely sudden and fatal to
which prisoners are liable, and there was only too much
reason to fear that you would be attacked by one of them.
There are other poisons, you know, besides the hemlock,
which the state administers to the condemned, and an adverse verdict is not always wanted before they are given.
Well; we were at our wits' end. You were obstinate—pardon me for using the word—and I would not tell you the
whole truth. Even if I had, it was doubtful, in the temper
of mind you were in, whether you would have believed me.
Then Hermione here came to the rescue. 'We must save
him,' she cried, 'against his will.' 'How can we do that?'
I asked; and I assure you that I had not the least idea of
what she meant. 'You must contrive to carry him off to
some safe place.' I was astonished. 'What!' I said, 'a
free citizen of Athens.' 'What will that help him, with the
men who are plotting to take his life?' she answered. Then
she told me her plan. I need not describe it to you. It was
carried out exactly. Now can you forgive her?"

"Oh! lady"—the young man began.

"Stop a moment," cried Hippocles. "I have something more to say, before you pronounce your judgment. You must take into account that if she has erred, she has already suffered."

"Oh! father," interrupted the girl, "it is enough; say nothing more. I am ready to bear the blame."

And she sank back into her seat and covered her face with her mantle.

Hippocles went on: "I say she has suffered. We did not reckon on that unlucky wind. It was bad enough to have carried you off against your will; but when it seemed that we might drown you as well, that looked serious. I was not much afraid, myself. I felt pretty sure that we should be able to pick you up. But still there was a chance of something going wrong. And she, of course, felt responsible for it all. It was true that it was the only way of saving you—that, I swear by Zeus and Athene, and all the gods above and below, is the simple, literal fact—but still, I must own, it was a trying moment, and if anything *had* happened — Then you were the last to be picked up, and just at the last moment, something went wrong. The clumsy fellow at the helm—I ought to have been there myself, but I wanted to help in getting you on board—the clumsy fellow at the helm, I say, gave us a wrong turn. We should have had a world of trouble in bringing the *Skylark* about again. Hermione saw it, sprang to the tiller, and put things right—I have always taught her how to steer. So you really owe her something for that. I don't exactly say that she saved your life, but you might have been in the water a little longer than you liked. Well, it was trying to the poor girl. **I can** imagine how she felt; **but** she bore up **till we got you on board.** Then she fainted; for the very first time in her life, I give you my word, for she is not given to that sort of thing. Now, say, can you forgive her **and** us? **We** really did it for the best, and thanks to Poseidon, it has ended pretty well, so far, **after all."**

"This is no case for forgiveness," cried the young Athenian earnestly; **"it** is a case of gratitude which **I** shall never exhaust as long as I live. **I am a headstrong young** fool, **a** silly child, in fact, and you were quite right in dealing with me as grown people must deal with a child, help it and do it good against its will. Forgive me, **lady," he** went on, and kneeling before her chair, he took one of **her** hands **in his** own, and carried it to his lips.

So far all was well. A bold achievement had ended hap**pily,** but the situation was **a little** strained, to use a common phrase, and Callias, like **the** well bred gentleman that he **was,** felt that it would be a relief to the girl if it was brought to an end. Happily, too, at that moment **the ludicrous side of** the affair struck him, and it was without any affectation that he sprang to his feet and burst into **a** hearty laugh.

"And now **that you** have captured me," **he said,** "what **is your pleasure? What are you going to do with** me?"

"You shall go where you please," said Hippocles. "Even **if you** want to return to Athens I **will** not hinder you. But my plan is this, subject of course, **to** your consent. Come with me as far **as Thasus.** I have business there, to look after my vineyard, or rather the vintage. My people, I find, are sadly apt to blunder **about it.** This will take me no little **time, and while I am engaged there, the** *Skylark* shall take you on to Alcibiades' **castle in Thrace. I** was going **to say** that I would **commend you to** him. But that will not be **necessary.** He is, **you** know, a distant kinsman, and is hospitality itself. In my judgment he has had hard **usage. It** would have **been** better for **Athens, if she had trusted him more.** But all that **is past. Meanwhile I think that his** castle is the safest place **for you just now. You** and he are very much in the same **case, I fancy. Athens has not** treated either of you fairly and yet you **wish well to her."**

" Your plan seems a good one," replied **Callias,** " **let me** think it over for a **few hours.** Anyhow you shall **have my** company as far as Thasus, **if you** will accept it."

Meanwhile the *Skylark* **was** making headway **gaily** through the well-sheltered waters **that lie** between Euboea and the mainland of Greece. When the shelter ceased the wind had fallen, shifting at the **same time to the** southwest. Nearly two hundred miles had yet to be traversed before Thasus could be sighted, and this was accomplished without accident or delay. The time of year was **later than** a Greek seaman commonly chose for a voyage of any **dura-** tion, for it was the latter end of October, **and the ninth of** November was the extreme limit of the sailing season.* Hippocles, however, was more venturesome in this way than most of his contemporaries, and his confidence was rewarded by a most pleasant and prosperous voyage. So blue were the cloudless skies, so deep the answering color of the seas, that it was only when the travellers saw the sunset tints on the forest-clad **ridge** of Thasus—" the ass's back-bone laden

---

*" The seas are closed," says Vegetius in his treatise *De **Re Militari,*** "from the ninth of November to the tenth of March."

with wood," as it was called—that they remembered that summer had long since given place to autumn.

Two days were spent in a visit to the vineyard which Hippocles had come to inspect, and then Callias, who had soon concluded to follow his friend's advice, resumed his voyage The course of the *Skylark* was now south-easterly. The voyage had all the interest of novelty for him, for he had never before visited these waters. When the *Skylark* started at early dawn there was a mist which contracted the horizon. As this cleared away under the increasing power of the sun the striking peak of Samothrace became visible in the distance. All day its bold outlines became more and more clearly defined. On the following morning —for the good ship pursued her course all night—it had been left behind, but another height, not less striking in appearance, and even more interesting in its associations, the snow-capped Ida, at whose feet lay the world-famed Trojan plains, took its place. As evening fell the *Skylark* was brought to land at the western end of the Hellespont, the rapid current of which could be better encountered by the rowers when they had been refreshed by a night's rest. Progress was now somewhat slow; and it was on the afternoon of the fourth day after the start from Thasus that the cliffs of Bisanthe and the northern shore of the Propontis came in sight. This was our hero's destination, for it was here that Alcibiades, after quitting Athens in the previous year, had fixed his abode.

CHAPTER XIII.

ALCIBIADES.

THE sun was just setting when the *Skylark* cast anchor about two hundred yards from the shore and opposite the castle with which the loftiest point of the cliffs was crowned. The signal flag which the captain ran up to his mast-head was answered by another from the castle, and in a few minutes a boat was seen to start from a little quay which had been built out into the sea at the foot of the cliff. Callias had written a letter to Alcibiades in which he briefly described himself and his errand, and Hippocles, though modestly depreciating the value of any thing that he could say, had also written, at the young man's request, a letter of introduction. These documents were handed over to the officer in charge of the boat, and conveyed by him to the castle. After a very short delay the boat returned again, this time in the charge of an officer of obviously higher rank. This higher personage mounted the side of the *Skylark*, and after giving a courteous greeting to Callias, delivered to him an invitation from Alcibiades to make his castle his home for as long a period as he might find it convenient to stay there, explaining at the same time that his master would have come in person to welcome his guest, if he had not been detained by business of importance with a neighboring chief. The young Athenian's baggage—for he had **been** liberally fitted out by the thoughtful and generous care of Hippocles—was transferred to **the boat,** and **in a** few minutes more he had set his foot **on** the landing-**place.**

He had been speculating as he neared the shore, about **the** way in which the castle was to be approached. An observer looking from the sea might have thought that there was no way of getting to it except by scaling the almost perpendicular base of the cliff. Once landed on the quay, however, the traveller discovered that a passage had **been** cut through the cliff. This passage, which could be closed at its lower end by a massive door, was something like a winding staircase. **It** was somewhat stifling and dark, though light and air were occasionally admitted by holes bored to the outer surface of **the rock.** Its upper **end** opened in to a courtyard round which the castle was **built.** The approach from the sea was, it will have been seen, sufficiently secure. **On** that side indeed the castle of Bisanthe was absolutely impregnable. From the land, it was, to say the least, safely defensible. **It** was approached by one narrow ridge, so formed that a few resolute men could hold it against a numerous body of assailants. The walls were lofty and massive, and so constructed that a galling fire of missiles could be kept up on either flank of an attacking force.

Callias was escorted to his chamber by a young Thracian **slave,** who informed him **in broken speech that a bath** room in which **he would find hot and cold water was at** his service, and further that his master hoped to have the pleasure of his company at supper in an hour's **time.** The chamber, it may be said, was furnished with a clepsydra, or water-clock, marked with divisions.*

Callias awaited his introduction to his host with no little curiosity. Alcibiades was, as has been said, a kinsman of his own, and he had heard of him—what Athenian, indeed, had not.—but he had never happened to see him. Callias' father had been an aristocrat of the old-fashioned type, and had so strongly disapproved of his cousin's reckless and extravagant behavior that he had broken off all intercourse with him, and had been particularly careful that his son should never come in contact with him. Callias was about fourteen when Alcibiades left Athens in command (along with two colleagues) of the Sicilian expedition. The absence thus begun lasted about eight years. For the first half of this time he was an exile; for the second half in command of the fleets and armies of Athens, but still postponing his return to his native city. Then came his brief visit, lasting it would seem, only a few days,† and at that time Callias, as it happened, had been absent in foreign service. He was now

---

* It is convenient in a narrative to speak of "hours," and the Greeks had a division of time that was so named. But it must not be supposed that these hours were exact periods of time such as we mean by the word. The day between sunrise and sunset was divided into twelve equal parts, which varied in length according to the season of the year. The divisions of the whole period of a day and night into twenty-four equal unvarying parts was later than the period of which I am writing, being attributed to Hipparchus, the astronomer, a native of Nicæa in Bithynia who lived in the second century B. C. The water-clock mentioned in the text may have been one of those large ones which served for the whole night (Plato is said to have had one). The slave in announcing to the guest the time at which the meal would be served would probably indicate it by pointing to this or that division marked upon it. The water-clock may be roughly compared to a sand-glass, but the water flowed through several orifices, which were very minute.

† He returned in May, 407, conducted in person the procession to Eleusis; a ceremony which had been discontinued for some time on account of the presence of the Spartan garrison at Decelea, and left again to take command of the fleet a few days afterward. He never saw Athens again.

in what **was or should have been, the** prime of life, having just completed his forty-fourth year, but the dissipation of his youth and early manhood and the anxieties of his later years had left their mark upon him, **and he looked** older than his age. Yet there were traces of the brilliant beauty that in earlier days **had** helped to make him the spoiled darling of Athens. The wrinkles had begun to gather about his eyes, but they were still singularly lustrous, and could either flash **with anger,** or melt with tenderness. His temples were hollow and his cheeks had somewhat fallen in; but his complexion was almost as brilliant as ever, while the abundant auburn curls that fell clustering about his neck had scarcely a streak of gray in them.

His greeting to his guest **was more than** courteous. It was affectionate, exactly such as was fitting from an older to a younger relative. Indeed then, as ever afterward during their acquaintance, Callias **was** greatly struck by the perfection of his manners. **It** seemed impossible that the stories told of his haughty insolence by which in former years he had made himself one of the best-hated **men in Athens** could possibly be true.

Supper was announced shortly after **Callias had been** ushered into the chamber. Alcibiades took his guest by the hand, led him into **the** dining-room, **and** assigned him a **place** next to himself. **Some other guests were present.** Two of these were officers **in the military** force which **Alci**biades maintained in his stronghold; the third was an **aged man,** who had been his tutor many years, and for whom he **retained** an affection **that** was honorable to both master and pupil. **The fourth was the** Thracian chief with whom Alcibiades had been engaged when the *Skylark* arrived.

The meal was simple. The chief feature was one of the huge turbot for which the Euxine was famous.

"That would have cost a fortune in the fish market at Athens," said the host pointing to the dish, "even if it could have been procured at all. Here a fisherman thinks himself well paid for such a monster by three, or at the most, four *drachmae*."*

A piece of venison and a platter of quails were the other dishes. The second course consisted of a maize pudding and some sweet-meats.

During the repast the conversation turned speedily on local matters, and was carried on (but not till after a courteous apology had been offered to the young Athenian) in the bastard Greek largely mixed with Thracian words, in which the chief was accustomed to express himself. The meal ended, a handsome silver cup was handed by the major-domo, a venerable looking man, who made the comfort of his master and his most honored guests his special care. Alcibiades took it and poured out a few drops upon the table, uttering as he did so, the words: "To Athene the Champion." This was equivalent to the loyal toasts of an English banquet. He then took a very moderate draught, the wine being unmixed, in obedience to the rule which demanded that all wine used in religious ceremonies—and this libation

---

* Three *drachmae* would be something more than half-a-dollar, (2 s. 5 d. in English money). This is taking silver at its present conventional value. What its purchasing power would be now it would be difficult to say, but it would certainly be greater than that of the sum by which it is represented.

was such a ceremony—should be pure.* He then tipped the cup to each guest in turn. All were equally moderate, for it was not the custom, even for a Greek drunkard, it may be said, to drink his wine unmixed. But when the cup came to the Thracian chief he drank a deep draught as if the liquor had been liberally diluted. Callias who had never been at table with a Thracian before, watched the man with amazement. He saw that while the other guests were supplied with the usual mixtures of wine and water the chief remained steadfast in his devotion to the undiluted liquid, and that he emptied his cup at a draught, and that the cup itself was of an unusual capacity. Nor did the drinker seem affected by these extraordinary potations, except that his voice became louder, and his manner more boastful. At last, however, and that without a moment's notice, he rolled over senseless on his back. So sudden was the change that it suggested the idea of a fit.

"Is he ill?" he whispered in some alarm, to his neighbor.

"Ill? not a whit. It is the way in which he always finishes his evenings. His slaves will carry him to bed, and he will awake to-morrow morning without the suspicion of a headache. Bacchus, I verily believe, has a special favor for these fellows, and, truly, they do worship him with a most admirable earnestness."

The Thracian's collapse was the signal for breaking up the party. Callias and the old tutor, Timanthes by name,

* So we have in Homer (Iliad II, 261) "the libations of wine unmingled" mentioned together with "the hand-holt trusted of yore," a thing that gave a solemn sanction to treaties. Similar references abound in the Greek and Latin poets.

declined to drink **any more, and the two officers, who** were on duty for the night, departed to make **their** round. Strong as **was** the place Alcibiades omitted no precautions **for** its safe custody. **Timanthes, who** was old and feeble **re-tired to rest.**

"**Come with me to my** own room," said Alcibiades **to his** guest, "we shall **be here alone.**"

The chamber to which he led the way was **little** like **what** one would have expected to find in free-booter's stronghold, for really the castle of Bisanthe was more of that than **any-thing** else. Art and letters were amply represented **in it.** On one wall **hung** a panel painting* **by Polygnotus, a** masterly composition, **of that serenity, that ethical mean-ing,** as the great **critic Aristotle** expresses it, **which was** characteristic of the artist. **This represented the gods in** council **at Olympus. It was faced on** the opposite **wall** by **an** exceedingly graceful painting from the **hand of** Xeuxis, Aphrodite and the Graces, and a spirited picture **by** the **same artist, of the** duel between **Ajax and Hector.** There **were other** works by men of **less note. Sculpture** was represented **by only a single specimen, a bust of** Socrates.

"Paintings are easily **carried about," Alcibiades** after-wards explained **to his guest, "but** sculpture is **inconven-iently** heavy. You will understand that a **man in my** situation has always to be ready **for a move; and I** always **like to have two or** three really **good things** that **I** can always take with me One bust, indeed, I have indulged

---

* The ancients painted on panel, not on canvass. Thus the Latin equivalent for 'picture' is tabula or tabella, words which may other-wise be used for a 'plank.'

myself with, that of my old teacher. Ah! if I had heard him to more purpose, I should **not be** here! **You** know him, of course?"

Callias said that he did.

"An excellent likeness! is **it not?** Who would think that such features concealed **a soul so** divinely beautiful? **Did** you have any talk with him when you were in Athens?"

"Yes," replied Callias, "**and I admired** above all things his practical wisdom. But what was that **to what I after-** wards saw **of him?**"

And he went on to relate how the philosopher stood firm, though in imminent peril of his life, **and had steadfastly** refused to put the unconstitutional proposal of Callixenus to the **assembly.**

Alcibiades heard the story with uncontrollable delight. He started up from his **seat,** and walked up and down the **room** with flashing eyes. "**Tell** me everything about it," he said, and he insisted upon the repetition of every detail. "That is magnificent," **he cried,** when his curiosity had been satisfied. "That is exactly what one **would have ex-** pected from Socrates. I suppose that **it is the very first time that he** ever acted **as** presiding magistrate—he had never been **so, I know, when I left Athens,** nor have I **heard** of his having been **since—and that first** time he did **what nobody else dared to do. You say** that the others **gave way?"**

"**Yes,** replied Callias, "**they** stood up against it at first, but gave in afterwards. Socrates was absolutely alone, and at **last** they put the question without him."

"**It is just** like him," cried Alcibiades **with** enthusiasm.

" He is simply the bravest and most enduring man alive. I could tell you stories about him that would astonish you. We served together in the campaign at Potidæa. Indeed we **were in the same mess.** When we had short commons, as we had **many a** time, there was no one like **him** in holding out. He seemed to be able to go without food altogether, **but** when **we had plenty, he** could enjoy it as well **as anybody. We had** a foolish way, as young men will, of making people drink whether they wished **it or not.** But nothing **ever** affected Socrates. No one ever saw him one whit the worse for what he had taken. **And** as for the way in which he bore **cold, it was** absolutely incredible, only **that** one saw it with one's own eyes. The winters here are terrible, as you will **find out, if, as I hope** you **will,** you stop **with** me, but he **used to make nothing of them.** During the very hardest frost we had, when every one who could, stayed in doors, and those **who** were obliged to go **out,** wrapped themselves till **you would hardly** know them, **he wore** nothing but his common cloak, and went absolutely barefoot.

"Once, I remember, something **came into his mind. That was in the early** morning. **Well, he stood trying to** think **it out till noon, and from noon he went on till** evening. **Some Greeks from Asia wanted to see how long** this would **go** on; **so,** after **dinner, they brought out their** mattresses, and took up their quarters for **the night in the** open air—it was summer-time, **you must understand.** Some of them slept, and some watched **him,** taking it by turns. Their report was that he stood **there till morning,** and the sun rose, and that then **he made a prayer to** the sun, and so **went to** his quarters.

"His courage, too, is astonishing. In one of the battles at Potidæa he saved my life. I had been wounded and must infallibly have been killed, if it had not been for him. He took me up and carried me off to our line. The generals gave me the prize for valor, when they ought, by right, to have given it to him. But they took account of my family and rank, and curiously enough, he was just as anxious as they were that I should have it and not he. Then at Delium, again, when the day went against us, and the army was in full retreat. I was in the cavalry; he was serving as a foot soldier. Our men would not keep together, and he and Laches—he was killed, afterward, at Mantinea—were making the best of their way back. I rode up to them and told them to keep up their courage and I would not leave them. A cavalry soldier has, you know, a great advantage in a retreat. There was no need to tell Socrates to keep up his courage. Laches, I could see, though a brave enough man, was terribly frightened; but Socrates was as cool as a man could be. He held up his head finely, and marched steadily on. It was plain enough to see that anyone who meddled with him would find out his mistake. The end of it was that he got back safe, and brought Laches back safe also. The fact is that at such times it is the men who are in a hurry to get away that are cut down. I do not think that there ever was a braver man than Socrates. And what you have just been telling me bears it out. A man may be brave enough in battle and be timidly frightened when the assembly is howling and raging against him. This has been a dismal business of the generals and I have never been so near despairing of my country, as I have since

I heard it. How is it possible to help a city that makes such a requital to those who save her? But still, while there are men like Socrates in her, all is not lost. But no more now; you must be weary, and ready to sleep. There will be plenty of time hereafter to talk. And now farewell."

CHAPTER XIV.

BISANTHE.

Life at Bisanthe would, in any case, have been remarkably attractive to Callias. The taste for sport was hereditary with him, as it was with most Athenians of his class. But, ever since his boyhood, circumstances had been altogether adverse to any indulgence of it. For a quarter of a century an Athenian's life had been perforce a city life.* The country outside the walls was not available for when it was not actually in the occupation of a hostile army, it was still in a state of desolation. Game, it is probable, had almost disappeared from it. It had long been too thickly populated for the larger animals to exist in it. These the sportsman had been obliged to seek in the mountain regions of Phocis, Doris, and Thessaly. Now the smaller such as the hare, always reckoned a special dainty in Athens, could scarcely be found, even when it was possible to seek for it. Callias was delighted to find a totally different condition of things at Bisanthe. Here there were to be found fierce and powerful animals the pursuit of which gave something of the delightful excitement of danger, the bear, the wild-boar, and the wolf. Lion, too, could be sometimes

* From 431 to 406 (the year of which I am now writing). The eight years from 424-416, during which the peace of Nicias and the truce that followed it were in force, must be excepted.

seen, though they were not so common as they had been some eighty years before when the army of Xerxes, marching through this very region, had had so many of the camels attacked and killed by them. Our young Athenian highly appreciated this abundance of noble game. He had had no experience, indeed, in the huntsman's craft, but he became fairly expert at it. He was an excellent rider; this accomplishment was a necessary part of the education of a well-born Athenian. He was expert in all martial exercises, especially in the use of the javelin and the spear; and, above all, he had a cool courage which his warlike experience by land and sea had admirably developed.

But there were more serious matters than sport to occupy him. The relation of his host to his neighbors, both Greek and barbarian, was of curious interest to a thoughtful young man. He had heard something of it at Athens, for Alcibiades was a much talked of personage, all of whose movements were earnestly, even anxiously, discussed both by friends and foes. Now he was, so to speak, behind the scenes, and saw and heard much that the outside world did not know or did not understand. The neighbors with whom his host came in contact, friendly or unfriendly, were three. There were the Greek cities along the northern coast of the Propontis; there was Seuthes, the king of Thrace; a potentate whose kingdom had many uncertain and varying boundaries, and there were the free or independent Thracians. Between these last and Alcibiades there was constant war. Accustomed for centuries to plunder their neighbors, they now found themselves repaid in their own coin. At the head of a picked force, highly disciplined and admirably armed, Alcibiades harried their country with an audacity and a skill which made his name a constant terror to them. The Greek cities, on the other hand, were uniformly friendly. Before his coming they had been sadly harrassed and distressed by their barbarian neighbors. They had not been able to call anything beyond their walls exactly their own, and even their walls had sometimes scarcely sufficed to protect them. All this was altered by the military genius of this remarkable man. The robber bands which had been accustomed to ride unchecked up to their fortifications were now compelled to keep at a respectful distance from them, and not only the cities themselves but their territories were practically safe. Land which it had been impossible to cultivate at all, or from which only a precarious crop could be snatched with imminent danger to the cultivator, was now covered with prosperous farms and pleasant homesteads. For this protection, enabling them as it did to save the exhausting expense of imported food, the cities were willing to pay, and considerable sums which were practically a tribute, only much more cheerfully paid, came regularly into the treasury at Bisanthe, and enabled its master to keep up a numerous and efficient force.

As for King Seuthes, his relations with the powerful stranger who had settled on these his territories were more doubtful. He was not an enemy, but he certainly was not a friend. All that Alcibiades could do in weakening the independent Thracians was altogether to his mind. Let them be weakened enough, and they would gladly seek protection by becoming his subjects. On the other hand he

did not approve the idea of any one but himself becoming
the patron of the Greek cities on his coast. What they
were willing to pay for protection ought to come, he felt,
into his coffers, not into those of an interloping adventurer.
Meanwhile he was content to remain an outwardly good
terms with the master of Bisanthe, and to await the develop-
ment of events.

In the little town of the same name that was dominated
by the castle of Bisanthe, the young Athenian found some
pleasant society. He was the more at home in it because it
was an Ionian colony, and the inhabitants were akin to
him in race and sympathies. They had the same culture, a
quality that always flourished more kindly in the Ionic
branch of the Hellenic race. Plays of the great dramatists
of his own country were performed in a small but well appointed theatre, and there was at least one circle in the
town in which literary topics were discussed with interest
and intelligence.

The resources available in the way of native society were
not great. Thracian habits in general were not unfairly
represented by the behavior of the chief to whom my readers
were introduced in the last chapter. Their hard drinking
habits had already made them notorious throughout Greece.
Our hero accordingly kept away from the entertainments
which his host felt it a matter of policy to attend. The one
great social function at which he assisted was the marriage
of a prince who was nearly related to King Seuthes.
Athenian habits were commonly frugal. Their public
buildings, whether for political or religious purposes, were
splendid in the extreme. On these, and on the ceremonies

of worship, they were accustomed to **spare no** expense. But **their private expenditure was, as a rule, not** large. **Our hero** was proportionately astonished at the profusion **which** prevailed **at the wedding** festivities **of the Thracian** Caranus. **There** were twenty guests. Each as he entered the banqueting chamber **had** a circle of gold put upon his head, **and in** taking his place was presented with a silver cup. These and indeed all the dishes, plates, and cups with which the guests were **furnished during** the entertainment, were supposed to become their actual property. A brass platter, covered with pastry, on which were birds of various kinds, was put before each, and after this another of silver, furnished with a variety of fresh meats. These disposed of —**they** were just tasted and handed to the slaves who stood behind the guests—two **flasks of** perfume, one of silver, the other of gold, fastened together with a link of gold, were **distributed. Each flask held about half** a pint. Then came a piece of quite barbarous extravagance—a silver gilt charger, large enough to hold **a porker** of considerable size. The creature lay on its back with its belly stuffed **with** thrushes, the yolks of eggs, **oysters,** scollops, and **other dainties. The** carrying capacity **of** the slaves was **nearly** exhausted, and the bridegroom received a hearty round of applause when he ordered his guests to be supplied with **baskets,** themselves richly ornamented with silver **in which** they might carry **away his bounty.**

At this point Alcibiades **and his friend made an excuse to** depart. "Caranus," said the former, as they returned to **Bisanthe, "** must have embarassed himself for life by this **silly** extravagance. **He** must have borrowed money largely before he could indulge in all this silver-ware, for though his estates are large, he is far from being wealthy. But it is a point of honor with these people to go as near to ruining themselves as the money-lender will permit them, when they celebrate a birth, a wedding, or a funeral."

But Callias found the chief interest of the months which he spent at Bisanthe in the frequent conversations which he held with his host. In these Alcibiades expressed himself with the utmost freedom and frankness. What he said was in fact at once a confession and an apology, the substance of them may be given as follows:

"You have heard I dare say very much evil of me, and I cannot deny that much of it is perfectly true. It ill becomes a man to complain of circumstances, for everyone, I take it, can make his own life and if he goes to ruin has only himself to blame for it. Yet the gods, or fate, or whatever it is that rules the world, were certainly adverse to me from the beginning. My father fell at Coronea when I was but a mere child, and the loss of a father is especially damaging when his son is rich and noble. Every one seems to agree in spoiling the boy, the lad, the young man, who is the master of his own fortune. I know that I was fooled to the top of my bent. However, that is all past, and the free man who lets others turn him about to their own purposes has nothing to say in his own defence; and I had at least one good thing on my side of which if I had been so minded I might have made good use. Socrates never wearied of convicting me out of my own mouth of folly and ignorance, and he knew my great weakness and told me of it in the most unsparing fashion. I remember once how he convicted me of what I know has been the great fault of my life. 'If,' he said, 'you can convince the Athenians that you deserve to be honored as no man, not even Pericles himself deserved, if you gain an equal name among the other Greeks and barbarians, if you cross over from Europe and meddle with matters in Asia, all these things will not satisfy you. You desire to be nothing less than master of the whole human race.' That perhaps was somewhat exaggerated, but I certainly have had big schemes in my head, bigger than I ever had, or could hope to have, the means of carrying out. My hopes took in all Greece, Persia, Carthage, the Western barbarians who inhabit the shores of the ocean, and I know not what else. It was too great a structure to build on the slight foundation of an Athenian dock-yard; it was piling Olympus and Ossa and Pelion on the hill of Hymettus, and such structures are sure to fall even without the thunder-bolt of Zeus. Yet it is only fair to myself to say that in my ambitions I did think of my country as well as of myself; and I think that I have not always had fair play in carrying them out. There was the expedition to Sicily, for instance. I suppose that no one will ever speak of it but as a piece of hair-brained folly into which I was the means of leading Athens. Looked at by the event, it seems so, I allow, and yet it might have succeeded. Indeed it was within an iota of succeeding, and this though the people showed the incredible folly of putting as senior in command, a man who hated the whole business. Even Nicias almost took Syracuse. If they had only left me without a colleague or with colleagues who would have yielded to my counsels! But what did they do? Just at the critical time they recalled the man whom everyone in the expedition, from the first to the last, identified with its success; and why did they recall me?   On that trumpery charge of having broken the Hermæ. * You would like to ask me, I know, whether I had anything to do with the matter. No; I had not, but I could have told them all about it if I had had the chance. As it was, they were ready to listen to any one but me. Why, there was an outrageous liar came forward, and declared he had seen the whole thing done by the light of the moon; and on the night it was done there was no moon at all. But I had enemies, personal enemies who would stick at nothing as long as they could injure me. And here I must confess a fault, a fault that has been fatal to me. I deserved to have enemies. I made them by my annoyance and insolence; and if they ruined me, and, as I think, my country with me, I have only myself to blame. You would like to know how I justify myself for what I did after my banishment, for getting Sparta to help Syracuse against my own country? I do not justify myself at all. It was madness, tho' it was only too successful. But it made me frantic to think what a chance, what a splendid opportunity for myself and for Athens, the fools who were in power at home were throwing away. No; on that point I have nothing to say for myself. But since then I have honestly tried to do the best that I could for the city. And if the Athenians could only have trusted me and had had a little more patience, I believe that I could have saved them.

* A day or two before the expedition started the pedestal statues of Hermes which stood at the street corners were broken down. Alcibiades was charged with being an accomplice in this outrage, refused an opportunity of defending himself, sent out in joint command, and recalled when the campaign was in progress.

But it is always the same story with them; they must have what they want at once, and if they don't get it, some one has to suffer. How could they expect that I **could** put right at once all that had been going wrong **for years?"**

Such was the substance of what Alcibiades said to his guest on the many occasions on which they discussed **these** matters, **said of course,** with a variety of details and **a** wealth of illustration, which it is impossible to reproduce. **More** than once Callias asked **his** host what were his views **and** expectations of the future of the war. He found that Alcibiades did not take **a cheerful view of the** prospects of the campaign that would be soon beginning.

"**I** was always afraid," **he** said, "that the victory **at** Arginusæ would be only a reprieve, **a** postponing of the evil day. The effort which Athens then made was too exhausting to be repeated—her next **fleet** will be nothing like as good as **the** last, and the **last** had hard enough work to win the day. And then there was the disastrous folly and crime of putting the **generals to death. Mind,** I don't **say** that they were not **to** blame; but I do say that to kill **the** only **good** officers the city had, even if they had deserved death **ten times** more than they did, was mere madness. Whom have they got to put in their place? Conon is a man who knows his business and would **do his** duty, but as for the **rest,"** he went on, anticipating **a** witticism which was **made many** hundred years afterwards by an English statesman, "**I can** only **say** that I **hope they** will inspire **the** enemy with half the terror with which they inspire me."

CHAPTER XV.

ALCIBIADES had established a system of communication with all the principal stations in the Ægean which gave him early information of what was going on.

Early in the new year (405) intelligence reached him at his castle, that Lysander was coming out from Sparta to assume the command of the allied fleet. This news affected Alcibiades very considerably.

"I anticipated this," he said to his guest after the evening meal on the day when the news had reached him, "and it is the worst thing that could have happened for Athens. There was just a chance that the Spartans, who, happily for us, are very stupid and obstinate, would stick to their rule that no man should be appointed naval commander-in-chief thrice. But they had, as I heard from a friend in Chios, a very strong requisition from the allies to appoint Lysander, and so they have sent him out again, saving their rule by appointing a nominal chief, a man called Arrachus, who, of course, is a mere figure head. Now Lysander is by far the ablest man that the Spartans have got; he is quite unscrupulous; he is a bitter enemy of ours; and what is worst of all, he can do anything that he pleases with Cyrus. You have not been campaigning for two or three years **without** finding out that the Persian money bags are the real weights that make the scales of fate go up and down. Last year Callicratidas was crippled because Cyrus, at this very Lysander's request, kept his purse strings tight. Now everything will be straight and easy, and **before** two months are **over** the Spartans will have as good **a fleet** as money **can make."** The year wore slowly on. The long Thracian winter, which Callias, though not unused to cold weather in Athens found exceedingly severe, yielded **at last to spring, and spring in its** turn **to summer.** All the **while the news** which **reached** Bisanthe **continued to have a gloomy** complexion. At Miletus, as well **as in other of the** mainland towns, thorough-going **partisans of Lysander were** installed in **power.** Cyrus had **been** called **away to** Upper **Asia, where** the old king, **his** father, **was** lying sick to death, and had left all his treasuries at **the** disposal of the Spartan **admiral.** With this supply of money the pay of the sailors had been increased, and new ships had been laid down **on the** stocks. In March the Athenian **fleet** sailed **for** the **seat** of war. It **was** larger than **any that** had been sent forth **by the city in recent years, for** it numbered **no** less than **one** hundred **and** eighty ships; but private letters **gave an** unfavorable **account of** the way in **which it** was equipped, and officered. **This** adverse opinion continued to be borne out by the news that arrived from time to time of its doings. It seemed **to be** moving about aimlessly and fruitlesly, always behind, always **in** the wrong place. It offered **battle to** Lysander, **who lay in** harbor near Ephesus, but in vain. **The** wary Spartan **had no mind to** fight but at his own time, and the Athenian admirals had no way of compelling him. Then the ships were scattered in plundering expeditions along the mainland coasts and among the islands which had accepted the Spartan alliance. The gain was small, for the booty was insignificant, but the demoralization and relaxation of discipline were great. About midsummer followed a bold maneuver on the part of Lysander. He sailed across the Ægean to the coast of Attica, where his sudden appearance caused no little consternation. The Athenian commanders were as usual behind hand. If they had heard of this movement as soon as they ought, and had been ready to follow immediately, it is quite possible that they might have inflicted a damaging blow on their adversaries. As it was, the news was long in reaching them, and when it came, found them with their fleet scattered and unprepared. Accordingly they missed their chance of forcing Lysander to an engagement off an hostile shore, an engagement, too, which he would hardly have been able to decline. Lysander crossed and recrossed the Ægean without molestation, and shortly afterward sailed northward.

Alcibiades, whose intelligence department was, as has been said, admirably organized, received information that this movement was intended, and in consequence took up his quarters at a little fort which he possessed at the extremity of the Chersonesus. He and his guest had not been there more than a day when the Spartan fleet came in sight. He watched it pass at a distance of two or three miles, with eager interest.

"They have a very formidable appearance," he said to Callias when he had scanned with his practical eye every detail of their equipment. "I shall be agreeably surprised if our ships have anything as good to show." On the following day the Athenian fleet appeared, showing only too plainly **how** just had been Alcibiades' forebodings. The effects of wind and weather—the ships had now **been** nearly six months at sea—were plainly visible; the sails, which, as there was a slight breeze from the west, they used to assist their progress, **were dirty and ragged;** the rowers were deplorably **out of time.**

"Things," he said to his companion, "are even worse than I expected; that fleet will be no match for its enemy, except under far more skillful management than it is likely **to have.** Still let us hope for the best; and it may be possible **to** give our friends some good advice, if they will take **it."** This, unfortunately, was the last thing that the Athenian admirals, certainly incompetent, and probably traitorous, were willing to **do.** The progress of events, briefly described, was this :

Lysander possessed himself, by a sudden attack, of the town of Lampsacus, which was in alliance with Athens. This conquest put him in possession of abundant supplies, and of what was more valuable, a safe and convenient base of operations. While securing these material advantages, he also, with a generosity which he could always assume on occasion, allowed the Lampsacenes to go unharmed. He gained thus not only a strong position but a friendly population. **On** the other hand **the** position occupied by the **Athenians** was by no means **so** favorable. They moved their fleet to the **mouth of a** little stream known by the **name of** Ægos **Potami, or the** Goat's River. This spot was directly **opposite** Lampsacus—the Hellespont here is somewhat less than two **miles broad**—but it had no conveniences for the purpose for which it was chosen. There **was no** harbor, the anchorage was indifferent, there were no houses in **the** neighborhood, **and the nearest point from** which supplies could be **obtained was the town of Sestos,** nearly two miles distant.

The opportunity **for offering advice which Alcibiades had** foreseen had now occurred, and he promptly took advantage **of it.** The morning after **the arrival of the fleet, he rode,** with Callias in **his company,** to the spot where the Athenian generals had pitched their **headquarters, and requested an** interview. He **was** introduced **into** the tent which they used for purposes of consultation, **and saw the two officers,** Menander and Tydeus by **name, who happened to be** detailed that **day** for duty on shore.

They received him **with a coldness and hauteur which** augured ill for the success of his **mission.**

"Allow me, gentlemen," he said, "to offer you a piece of advice which, from my knowledge of the country, **I feel** sure will be **useful.** Transfer **your** fleet from this position, which, **you** must allow me to say, has nothing to recommend it, to Sestos. You must go to Sestos for **your supplies; why** not stay **there** altogether. The harbor is good and you will **be able to do what you please, fight, or** not fight, as it may **seem best.** Here, if it comes on **a blow from** the south and —you will remember that the equinox is near—you will be in a very awkward predicament ; and, anyhow, **I** do not see how you are to keep your men together when they **have to forage in this manner** for supplies."

"We are obliged to you for the trouble you have taken in coming," said Menander, "but you must allow us to remind you that it is we, and not you whom the Athenian people have appointed to the command of this fleet."

"The gods prosper you in it." replied Alcibiades with unruffled coolness. "And now, farewell."

"I have done all that I could," observed Alcibiades to his companion, who had been expecting his return outside the tent. "Now we can only await the event. As for these men, I would say of them that the gods strike with madness those whom they are determined to destroy, but for one thing. There may be a method in their madness. They may *mean* to bring about a disaster. In a word they may have sold their country. It is a hard thing to say of any man, but could any admiral, not being a madman or a traitor, keep his fleet in such a place as this? And yet I do not know. I have seen honest men act with a folly so outrageous that one could not help suspecting something more. Let us go home, and prepare for the worst. But stay—there is yet a chance. There is Conon. He must know better than this. Will you see him? I cannot, for there is too deadly a feud between us. Do you know him?"

"Yes," said Callias, "I was with him last year when he was shut up in Mitylene, and he sent me with despatches to Athens."

"And will you go to him?"

"Certainly, if it would not seem too presumptuous."

"You can give your authority; he will understand why I did not come myself; and he is too sensible not to listen to good advice from whomsoever it may come."

Conon was on board his ship in which **he was** practicing some maneuvers about half a mile from the shore. The young Athenian was rowed out to see him, and returned in **about an hour.** The **report** which he brought back was this:

"**Conon was very** reserved, **but courteous. He wished** me to thank you for your message, and to say he **was sure** you wished well to Athens. **He** would do what he could, but he was only one out of many, and he might be out-voted. Anyhow, he would keep his own men from straggling."

"Then," said Alcibiades, "we have shot our last bolt, **let** us go back."

For some days the two companions waited for news in a suspense that they often felt to be almost beyond bearing. One night—it was the night of the fifteenth of September— they had watched through the hours of darkness till the day **began** to show itself in the eastern sky. **Both had felt the** presentiment that their waiting was about to end, though neither had acknowledged it **to** the other.

"**Is it** never coming?" said the elder man, as he rose from his seat, and looked from the window across the sea, just beginning to glitter with the morning light. **In a moment** his attitude of weariness changed to one of eager attention.

"Look!" he cried to Callias. "What is that?" and he pointed to a boat that had just rounded the nearest point to **the westward.** It was a fishing boat, manned, apparently, by seven or eight men, and making **all the** speed it could **with both oars and sails. The two men** hurried **down to the** castle pier, and awaited the **arrival of what they were sure** was the long expected message.

The boat was still about two hundred yards away when Alcibiades recognized the steersman.

"**Ah !**" he cried, "it **is** old Hipparchus." **And** he waved his hand with a friendly gesture.

"It is a bad news he brings," he said again after a quiet **pause,** "he makes no reply."

A few more strokes brought the boat alongside of the pier. Alcibiades reached his hand to the steersman, and helped him to disembark. **That** his **errand** was bad was only too evident from his look. He was deadly pale, and in his eyes was the expression of one who had lately seen some terrible sight.

"It is all over," he said, "Athens is lost."

For a few minutes the three men stood **silent. Perhaps** it was then that Alcibiades felt the keenest remorse of his life. **After all,** it was he who, more than any living man, had brought **this ruin to his country. He** had led her into an enterprise which overmatched her strength; and he had suggested **to her enemies, the** too successful policy that had ended in her overthrow. If Athens was indeed lost it was his doing—and yet he loved her. Much of this the younger man could guess **at,** for he had not been at Bisanthe for now nearly a year without learning something of his host's inner thoughts. He turned away his face unwilling to witness the emotion which he felt could be seen **in the** other's counte- **nance.** The messenger from the scene of the disaster stood with downcast eyes, absorbed in the dismal recollections of what he had lately witnessed.

"Tell us how it happened," **said** Alcibiades.

" For five days," **so he** began, "we manned our ships

every morning about the **third hour, formed** them in line of battle, and moved across the **strait** to the harbor of Lampsacus. **The** Spartan fleet was ranged in line outside the harbor with their army drawn up upon the shore on either side. Our admirals did not venture to attack; and so we sailed back. I noticed that a few quick-sailing **galleys** followed us at about half a mile distance. When we **got** back to our station, **our men** used to scatter in search of provisions for their noonday meal—our commissariat, you must **know,** was very ill-supplied. Some went up the country, but most made their way to Sestos. **None of our admirals,** except Conon, seemed to have a notion that this was dangerous, though some of us old sailors could have warned **them** if **we** had dared. Conon always kept **his men together.** Well, on the fifth day—our men, you must understand, had been growing more and more careless—about an **hour after** we got back, a shield was run up to the masthead of one of the Spartan swift-sailing galleys. I saw it flash in the sunshine; and **a few** moments afterwards the **whole** Spartan fleet rowed from their anchorage **and made their** way across **the strait.** They caught us **entirely unprepared.** There was no battle; scarcely **a** blow **was struck.** I can easily believe that they did not lose a single man. **Some of our ships they found** absolutely deserted. **None of them had more** than **two-thirds of their complement. No, I should not say** none; twelve were ready, Conon's **eight and four others, one** of which was the Parelus.* **I was on board**

* The Parelus was one of the two consecrated ships, (the other being the Salaminia) which were used for such purposes as the conveyance of ambassadors, the carrying of offerings to shrines, and, in case of need, the conveyance of important tidings. They **were** always manned with picked crews.

Menander's own ship, of which I was steersman. There were eight others with me. We hurried as fast as we could to **Sestos.** There, the next day, I was able to hire this boat, and **thought the** best thing **that** I could do was to come here."

"**You say that** twelve ships escaped," said Alcibiades, "how **many then** were taken?"

" About a hundred and seventy," answered the man.

"**And** how many prisoners?"

" I cannot **say,** but **certainly several thousand. Before** we came away, a boat from Lampsacus brought an awful story of what had been **done** there. **All** the Athenian prisoners were put to death, between three **and four thousand.** Only the admiral Adeimantus was spared."

"**Ah!** I see," cried Alcibiades, " he was the traitor."

CHAPTER XVI.

THERE was little sleep that night for the inhabitants of the castle of Bisanthe. Every one felt that the situation was full of peril. If it had not been for the confidence which every one brought into contact with Alcibiades felt in his capacities of leadership there would have been something like a panic. As it was, the garrison awaited with calmness, though not without intense anxiety, the course of action which their commander would take for himself, and recommend to them. They were not kept long in suspense.

Shortly after dawn the notes of a trumpet were heard through the castle giving the well known signal by which a general assembly of the garrison was called. A few minutes sufficed to collect the men. The meeting was held in the central court of the castle, and Alcibiades, taking his stand on the topmost step of an outside staircase which led up to one of the chambers, addressed them.

"Comrades," he said, "you have heard of the disaster by which Athens has lost its last fleet. I will blame no man for what happened or inquire whether it might not have been averted—"

The speaker was interrupted by loud cries of "Long live Alcibiades, the invincible!"

A flush of pleasure **passed** over the **speaker's face, but he made a** gesture imperative of silence, and continued.

"**The only** thing that remains for us is to consider what it is most expedient to **do.** Here, my friends, **we** cannot **stay.** Bisanthe indeed, protected by its situation, its walls, **and** stout hands **and tried valor,** it would not be easy **to take.** But, with both sea **and** land hostile, with all the country and cities from which we have drawn our supplies in the hands of the Spartans, **we** cannot long continue to hold it. What then shall we do? You, my friends, I can only advise, for from this day I of necessity cease to command. Go, then, I would say, **to King** Seuthes, and offer yourselves to him. He will receive you kindly. **Brave men—and your valor has** been shown times without number—are always valued and honored by him, and now that, for a time at least, the Spartans and their allies have became supreme in **these** parts, he will want men more than ever. If you require it, you shall **have my good** word; but your reputation will speak for you more effectually than I can. My gratitude to you, who have served me so well, I can never express. Yet such return as I can make shall not be left undone. The paymaster will pay you all arrears of pay, with a donation of thrice as much again."

A loud burst of applause followed this announcement.

The speaker continued: "This gift would be many times greater, if my means were equal to my sense of your courage and **your** services. **From** some of **you** I have a favor **to** ask. **It** is not expedient publicly to declare my plans; but I may say that I shall need a few associates in them. For these I shall not ask you, not because I am doubtful of raising them, **but** because **I know that** you would all offer yourselves—"

A roar of assent went up from the whole assembly.

"I have already exercised the choice which in any **case** I should have been compelled afterwards to make. Twelve companions—more I am forbidden **by circumstances to take** —will go with me. **To the rest I say, ' Farewell.' The gods** grant that at some happier time we may again render **our service to Athens and to Greece.** Till then, Farewell !"

A loud answering cry of farewell **went up** from the men, which was renewed again and again as the speaker entered **the room at** the head of the staircase. Here the twelve chosen associates were assembled, Callias and Hipparchus, the messenger from the scene of the **late** conflict, making up the number to fourteen. Alcibiades addressed them:

" I have long since anticipated and prepared **myself** for this misfortune which has now overtaken us, **though the** blow has fallen more suddenly and more heavily **than I had** feared. To you, **my chosen** friends, I reveal the counsels which it would not have **been** expedient to publish **to a** multitude. Briefly **they** are these: Lysander has con- **quered by the help** of the Persians, for had it not been for the gold of Cyrus, his **fleet** could never have been kept together. We also must go to the Persians for help. It is an evil neces- **sity, I** confess, that makes free-born Greeks court the favor of their slaves; but a necessity it is. And the time favors us **for using** it. Cyrus covets the throne of Persia which he claims against his elder brother Artaxerxes as having been born after his **father's accession** whereas Artaxerxes was born before it. **As Lysander,** then, has used Cyrus against us, so we must use Artaxerxes against **Cyrus.** 'How,' you will ask, 'is Artaxerxes to be approached?' Through Pharnabazus, the Satrap, with whom I have a warm friendship of now some years' standing. To Pharnabazus, **there-fore,** I now purpose to go. I shall demand of him that which he will himself be most willing to grant—for he is **no** friend to **Cyrus—that he send me up** to Susa. This Themistocles did before me; but he, at least in word, went as the **enemy of his country, though indeed he was** unwilling **to harm it. I shall go,** both in word and in deed, as its friend. And now for other things. For my most valuable possessions **I** have prepared hiding-places. Much I shall leave to King Seuthes, to whom I sent a message concerning my immedi-**ate** departure. This morning, my friends, I would ask you **to** receive at my hands a year's pay. Do not hesitate to receive it; I can give it now, I may not be able so to do a year hence. **We** will start this **day** at sunset. There is no time to be lost. To-morrow, I doubt not, or the next day at the latest, Lysander will be here."

With Callias, after the rest had departed **to** make preparations for their departure, Alcibiades had some private conversation as to the subject of ways and means.

" You must let me be your banker," he began **by** saying.

Callias thanked him heartily, but declined to receive anything more than would suffice for immediate **needs.**

" You may as well take it," returned his host, " there is a good deal more here than I can take with me; and why should you not? For myself, I carry most of my possessions **about** with me **in this** fashion,"—and he showed a leather **purse** filled with pearls and precious stones. "**Gold is** too cumbrous to carry in any quantity. This no man will take as long as I am alive. Besides this, my worthy friend Hippocles, who, as you know, is as trustworthy as the treasury of Delphi, has most of my property in his hands. And, if we once get safely to Pharnabazus, we need not trouble any more about this matter. I must do the Persians the justice to say that they are always open-handed. And they can afford to be. It is not too much to say that for one talent of gold that we have in Greece they have at least a hundred. Any one who should have the ransacking of one of their great treasure cities—and they have others besides Susa; Babylon, for instance, and Persepolis and Pasargadæ—would see something that would astonish them. And " he added, with a profound sigh—" if only things had gone straight, I might have been the man."

The journey along the northern shore of the Propontis was accomplished in safety. No Spartan ship had as yet made its way so far eastward. At a little town on the Asiatic shore Alcibiades provided his party with horses for riding and serviceable mules for the conveyance of their baggage and of such a selection of his own possessions as he had thought it well to take with him. The old sailor Hipparchus here wanted to leave them, and to make his way to Byzantium, where he had relatives. The remainder Alcibiades addressed before setting out, to the following effect :

" We have to make our way to Gordium in Phrygia, for it is there that, if he keeps to his usual habits, we shall find the Satrap Pharnabazus. He is accustomed to winter there. But we shall not find it easy to get there. These Bithynlans are not effeminate Asiatics, a hundred of whom will fly before five stout Greeks. They are Thracians from the other side of the sea, and we all know how hard are their heads, and how strong their arms. We cannot force our way through them; we must elude them if we can."

The route which the party followed lay for some time within sight of the sea. This was commonly followed by travellers, as the mountaineers seldom ventured within the border of the maritime plain. When they had reached the head of the Gulf of Olbia they struck inland. The road usually followed would have taken them by the valley of Sangarius, a river which divides the great chain of the Mysian Olympus. Their guide strongly dissuaded them from taking it. It was constantly watched, he said, by the mountaineers. No one could hope to escape them, and only a very strong party could force its way through. The safest plan would be by certain paths which he knew, and by which they might hope to cross Olympus unmolested. Only hunters and shepherds know them, or a chance traveller on foot for whom it would not be worth the robbers' while to wait. It was a toilsome and even dangerous journey. The first snows of Autumn had began to fall, and even the practical eye of the guide found it difficult to discover the path, while the sufferings of the travellers, who had to bivouac for several nights in the open air, with but scanty fire to warm them, were exceedingly severe. Still, but for one unlucky incident, it would have been accomplished in safety. The party was now half-way down the southern slopes of Olympus when they halted for the night at a road-side inn, or rather caravansary. They found the large reception chamber—it contained two only—already occupied by a party of the vagrant priests of Cybele. While Alcibiades and Callias found accommodation, such as it was, in the smaller room, the rest of the party were thrown upon the hospitality of the priests, unless indeed, they chose to bivouac outside. Unluckily, the priests were only too hospitable. They invited the new comers to an entertainment which was prolonged into a revel. During the passage of the mountains the allowances of food had been small, and for drink the party had had perforce to be satisfied with the wayside springs or even with melted snow. When they found themselves under shelter, in a room which was at least weather-tight, and warmed with a blazing fire, the sense of contrast tended to relax their powers of self-restraint. The priests had roasted a couple of sheep, and broached a cask of the heady wine of Mount Tmolus, with which a wealthy devotee had presented them. This they drank, and insisted on their guests drinking, unmixed. By the time the mutton bones had been picked bare, and the cask drained to its dregs, not a man out of the twelve was sober. A heavy slumber, lasting late into the morning, was the natural consequence of this debauch, and when the sleepers were at last aroused, they set about the preparation for a start in a very languid fashion. It was nearly noon before the party was fairly on its way. Darkness came on before the next stage could be reached. It was while the travellers were bivouacking in a wholly unprotected situation that a company of marauders, who had indeed been watching their movements for some days in the hopes of finding such an opportunity, fell upon them. The result was disastrous.	Alcibiades and **Callias**, who had been sleeping with their horses picketed close to their camp fire, were roused by **the noise**, and springing to their saddles made their escape. Not one of their followers **was** equally fortunate. **Some** were cut down in their sleep, others as they were endeavoring to **collect** their senses. The sumpter-horses and **their** burdens of course fell into the hands of the **assailants. It was** only with what they carried on their own persons **that** the two survivors of the party made their way about **six days** afterward to the Satrap's winter palace at Gordium.

CHAPTER XVII.

"I FEEL that my place is at Athens," said Callias to his host a few days after their arrival.

"In spite of the past?"

"Yes. At such a time no one thinks of the past, but only of the future."

"Well; I cannot say that you are wrong. If you think fit to go, I shall not seek to hold you back. I must frankly say that I see little hope."

"And you?" Callias went on after a pause. "What shall you do, if I may make so bold as to ask?"

"If I can save my country at all, it will be here. The only hope now is to detach Persia from Sparta. Perhaps now that Athens has fallen so low, the Persians will see what their true interests are. The worst of it is that there is no real ruler, no one to carry out a consistent policy. The great king is absolute at the capital, but in the provinces he is little more than a name. The satraps do almost as they please; they actually make war on each other if it suits their purpose. So, it is not what is best for Persia, but what Tissaphernes or Pharnabazus may think best for himself that will be done. Still there is a chance left; only I must be on the spot to seize it if it comes. Were I to go to Athens, I should be only one man among a useless crowd, and you, my young friend, will, I very much fear, be little more."

"Anyhow I shall go," replied the young man, "at all events there will be one sword more to be drawn for Athens."

"Yes," muttered Alcibiades to himself, as his companion left the room, "if you get the chance of drawing it. I rather think that with that fox Lysander in command, you will do nothing more for Athens than bring one more mouth to be fed."

Callias made his way to the coast with no difficulty. Assuming, at the suggestion of Alcibiades, a citizen's dress, he joined a caravan of traders which was on its way westward, and in their company travelled pleasantly and safely. Arrived at Miletus he took passage in a merchant ship that was bound for Ægina, hoping if he could only get so far, to be able to make his way somehow into the city. At one time, indeed, he was terribly afraid that this hope would be disappointed. The *Swallow*—this was the name of the vessel of Ægina—was challenged and overhauled by a Corinthian ship of war. Callias made no attempt to conceal his nationality. Indeed it would have been useless, for an Athenian in those days was about as easily recognized over the whole of the Greek world as an Englishman is recognized in these, anywhere in Europe. To his great surprise the Corinthian captain simply said: "You can go; I have no order to detain you." That there was no kindness in his permission Callias was perfectly well aware, for the hatred of Corinth for Athens was tenfold more bitter than that of Sparta.

It was a quarrel between Athens and Corinth, on the tender point of a rebellious Corinthian colony, that had been the immediate cause of the Peloponnesian War; and even before this there had always been the potent influence of commercial rivalry to set the two states against each other. The young Athenian noticed also a sinister smile on the captain's face; but what it meant he was at a loss to determine.

Landed at Ægina he lost no time in enquiring how he might best reach his destination.

"Oh! you will get in easily enough," said the Æginetan merchant, the owner of the *Swallow*, to whom he stated his case.

"Is not the city blockaded then?"

"Yes, in a way," replied the man.

"Please to explain what you mean," said Callias, who was getting a little heated by these mysterious remarks.

"Well," said the merchant, "King Pausanias is encamped outside the city in some place that they call the Grove of Academus, I think. Do you know it?"

Callias assented with a nod.

"And Lysander has a hundred and fifty ships off the Piraeus. Still I think that you will be able to get in. The blockade is not kept very strictly."

"Had I best go by night?"

"Perhaps it would be better."

"Can you help me to a boat?"

"Certainly; but you will have to pay the boatman pretty highly, for, of course, it is a risk, though it can be done.

"Will you make the arrangements if I pay you the money in advance?"

"Certainly, if you do not mind going so far as a *mina.* It is really worth the money."

Callias paid the money, and was told to be in readiness to embark at midnight.

It would have enlightened him considerably if he could have seen the merchant's behavior as soon as he was safely out of the room.

"Ah, you young serpent," the man cried, "you will be allowed to creep into your hole easily enough; but if we don't suffocate you and your whole brood when we have got you there, my name is not Timagenes."

The fact was that a revolution of which Callias knew nothing had taken place at Ægina. An old rival and enemy of Athens, the city had been conquered many years before, and the anti-Athenian party expelled. And now everything was changed. Lysander had brought back the exiles, and though Athens had still friends, it was the hostile party that was in power. Callias had observed a certain change in the demeanor of the people, but was too much engrossed in his own affairs to think much about it.

The blockade was run as easily as the Æginetan had foretold. The boat passed within fifty yards of one of the squadron, and Callias could have sworn that he saw a sentinel on the watch pacing the vessel's deck. But the man did not challenge, and the Piraeus was reached without any difficulty.

It was not long before all the mystery was explained.

"This is just what I feared," said Hippocles, to whose house the young Athenian hastened. "I knew that you would come back, and I could not warn you."

"What do you mean," cried the young man in astonishment. "Was it not my duty to return?"

"Yes, in one way it was. But tell me how you got here?"

Callias related the incidents of his journey, and expressed some surprise that the Corinthian captain had not taken him prisoner, and that the blockade was so negligently kept.

"And you did not understand what all this meant?"

"No; I understood nothing."

"My dear friend," said the merchant, "it simply means that Lysander is going to starve us out, and that the more there are of us the easier and the speedier his work will be. This has been his policy all along. He has taken no prisoners. Whenever he has taken a city, and there is hardly one that has not either been taken or given itself up, he has sent every Athenian citizen home. They are simply put on their parole to come here. The consequence is that the city is fairly swarming with people, and that there is next to no food. I have a good store—for some time past I have kept myself well provisioned, not knowing what might happen—and I am able to do something for my poor neighbors. But the state of things in the city is simply awful. People, and people too whom I know as really well-to-do citizens, are dying of sheer starvation. As for the poor women and children it is truly heart breaking. Oh, my dear friend, if you had only stopped away ; for here you can do nothing. But I knew you would come back, and I honor you for it."

"But can nothing be done?" cried the young man. "It is better to die than be starved like a wolf in his den."

"The people have lost all heart. And indeed, if they were all brave as lions, we are hopelessly outnumbered. Pausanias must have as many as forty thousand men outside the city, for every city in the Island* except Argos, has sent its contingent; and we could not muster a fourth part of the number, and such troops too! And where is our fleet? At the bottom of the Ægean, or in the arsenals of the enemy. I do not suppose that there are fifty ships, all told, in our docks. And of these a third are not seaworthy. No, we must submit; and yet it is almost as much as a man's life is worth to mention the word."

"But could we not make terms of some kind, not good terms I fear, but still such as would be endurable? Has anything been done?"

"The Senate sent to Agis, who was at Deceleia,† and proposed peace on these terms: Athens was to become the ally of Sparta on the condition of having the same friends and the same enemies, but was to be allowed to keep the Long Walls‡ and the Piraeus. Agis said that he had no authority to treat, and bade the envoys go to Sparta. So they came back here, and were directed to go. They reached a place on the borders of Laconia and sent on their message to the ephors at Sparta, not being allowed to proceed any further themselves. The ephors sent back this answer: ' Begone instantly; if the Athenians really desire peace, let them send you again with other proposals, such as having re-

---

*The Peloponnesus or Island of Pelops.

† Deceleia was the fort established in Athenian territory by the Peloponnesians early in the war and used as their headquarters during their annual invasion of the country.

‡ The Long Walls were the great strength of Athens. They joined the harbor of the Piraeus to the city.

flected more wisely they may be disposed to make.' So
the envoys returned. Some had hoped that they would do
some good. I must confess that I had not. There was
terrible dismay. At last one Archistratus plucked up
courage to speak. ' The Lacedaemonians can force us to
accept what conditions they please. Let us acknowledge
what we cannot deny, and make peace with them on their
own terms.' There was a howl of rage at this, for in truth
the Lacedaemonian terms were nothing less than this:
' Pull down a mile of the Long Walls, and give up your
fleet.' The unlucky Archistratus was thrown into prison
where he lies still. Well, one said one thing, one another.
At last Theramenes got up and said : ' The real manager of
affairs is neither Agis nor Pausanias, nor even the Ephors,
but Lysander. Send me to him—he is a personal friend of
mine own—and I will make the best terms I can with him.'
To this the assembly agreed, having indeed nothing better
to do. That was three or four days ago. Theramenes
started the same night. I very much doubt whether
he will be able to do any good. I am not even sure that he
means to. But we shall see."

A miserable period of waiting followed. Day after day
passed, and the envoy neither returned nor sent any communication to his fellow countrymen. No one knew where
he was. Whether he was still with Lysander or had gone
on to Sparta—all was a mystery. Meanwhile the distress in
the city grew more and more acute. Callias had taken up
his abode with Hippocles, and was so out of absolute want.
He was perfectly ready to acquiesce in the extreme frugality
which was the rule of the house. Free and bond all fared

alike, and none had anything beyond the most absolute necessaries of life. Whatever could be spared was devoted to the relief of the needy.

Not the least trying part of the situation was the forced inaction. Not even a sally was made. Indeed, it would have been a useless waste of life. Not only were the forces of the enemy vastly superior, but the besieged soldiers were almost unable to support the weight of their arms, so scanty was the fare to which they were reduced. There were times when Callias was disposed to rush sword in hand on some outpost of the enemy, sell his life as dearly as he could, and perish.

Two things held him back from carrying this idea into execution, things curiously unlike, yet working together for the same result. One was his love for Hermione. Life had not lost all its charm, his horizon was not wholly dark, while there remained the light of this hope. Indeed it was the one consolation of his life that he was permitted to help her in her daily ministration among her needy neighbors. A string of pensioners presented themselves at the merchant's gates, and received such relief as he could give. But Hermione was not content with this. There were some, she knew, whose pride would not permit them to mingle in the train of mendicants; there were others whose strength did not permit them to come abroad. These she sought out in their own homes. Callias found a melancholy pleasure in accompanying and helping her. Not a word of love passed his lips. He would have scorned himself if he had added the smallest grain to the burden of care that she bore. But he never failed in his attendance, and he was hailed by many a poor sufferer with a pleasure only second to that which greeted the gracious presence of the girl. When, as happened before long, fever the unfailing follower of famine, began to spread its ravages over the Piraeus, his labors and hers grew more arduous. Battling with these two fearful enemies within the walls, Callias almost forgot the foes that were without.

The other restraining and strengthening influence was that which Socrates exercised on the young man's mind. All the time that Callias could spare from the labors that he shared with Hermione was given to the society of the philosopher. The sage's indomitable courage and endurance were in themselves an encouragement of the highest order. Doubtless his physical strength, which made him capable of bearing an almost incredible degree of cold and hunger, helped him to show a dauntless heart to the troubles which were breaking down so many. Indeed he seemed scarcely to want food or drink. But the steadfastness with which he pursued his usual course of life, still keeping up his untiring search for wisdom was a spectacle nothing less than splendid, while nothing could exceed his practical sagacity. Anyone who wanted shrewd advice in the actual circumstances of life, anyone who desired to be lifted out of the sordid present, with its miserable hopes and cares, on to a higher plane of life, came to Socrates and did not come in vain.

At length, when nearly three months had passed, the long period of suspense seemed about to come to an end. The report ran through the city that Theramenes had returned. What were the terms he had brought back, no one knew. On that point he remained obstinately silent. In fact he had nothing to say, nothing further, that is, than the fact that Lysander professed himself unable to treat; the Ephors must be approached, if anything was to be done.

Had Lysander amused him with hopes that instructions and power to treat would soon be sent down to him from Sparta, or had he deliberately waited till the city should be reduced to such a pitch of starvation that it would be ready to consent to any terms? There was a brutal, cold-blooded cruelty in such conduct that makes it difficult to credit; yet many believed it to be the true explanation of the delay.* To picture the dismay that prevailed through the assembly when Theramenes had given his report of the negotiations which he had *not* concluded would be impossible. There was nothing to be done but accept the bitter necessity. Theramenes, with nine others, was sent to Sparta with full power to treat. They were to accept any terms that might be offered. The proud city had fallen as low as that.

Then came another time of waiting. Happily it was not long. Theramenes felt that the endurance of his countrymen had been tried to the uttermost, and that nothing more was to be gained. Athens was on her knees. It did not suit him and his purposes—for he had purposes of his own, possibly a tyranny, certainly power—that she should be actually prostrate. He and his colleagues made all the haste that they could; and as their instructions were

* Xenophon distinctly says that he lingered with Lysander, waiting for the time when the Athenians, at the last pinch of starvation, should be ready to accept any terms that might be offered.

THE PARTHENON AT THE PRESENT DAY.

simple—to accept anything that might be offered—there was little to delay them.

At the end of about twelve days they returned. It was in the midst of a breathless suspense that Theramenes stood up to make his report. What he said may be thus given in outline.

" We went with all speed to Sellasia * and there waited, having sent on a message to the Ephors that we had come with full power to treat. On the second day we were summoned to Sparta. There we found envoys assembled from the allies of the Lacedaemonians. Aristides also was there.

" At the mention of the name of Aristides a murmur of fear and rage ran through the assembly. The man was one of the most notorious of the anti-patriotic party. He had been in exile for many years, and was believed to have done more harm than any one else to his native city.

" The senior of the Ephors stood up, and said : ' Friends and allies, the Athenians seek for peace. What say you? Shall we grant it to them?' One after another the envoys rose in their places. They did not use many words. It was not the custom of the place to be long in speech as they knew. All said the same thing. ' We give our vote against peace. Let Athens be destroyed. There will be no true peace so long as she is permitted to exist.' When all had spoken we were called on to speak. ' You hear what these say,' said the Ephor who had not spoken before. ' What have you to reply?' I answered that the Athenians were ready to give all pledges that might be asked from them

---

* Sellasia was a town on the border where the previous embassy had been bidden to wait till the Ephors could be communicated with.

that they would not harm either Sparta or her allies or any city of the Greeks. After this we were all commanded to withdraw. In about the space of an hour we were summoned again into the chamber. The Ephor rose in his place and spoke. 'The Corinthians and the other allies demand that Athens should be destroyed. Nor do they this without reason. The Athenians have destroyed many cities of the Greeks. Yet can we not forget that they have also in time past done good service to Greece. But of these things which you all know it is needless to speak. Our sentence is this: Let the Athenians pull down their Long Walls for the space of a mile. Let them also surrender their fleet, keeping only twelve ships. On these terms they shall have peace. These then, O men of Athens,' the speaker continued, 'are the conditions which the Spartans demand. I confess that they are hard. Yet they are better than those which the rest of Greece would impose upon you. Truly the Lacedaemonians stand between us and utter destruction. And there is nothing beyond remedy in what they would lay upon us. Walls that are broken down may be repaired, and for ships that have been given up many others may be built; but of a city against which the decree of destruction has gone forth, there is an end. Therefore I propose that peace be made with the Lacedaemonians on these terms.

"One or two speakers ventured to rise in opposition. But they could scarcely get a hearing. Probably they only went through the form of opposing in order that they might be able at some future time to say that they had done so. With but short delay the proposition was put to the vote and carried by an overwhelming majority. The same evening envoys were sent to Lysander announcing that the Spartan conditions had been accepted.

"The next day the gates of the city were thrown open, and the fleet of Lysander sailed into the Piraeus. The ships of war were handed over to him. Many were destroyed, and indeed the once famous and powerful fleet of Atticus had been reduced to a state of most deplorable weakness. The sacrifice of the fleet, such as it was, was not so very costly after all. The few sea-worthy ships that remained, besides the twelve that the city was permitted to retain, were sent off to the Lacedaemonian arsenal of Gytheum. This done, the next thing was to beat down the Long Walls. 'This is the first day of the freedom of Greece,' said Lysander, 'we must keep it as a festival. Send for the flute players.' Accordingly the services of every flute player in Attica were requisitioned; and to the sound of the gayest tunes which they could find in their *repertoire* the work of demolition went on. Every decent Athenian whatever his policy, kept, of course, close within doors; but there was nevertheless a vast concourse of spectators, the rabble who will crowd to any sight, however brutal and humiliating, the army of Pausanias and the crews of Lysander's fleet, with a miscellaneous crowd of foreigners who had come to gloat over the downfall of the haughty city. Loud was the shout that went up when a clean breach was made through the walls. The general feeling was that Athens had suffered a blow from which she could never recover. But there were some who doubted. 'You have scratched the snake, not killed it,' said a Corinthian, as he turned away."

CHAPTER XVIII.

"NOBLESSE OBLIGE."

SOME fourteen or fifteen days have passed since the humiliation of Athens was completed. To have come to the end, bitter as it was, was in one way a relief. To know the worst always brings a certain comfort, and that worst might have been, was, in fact, very near being far more terrible than what actually happened. Then there was a great material relief. The pressure of famine was removed. Supplies poured plentifully into Athens, for the city, in spite of all its sacrifices and losses, was still rich. If fever still remained—it always lingers a while after its precursor, hunger, has departed—it was now possible to cope with it effectually. And then, last not least, it was the delightful season of spring. The Athenians could once more enjoy the delights of that country life from which they had been shut out so long, but which they had never ceased to love. Attica, indeed, had suffered sadly from the presence, repeated year after year, of the invading host; but it had suffered less than might have been expected. The olive yards in particular, had not been touched. A religious feeling had forbidden any injury to a tree which was supposed to be under the special protection of the patron goddess of the land. The sacred groves also of the heroes, that were scattered about the country, had not been harmed. Not a few houses with their gardens had been saved by having served as residences for officers high in command in the Peloponnesian army. And now Nature, the restorer, was busy in the genial season of growth in healing or at least hiding the wounds that had been made by the ravages of war.

"What do you say to a trip to Marathon?" said Hippocles one day, to his daughter and Callias. "You both of you look as if a little fresh air would do you good."

"An excellent idea," cried Hermione, clapping her hands, "it is years since I have seen the place."

"What say you, Callias?" said Hippocles, turning to the young man.

Callias was only too glad to join any expedition when he was to have the company of Hermione. He did not give this reason, but he assented to the proposal very heartily.

"But, father, how shall we go?" said Hermione. "There is scarcely a horse to be found, I suppose."

"Why not go by sea?" was her father's reply. "I have a pinnace which would just suit us. We will go to-morrow if the weather holds fine, stop the first night at Sunium, and the second at Marathon. At Sunium there is my villa, and at Marathon there is a little house of which I can get the use, and which will serve us if we do not mind roughing it a little. We can return the next day. Only we must take provisions, for except such fish as we may catch in the Marathon stream, and possibly, some goats' milk, if all the goats have not been eaten up, we shall have nothing but what we bring. That must be your care, Hermione."

"Trust me, father," cried the girl joyously. "If you have gone through four months' famine, depend upon it you shall not be starved now."

The weather on the following day was all that could be desired. A warm and gentle west wind was blowing. This served them very well as they sailed southward to Sunium. In such good time did they reach the promontory, that by unanimous vote they agreed to finish their journey that same day. Sailing northward was as easy as sailing southward, and the sun was still an hour from setting when they reached the northern end of the plain, having travelled a distance of upwards of sixty miles. This was about four times as far as they would have had to go, had they made the journey by land. No one, however, regretted having followed **Hippocles'** suggestion. The voyage was indeed as delightful an excursion as could have been devised. The deep blue sky overhead, the sea, borrowing from the heavens a color as intense, and only touched here and there with a speck of white where a little wave swelled and broke, sea birds now flying high in the air, now darting for their prey into the waters, the white cliffs tipped with the fresh green of spring that framed the coast line, made a picture that the party intensely enjoyed, although they did not put their enjoyment into words with the fluency and ease which would have come readily to a modern. The ancients loved nature, but, as a rule, they felt this love much more than they expressed it.

The little house at Marathon was one that had escaped destruction by having been occupied by a Spartan officer. It was bare indeed of furniture, but it was habitable;

and the party had brought with them the few things that were absolutely necessary, far fewer, we must remember, than what we now consider to be indispensable. Supper was felt by all to be a most enjoyable meal. The room in which they sat was bare, for, of course, the luxurious couches on which it was the fashion to recline were absent. There was not even a table, and there was but one broken chair, which was naturally resigned to Hermione. But it was lightened with a cheerful fire, which was not unwelcome after seven or eight hours' exposure to a high wind. Happily the late occupant had left a store of logs, which had been cut on the slopes of Pentelicus in the previous autumn, and which now blazed up most cheerfully. The meal was declared by both Hippocles and Callias to be good enough for a State-banquet in the Prytaneum. One of the sailors had caught a basketful of fish in the stream, and these Hermione had cooked with her own hands. An Athenian who had plenty of fish, seldom wanted anything in the way of flesh, and the provisions which Hermione, not liking to trust to the skill or the luck of the anglers had brought with her, were not touched. A cold maize pudding, some of the famous Attic figs, which had been preserved through the winter, bread with honey from Hymettus, and dried grapes completed the repast. Some of the goats, it turned out, had survived, and a jug of their milk was forthcoming for Hermione. The two men had a flask of wine which they largely diluted with water. When, after the libation, Hippocles proposed the toast of the evening, as, in consideration of the locality it might fairly be called, "To the memory of the Heroes of Marathon," Hermione honored it by putting her lips to the cup. It was the first time that wine had ever passed them, but she could not refuse this tribute to the chief glory of the city of her adoption.

Hermione, fatigued, it may be said, with all the delights of the day, retired early to rest. Soon after she had gone Callias took the opportunity of opening his heart to his companion on a subject which had long occupied his thoughts.

"We have peace at last," he said, "not such a peace as I had ever hoped for, but still better than the utter ruin which lately I had begun to fear. A good citizen may now begin to think of himself and of his own happiness. You, sir, can hardly have failed to observe why I have begun to look for that happiness. If your daughter will only consent to share my life, I feel that I shall have to ask the gods for nothing more. She is free as far as I know. And me you have known from my childhood. You were my father's friend and since he died you have stood in his place. Can you give her to me?"

Hippocles caught his young companion's hand, and gave it a hearty grasp.

"I will not pretend," he said, "not to have observed something of what you say; nor will I deny that I have observed it with pleasure. What father would not be glad if Callias, the son of Hipponicus, loved his daughter? Of Hermione's feelings I say nothing, indeed I know nothing, save that she has regarded you since childhood with a strong affection, and that as you say she is free. But there are facts which neither you nor I can forget; and the chief of them is this, that while you are Callias, son of Hipponicus, an

Eupatrid of the Eupatrids,* I am Hippocles, the Alien. I am well-born in my own country, but that is nothing here. I am wealthy—so wealthy that I care not a single drachma whether my future son-in-law has a thousand talents for his patrimony or one. I am, I hope and believe, not without honor in the city of my adoption. But I am an alien, my child is an alien. Whether you have thought of all that this means I know not—love is apt to hide these difficulties from a man's eyes—but the fact must be faced; you and my daughter must face it. You speak of my giving her to you. But, if Hermione is a Greek, she is also an Italian. The Italian women choose for themselves. I could not if I would constrain her will. She must decide, and she must answer."

"There is nothing that I should desire better. But you do not tell me, sir, what you yourself wish. Have I your consent and your good wishes?"

"Yes," said Hippocles, "you have. I have thought over the difficulties, for I foresaw that you would some day speak to me on this subject. As far as I am concerned I am ready to waive them. But then, they do not concern me in the first place."

The two men sat in silence for some time after this conversation had passed between them, buried each of them in his own thoughts. At last Hippocles rose from his seat.

"It is time to sleep," he said; " I will speak to my daughter to-morrow; you shall not want my good word, but I can do nothing more. You must speak to her yourself. That

*The class name of the Athenian nobility.

is, I think, what few fathers in Greece would tell a suitor to do. But then Hermione is not as other maidens."

Callias passed a restless night, and was glad, to make his way into the open air when the first streaks of dawn appeared on the Eubœan hills, which were in full view from the house. He shrank from meeting Hermione till he could meet her alone, and ask the momentous question which was occupying his whole mind. Partly to employ the time, partly to banish thought, if it might be done by severe bodily exercise, he started to climb the height of Pentelicus, which rose on the southern side of the Marathonian plain. The excursion occupied him the whole morning. On his way back he traversed the hills which skirted the western side of the plain, and, following what was evidently a well-beaten track, came at last in view of the mound under which reposed the Athenian dead who had fallen in that great battle. His quick eye soon perceived a familiar figure, conspicuous in its white garments among the monuments which stood on the top of the mound. Hippocles had fulfilled his promise, and had said all that he could to Hermione in favor of her suitor. He had dwelt upon his noble birth, the reputation as a soldier which he had already won, his culture and taste for philosophy, and his blameless life. " As for wealth," he ended by saying, " that is of little account where my daughter is concerned. Yet a man should be independent of his wife, and I may tell you as one who knows—and I have had charge of his property for some years past—that Callias is one of the richest men in Athens. That will not weigh with you I know, but I would have you know all the circumstances."

Hermione said nothing; she took her father's hand **and** kissed it. A tear dropped on it as she raised it **to her lips.** As she turned away, Hippocles noticed that she was shaken **by a sob.**

An instinct in the **girl's heart told** her that it **was on the** mound that her lover would speak to her, and **it was here** that she wished **to give her answer to him.** It was not the first time that she had **visited it.** Indeed there **was not a** woman, **and not many men in** Athens who **knew so much** about its records.

On the top **of this tumulus, which still** rises **thirty feet** above the surrounding plain, and which was then, **it is probable,** considerably **higher, there** stood in those days eleven stone columns inscribed with the names of those who had fallen in the great battle. Each **of the ten** Athenian **tribes had its** own peculiar column, while **the eleventh com-**memorated the **gallant men** of **Plataea, Plataea, which** alone among the **cities of Greece,** had sent her **sons on that** day to stand shoulder to shoulder with the **soldiers of** Athens.

Hermione **was apparently** engrossed in the task of de-ciphering the names, **now** grown somewhat obliterated by time, which **were engraved on one** of the columns. So in-tent was she **on this occupation that she** did not notice the young **man's approach.** Turning suddenly round, she faced him. **At** that moment, **though she had expected him** to come, his actual **coming was a surprise, and the hot blood** crimsoned **her face and neck.**

"Hermione," **he said,** "I have spoken to your father, and he bids me speak **to you.** You can hardly have failed to **read** my heart, and if I have not spoken to you before, **it has been because I** have not presumed. **You know all** that needs be known about me, and though I do not think myself worthy **of you, I need** not be ashamed **of my fathers or** of myself."

The brilliant color had faded from the girl's cheek, **her** hand trembled, her bosom heaved. Twice she opened her lips; twice the voice seemed to fail **her.** At last she spoke.

"You speak **of your** fathers. You are, I think, of the tribe of Pandion?"

"I am," said Callias.

"And this is the column **of their tribe, and this"—she** pointed as she spoke—"**the name of** an ancestor of yours?"

"Yes," replied the young man, "this Hipponicus whose **name you see** engraved here was my great grandfather."

"He had been Archon at Athens the year before **the great battle.** You see," she added with **a** faint smile, **"I** know something **of your family** history."

"It was so."

"And his son, a Callias like yourself, was Archon general many times—held, **in** fact, every honor that Athens could bestow?"

"Yes, there was no more distinguished **man** in the city **than he."**

"And your father ; he died, I think **I** have heard, in early manhood; but he **was already far** advanced in the career of **honor ?"**

"Doubtless had he lived he would not have been inferior in distinction to my grandfather."

"And you have started well in the same course? I need **not ask** you that. We all know it better, perhaps, than you know it yourself, and we are proud of it. My dear brother," the girl's voice which hitherto had been clear and even commanding in its tones, faltered at the mention of the dead, "my dear brother used to say that there was nothing that you might not hope for, nothing to which you might not rise."

"You speak too well of me; but I hope that I am not altogether unworthy of my ancestors."

The girl paused for a while. She seemed unable to utter what she had next to say. The flush mounted again to her cheek, and she stood silent and with downcast eyes.

Meanwhile the young man stood in utter perplexity. He had heard nothing from the girl's lips but what might have made any man proud to hear. She knew, as she had said, the history of his race, and she believed him to be not unworthy of it. Yet this was not the way in which he had hoped to hear her speak. He was conscious that there was something behind that did not promise well for his hopes.

At last she went on. Her voice was low but distinct, her eyes were still bent on the ground.

"And what your fathers have been in Athens, what you hope to be yourself, you would have your son to be after you?"

"Surely," he answered without thinking of what he was admitting.

"Could it be so if I—" she altered the phrase—"if a woman not of Athenian blood were his mother?"

He was struck dumb. So this was the end she had before her when she enumerated the honors and distinctions of his race.

"Mind," she said, "I do not say that my race is unworthy of yours. I am not ashamed of my ancestors. They were chiefs; they were good men. I am proud to be their daughter. But here in Athens their goodness and their nobility goes for nothing. I am Hermione, the daughter of Hippocles, the Alien. Marrying me you shut out, not perhaps yourself, but your children from the career which is their inheritance. I am too proud,"—and here the girl dropped her voice to a whisper,—"and I love you too well for that."

"What is my career to your love?" cried the young man passionately; "I am ready to give up country and all for that."

"That," said Hermione, "is the only unworthy thing that I ever heard you say. Your better thoughts will make you withdraw it. Athens has fallen; the gods know that it has wrung my heart to see it. But she needs all the more such sons as you are. She has little now to offer. It is a thankless office, perhaps, to command her fleets and armies. All the more honor to those who cling to her still and cherish her still. You must not leave her or betray her. I should think foul shame of myself if I tempted you for a moment to waver in your loyalty to her. I may not love you—that the gods have forbidden me—but you will let me be proud of you."

The young man turned away. The final word, he knew, had been spoken. This resolution was not to be shaken by indignant reproaches or by tender pleadings. All that remained was to forget, if that was possible. He would not see Hippocles or his daughter again till the wound of this bitter disappointment had had time to heal. Returning to the house, which he found empty but for a single **attendant**, he snatched a hasty meal, and then set out to return over-land to Athens.

CHAPTER XIX.

THREE days after the events recorded in the last chapter
—it took so much time for the young man to screw up his
courage to the point—Callias made his way to the ship-yard
of Hippocles at an hour when he knew that he would be
pretty certain to find the master there.   He was not disappointed, nor could he help being touched by the warm sympathy with which he was received.

"Ah! my dear friend," cried the merchant, "this has
been a great disappointment to me.   I must own that I had
my fears.   I know something, you see, of my daughter's
temper.   I knew that she had always chafed under our
disabilities.   Things that have ceased to trouble me—and I
must own that they never troubled me much—are grievous
to her.   You see that I have a power of my own which is
quite enough to satisfy any reasonable man.   I can't speak
or vote in your assembly, but I have a voice, if I choose to
use it, in your policy.   She knows very little about this, and
would not appreciate it if she did.   Besides it would not
avail her.   No; she feels herself an inferior here, and it galls
her; yet that is scarcely the way to put it, for she was thinking much more of you than of herself.   I believe that she loves
you—she has not confided in me, you must understand,

but I guess as much—and she would sooner cut off her right hand than injure you or yours. And then her pride comes in also. 'Am I, daughter of kings as I am,' she says to herself, 'am I to be one to bring humiliation into an ancient house?' Her mother's forefathers would be called barbarians here, but they were kings and heroes for all that. And that is the bitterness of it to her : to feel herself your equal in birth, and yet to know that to marry you would be to drag you down."

" I understand," said Callias, "it is noble; but just now my heart rebels very loudly against it. Let us say no more. I have come to ask you what you would advise. For the present I cannot stay at Athens."

"That," said Hippocles, "is exactly what I wanted to talk to you about; if you had not come to-day I should have sought for you. You wish to leave Athens, you say. It is well, for it would not be safe for you to stay. We shall have a bad time in Athens for the next few months, perhaps for longer. The exiles have come back full of rage and thirsting for revenge. And then there is Theramenes; he is the man you have to fear. He has the murder of the generals on his soul. That, perhaps, would not trouble him much but he fears all who might be disposed to call him to account for it. He knows that you were the kinsman and dear friend of Diomedon, and he will take the first opportunity that may occur of doing you a mischief. And opportunities will not be wanting. I suspect that for some time to come, with the Oligarchs in power and the Lacedaemonians to back them up, laws and constitutional forms will not go for much in Athens."

"And you advise me to go?" said **Callias.**

"Certainly there is nothing to keep you. For the present **there is no career for you here.** I don't despair **of Athens; but for some time to come she will have a very humble part to play.**"

"Have you anything to suggest?"

"I have been thinking over it for two or three days. Many things have occurred to **me, but** nothing so **good as** was suggested by a letter which **I received this morning.** It came from a merchant in Rhodes with whom I have had dealings for some years **past. My correspondent** asks for a **large advance in** money for a commercial speculation which **he says promises large profits.** I have always found **the man honest; in fact** the outcomes **of** my dealings with him in the past **have** been quite satisfactory. But this new venture that **he proposes** is a very large one indeed. I like what he tells me of it. **It opens up** quite a new field **of** enterprise; and new fields, I need hardly tell you, have a great charm for a man in my position. **The ordinary rou**tine of commerce does not interest me **very much; but** something new is **very** attractive. **Now I want you to go** to Rhodes for me. Make all the **enquiries you can about** the character and standing of my correspondent, whom, curiously enough, **I** have never seen. **I will** give you introductions to those **who will put you in** the way of hearing **all** that is to be heard. **If the** man's credit is shaky at all, **then I** shall know **that** this proposition **of his is a desperate venture.** If all is sound, I shall feel pretty **sure that he has got** hold **of** a really good thing."

" I know very little of such matters," said the young Callias after a pause.

" I do not ask you to go that you may judge of this particular enterprise; I simply want you to find out what people are saying about Diagoras—that is my correspondent's name; you will be simply an Athenian gentleman on his travels. Keep your ears open and you will be sure to hear something."

" Well," said Callias, "I will do my best; but don't expect too much."

" Can you start to-morrow ? "

" Yes, if you think it necessary."

" Well, my affair is not urgent for some days, at least. But for yourself, I fancy you cannot get out of the way too soon. I don't think that Theramenes and his friends will stick much at forms and ceremonies. I own that I shall feel much happier when there are two or three hundred miles of sea between you and them. Be here an hour after sunset to-morrow. By that time I shall have arranged for your passage and got ready your letters of introduction and the rest of it."

" Well," said the young man to himself as he went to make his preparations for departure, "this, it must be confessed, is a little hard on me. Hermione says, 'Stop in Athens and stick to your career'; her father says, 'If you stop in Athens you are as good as a dead man, and your career will be cut short by the hemlock cup.' I have to give up my love for my career and then give up my career for my life."

It is needless to relate the incidents of my hero's voyage to Rhodes or of his stay on that island. His special mission he was able **to accomplish** easily enough.   Diagoras' speculation was, **as he soon found out,** the last resource of an embarrassed man; and the loan for which he asked would be **a** risk too great for any prudent person to undertake. The letter in which he communicated what he had heard to Hippocles was crossed by one from Athens. From this he learned that the political anticipations of the merchant had been more than fulfilled. The oligarchical revolution had been carried on with the most outrageous violence.   **On the very day on** which he had left Athens, an officer of the government had come with an order for his arrest.

All this was interesting; still more so was a brief communication from Alcibiades which the merchant enclosed. **It ran thus:**

"Alcibiades to Callias son of Hipponicus, greeting. **Great** things are possible now to the bold of whom I know you to **be one. More I** do not say, but come to me as soon as you can.   Farewell."

The merchant had added a postscript. **"I leave** this for your consideration. Alcibiades has a certain knack of **success.** But the risk will be great."

"What is risk to me?" said Callias, "**I can't** spend my life idling here."

The next day he left the island, **taking his** passage in **a** merchant ship which, by great good luck was just starting **for Smyrna.** Smyrna was reached without any mishap. Four **days afterwards, he started** with a guide for the little village in Phrygia from which Alcibiades had **dated his** note. Halting at noon on **the** first day's journey to **rest** their horses, they **were** accosted **by a miserable looking** wayfarer, who begged for **some** scraps of **food,** declaring **that he** had not broken his fast for four and twenty hours. **Something in** the man's voice and face struck Callias as familiar, and he puzzled in vain **for a** solution of the mystery, while the stranger sat eagerly devouring **the** meal with which he had been furnished.

"Here," said Callias, when the man had **finished his re**past and was thanking him, "here is something to **help you** along till you can find friends **or** employment." And he gave him **four** or five silver pieces.

It was the first time he had spoken in the fugitive's **hearing,** and the man, who, now that his ravenous hunger **was** appeased, had leisure **to notice other things,** started at the sound of his **voice. He, on** his part, **seemed to** recognize something.

"Many thanks, sir," **he said;** "the gods **pay** you back ten-fold. **But surely,"** he went on, "**I have seen you** before. Ah! now **I remember.** You are Callias **the son of** Hipponicus, and you were my master's guest in Thrace."

A light flashed on the young Athenian's mind. **The man** had been one of **Alcibiades'** attendants in his Thracian **castle.**

"Ah! I remember," he cried, "and your master was Alcibiades. **But what do you** here? **How does** he fare?"

The man burst into tears. "Ah, **sir, he is** dead, cruelly **killed by those** villains of Spartans. **He was the very best** of masters. I never had a rough **word from him. We all** loved him."

"Tell me," said Callias, "how it happened. **I was on my** way to him," and he read to the man the **brief note that had** been forwarded to him at **Rhodes.**

"**Yes, I understand. I** know when that was written. He **had** great hopes of being able to do something. I did not rightly understand what **it was, but the common talk** among us who were of his household was that he was going to the Great King to persuade him that the best thing that he could do would be to set Athens on her feet again to help him against Sparta. Oh! he was a wonderful man to persuade, was my **master.** Nobody could help being taken by him."

"But tell me the story," said the young man.

"Well, it happened in this way. My **master had gone up** to see Pharnabazus, the Satrap, who had **promised to aid him on** his way up to Susa **to see the Great King. There** were six **of** us with him; his secretary, myself **and four** slaves. There **was Timandra,** also, whom he used to call his wife; but his real wife was an Athenian lady, Hipparete, I have heard say."

"Yes," interrupted Callias, "I knew her; a cousin **of my** own; a most unhappy marriage. But go on."

"Well, Pharnabazus received him most hospitably. There was no good house in the village, **so we had three** cottages. Alcibiades had one; the secretary **and I another,** and the slaves, a third. Every day the satrap **sent a handsome** supply of provisions for us; dishes and wine from his own table for my master, and for **us** all that we could want **for** ourselves. I never fared better in my **life. And** my master had long talks with him and seemed in excellent spirits. Everything was going on as well as possible. **Then** there came **a** change. I never could find out whether my master had heard anything to make him suspicious. If he

had, he certainly told the secretary **nothing about it. But**
he was very much depressed. First he sent Timandra away.
She was very unwilling to go, poor lady, **for** she did love
my master very much, though, as I say, she was not really
his wife. But my master insisted **on it,** so she went away
to stay with some friends. After that his spirits grew worse
and worse. He used **to tell his** secretary **the dreams he**
had. Once he dreamt **he was dressed in Timandra's**
clothes, and that she was putting **rouge and powder** on his
face. At another time he seemed to see himself laid on a
funeral pyre **and the people standing round ready to set it**
on fire. **The very** night **after he** had that dream
we were awakened by **a** tremendous uproar; the
secretary **and I got up** and looked out. The master's
cottage, which was about a stadium * **away from ours**
was on fire, and there were **a** number of Persians, **about**
fifty or sixty, standing round **it,** shouting **out** and cursing
him. The next moment **we saw the door of the** cottage
open, and **the master ran out** with **a** cloak **round his head,**
to keep himself from being choked by the smoke, **and with**
a sword in his hand. As soon as he was clear of the
burning cottage he threw **down** the cloak **and rushed**
straight at the nearest Persian. **The man** turned and **ran.**
There was not one of them that dared stand for a moment.
But they shot **at him with arrows.** They had fastened the
gates of the enclosure in which the cottages stood, you must
understand, so that **he could not escape. In** fact he **was**
climbing over one of them when he was killed."

"And you ; what did you do?"

* A stadium was nearly a furlong ; to be exact, 202 yards.

"Ah ! sir," cried the man, "we were helpless, we had not a sword **between us.** We hid ourselves, **and** the next morning took our master's body **and** carried it to Timandra. **She** made a great funeral, spending upon it, poor thing, nearly every drachma she had. When we had seen the last of my dear master, the secretary said that he had friends at Tarsus, and set out **to** go there. I thought that I had best make my way **to** Smyrna. Thanks to **your** goodness, I shall now be able to get there, but **I** was very nearly dying of starvation. But what, if **I may ask, are you thinking of doing?"**

"That I can't tell," **replied the Athenian; "as I told you,** I was on my way to Alcibiades."

"Well, sir, **I can tell** you this," rejoined the stranger, "no **friends of my master's** will **be** safe here. Pharnabazus, **I feel sure, had no great love for him,** notwithstanding all his politeness; as for the Spartans, they hated him; and I did hear that the people who are now in power at Athens had **sent to say that** peace could not last unless he were put out of the way. Yes, sir, if anyone recognizes that you are my **master's friend, you are a** dead **man."**

"**Why,**" said Callias, "I have made no secret of it. **In** Smyrna **I** spoke about him to the people **with whom I was staying.** No one said a word against him."

"Very likely not," replied the man, "for they thought **that** he was alive, **and** no one liked to have my master for an enemy. He had **a wonderful** way of making friends to **have the** upper hand and contriving that his adversaries **should** have the worst **of it.** But now that he is dead **you** will find things very different."

" What is to be done?" asked the young Athenian.

" Can you trust your guide?"

" I know nothing of the man. I simply hired him because I was told that he was a fairly honest fellow, knew the country very well, and would not run away if a robber made his appearance."

" Well, then get rid of him."

" But how?"

"Tell him that you have a headache, and that you will come on after him when you have rested a little and the sun is not so hot, and that he had better go on, get quarters at the next stage and have everything ready for you when you shall arrive. As soon as he is gone, get back as fast as you can to Smyrna. The news will hardly have reached that place yet, indeed we may be sure that it has not, or you would have heard of it before you started. Go down to the docks, and take your passage in any ship that you can find ready to start. Even if it is going to Athens never mind; you will be able to leave it on the way. Anyhow, get out of Asia at any risk."

" And you?"

" Oh, no one will care about me. I am a very insignificant person. But, as a matter of fact, I shall try to get to Syracuse. I was born there."

" Syracuse will do as well for me as any other place. Why not come with me if it can be managed? I was able to do you a little service, and you have done me a great one. Let us go together."

The plan was carried out with the greatest success. Callias made the best of his way to Smyrna, and left his horse at

an inn, not, of course, the one from which he had started. As
he had plenty of money for immediate wants, besides letters
of credit from Hippocles, he thought it safer not to attempt
to sell the animal. He then provided himself with different
clothes, purchasing at the same time a suit for his new acquaintance. These he ordered to be sent to a small house of
entertainment near the docks which they had arranged
should be the place of meeting. Shortly before sunset the
man appeared. Meanwhile Callias had arranged for a passage for himself and his servant in a ship bound for Corinth.
They would not venture into Corinth itself, but would
transfer themselves at the port of Cenchreae into some ship
bound for Sicily.

Before the morning of the next day the two were on their
way westward. Everything went well. At Cenchreae they
found a Syracusan merchantman just about to start, shipped
on board her, and after a prosperous voyage found themselves in the chief city of Sicily.

CHAPTER XX.

It was with no common emotion that the young Athenian entered the great harbor of Syracuse. It was here that the really fatal blow had been struck from which his country had never recovered. She had struggled gallantly on for nearly ten years after she had lost the most magnificent armament that she had ever sent forth, but the wound had been mortal. Thenceforward she had been as a man of whose life-blood a half had been drained away. Callias had read, shortly before leaving Athens for the last time, the magnificent passage, then recently published, in which the great historian of Athens had described the decisive battle in the harbor.* The sight of the place now enabled him to realize it to himself in the most vivid way. He seemed to see the hostile fleets crowded together in a way for which there was no precedent, two hundred war galleys in a space so narrow that manœuvre was impossible, and nothing availed but sheer fighting and hard blows; while the shores seemed alive again as they had been on that eventful day with a crowd of eager spectators, the armies of the two contending powers, who looked on with passionate cries and gestures at such a spectacle as human eyes had scarcely wit-

* See Thucydides, VII. 71.

nessed before, a mighty war-game in which their own **liberties** and lives were the stake. The heights **that** ran above
the harbor were **scarcely** less **significant. There,** its **re-**
mains still **visible, had been the** Athenian **line** of invest-
ment. If only a few **yards** more had been completed, **the**
young man thought to himself, **the** whole course of **history**
might have **been changed.*** Not far away was the spot
where **the sturdy** infantry of Thebes had withstood the fiery
shock of his **own** countrymen, and so, not **for the first** time,
wrested from them the empire that **seemed almost within**
their grasp.† And somewhere—no one knew where—his own
father had fallen, one of the thousands of noble victims who
had been sacrificed to the greed and ambition of **a restless**
democracy.

The noble house of **which Callias** was the representative
had, of course, its hereditary guest-friend at Syracuse.
Naturally there **had been very** little intercourse between
citizens of the two states **in late** years; but the old tie remained **unbroken,** and Medon, for that was the Syracusan's
name, was as ready to give a hospitable **welcome** to the
young Athenian, as if he had **been a citizen of one of his**
country's allies, a merchant prince of Corinth, **or a scion of**
one of the two royal houses of Sparta. **He** insisted upon his
guest taking up his quarters in his **house, and exerted** himself to the utmost to supply and **even** anticipate every
want.

---

* A very small space yet remained to be erected when Gylippus and
his Lacedaemonians broke through, relieved Syracuse, and practically
decided the issue of the campaign.

† Coronea (447) and Delium (424) had been defeats inflicted by the
Bœotians on the Athenian army at very critical periods when the vic-
tory of the latter must have had very far reaching results.

"Now you have seen something of the outside of our city," said Medon to his friend as they sat together after the evening meal on the third day after his arrival, "you should know something of its politics. But first let me make sure that we are alone."

The dining chamber in which the two were sitting had an ante-room. The door of this the Syracusan proceeded to bolt.

"Now," he said, "we shall have no eavesdroppers. Any inquisitive friend may listen at that other door, with all this space between us and him, without getting much idea of what we are talking about. All the other walls are outer walls, as you know, and unless a certain great personage has the birds of the air in his pay, we may talk without reserve. You look surprised. Well, you will understand things a little better when you have heard what I have to tell you. You know something, I suppose, of what has been happening here of late years. The fact is we have been going through an awful time. No sooner were we free of the danger that you put us in—you must pardon me for alluding to it—than we were confronted with another which was every whit as formidable. Another wretched quarrel between two towns in the island—curiously enough the very same two that were concerned in your expedition against us*—brought in a foreign invader. This time it was the Carthaginians. They had had settlements in the island for many years, had always coveted the dominion of the whole, and more than once had been very near getting it.

* The two were Selinus and Egesta.

They were not far from success this time. First they took Selinus and massacred every creature in it; then they took Acragas;* then they utterly destroyed Himera. Something made them hold their hands, and we had a short breathing space. Four years **afterwards** they came **back in** greater force than ever. Acragas was besieged; it held out bravely, but at last the population had to leave it; only Syracuse was left. Again when in the full tide of victory, the Carthaginians held their hand. **Do you ask me why**? I cannot tell you. But listen to the fourth article **of** the treaty of peace." In spite of the precautions that he had taken against being overheard, Medon, at this point lowered his voice. **"Syracuse is to** be under the rule **of Dionysius. Yes; the secret** is there; it was he that made it worth their while to **go;** and you may be sure that it was worth his while **to** buy them off. I must allow that **he was** the only man who showed a grain of sense or courage in the whole matter; the other generals as **they were** called were hopelessly imbecile. Well, they went, and Dionysius became, shall we call it, 'commander-in-chief,' or perhaps **as** we are **quite** alone, 'tyrant?' He had not an easy time **of it at first; I** don't suppose that he will ever have **an easy time, tyrants** seldom do. The nobles and the **heads of** the democratic party leagued together against him, and drove him out. That did not last long. Of course the conquerors used their **victory most** brutally. They were furious that Dionysius had slipped out of their hands, and wreaked their **vengeance** on his poor wife. I can't tell you the horrible way in which **they** killed **her.** She was **the daughter, too,** of Hermo-

* Commonly known by its Latinized name of Agrigentum.

crates, one of the very **best** and noblest men that Syracuse ever had.   Equally of course they quarrelled over the spoils. **Naturally,** before long they had nothing left to quarrel **over.**   Dionysius hired a force of Campanian mercenaries, the hardest hitters, by the way, that **I** ever saw, and **drove** them out of the city.   **Now, I** fancy, he is pretty firmly seated.   The people like him ; they were never as fit, **you** must know, for popular government as yours are.   He gives them plenty of employment and amusements, wrings **the** money out of us with **a** tight hand, **and** scatters it **among** them with **an open one. Of course a** dagger may reach him, and there are **not a** few that are kept ready sharpened for **the** chance.   Barring **that,** he is likely to be master here **as** long as he lives.   And to tell you the truth, though personally I hate the idea, as any noble must—it is the nobles that always hate a tyrant most—yet I do not see that anything **could** be better for Syracuse.   The Carthaginian danger is not over yet, and Dionysius **is** the very **ablest** soldier and administrator that we **have. Of** course **the** pinch will come later. **A** ruler of this sort always becomes harder, more **cruel, more suspicious as** he grows older. **And if** he has a son, brought up in the **bad** atmosphere of tyranny, the country has a terrible time of **it.**   Happily **the son** is generally **a fool,** and brings **the whole thing down with a crash. But all this is far off.**   Dionysius **is still a young** man, **not more than** twenty-six **years old, I fancy.** However, you shall see him—we are very **good** friends in public—and judge for yourself."

Callias, who had the hereditary abhorrence of his race for

anything like tyranny,* demurred at the proposed introduction to the despot. Medon was very urgent in over-
ruling his objection. "Don't mistake Sicily for Greece," he
said; "we are half barbarous, and what would be monstrous
with you is quite in its right place here. I grant you that
an honest man should have no dealings with a tyrant who
should set himself up at Thebes, or Corinth, or Argos. But
it is different here. I am sure that the man governs us better than we should be governed by the people, or, for the
matter of that, by the nobles either."

At last the Athenian consented. "Very good," cried
Medon, "you will go. Then we will lose no time about it.
Depend upon it, Dionysius knows all about you; and if you
do not pay your respects to him without loss of time he will
be suspicious. Suspicion is the bane of his situation. Servant, friend, wife; he trusts nobody."

The next day Medon and his guest presented themselves
at the palace. The Athenian had half turned back when
he found that he must be searched. No one was admitted
into the presence until that precaution had been taken, and
his freeman's pride revolted. Medon simply shrugged his
shoulders. "He is quite right," he whispered to his indignant friend, "he would not live a month if he did not do it."

Dionysius was, or pretended to be, busy with his studies,
when the two visitors were announced. A slave was reading to him from a roll, and he was taking notes on a wax

---

* Tyranny, in its Greek sense, it may be explained, is the unconstitutional rule of a single person. It does not necessarily connote, as in
English, cruelty or oppression. Except in Sparta, where the kings, indeed, were only hereditary commanders-in-chief, there was no king in
any Greek state. Wherever an individual ruled, he was, of necessity, a
tyrant.

tablet. He welcomed the newcomers with much cordiality.

"So, Medon, you have brought your Athenian friend at last. **I hope** that you have not been slandering me to him."

"My lord," answered Medon with a courtly bow, "I have told him the history of the last five years, and **have taken him to see** Syracuse. That is not the **way** to slander you."

"Good," said Dionysius, "I shall have you a courtier yet."

He then turned to the Athenian, asked him a **few questions,** all with the nicest tact, about **his movements, and** finally named a time when he should **be** at leisure to have some real conversation with him.

"Believe me," he **said, "I honor the** Athenians more than any other people in **Greece;** a strange thing you may think for a Syracusan **to say, but it is true."**

Certainly when Callias presented himself at the appointed time, everything that his royal host had said seemed to bear out this assurance. "After to-day," **he said, "** politics shall be banished from our talk. Don't suppose for a moment that if I had been a citizen of Athens, I should have attempted, that I should even have wished, to be what I am here. **But Syra-**cuse is not capable of **being what Athens is.** Even **you find** liberty **a** little hard to manage sometimes. Here it is a farce, only a very **bloody farce.** Listen to **what** happened to **my** father-in-law, Hermocrates. There **never was an abler man in the** country. **If it had not** been for him, I **verily** believe **that you** would **have conquered us.** He saved the city; and then, **a** little time **afterwards, because he did** not do what ten **years before no one would have dreamt of** doing, that is, **conquer you Athenians in a sea-fight,** they banished him. **Can you imagine such ingratitude,** such folly? Well; he was not disposed to put up with it; **he saw what** I see, that the Syracusans are not fit to govern themselves, and if it had not been for an accident, perhaps I ought rather to say his own reckless courage, he would have been **in my place now.*** What he intended to do I have done. I saved Syracuse as he saved her from Athens; and I dare say that in **a year** or two my grateful countrymen would have banished me as they banished him. Only **I** have been beforehand **with them.** So much for politics; **now let us talk** of something more pleasant and more profitable."

"Tell me now, do you know one **Socrates in your city, a** very wise man they tell **me?**"

"Yes, I know him well."

"**And he is wise?**"

"Yes, indeed; there **is no** one like him ; and so the **god** thought, **for the Pythia declared him** to be the wisest **of** men."

"I should dearly like to see him. Do you think it likely that he would come here, if I were to invite him? **I would** make it worth his while."

"I fear there is no chance of it. He never leaves Athens; **never has** left it **except** when **he served abroad with the** army, and as for money, he is quite careless about **it.**"

"**But he takes a fee for his teaching, I suppose. **"

"**Not a drachma.**"

* Hermocrates, resenting the decree of banishment that had been passed against him, attempted to make himself master of the city. He marched with the force that he had raised from Selinus, where he was encamped, and made such haste that he found himself with only a few companions far in advance, and close to the gates of Syracuse. While **he** halted to allow the army to come up, the leaders within the walls sallied out, overpowered the little party, and killed their leader. There is very little doubt but that he had resolved to seize absolute power.

"Well, **that astonishes** me. Why, Georgias **would not** teach anyone for less than half a talent, **and** has got together, I suppose, a pretty heap of money by this time. But, perhaps, **if I** could not get the great man himself, I might get one of his disciples. **Whom do men reckon to be** the first among them?"

"I think that one **Plato is** the most famous. **He was a** poet when he was quite young, indeed **he is young now,** and had a great reputation; **but he** has given up poetry for philosophy."

"That seems a pity. **I** don't see why a **man** should not be both poet and philosopher. I am a little of both myself. Can you remember anything that he has written?"

"**Yes; there was an epigram** which everyone was repeating when I left Athens. **It was written** for the tomb **of one** of his fellow **disciples.**"

"Let me hear it."

Callias repeated,

> **"In life like** Morning star thy shining head ;
> And now the star of Evening 'mid the dead."

"Very pretty indeed. I have something very **like it of** my own. Would you like to hear it?"

Callias of course politely assented and expressed as much admiration **as his conscience** permitted, possibly **a little** more, for the composition was vapid and clumsy.

But though Dionysius was **an indifferent** composer, he had really a **very** strong interest in **literary matters.** Personal vanity had something to do with it, for he was fully convinced of **his own** abilities **in** this way; but he had a genuine pleasure in **talking on** the subject. This was indeed

the first of many conversations which the young **Athenian**
had with **him.** Politics were never mentioned again, **but**
poetry, the drama, indeed every kind of literary work, supplied topics of unfailing interest. The drama was, perhaps,
the despot's favorite topic. He had received not long before
Callias' arrival, **a copy of** the **play** which **was**
described **in** my first chapter, **and was** never tired **of**
asking questions **about various points of** interest **in it.**
It soon became **evident** that his special ambition **lay in** this
direction.

"So, now that your two great men are gone," **he said to**
the young Athenian, "you have **no** man of really the first
rank among your dramatists?"

"I should say not," replied Callias. "Some think well **of**
Iophon, who **is the son of** Sophocles. Others say that **he**
would **be** nothing without his father. They declare that
the old man helped him when he was alive, and that what
he has brought out since his father's death is really not his
own."

"Well," said Dionysius, "the **stock** will be exhausted before long. And there **is no** one, **you say,** besides
him?"

"No one, certainly **of** any reputation."

"Then there would be a chance for **an** outsider? But
would a dramatist that was not an Athenian be allowed to
exhibit?"

"I know nothing to **the** contrary. But I do not know
that there has ever been **a case.** Anyhow it would be easy
to **exhibit** in the name of a citizen."

"An excellent idea! I shall certainly manage it somehow.

The first prize at your festival would **be almost as well** worth having **as** the tyranny itself."*

It is not surprising that a ruler who cherished such tastes should have reckoned a library among the ornaments which **were to make** Syracuse the most splendid among Greek **cities. In** his Athenian guest he believed himself **to** have found a competent agent **for** carrying **this purpose into** effect; and Callias was in **truth a** well **educated person** who knew what books **were worth buying. He was** well acquainted with the literature of his own country **and** had a fairly competent knowledge of what had **been produced** elsewhere in Greece. For the next three years it was his employment, and one, **on** the whole not uncongenial to his tastes, to collect volumes for Dionysius. In Sicily there was little culture, but the Greek cities **of** Italy furnished a more fertile field. There was not indeed much in the **way** of *belles-lettres.* Works of this kind had to be imported for the most **part,** either **from Athens,** or from **Lesbos,** where the traditions **of the** school of Sappho and Alcæus were not extinct, **but** books on philosophy and science, could be secured in considerable numbers. At Crotona, **for** instance, Callias was fortunate enough to **secure** a valuable scientific library which **had been** for some **years in the** family of Democedes, while at Tarentum he purchased a handsome collection of treatises by teachers of the school of Pythagoras.

This **occupation was varied in the second year of his resi-**

* Dionysius **did** actually compete many times. He is said to have gained the second and third prizes more than once; and finally in the last year of his life won **the** first honors for a play entitled "The Ransoming of Hector." One of the various accounts of his death attributes it to the excessive feasting **in** which he indulged on hearing of his victory.

dence by an interesting mission **to Rome.   That city, the**
rising greatness **of** which so keen an observer as Dionysius
was able to discern, was at this time sorely distressed by a
visitation of famine, and had applied far and wide for help.
The harvests of Sicily had **been** remarkably **abundant, and**
Dionysius sent a magnificent present of a hundred thousand
bushels of **wheat,** putting Callias in charge of the mission.

In spite of these **honorable and not** distasteful employ-
ments the young Athenian did not greatly like his **position.**
It would indeed have been scarcely endurable to a soul that
had been reared in an atmosphere of liberty, but for the fact
that his work took him much away from Syracuse. Dionysius
was all courtesy and generosity in **his dealings with** him;
but he was a tyrant; there **was iron under his** velvet glove.
It was therefore with a considerable feeling of relief that in
the early spring **of the third (or** according **to** classical
reckoning) the fourth year after the fall of Athens, he received a missive from Xenophon couched in the following
terms. *

"**Meet me** at Tarsus with all the speed **you can.** Great
things lie before us, of which **you will hear more at** the
proper time. Farewell."

Leave of absence was obtained **with some difficulty, and**
towards the end of June, Callias found himself at **the ap-**
pointed place.

---

* Athens capitulated in March, **404;** Callias is supposed to have received the letter about August, 401.

CHAPTER XXI.

CYRUS THE YOUNGER.

ALMOST the first person that the Athenian saw when he disembarked at Tarsus was Xenophon. The latter was evidently in the highest spirits.

" You are come at exactly the right moment," he cried. " All is going well; but, three days ago, I should have said that all would end badly. Cyrus and Clearchus have thrown for great stakes, and they have won; but at first the dice were against them. But I forget; you know nothing of what happened. I will explain. You know something about Cyrus, the Great King's brother ? "

Callias assented.

" You know that he was scarcely contented to be what he was, in fact that he was disposed to claim the throne."

" I heard some talk of the kind when I was with Alcibiades."

" Listen then to what happened. Cyrus, to put a long story in a few words, collected by one means or another about thirteen thousand Greek soldiers. He gave out that he was going to lead them against the mountain tribes of Cilicia. But his real object has all along been to march up to Susa, and drive the King from his throne. Clearchus knew this; I fancy some others guessed it; I know I did for

one. But the army knew nothing about it. Of course it
had to come out at last. When we came to Tarsus, the men
had to be told. If we were going to act against the Cicilian
mountaineers, now was the time. If not, why had we been
brought so far? When the truth was known there was a
frightful uproar. The men declared that they would go
back. It was madness, they said, for a few thousand men to
march against the Great King. For four days I thought all
was lost. Clearchus and Cyrus managed admirably. I will
tell you all about it some day. Meanwhile it is enough to
say that all is settled. The men have changed their tone
completely. They talk of nothing but ransacking the
treasuries of the King, and Cyrus is quite magnificent in his
promises. He gives a great banquet to the officers to-night.
I am going with Proxenus, who is my special friend among
the generals, and I have no doubt that I can take you.
Cyrus, I assure you, is a man worth knowing, and, though
we should call him a barbarian, worth serving."

The Persian prince, when Callias came to make his acquaintance, bore out, and more than bore out, the high
character which Xenophon had given of him. A more
princely man in look and bearing never lived. That he was
a stern ruler was well known, but his subjects needed stern
methods; but for courtesy and generosity he could not be
matched, and he had that genial manner which makes
these qualities current coin in the market of the world. He
was of unusual stature, his frame well knit and well propor-
tioned, and his face, though slightly disfigured by scars
which he had received in early life in a fierce death struggle
with a bear, singularly handsome. Proxenus introduced

his friend's friend as a young Athenian who had come to
put his sword at his disposal, and Cyrus at once greeted
him with that manner of friendliness and even comradeship
which made him so popular. At the same time he made
some complimentary remark about Athens, saying that the
Athenians had been formidable enemies, and would hereafter, he hoped, be valuable friends.

The banquet could not fail, under such circumstances, of
being a great success. Everyone was in the highest spirits, and
when Cyrus, in thanking his guests for their company,
said that though Greece and Persia had been enemies in the
past they would be firm friends in the future, he was greeted
with a burst of tumultuous applause.

The next day the army set out, their last remaining
scruples dispelled by an increase of pay.*   There was still a
certain reserve in speaking about the object of the campaign
but every one knew that it was directed against the Great
King. Two days' march took them to Issi, a town destined
to become famous in later days.† The difficult pass of the
Cicilian Gate was found unguarded. About a month later
the ford of the Euphrates at Thapsacus‡ was reached.
Then all disguise was thrown off. Cyrus was marching
against his brother, and he would give each man a bonus of
a year's pay when he had reached Babylon.

So the long and tedious march went on. The King made
no signs of resistance.   Line after line of defense was found
unguarded. At last, just ten weeks after the army had
marched out of Tarsus, a Persian horseman attached to

---

* From one daric to one daric and a half per month, $5 to $7.50.
† For the second of the great victories of Alexander.
‡ Thipsach or " The Passage."

Cyrus' person, came galloping up with the news, which he shouted out in Greek and Persian, "The King is coming with a great army ready for battle."

Something like a panic followed, for the invaders had almost begun to think that they would not have to fight. Cyrus sprang from the carriage in which he had been riding, donned his corslet, and mounted his charger; the Greeks rushed to the wagons in which they had deposited their armor and weapons, and prepared themselves hastily for battle.

By mid-day all was ready. Clearchus was in command of the right wing, which consisted of the heavy-armed Greeks, and rested on the Euphrates the light-armed Greeks, with some Paphlagonian cavalry, stood in the center; on the left were the Persians under Ariæus, Cyrus' second in command. The extreme left of all was occupied by Cyrus himself with his body guard of six hundred horsemen. All wore cuirasses, cuisses and helmets; but Cyrus, wishing to be easily recognized, rode bareheaded.

It was afternoon before the enemy came in sight. First, a white cloud of dust became visible; then something like a black pall spread far and wide over the plain, with now and then a spear point or bronze helmet gleaming through the darkness. Silently the huge host advanced, its left on the river, its right far overlapping Cyrus' left, so great was its superiority in numbers. "Strike at the center," said the Prince to Clearchus, as he rode along the line, "then our work will be done."

He knew his countrymen; the King himself was in the center. If he should be killed or driven from the field, victory was assured.

The hostile lines were only two furlongs apart, when the Greeks raised the battle shout, and charged at a quick pace, which soon became a run. A few minutes afterwards the Persians broke. Their front line, consisting of scythe-armed chariots, for the most part, turned and drove helter skelter through the ranks of their countrymen; the few that charged the advancing foe did, perhaps attempted to do, no harm. The ranks were opened to let them through, and they took no further part in the battle. Anyhow the Greeks won the victory without losing a single man.

Meanwhile the King, posted, as has been said, in the center, seeing no one to oppose him, advanced as if he would take the Greeks on their flank. Cyrus, seeing this, charged with his six hundred, and broke the line in front of the King. The troopers were scattered in the ardor of pursuit, and the Prince was left alone with a handful of men. Even then all might have been well but for the fit of ungovernable rage which seized him. He spied his brother the King in the throng, and, crying out, "There is the man," pressed furiously towards him. One blow he dealt him, piercing his corslet, and making a slight wound. Then one of the King's attendants struck Cyrus with a javelin under the eye. The two brothers closed for a moment in a hand-to-hand struggle. But Cyrus and his followers were hopelessly overmatched. In a few minutes the Prince and eight of his companions were stretched on the ground. One desperate effort was made to save him. Artapates, the closest of his friends, leaped from his horse, and threw his arms around his body. It did but delay the fatal blow for the briefest space. The next moment Cyrus was dead.

CHAPTER XXII.

THE RETREAT.

SEVEN weeks have passed since the catastrophe recorded in my last chapter.* Curiously enough the Greeks had returned to their camp after their easily won victory without any suspicion of what had happened on the other side of the battle field. They wondered, indeed, that Cyrus neither came nor sent to congratulate them on their success, but the news of his death which was brought to them next morning by an Ionian Greek, who had been in the service of Cyrus, came upon them like a thunderclap. Then had followed a period of indecision and perplexity. So long as they had to answer insolent messages from the King or Tissaphernes, bidding them give up their arms and be content with such chance of pardon as they might have, their course was plain. To such demands only one answer was possible. "We will die sooner than give them up," had been the reply which Cleanor the Arcadian, the senior officer, had made. But when the Persians began to treat, when they agreed upon a truce, and even allowed the Greeks to provision themselves, the course to be followed became less plain. Tissaphernes made indeed the most

---

* The battle of Cunaxa, in which Cyrus fell, was fought on Sept. 3d. The day at which we have now arrived is Oct. 31st.

liberal offers. "We will lead you back to Greece," he said, "and find you provisions at a fair price. If we do not furnish them, you are at liberty to take them for yourselves, only you must swear that you will behave as if you were marching through the country of friends." There were some who roundly said that the Greeks had best have no dealings with the man; he was known to be treacherous and false; this was only his way of luring them on to their death. On the other hand it was difficult to refuse terms so advantageous. It was possible that the satrap, though not in the least friendly, was genuinely afraid, and would be glad to get rid at any price of visitants so unwelcome. This was the common opinion. If the army could find its way home without fighting, it would be madness to reject the chance. For many days past, every thing had gone smoothly; relations between the Greeks and Tissaphernes seemed to become more and more friendly. Clearchus, the general, commanding in chief, had even dined with the satrap, had been treated in the most friendly fashion, and was now come back to the camp with a proposition from him for a formal conference at which the Greeks were to be represented by their principal generals. Some voices were raised against this proposal. "No one ever trusted Tissaphernes without repenting it," was the sentiment of not a few, Xenophon amongst the number. But the opposition was overruled. Five generals and twenty inferior officers proceeded to the tent of Tissaphernes, followed by a troop of stragglers, who availed themselves of the favorable opportunity. as they thought it, of marketing within the enemy's lines.

"Callias," said Xenophon to his friend on the **morning of this** eventful day, "my mind misgives me. The soothsayer tells me that, though the sacrifices **have been generally** favorable, there have always been some sinister indications. And certain it is that we have never put ourselves so completely in the enemy's power **as we** have this day. Tissaphernes has only to say the word and our most skillful leaders are dead men. But, hark, what is that?"

A cry of surprise **and** wrath went up from the camp, and the two Athenians rushed out of the tent in which they had been sitting, **to ascertain the cause. One glance was enough.** The stragglers were hurrying back at the top of **their speed with the Persians in hot pursuit.** Among the foremost of the fugitives was an Arcadian officer, **who, fearfully** wounded as he **was,** managed to make his **way to** the camp. "To arms!" **he cried,** "Clearchus and the rest are either dead or **prisoners."** Instantly there was a wild **rush** for arms. Everyone expected that the next moment would **bring the whole** Persian army in sight. But the King **and his** satraps knew how formidable the Greeks really **were.** As long as they had a chance of succeeding by **fraud,** they would not use force.

Fraud was immediately attempted. **Ariæus, who by this** time had made his peace with **the King,** rode up to within a short distance of **the camp, and said, "Let** the Greeks send some one that is in authority to **bear a message from** the King." The veteran Cleanor accordingly went forward.

"**Let me go with you,**" cried Xenophon, "I am eager to hear what has become of my friend Proxenus. Come you, too," he whispered to Callias.

Ariæus addressed them: "Thus saith the King; Clearchus, having forsworn himself and broken the truth, has been put to death. Proxenus and Medon are honorably treated. As for you, the King demands your arms, seeing that they belonged to Cyrus, who was his slave."

Cleanor's answer was brief and emphatic, "Thou villain, Ariæus, and the rest of you, have you no shame before gods or men, that you betray us in this fashion, and make friends with that perjurer Tissaphernes?"

Ariæus could only repeat that Clearchus was a traitor. "Then," cried Xenophon, "why send us not back Proxenus and Medon, good men you say, who would advise both you and us for the best?"

To this no answer was made; and the party slowly made their way back to the camp. The worst had happened. They were in the midst of their enemies, more than a thousand miles from the sea, and they had lost their leaders.

The two Athenians, who shared the same tent, lay down to rest at an early hour. It still wanted some time to midnight, when Xenophon surprised his companion by suddenly starting up.

"I believe," he cried, "all will be well after all. I have had a most encouraging dream."

"What was it?" asked Callias.

"I dreamed," returned the other, "that I was at home and that there was a great storm of thunder and lightning and that the lightning struck the house and that it blazed up all over."

Callias stared. "But that does not sound very encouraging."

"Ah! but listen **to what I have** to tell you. **When** Proxenus asked me to come with him on this expedition, **I applied to** Socrates for his advice. **'Ask** the **god** at Delphi,' he said. So I asked the god but not, as he meant me to do, whether I should go **or** not, but to what gods, if I went, I should sacrifice. Well, this has been a great trouble to me, and I look upon this dream as an answer. First—this is the encouragement—Zeus shows **me a** light **in** darkness. The house all on a blaze, I take **it, means** that we are surrounded with dangers."

"**May** it turn out well," was all that Callias could find it in his heart to say. But if he was tempted to think meanly of his companion, he had **soon reason** to alter his opinion.

"Whether my dream means what I think **or** any thing else," Xenophon went on, "**we** must act. To fall into the **hands of the King means death,** and death in the most shameful form. And yet no one stirs hand or foot to **avoid** it; we lie quiet, as though it were time to take **our rest. I** shall go and talk to my comrades about it."

The first **thing was** to call **together** his own particular friends, the officers of Proxenus' division. **He found them** as wakeful as himself.

"Friends," **he** said, "we must get out of the King's clutches. You know what he did to his own brother. **The** man was dead; but he must nail his body to a cross. **What** will he do, think you, **to us?** No; we must get out of his reach. But how? Not by making terms with him. **That** only gives him **time to hem us** in more and **more** completely. **No;** we must fight him; and we, who **are more** enduring and brave than **our enemies,** have a right **to** hope that we shall **fight to** good purpose. **And surely the gods** will help us rather than **them.** For are **they not** faithless and **forsworn?**

"**But, if we are to fight, we** must have leaders. **Let us** choose them then. As for **me, I** will follow another, **or, if** you will have it so, **I will lead myself. Young I am, but I** am at least of an age to take care of myself."

Then there was a **loud cry—**"Xenophon for **general!"** Only one voice was **raised in** protest, that of a **captain, who** spoke in very broad Bœotian. "**Escape is impossible; we** should better try persuasion." Such was the burden of his speech.

Xenophon **turned on** him fiercely. "Escape impossible! And yet you know what the ·**King did.** First **came a** haughty command that we should give up our arms. When we refused, he took to soft words **and cajolery.** He is afraid of us; but if we trust to persuasion we are lost." **Then turn-** ing to the others, he cried, "**Is this man fit to be a captain?** Make him a bearer **of** burdens. **He is a disgrace to the** name of Greek."

"Greek," cried an Arcadian captain, "**he is no Bœotian,** nor Greek at all. **He is a** Mysian slave. **I see his ears are** bored." And the **man** was promptly turned out of **camp.**

Not **a moment was now lost. A representative body of** officers from the whole army **was promptly collected, and** Xenophon was asked to repeat **what he had said to the smaller** gathering. The meeting **ended in the** election **of five** generals to **replace** those who had been murdered. **Chiri-** **sophus,** a Spartan, **made the sixth,** having held the office before.

The day was now beginning to dawn.   It was scarcely light when the whole army assembled in obedience to a **hasty summons** which had been sent through the camp.

Chirisophus opened the proceedings.   **"We have fared ill, fellow soldiers," he** said, "in that we have been robbed **of so** many officers and have been deserted by our allies. Still we must not give in.   If we cannot conquer, at least we can die gloriously.   **Anyhow we must not** fall alive into the hands of the King."

After an address by another **general,** Xenophon stood up. **He** had dressed himself in his best **apparel.**   "Fine clothes **will suit victory best," he said to himself,** "and if I die, let me at least die like a gentleman."

"Gentlemen," he said, "if we were going to treat with the barbarians, then, knowing how faithless they are, we might well despair; **but** if we mean, taking our good **swords** in our hands, to punish them for what they have done, **and to secure our** own safety, then **we** may hope for **the** best."

At this point, a soldier sneezed.   A sneeze was a lucky **omen,** and by a common impulse all **the soldiers bowed their heads.**   Xenophon seized the **opportunity.**

"I spoke of safety, gentlemen, and as I was speaking, Zeus the Savior, sent us **an omen of** good fortune.   **Let us** therefore vow **to him** a thank-offering **for deliverance, if we ever** reach our native country.   This let us do as an army; and besides, let everyone vow to offer according to his ability in return for his own safe arrival."

These propositions were unanimously accepted, and the **hymn** of battle was solemnly sung by the whole army.

"Now," said the speaker, "we have set ourselves right with the gods, who will doubtless reward our piety, while they will punish these perjurers and traitors who seek to destroy us."

Then, after appealing to the glorious memories of the past, when the Greeks, fighting against overwhelming odds, had once and again turned back the tide of Persian invasion, he addressed himself to deal with the circumstances of the situation. "Our allies have deserted us; but we shall fight better without such cowards. We have no cavalry; but battles are won by the sword; our foes will have the better only in being able to run away more quickly. No market will be given us; but it is better to take our food than to buy it. If rivers bar our way, we have only to cross them higher up. Verily, I believe that not only can we get away, but that if the King saw us preparing to settle here, he would be glad to send us away in coaches and four, so terribly afraid is he of us.

"But how shall we go? Let us burn our tents and all superfluous baggage. The baggage too often commands the army. That is the first thing to do. Our arms are our chief possession. If we use them aright, everything in the country is ours. Let us march in a hollow square, with the baggage animals and the camp followers in the middle. And let us settle at once who is to command each section of the army."

All this was accepted without demur. Chirisophus was appointed to command the van, Xenophon, with a colleague, as the youngest of the generals, the rear. Practically these two divided the command between them.

The first experience of an encounter with the enemy was not reassuring; in fact **it** was almost disastrous. Early in the first day's march, **one** Mithridates, a personage well known to the Greeks, for he had **been high** in Cyrus' confidence, **rode up with a couple of hundred** horsemen **and** twice as **many** slingers and bowmen. He had a look of coming as a friend; indeed, earlier in that day he had come with what purported to be a conciliatory message from **Tissaphernes. But on arriving within** a moderate distance of the Greeks he halted, and the **next** moment there was **a** shower of bullets and **arrows from the** slings and bows. **The Greeks** were helpless. **They suffered** severely, but could do nothing **to the enemy in return.** The **Cretan** archers had a shorter **range than** that of the Persian bows, **and** the javelin could **not, of** course, come anywhere near the slingers. **At last** Xenophon gave the order to charge. Charge the **men did,** heavy-armed and light-armed alike. Possibly it was better than standing still to be shot at. But they did not contrive to catch a single man. **As** foot soldiers they were fairly outpaced ; **and they had no** cavalry. Only three miles were accomplished **that day,** and the army reached the villages **in** which they **were to bivouac,** in a state of great despondency. **Unless such** attacks could be resisted with better success, **the fate of** the army was sealed.

Xenophon was severely **blamed** by his colleagues for his **action in** charging. **He** frankly acknowledged his fault. "I could not stand still," he said, "and see the men falling **round me** without striking a blow, but the charge was no good. We caught none of them, and we did not find it **easy to** get back. Thanks to the gods, there were not very many of them; if they had come on in force, we must have been cut to pieces."

After a short silence, he addressed his colleagues again. "We are at a great disadvantage. Our Cretans cannot shoot as far as their Persian archers; and our hand throwers are useless against the slingers. As for the foot soldiers, no man, however fleet of foot, can overtake another who has a bowshot's start of him, especially as we cannot push the pursuit far from the main body. The simple truth is that we must have slingers and horsemen of our own. I know that there are Rhodians in the army who can sling leaden bullets to a much greater distance than these Persian slings can reach. I propose, first, that we find out who among them have slings of their own; these we will buy at the proper value; if any know how to plait some more, we will pay them the proper price for doing it; the slings thus obtained, we shall soon get a corps of slingers to use them. Give them some advantage and they will enroll themselves fast enough. Now for the cavalry. We have some horses I know. There are some in the rear-guard with me; there are others that belonged to Clearchus; a good many have been taken from the enemy, and are being used as baggage animals. Let us take the pick of these and equip them for the use of cavalry; we shall soon have some very capable horsemen at our service."

The idea was promptly carried out. That very night a couple of hundred slingers were enrolled, and the next day, which was spent without any attempt to advance, fifty horsemen passed muster, fairly well-mounted and duly furnished with buff' jackets and cuirasses. This was only the

first of many **instances in** which Xenophon showed the
fertility and readiness of device which did so much to save
the army.

The very next **day** the new forces were **brought into ac-**
tion with the happiest results. Mithridates came up again
with his archers **and** slingers, but encountered **a** reception
on which he had not calculated. The cavalry made a brilliant charge, cutting **down a** number of the infantry **and**
taking prisoners some seventeen horsemen. At the end **of**
the day's **march, the army reached the Tigris. Fourteen
weeks of hard and** perilous marching **lay before** them ; but
they were fairly well-equipped for the work. I shall take
an account **of some of** the principal incidents **of the journey
from a diary** kept by Callias, **who** acted **throughout as aid-**
de-camp to **Xenophon.**

CHAPTER XXIII.

THE DIARY.

OCTOBER 27.*—Our new corps have covered themselves with glory to-day. About noon Tissaphernes himself appeared with a large force of cavalry. He had his **own regiments** with him ; among the others we recognized some of Cyrus' Persian troops. They want, I suppose, **to make the** King forget their rebellion. The satrap did **not wish to** come to close quarters ; but he found after all that the quarters were closer than he liked. He was well within range ; and as his men were posted in great masses every arrow and every bullet told. It would, in fact, have been impossible to miss, with such a mark to aim at. As for the Persian archers they did no damage at all. But we found **their arrows** very **useful.** Our men are now well-equipped, for we discovered an abundant store of bow-strings and lead for the sling bullets in the villages.

NOVEMBER 3.—Things have not been going so well to-day. The barbarians occupied a post of vantage on **our route and** showered down darts, stones, and arrows upon us as we

---

* For convenience' **sake** I have translated the dates of the Attic year which Callias, of course, used with the corresponding days in our reckoning. October 27 would be the "fifth day of the middle of Boedromia." Each month was divided into three portions, of ten days each, respectively called beginning, middle, and ending. The days of the last were reckoned backwards. If this month had twenty-nine days only, the third division had nine.

passed. **Our** light-armed were easily driven in. When the heavy-armed tried to scale the height, they found the climbing **very hard work, and of** course the enemy were gone by the time **that they reached the top.** Three times this was done, **and I was never more** pleased in my life than when **at last** we **got** to the end of our day's march. Eight surgeons are busy attending to the wounded, **of whom there is** a terrible number. We are going to stop here three days, Xenophon tells me. Meanwhile we are **in a land of** plenty. **There are** granaries full **of** wheat, **and** cellars of wine, and barley enough to supply our horses if we had fifty times as **many.** Hereafter we are to follow a new **plan.** As soon as we are attacked, we halt. **To march** and fight at the **same** time puts us at a disadvantage. **And** we are to **try to get as** far in advance as possible.

NOVEMBER 9.—We had **our** three days' **rest, and then** three **days'** quick marching. **To-day**, however, there has been a smart brush with the **enemy. They had** occupied a ridge commanding our **route, which just then** descended from the hills into the plain. **Chirisophus sent for** Xenophon to bring his **light-armed to the front. This, of** course, was a serious thing to do, **as** Tissaphernes **was not far from our rear. Xenophon** accordingly **galloped to the front to** confer with his colleague. **"Certainly,"** he said, when he **saw how** the enemy was **posted, "** these fellows must be dislodged, **but we can't uncover** our rear. You must give me some troops, **and** I will do my best." Just at that moment **he caught** sight of a height **rising** above us just on our right —he has **a** true general's eye—and saw that it gave an approach **to the enemy's** position. "That is the place for us to take," he cried. "**If we get that,** the barbarians can't stay where they are." **As soon** as the troops were told off for **service,** we started; and lo! as soon as we were **off, the bar-** barians seeing what we were after started too. **It was a race** who should get there first. Xenophon rode beside **the men,** and urged them on. "**Now** for it, **brave sirs!**" he cried. "**'Tis for Hellas!** 'Tis for wives and children! **Win the race,** and you will march on in peace! Now for it!" The men **did their best,** but of course it was hard work. **I never had** harder in my life. **At last a grumbling fellow in the ranks** growled out, "We are not on equal terms, Xenophon. **You** are on horseback, and I have got to carry my shield." **In a** moment Xenophon was off his horse. He snatched the fel- low's shield from him, **and** marched on **with the rest. That** was hard work indeed, for he **had his horseman's cuirass on;** still he kept up. Then the men **fell** on **the** grumbler. **They abused him, pelted** him, and cuffed him, till he was glad **enough to take his shield again.** Then Xenophon re-mounted, and **rode on** as **before as** far **as the horse could go.** Then he left **him tethered to a tree, and went** on **foot. In** the end we won **the race; and the** barbarians left the **way clear.**

NOVEMBER 10.—We had **a** great disappointment **to-day. The route lay** either across a river which was too deep to ford—we tried **it with our** spears, and **could find no bottom** —or through a mountainous region **inhabited by a set of** fierce savages whom the **King has never been able to sub- due. He** once **sent an** army **of a** hundred thousand men among them, **they say, and** not a single soldier ever came back! First **we** considered **about** crossing **the river. A**

Rhodian had a grand **plan,** he said, for taking the army across. He would sell it for a talent. I must confess, by the way, **that I** am more and more disgusted by the manner in which everything is for sale. Citizen soldiers think of the **common** good, though, it must be confessed, they are not so sturdy in action as these fellows ; mercenaries think only of the private purse. However, the Rhodian never got his talent. His plan was clever enough, making floats of skins, but impracticable, seeing that the enemy occupied the other **shore in** force. Nothing, then, remained for it but to take **to the** mountains. We must **do** our best to fight our way through them, if the mountaineers won't be friends. This **done,** we shall find ourselves **in** Armenia ; once there, we shall be able to go anywhere we please.

November 14.—We **have had** three awful days. **The** Carduchians—so they **call the** barbarians—are **as** hostile **and as** fierce as they can be. It seems unreasonable, for they must **hate** the Great King as much as we do. Still they will **not** listen to our overtures for friendly intercourse, but keep up an incessant attack. **To-day** there was very **near** being a positive **disaster. We in the** rear-guard had, of course, the worst of it. Generally **when we** find our work particularly hard we pass on the word **to** the van, and they slacken their pace ; **otherwise** we should get divided from the main **army.** To-day no attention was paid to our messages ; Chirisophus **did** nothing but send back word that we must hurry **on.** Consequently our march became something very like a **rout, and we** lost two of our best men. **At the first** halt Xenophon rode to the front.

"Why this hurry?" he **asked.** " It has cost us two men,

and we had to leave their bodies behind." "See you that?" said Chirisophus, and he pointed to a height straight before us, which was strongly held by the enemy. "I wanted to get there first, for the guide says that there is no other way." "Says he so?" said Xenophon. "Let us hear what my fellows have to say. I laid an ambush, you must know, and caught two barbarians. They would be useful, I thought, as guides!" The two were brought up and questioned. "Is there any other way than what we see?" "No," said the first. Try all we could, he would make no other answer. At last Chirisophus had him killed. "Now," he said, turning to the other, "can you tell us anything more?" "O yes," said the man, "there is another way, and one that horses can pass over. But the other would not say anything about it, because he had kinsfolk living near it, and was afraid that you would do them an injury." Poor fellow! I was sorry for him, when I knew how loyal he had been. But I don't know what else could have been done. The second man told us that there was a height which we must occupy if we would make the new route practicable. Two thousand men have set off to get hold of it. If they fail, we shall be in terrible straits.

November 16.—The army is safe for the present, but some—I among the number—have had a very narrow escape. The two thousand found their work very much harder than at first they thought it was going to be. They took the first height without any difficulty, and fancied they had done all that was wanted. But there were no less than three heights beyond, and each of these had to be stormed. My part in the business was this. Xenophon thought that the second of the four heights—there were four in all—ought to be held permanently till our army had **passed.** Some two hundred men were told off for this duty, and **I** volunteered to be one of them. All of a sudden we found ourselves attacked by a whole swarm of mountaineers. They outnumbered us by at least ten to one. It was a case for running, for there was really no position that we could hold. But running was no easy matter. Our only chance was to climb down **a** very steep mountain side to the pass below, where the last columns of the van-guard were just making their way. Some of the men did not like to try it; and, indeed, it did look desperately dangerous. **While they were** hesitating, the barbarians were upon **them. As for myself, I** felt that **I** would sooner break my neck than **fall** into the enemy's hands, so I started off at full pace, and was **safe.** Nor do I think that any who followed my example were seriously hurt, though some got very nasty falls. **Those** who stayed behind were killed to a man. Just now we are **in** comfortable quarters. Wine is in such plenty hereabouts that positively the people keep it in great cisterns.

NOVEMBER 19.—We have crossed the Centrites, which is the Eastern branch of the Tigris.

NOVEMBER 30.—The march through Armenia has been on the whole as pleasant as we had hoped. The Lieutenant **Governor,** one Tiribazus, made an agreement with our generals that **he** would do us no harm, if we would not burn the houses, but content ourselves with taking such provisions as we wanted. Four days ago, we had a heavy fall of snow, and the general thought it as well to billet out the army in **the** villages, which are very thick in these parts.

There was no enemy in sight, and, as we had no tents, bivouacking in the open would be neither pleasant nor safe. We all enjoyed it vastly, particularly **as the villages were** full of good things, oxen, and sheep, and wine, some of the **very best** I ever tasted, and raisins, and vegetables of **all** kinds. But after the first night we had an alarm. **A great** army was reported in sight; and certainly there **were** watchfires in every direction. The generals thereupon **determined** to bring the army together again, and to bivouac on the plain. The weather too, promised to be fine. **But in** the night there was another heavy snow fall, so heavy that it covered us all up. It was not uncomfortable lying there under the snow; in fact, it felt quite warm; but of course it was not safe. I have heard of people going to sleep under such circumstances and not waking up again. Anyhow Xenophon set the example of getting up, and setting to work splitting wood. Before long we were all busy. But there was no more bivouacking in the open. We went to the villages again; and some foolish fellows who had wantonly set their houses on fire **were now** punished for their folly.

December 8.—The weather becomes colder and **colder,** and is our worst enemy now. The other day there was a cutting north wind, which drifted the snow till it was more than six feet deep in places. Xenophon, **whose faith and** piety are admirable, suggested a sacrifice to the north wind. This was made; and certainly the weather did begin to abate shortly afterwards. The doubters say that the wind always does go down after a time. These are matters on which I do not pretend **to judge; but I do see** that Xenophon's

pious belief makes him very cheerful and courageous.
The day before yesterday many of our men were afflicted.
what with the long march and what with the cold, with a
sort of ravenous hunger. They fell down, and either would
not, or could not, move a step forward. At first we did not
know what was the matter with them ; but then some one
who had campaigned before in cold countries suggested the
real cause. When we gave them a little food we found that
they recovered. Yesterday we nearly lost a number of men
who were simply overpowered with the cold. The enemy
was close behind, and we tried to raise the poor fellows up ;
but they would not stir. "Kill us," they said, "but leave
us alone." They were simply stupid with cold. All that
could be done was to frighten the enemy away. On the
barbarians came, till the rear guard, who were lying in ambush, dashed out upon them, and at the same time the sick
men shouted as loud as they could, and rattled their spears
against their shields. The enemy fled in a hurry, and we
saw and heard no more of them. But what would have
happened if they had persisted, is more than I can say. The
whole army was demoralized with the cold. The men lay
down as they could with their cloaks round them. There
was not a single guard placed anywhere. As it was, no
harm was done ; and in the afternoon to-day the sick men
were brought safe into good quarters. We are now in excellent quarters, with all that we could wish to eat and drink.

DECEMBER 9.—Just as I had finished my entries yesterday an Athenian with whom I have struck up a great
friendship asked me to come with him on an expedition.
His name is Polycrates, and he is the captain of a company.

' Let us raid that village," he said, " before the people have time to get away." So we did, and we had a fine catch. We laid hands on the villagers and their head man. With the head man was his daughter who had been married only eight days before. Her husband was out hare-hunting, and so escaped. The village was a curious place. All the houses were underground ; beasts and men lived there together, the beasts entering by a sloping way, the men by a ladder. There were great stores of barley, and wheat, and green stuff of all kinds. The drink was barley wine, which they keep in great bowls. You have to suck it up by a reed. It is very strong. As to the flavor I feel a little doubtful. To-day Xenophon has been taking the head man, whom he had to sup with him last night, all round the camp, by which I mean the villages, for the men are encamped in them. At Chirisophus' quarters there was a strange sight. The men were feasting with wisps of hay round their heads, for lack of flowers ; and Armenian boys, in the costume of their country, were waiting on them. Everything of course had to be explained by signs, for neither soldiers nor waiters knew a word of each other's language. Xenophon gave the head man his old charger, which indeed was pretty well worn out with marching, and took for himself and his officers a number of young horses which were going to be sent, we were told, as part of the King's tribute.

DECEMBER 27.—Nothing of much moment has happened, except it be a quarrel, the first that has taken place—and I devoutly hope the last—between our generals. After resting in the villages for a week, we started again, taking the head man with us as a guide. If he did this duty properly, he was to be allowed to depart and to take his son with him, for he had a young son in his company.   All the rest of his **family** were safe in his own village with **a very** handsome lot of presents.   At the end of the third day Chirisophus got into a great rage because the head man had not taken them to any village.   The man declared that there was no village **near.**   But Chirisophus would not **listen, and** struck the man.   The next night he ran away.   Xenophon was very angry.   " You ought not to have struck him," he said ; "but having struck him, you certainly ought to have kept a doubly strict guard on him."

DECEMBER 30.—We have crossed the river Phasis, and got **through** what **is, I hope, our last** difficult pass.   I have not time to write about it ; but **I must** record an amusing little controversy that took place between our two generals.   **It** shows anyhow that they have made up their quarrel. Xenophon had been insisting that they must do as much as they could by craft, and had been speaking of *stealing* somewhere at night, *stealing* a march, and so forth.   Then he **went on,** " But why do I talk about stealing **in your** presence Chirisophus, for you Spartans are **experts** in the art. You practice it I am told, **from your youth up.   It is** honorable among you to take anything except what the law forbids.   But **to** encourage you **and to** make you master thieves you get a whipping if you are found out.   I must not therefore presume to instruct you about *stealing*." "Nay," replied the other, " you have the best possible right to do it. You Athenians, **I** am told, are wonderfully clever **hands at** stealing **the** public money and the best men among you do it the most.   **No ;** we Spartans must yield to you." In the end the pass was carried without much loss.

JANUARY 3.—For several days we have been on very short commons. The Taochi, through whose country we are passing, have collected all their possessions, alive and dead, into strong places. At last we felt that something had to be done, for we were simply starving. Accordingly, when we came about noon to-day to one of these strongholds which happened to lie directly on our route, Chirisophus made up his mind to take it. It could be seen to be full of flocks and herds besides a mixed crowd of men, women and children. First one regiment went up against it; then a second; then a third. They could do nothing with it; the slingers and archers, which were the only troops we could use, made no impression at all. Just then Xenophon came up with the rear-guard, I being close behind him. "You have come just in the nick of time my friend," said Chirisophus, "we must take this place or starve." "But what," Xenophon asked, "is to hinder our simply walking in?" Chirisophus answered, "You see that one narrow path, that is the only way of approaching the place. Whenever anyone attempts to go by it, these fellows roll down huge masses of rock from the crag up there," and he pointed to a cliff that overhung the plain. "See what has happened to some of my poor fellows who were unlucky enough to get in the way!" And sure enough there was one man with one leg broken and another with both, and a third with his ribs crushed in. "But," said my own general, "when these fellows have expended their ammunition—and they can't have a perpetual supply of it—there will be nothing else to hinder our going in. I can only

see a very few men, and of these not more than two or three
are armed. As for the distance that we have to get across, it
cannot be more than one hundred and fifty yards; and two-
thirds of this are covered at intervals by great pine trees.
As long as we are among these, stones cannot hurt us.
These past, there are only fifty yards more to be crossed."
"Very good," said Chirisophus, "but the moment we get
near, the fire of stones begins again." "All the better,"
said Xenophon, "the hotter their fire, the quicker the
enemy will use up their ammunition. However, let us
begin by picking out the place where the run across the open
space will be shortest."

First we occupied the trees. I had the luck, by special
favor of Xenophon, to be among them. We were only
seventy, for no more could find proper shelter behind the
pines. Then one of us came forward a yard or two from under
cover of the pines. No sooner did the Taochi see him than
they sent down a vast quantity of stones. Before they
reached him he was under cover again. This he did several
times; and every time a wagon-load of rocks, at the very
least, must have been whizzing and whistling down the
slope. Before long, however, the ammunition gave signs of
not holding out. As soon as Agasias, an Arcadian from
Lake Stymphalus, perceived this, he ran forward at full
speed. The man who had been amusing himself with the
rocks, caught hold of his shield as he ran by. Then two
other men started. Altogether it was a splendid race, and
curiously enough not another stone was thrown. Then the
rest of us followed. But when I saw the horrible thing that
ensued, I was inclined to be sorry that I had anything to

do with it. The women threw their children over the cliff, and then threw themselves after them, and the men did the same. I caught hold of one man to stop him, but he wriggled out of my grasp, and threw himself over the top. It was well for me that he did so or else I might have fared as Æneas of Stymphalus did. He saw a man very finely dressed just about to throw himself over, and tried to hold him. The man did not try to get away, but clasped Æneas tightly in his arms. The next moment both had fallen headlong over the edge. Of course they were both killed. We took very few prisoners, but flocks and herds as many as we wanted and more.

JANUARY 26.—The marching has been easy enough on the whole, though we have met with the bravest enemies that we have yet come across, the Chalybes, they are called. They did not hang on our rear, taking care never to fight unless they had some vantage ground, but met us fairly face to face. They were not as well armed as we. Indeed, they had no armor on the body except cuirasses of linen. Their chief weapon was a very long and clumsy spear. Nevertheless they made a good fight of it; and if they did kill a man they cut his head off directly with a short sabre that they carried at their waists. We got nothing but hard knocks here. All the property of the country was stored away in strongholds; still what we got from the Taochi has lasted us up to this time, and will supply us for some days to come. The country of the Chalybes past, we came to the city, the first, by the way, that we have seen. It seemed very populous and rich, and its governor was extremely civil. He gave us a guide who told us the best news that

we had heard for a long time. "Within five days you shall **see the sea**," he said. "**If I** fail, my life shall be the forfeit." According to this we **ought to see it to-morrow.**

JANUARY 27.—**We have seen it! I was in the van-guard** as usual. **We had our** hands full, **for the** people of the country **were up** in arms against us. Our friend, the guide, had been **very** urgent with us **to** ravage and burn the country; and the men had not been backward in following his advice. So now there was **a whole swarm of** enemies hanging on our heels, **and we of the rear** guard had to keep them in check. **All of a sudden we** heard a tremendous uproar. "There is another attack **on the van**," **cried** Xenophon, "this looks serious." But the shouting grew louder **and nearer. As soon as** a company came **up,** it began racing towards the shouters, **and** then took to shouting **itself.** Xenophon mounted his horse to see for himself what had happened. He took the cavalry with him in case anything should have happened, and I made the best of my way after **them.** Presently we could distinguish the words. The men were shouting, *The sea! The sea!* Then everybody started running, **rear guard and all**; even the very baggage horses were taken with it and came galloping up. And, sure enough, there it was, **right** before our eyes, a **glimpse of blue in the distance with** the sunshine upon it. What a scene it was! We all fell to embracing one another; rank was forgotten; generals, officers, and common men were friends. **Indeed the** gods could not have given to our eyes a more delightful sight. Presently the soldiers fell to erecting a great cairn of stones. On this they put skins and staves and wicker shields that we **had** taken from the enemy. Of course the guide had a very handsome present from the common store, a purse, a silver bowl, a Persian dress, and ten gold pieces. Then he begged some rings, and got not a few. The soldiers were ready to give him anything.

FEBRUARY 2.—We have passed safely through another country. The people were drawn out in order of battle when the luckiest thing happened, saving, I doubt not, many lives. One of the men came up to Xenophon and said : "I think I know the language these people talk. I verily believe that it is my own." And so it turned out to be. The man had been a slave in Athens. He explained to them that we did not wish to do them any harm, but simply wanted to get back to our own country. Since then it has been peaceful. The people—Macrones they call themselves—have been as helpful as possible, making roads for us, and supplying us with as good food as they possessed.

FEBRUARY 7.—Yesterday I really thought that after all that I had gone through, I was going to die of eating a mouthful of honey. We found a great store of this in one of the Colchian villages that we came to, and of course ate it freely. It was poisonous, at least to persons not used to it. I know that I was desperately ill and so were many of my comrades. Happily no one died. We reach Trapezus to-morrow. We are in Greece again. Thanks be to Zeus and all the gods !

CHAPTER XXIV.

A THANKSGIVING.

THE worst severity of the winter was over when the army reached Trapezus. The days were longer, for it was already half way between the winter solstice and the spring equinox, and though the nights were still bitterly cold, the sun was daily gaining power. Sometimes a breeze from the west gave to the air quite a feeling of spring. Still Callias was very thankful to find quarters in the city. He discovered but scarcely with surprise, that as soon as he returned within the circle of Greek influence, the credentials furnished him by Hippocles made life much smoother for him. Trapezus was the very farthest outpost of civilization; it was at least nine hundred miles from Athens, yet the name of Hippocles seemed as well known and his credit as good as if it had been the Piraeus itself. As soon as permission could be obtained to enter the town—for the people of Trapezus, though kind and even generous to the new arrivals, kept their gates jealously shut—Callias made his way to the house of a citizen who was, he was told, the principal merchant in the place. Nothing could have been warmer than the welcome which he received, when he produced the slip of parchment to which Hippocles had affixed his seal and signature.

"All I have is at your disposal," cried Demochares; this was the name of the Trapezuntine merchant. "I cannot do too much for any friend of Hippocles. You will, of course, take up your quarters with me; and any advance that you may want,—unless," he added with a smile, "you have learnt extravagance among the Persians, for we are not very rich here in Trapezus—any advance within reason you have only to ask for."

The young Athenian ventured to borrow fifty gold pieces, astonishing his new friend by the moderation of his demand. He knew that some of his comrades, mercenaries who had not received an *obolus* of pay for several months, must be very badly off, and he was glad to make a slight return for many little services that he had received, and acts of kindness and good fellowship that had been done for him on the march. As for hospitality, he begged to be allowed to postpone his answer till he could consult his general.

"I don't like to leave you, sir," he said when he broached the subject to Xenophon after their evening meal. "Why should I have the comforts of a house, lie soft, and feed well, while you are sleeping on the ground, and getting or not getting a meal, as good luck or bad luck will have it?"

"My dear fellow," replied Xenophon, "there is no reason why you should not take the good the gods provide you. You are not one of us; you never have been. You came as a volunteer, and a volunteer you have remained. You are perfectly free to do as you please. Besides, if you want anything more to satisfy you, you are attached to my command, and I formally give you leave."

Callias, accordingly, took up his quarters in the merchant's

house. **Never** was guest more handsomely **treated. Demochares and his** family were never wearied of his adventures,
a story which has indeed interested the **world** ever since,
and which to these Greeks of Trapezus **had a meaning**
which it had lost for us. Living as they did on the farthest
boundaries of the Greater Greece, the Greece of the colonies,
they were keenly alive to all that could be known about the
barbarian world with which they were brought **in** constant
contact. The young Athenian, **indeed, held** a sort of levee
which was thronged day after day with visitors young and
old. All that he had to tell them about the Great King, on
whose dominions they were in **some sort** trespassers, and
about the unknown tribes who dwelt between the sea and
the Persian capital, was eagerly **listened to.** Pleasant as his
sojourn was to himself, it **was** not without some advantage
to his old comrades. His host was an important person in
Trapezus, holding indeed the chief magistracy for the year,
and he had much to do with the liberal **present of oxen,**
corn, and wine which the town voted to the army.

A month passed **in a** sufficiently pleasant way. **Meanwhile the army** was preparing to offer a solemn thanksgiving for the safe completion of the **most perilous part of
its journey. The vows made at the** moment of its greatest
danger were now to be paid, and paid, after the usual Greek
fashion, in a way that would combine religion and festivity.
There was to be a sacrifice ; the sacrifice was to be followed
by a feast, and **the feast again** by a celebration which was,
of course, in a great measure an entertainment, **but was also,
in a** way, a function **of worship.** Wrestlers, boxers, and
runners not only amused **the** spectators **and** contended for

glory and prizes, but were also supposed in some way to be doing honor to the gods.

The sacrifice and the feast it is not necessary to describe. Necessarily there was nothing very splendid or costly about them. The purses of the soldiers were empty, though they had a good deal of property, chiefly in the way of prisoners whom they had captured on the way, and whom they would sell in the slave markets as the opportunity might come. Trapezus, however, and the friendly Colchian tribes in the neighborhood furnished a fair supply of sheep and oxen to serve as victims, and a sufficient quantity of bread, wine, dried fruit and olive oil, this last being a luxury which the Greeks had greatly missed during their march, and which they highly appreciated. A few of the officers, the pious Xenophon among them, went to the expense of gilding the horns of the beasts which were their special offerings ; but for the most part the arrangements were of a plain and frugal kind.

The games had at least the merit of affording a vast amount of entertainment to a huge multitude of spectators. They were celebrated, it may be easily understood, under considerable difficulties, for Trapezus did not possess any regular race course, and the only rings for wrestling and boxing were within the walls, and therefore not available on this occasion. By common consent the management of the affair was handed over to a certain Dracontius. He was a Spartan, and to the Spartans, who had been undisputed lords of Greece since the fall of Athens, had been conceded a certain right of precedence on all such occasions as these. Dracontius, too, was a man of superior rank to his comrades.

He belonged to one of the two royal houses of Sparta, but **had been** banished from his country in consequence of **an** unlucky accident. In one of the rough sports which the Spartan lads were accustomed to practice, sports which were commonly a more or less close mimicry of war, a blow of his dagger, dealt without evil intention but with a criminal carelessness, had been fatal **to a** companion. Hence, from boyhood, he had been an exile; cut off from the more honorable career to which he might have looked forward in the service of his country, **he had** been content to enlist as a mercenary.

Dracontius, accordingly, was made president of the games. The skins of the sacrificed animals were presented to him, as his **fee,** and he was asked to lead the way to the race-**course** where the contests were to be held.

" Race course!" cried the Spartan, with the *brusquerie* which it was the fashion of his country to use, " Race course ! **What more** do you want than what we have here?"

A murmur of astonishment ran through the army. **In-**deed there could have been nothing less like a race course than the ground on which they were standing. It was the slope of a hill, a slope that sometimes became almost precipi-tous. Most of it was covered with brushwood and heather. Grass there was none, except here and there where it covered with a treacherously smooth surface some dangerous quag-mire. Here and there, the limestone rock cropped up with jagged points.

" But where shall we wrestle?" asked Timagenes, an Ar-cadian athlete, who had **won the** prize for wrestling two or three years before at the Lithurian games, and who naturally considered himself as an authority on the subject.

"Here of course," was the president's reply.

"But how can a man wrestle on ground so hard and so rough?" asked the Arcadian, who had no idea of practising his art except in a regular ring.

"Well enough," said **Dracontius,** "but those who are thrown will get worse knocks."

The wrestler's face fell and he walked off amid a general laugh. His comrades fancied, **not** without reason, **that he was** a great deal too careful of his person.

But if the ground, broken with rocks and overgrown with wood was not suited to scientific wrestling, it certainly helped to make some of the other sports more than usually amusing. The first contest was a mile race for boys. **Most** of the competitors were lads who had been taken prisoners on the march, but a few Colchians entered for the prize, as did **also** two or three boys of Trapezus, who had the reputation of being particularly fleet of foot. But the natives of the plain, still more the inhabitants **of the town,** found themselves entirely **outpaced on this** novel race course **by** the young mountaineers. A Carduchian came in first, and was presented with his liberty, **his** master being compensated out of the prize fund which had been subscribed by the army. **As** soon as he understood that he was free, he set out at full speed **in the** direction **of his home.** A true mountaineer, he **sickened** for his native hills, and in the **hope** of seeing **them** again **was ready to** brave alone the perils which an **army had scarcely** survived.

A foot race for men followed, **but** the distance to be traversed was, according **to** the common custom of the great games, only two hundred yards. There were as many as sixty competitors ; but curiously enough, they were to a man Cretans. Another foot race, this time for men in heavy armor, was next run. The president had a Spartan's admiration for all exercises that had a real bearing on military training, and the race of the heavy armed was unquestionably one of these. It was won by a gigantic Arcadian, an Ætolian whose diminutive stature made a curious contrast to his competitor, coming in close behind him.

Next came the great event of the day, the " Contest of the Five Exercises," or " Pentathlon." The five were leaping, wrestling, running, quoit-throwing, and javelin-throwing. The competitor who won most successes had the prize adjudged to him.* Callias had been trained for some time at home with the intention of becoming a competitor at Olympia ; but various causes had hindered him from carrying out his purpose, and, of course, he was now wholly out of practice. He was sitting quietly among the spectators when he felt a hand upon his shoulder and looking up, saw his general standing by.

"Stand up for the honor of Athens," said Xenophon, "don't let the men of the Island† carry everything before them."

"But I am not in training," said Callias.

" You are in as good training, I fancy," replied the general, "as are any of these ; better I should say, to judge from the

* According to some accounts no competitor was crowned unless he was successful in all. But victory in five exercises so dissimilar could seldom, if ever, have been gained. Quoit-throwing, for instance, corresponding to our " putting the stone," required lofty stature and great muscular strength, and would very seldom be the specialty of a very fleet runner.
† The Island of Pelops or Peloponnesus.

way in which they have been eating and drinking since the **retreat** was ended. Besides, it is only **the boxers who** absolutely **require** anything very severe in that way. And you **have** youth."

Callias still made objections, but yielded when his general made the matter **a** personal favor.

The competitors were five in number, the winner of the foot-race, the tall Arcadian and his diminutive **rival** from Ætolia, two Achaeans, and Callias.

The first contest was leaping at the bar. Here the Arcadian's long legs served him well. He was a singularly **un**gainly fellow, and threw himself over the bar, **if I** may be allowed the expression, in a lump. Every time the bar was raised, he managed just **to clear** it, though the spectators could not understand how his clumsy legs, which seemed sprawling everywhere, managed to avoid touching it. Still they did manage it, and when he had cleared four cubits short **of a** palm, which may be translated into the English measure of five feet nine inches, his rivals had to own themselves beaten. Callias, who came second, declared that he had been balked by the infamous playing of the flute player, whose music according to the custom followed at **Olympia,** accompanied the jumping. "The wretch," he declared **to** the friends who condoled with him on the loss of what they had put down to him for **a** certainty, "**the** wretch **played a false note just as I** was at my last trial. **If I had** not heard him do the same at least half-a-dozen times before, I should **have said** that he did it on purpose."

If chance or fraud had been against him in this trial, in the next **he** was decidedly favored by fortune. This was the foot race. **The** course was, **as** usual, round a post fixed about a hundred yards from the starting point, and **home again.** Whenever a **turn has** to be made, a certain advantage falls to the competitor who has the inner place, and when, as in this case, the distance is short, the advantage is considerable. The places were determined by lot. The innermost fell to the Arcadian ; Callias came next **to him ;** fortunately for him, his most dangerous competitor, **the** Cretan who had won the foot race, had the outermost, *i. e.,* the worst station. The Arcadian jumped **away with a lead,** and for fifty yards managed, thanks **to the long** strides which his long legs enabled him to take, to keep in front ; but **the effort was soon** spent ; **by** the time that the turning point was reached, **Callias had** gained enough upon him to attempt the dangerous manœuvre of taking his ground. **If** it had not been for this, he must have been beaten, for the fleet-footed Cretan, weighted though he was by his disadvantageous place, ran a dead heat with him.

In the quoit-throwing, **the** Arcadian's strength **and** stature brought him to the front **again.** With us quoit-playing is a trial of skill as well as of strength. The quoit is thrown at a mark, and the player who contrives to go nearest to this mark, without touching it (for to touch it commonly ends in disaster) wins. At the same time the throw does not count unless the quoit either sticks into **the** ground or lies flat upon it with the right side uppermost. In the Greek game there were no requirements of this **kind.** The quoit was a huge mass of metal with notches by which it could be conveniently grasped, or, sometimes, a hole in the middle through which a leather strap or wooden handle could be put. He who threw it farthest was the winner. Some little knack was required, as is indeed the case in every feat of strength, and, as has been said before, stature was the chief qualification. The Arcadian hurled the quoit, a mass of iron weighing ten pounds, to the vast distance of forty-two feet. None of his rivals came near him. As he had now won two events out of three, and his gigantic height and weight would make him, to say the least, a formidable opponent in the wrestling, he was a favorite for the prize. His Arcadian countrymen, who formed, as has been said, a large proportion of the army, were in high hope, and staked sums that were far beyond their means on his success.

The quoit-throwing was followed by hurling the javelin at a mark. Here the Arcadian was hopelessly distanced, for here skill was as much wanted as strength had been in the preceding trial. He threw the javelin indeed with prodigious force, but threw it wholly wide of the mark. Indeed, when he was performing, the near neighborhood of the mark would have been the safest place to stand. The spectators were more than once in danger of their lives, so at random and at the same time so vigorous were his strokes. The first mark was a post rudely fashioned into the figure of a man. To hit the head was the best aim that could be made ; to hit a space marked out upon the body and roughly representing the heart was the next; the third in merit was a blow that fell on some other part of the body. The legs counted for nothing. Callias and the Cretan scored precisely the same. The Athenian hit the head twice, scoring six for the two blows. The third time his javelin missed altogether.

The Cretan, on the other hand, in his three strokes hit the third, second, and the first places successively, **scoring for** them **one, two, and three** respectively. Further trials of skill were **now given.** A wand about three fingers wide was set up at a distance of twelve yards. The Cretan's javelin pierced it, making it, as may **be** supposed, an exceedingly difficult thing for a rival to equal, much more to surpass the performance. But Callias was equal to the occasion. Amid tumultuous **applause** from the spectators, **for his courtesy** and carriage had made him a great favorite, he hurled his javelin **with such** accuracy **that he split that** which was already sticking in the mark. Again the Cretan and he were pronounced to have made a **tie.**

The two Achaeans and the Ætolian did creditably, **scor-**ing five each. **As they had** failed in four out of the five contests, **the prize was** clearly out of their reach, and they stood out of the **last** competition, the wrestling.

And now came the last and deciding struggle. Here **again** fortune decidedly favored the Athenian. **The presi-**dent, following the rule always observed at Olympia, ordered three lots marked A, B, and C, and representing respectively Callias, the Arcadian, and the Cretan, to **be put into an urn.** The two first drawn were to contend in the first heat, the **third was** to have what is technically **called a "bye." The** "bye" fell to the lot of Callias, and with it, it need **hardly** be said, the not inconsiderable advantage of coming fresh to **contend with a rival** who had undergone the fatigue **of a** previous struggle.

The issue of the contest between the Arcadian and the Cretan was not long in doubt. The latter was an agile fellow,

who would have had a very good chance with "light-
weights," to use again a technical term, if the competitors
had been so classed, as indeed they are by the customs of the
modern wrestling ring. But against his gigantic opponent
he had scarcely a chance. In the first bout the Arcadian
lifted his antagonist clean from the ground, and threw him
down at full length without more ado. The second was
more equal. The Cretan struck his antagonist's left ankle
so sharply with his foot that the giant fell, but he could
not loose the other's hold, and fell also, scoring only the advantage of being the uppermost. If there had been a tie in
the other two bouts this might have sufficed to give him the
victory, or the president might have ordered a fresh trial.
But the third bout was decisive. It was in fact a repetition
of the first, only, if possible, still more decisive. The Cretan
was again lifted from the ground, before he had the chance
of practising any of his devices, and again hurled at full
length upon the ground. This time he was stunned, and
carried insensible from the ground by his companions.

A brief interval was now allowed. It was thought unfair
that the Arcadian should be called upon to engage a fresh
antagonist without some chance of resting himself. But
what was meant for an advantage turned out to be exactly
the contrary. The man was not particularly tired, but he
was exceedingly thirsty, and he had not learnt the habit of
self-control. Regardless of the remonstrance of his companions, he indulged himself with a huge goblet of wine
and water. So imprudent was he indeed that he put less
water than was usual in the mixture, and slightly confused
his brain by the potency of the draught. When he came

forth to meet his antagonist, he had not only damaged his wind but had made his footing somewhat unsteady. Three bouts, as before, were fought. The Arcadian first tried the simple tactics which had been successful with the Cretan. He did his best to lift the Athenian from the ground, and Callias had all he could do **to** prevent it. But his weight and his strength, which he made the most of by his coolness, stood him in good stead. After a fierce struggle both fell together, and fell in such a way that the president declared that neither had gained any advantage. Practically, however, the victory was decided in favor of Callias. The Arcadian's strength was impaired, **and he** was so scant of breath that he could not use what was left to him. And he had little skill to fall back upon, whereas his antagonist had been the favorite pupil of one of the best trainers in Athens. In the second bout Callias struck the Arcadian on the right foot with his own left; in the third he simply reversed the device, striking the left with his right. In both he contrived to free himself when his opponent fell. Thus the fifth contest ended for him in an unquestioned victory.

The prize of victory was an ox and a purse of twenty-five gold pieces, for soldiers who fought for **pay** would not have relished the barren honor of a wreath **of** wild olive with which the Olympian judges were accustomed to reward the victors. Callias won golden opinions from his comrades by the liberality with which he disposed of his gains. The ox **he presented to** the company to which he had been attached; the money he divided, in such proportion as seemed right, among the unsuccessful competitors.

One more contest remained, and it turned out to be the

most entertaining of them all. This was a horse race. The competitors were to make their way from the hill-top to the shore and back again. The headlong, break-neck speed at which they galloped **down,** and the slow and painful effort by which they crawled back again, were witnessed with inextinguishable laughter by the assembled **crowds.** Xenophon himself took **a part** in this sport, and gained great **favor not** only by his **condescension but by** his skillful riding. He did not win indeed, for the animal which **he rode was** hopelessly inferior, but his performance did not discredit the land which claimed by the bounty of the **god** of the sea to have been the birthplace of the horse.* The piety of Xenophon always ready to show itself, did not fail **to** improve the occasion **of his** young friend's success.

" You have gained the prize," **he said in a tone of the deepest** earnestness, "**nor** did you **fail to** deserve it. Prize it **the** more because **it is** manifest that the gods **favor you.** Youth and strength pass away, but piety **you can cherish** always, and cherishing piety, **you** have **also the favor of** the gods."

* The legend was that Poseidon and Athene contended together for the honor of being the patron Deity of Attica. This was to be adjudged to the Power which should present it with the most useful gift. Poseidon struck the ground with his trident, and produced the horse ; Athene bade the olive spring forth, and was judged to have surpassed her rival. Reference is made to this legend in the most beautiful of the choral odes of Sophocles, the " Praise of Colonas " in the second of the two plays in the Story of Œdipus.

CHAPTER XXV.

BUSINESS AND PLEASURE.

Its religious obligations discharged, for the **games, as has
been already** said, were regarded as a service of thanksgiving
for deliverance, the **army turned its** attention to secular
affairs. One indispensable duty, one curiously characteristic,
by the way, of the Greek soldier's **temper of mind, was to
call the generals to** account. **For a Greek soldier, even** when
he was selling **his sword to the highest bidder, never forgot
that he was a citizen, and** that **as a** citizen he had the right
of satisfying himself **that his** superiors had done their duty
with due care and with integrity. The Ten Thousand
accordingly put aside for the time their military **character,**
and resolved themselves into a civil assembly. Their generals
were no longer the commanding officers to whom they owed
an unhesitating obedience, but the magistrates who had just
completed their term of office, **and** had now to render their
accounts† to those who had elected them.

The meeting of the army, perhaps I should rather say the
assembly, **was held on the** same ground which had served

---

† The examination of accounts (euthuna) was one of the most important constitutional usages in the Athenian commonwealth. All magistrates on coming out of office, and ambassadors returning from a mission
had to undergo it. The existence of this usage would make the difference in the eyes of an Athenian between a constitutional and a despotic
government. The other Greek States, though we know but little of
their internal arrangements, probably had some similar institution.

for a race course. One by one the officers were called to
answer for themselves. With many, indeed, the proceeding
was purely formal. The name **was** called, and the man
stepped forward **on** a platform which had been erected
where it could be best seen by the whole meeting. **If** no
one appeared **to make** a complaint or to ask **a question, the**
soldiers gave him a round of applause, if I may use the word
of the **noise** made by clashing their spears against their
shields ; this **was a** verdict of acquittal and the officer **re-**
tired with a bow. And this was what commonly happened.
After all, the leaders had, **on the** whole, done their duty
sufficiently well ; there was proof of that in the simple fact
that such a meeting was being held. But all did not escape
so easily. If, indeed, **only a few** voices of dissatisfaction were
heard, the matter was not pushed any further. When the
second appeal was made by the malcontents, they, seeing
that they were not supported by their comrades, preferred
to keep silence. The man would, in all probability, **be** their
officer again **and** he would not be likely to think pleasantly
of any one who had accused him. But where, on the other
hand, there was anything like an agreement of dissatisfied
voices, the complainants took courage to come forward, **and**
the examination was proceeded with in earnest. **One officer**
had had charge of some of the property of the army ; **there**
was a deficiency in his accounts and he was fined twenty
himal * to make it good. Another **was** accused of careless-
ness in his duties as leader, **and** had to pay half this sum.
Then came the *cause celebre*, as it may be called, of the day,
the trial of Xenophon **himself.** Xenophon **was** generally

---

* Rather more than £400.

popular with the army, as, indeed, he could scarcely fail to be, considering all that he had **done** for it ; but he had enemies. The mere fact of his being an Athenian made him an object of dislike to some ; others, as will be seen, he had been compelled to offend in the discharge of his duty.

"Xenophon, the son of Gryllus," shouted the herald at the top of his voice.

The Athenian stepped on to the platform.

An Arcadian soldier, Nicharchus by name, came forward and said, "I accuse Xenophon the Athenian of violence and outrage."

A few voices of assent were heard throughout the meeting ; and some half dozen men **came forward to support the the prosecutor. Accuser and accused were now confronted.**

"Of what do you accuse me ?" asked Xenophon.

"Of wantonly striking me," replied the man.

"When and where did you suffer these blows ?"

"**After** we had crossed the Euphrates, when there was **a** heavy fall of snow."

"I remember. You are right. The weather was terrible ; our provisions had run out ; **the wine could not** so much as be smelt ; many men **were** dropping down, **half** dead with fatigue ; the enemy were close upon our heels. **Were not** these things so ?"

"It is true. Things were as bad as **you say, or even worse.**"

"You hear," said Xenophon, turning to the assembly, "how we were situated, and indeed, seeing that you suffered these things yourself, you are not likely to forget them. Verily, if in such a condition of things, I struck this man wantonly and without **cause, you** might fairly count me more brutal than an ass. **But say—**" he went on, addressing himself again to his accuser, "was there **not** a cause for **my** beating you?"

" **Yes,** there was a cause," the fellow sullenly admitted.

" Did I ask you for something, and strike you because **you** refused to **give it?"**

"**No."**

"Did I demand payment **for a** debt, **and lose my** temper **because the money** was not forthcoming?"

" No."

" **Was I drunken ?"**

"No."

" **Tell me now ; are you a heavy-armed soldier?"**

"No ; I am not."

" Are you a light-armed then ?"

"No; nor yet a light-armed."

"What were you doing then ?"

" I was driving a mule."

" **Being** a slave ?"

" Not so ; **I am free ; but my commander compelled me** to drive **it."**

A light broke in upon Xenophon. He had had a general recollection of the occasion, but could not remember the particular incident. Now it all came back to him.

" Ah," he cried, "I remember ; it was you who were carrying the sick man ?"

" Yes," the man confessed, " I did so, by your compulsion ; and a pretty mess was made of **the kit that I had upon the** mule's back."

" Nay, **not so ; the men carried** the things themselves, and nothing was lost. But hear the rest of the story," he went on, turning to the assembly, "and, indeed it is worth hearing. **I** found a poor fellow lying **upon the** ground, who could not move a step further. **I knew the man,** and knew him as one who had done good service. And **I** compelled you, sir," addressing Nicharchus, "to carry him. For if I mistake **not, the enemy were close** behind us."

The Arcadian nodded assent.

"Well then ; **I sent** you forward **with your** burden, **and after** a while, overtook you again, when **I** came up with the rear-guard. You were digging a trench in which to bury the man. **I** thought **it** a pious act, **and** praised you **for it.** But, lo ! while I was speaking, the **dead** man, as I thought he was, twitched his leg. **'Why** he's alive,' **the** bystanders cried out. **'Alive** or dead, **as** he pleases,' **you said, 'but I am not going** to carry him any further.' Then **I struck you.** I acknowledge **it.** It seemed to me that you were going to bury the poor fellow alive."

"Well," said the Arcadian, "you won't deny, I suppose, **that the** man died after all."

"Yes," replied Xenophon, **"he died, I acknowledge.** We **must** all die some day ; but, meanwhile, **there is** no reason why we should be buried alive."

The man hung his head and **said** nothing.

"What say you, comrades ?" cried **Xenophon.**

One of the oldest men in the ranks got up and said, **"If** Xenophon had given the scoundrel a few more blows he had **done well."**

A deafening clash of swords and spears followed, and **the** verdict was accepted.

The other complainants were now called to state the particulars of their grievances. Dismayed by the reception which their spokesman had met with, they remained silent, **one** and all. Xenophon then entered upon a general defence of his conduct.

"Comrades," he said, "I confess that I have many times struck men for want of discipline. **These** were men **who,** leaving others to provide for their safety, thought only of their own **gain.** While we were fighting they would leave their place in the ranks to plunder, and so enriched themselves at our expense. Some **also I** have struck, when I found them playing the coward and **ready** to give themselves helplessly up to the enemy. Then **I** forced them to **march on,** and so saved their lives. For I know, having once myself sat down in a sharp frost, while I was waiting for my comrades, how loath one is to rise again. Therefore, for their sake, I raised them even with blows, as I should myself wish, were I so found, to be raised. Others also have I struck whom I found straggling behind that they might **rest. I** struck them for your sake, for they were hindering both you that were in front, and us that were behind, and **I** struck them for their own sake. For verily it was a lighter thing to have a **blow with** the fist from me than a **spear's** thrust from the enemy. Of a truth, if they are able to stand up now **to accuse me, it is because I saved them thus.** Had they fallen into the enemy's **hand,** what satisfaction would they be able to get, even if their wrongs were ten times worse than that Nicharchus complains of? **No,"** he went on, "my friends, I have done nothing more to any one than what a wise father **does to** his child, or a good **physician** does to his patient. You see how I behave myself now. I am in better case; I fare better; I have food and wine in plenty. Yet I strike no one. Why? Because there is no need; because we have weathered the storm, **and** are in smooth **water. I** need **no** more defence; you have, I see, acquitted me. Yet I cannot forbear to say that I take it ill that this accusation has been made. You remember **the** times when I had for your **good** to incur your dislike; but the times when I eased the burden of storm or winter for any of you, when I beat off an enemy, when I ministered to you in sickness or in want, these no one remembers—" and here the speaker's voice half broke, partly with real emotion, partly **at** the suggestion of the orator's art. A **thrill of** sympathy ran through the audience. "And you forget," he went on, "that **I never** failed to praise the doer of any noble deed, or to do such honor as I could, to the brave, living or dead. Yet, surely it were more noble, more just, more after the mind of the gods, a sweeter and kindlier act, to treasure the memory of the good than to cherish these hateful thoughts."

When the speaker sat down, there was nothing that he might not have obtained from his **comrades.**

That night there was a great banquet. **This** served **a** double purpose. Quarrels were made up, and **some other** difficult relations of the army to its neighbors were satisfactorily adjusted. The fact was, that the Greeks, partly from their want, and partly in the hope of filling their pockets after **a** long and profitless campaign, had been plundering right and left. The natives, on the other hand, had not been slow to retaliate. Plundering cannot be done satisfactorily in company ; but any who ventured to do a little business on his own account ran a great chance of being cut off. Under these circumstances both parties thought it might be possible to come to an agreement. If the Greeks would not plunder, the natives would leave them unmolested and even furnish them with supplies. The chief of the country, accordingly, sent an embassy, with a handsome present of horses and robes of native manufacture. The generals entertained them at a banquet, to which, at the same time, they invited the most influential men of the army. The chief's proposals would be informally discussed, and proposed in regular form at a general meeting the next day.

The generals did their best to impress their guests. Meat, bread and wine were in plenty ; and the eparch of Trapezus sent one of the magnificent turbots for which the waters of the Black Sea were famous. All the plate that was in the camp was put into requisition to make as brave a show as possible ; and, at the instance of Callias, some handsome vessels of gold and silver were lent by the town authorities.

But, in the eyes of the guests, the most impressive part of the entertainment was in the performances which followed it. The libation having been made and the hymn, which supplied the part of grace after meat, having been sung, some of the Thracian soldiers came upon the platform which had been prepared for the performers. They wore the usual armor of their country, a helmet, greaves, light cuirass, and sword, and danced a national dance to the sound of a flute, leaping into the air with extraordinary nimbleness, and brandishing their swords. One pair of dancers were conspicuous for their agility. Faster and faster grew their movements, and with **gestures** of defiance they alternately retreated and advanced. At last, one of them, carried, it seemed, out of himself by his rage, thrust at his fellow with his sword. **The** man fell.

" He is killed !" screamed out the guests, and rose from their seats.

Indeed, the man had fallen so artistically and lay so **still** that any one would have thought that he **had** received a fatal blow. The Greeks, however, looked on unmoved, and the strangers, not knowing whether this wonderful people might not be wont to kill each other for the entertainment of their guests, resumed their seats. The dancer **who had** dealt the blow stripped the other of his arms, and hurried off, singing the Thracian national song :

> " All praise to Sitalces,
>   Invisible Lord,
> **The** spear point that errs not,
>   The death-dealing sword,
> The chariot that scatters
>   The close ranks of war,
> Red Ruin behind it,
>   Blind Panic before !"

When he had left the stage a party of Thracians appeared **and** carried off the fallen man, **who had** remained without giving the slightest **sign of life.**

Another dance in **armor succeeded,** performed this **time** by Æolian tribesmen **from the** Menalian coast. **A man** came on the stage, and, laying aside his arms, made believe to drive a yoke of oxen, and to sow as he drove. Every now and then he looked round, with an admirable imitation of expecting some unpleasant interruption. This came in the shape of another armed man, who was supposed to represent a cattle-lifter. The ploughman caught **up his** arms, and ran to encounter him. The two fought in front of the team, keeping time as they struck and parried to the sound of the flute. At last the robber appeared **to** vanquish his adversary, to bind him, strip him of his arms, and drive off the **team.**

The next performer was a Mysian, who danced, again **in armor, what we** should **call a** *pas scul.* **He had a** light **shield** in each hand, and seemed to be fighting with two **adversaries** at **once; his** action was extraordinarily life-like and his agility almost more than human. In curious contrast with his performance was the stately movement of some Arcadians heavy-armed, who, **with** all the weight of their armor and accoutrements **upon them, moved to the** tune of the **warriors'** march with as **much ease as if they** had been perfectly unencumbered.

"**Good** Heavens !" **cried** one of the envoys to his next neighbor, "what men **these are !** Their armor seems **not one** whit **heavier to** them than **a shirt,** and **they carry their swords and their spears as if they were** twigs of osier."

One of the Mysians, **whose** dialect was **not** very different **from that of the** speaker, overheard the **remark. "Ah !"** he said to himself, "**we will** astonish **these gentlemen still** more."

He drew one of the Arcadians who had just performed, aside. "**Send** Cleone on the stage," **he said.**

Cleone was a dancing-girl, famous for her agility.

By good luck she was **at hand,** having indeed **expected to perform** for the amusement of the company. **The Arca-**

dian made her put on a light cuirass of silvered steel, which she wore over a scarlet tunic. She had a short gilded helmet, buskins of purple, and sandals tied with **crimson** strings. In her left hand she carried a small shield, and **in her right, a light spear.** Thus accoutred, she came on the **stage** and danced the Pyrrhic dance **with** tremendous applause from **all the spectators.**

The astonishment of the native guests **was beyond all expression.**

"What!" cried their chief, **"do your women fight?"**

"Of course," said the General whom he addressed, **"of** course they fight, and very pretty soldiers they make."

"Women soldiers!" gasped the man.

"Why," said his host, "did you not know **that it was the** women who routed the **Great King, and drove him out of** our camp?"

CHAPTER XXVI.

INVALIDED.

CALLIAS found it very hard to sit out the banquet and the entertainment that followed it. He had felt a headache before sitting, or to speak more correctly, lying down, and this grew so bad during the evening that he gladly took the earliest opportunity of leaving. The fact was that he had been ailing for some days; the excitement of the games had carried him through the labors of the day, but he suffered doubly from the reaction, and before nightfall he was seriously ill.

And now he found the advantage of having followed Xenophon's advice and taken up his quarters in the town. Had he been reduced to such nursing and attendance as the camp could have supplied, his chances of moving would have been small indeed. At the house of Demochares, on the contrary, he had everything in his favor, an exceptionally good nurse, and an exceptionally skillful physician. In those days neither branch of the healing art, for nursing has certainly as much to do with healing as physicking, was very successfully cultivated. Women nursed the sick, indeed, often with kindness and devotion, for woman's nature was substantially the same then as it is now, but they did it in a blind and ignorant fashion. As for the

practice of medicine it was a mass of curious superstitions
and prejudices, leavened here and there with a few grains
of experience, and, if the practitioner happened to have that
inestimable quality, of good sense. Of systems there was
only the beginning. The great physician Hippocrates had
indeed acquired a vast reputation, and was beginning to influence the opinion of the faculty throughout Greece ; but
the medical profession has always been slow to adopt new
ideas—what profession, indeed, has not?—the means of
communication, too, were very limited, and as yet his teaching had had but little effect.

But Callias happened to be exceedingly fortunate both in
his nurse and in his doctor. The house of Demochares was
kept by his sister, a widow, who after her husband's death
had returned to her old home, and had devoted herself to a
life of kindness and charity. The young Athenian had won
her heart, not only by his sunny temper and gracious manners, but by his resemblance to a son of her own whose
early death—he had been slain in a skirmish with the barbarian neighbors of Trapezus—had been the second great
sorrow of her life. His illness called forth her tenderest
sympathies, and nothing could have exceeded the devotion
with which she ministered to her patient.

The physician, Demoleon by name, was a very remarkable man. He was a native of the island of Cos, and was at
this time between fifty and sixty years of age. He had been
one of the first pupils of the famous Hippocrates, who was
a native of the same island, and had lived on terms of great
intimacy with his teacher whom he assisted in his
private practice. When Hippocrates was summoned to the

plague-stricken **city of Athens,** Demoleon accompanied him, and, by a curious coincidence, in the course of his residence there had treated the father of Callias. Whatever the benefit that followed the prescriptions **of Hippocrates, it is certain** that the fact of his being called in to administer them by the most famous citizen of Greece, largely **increased** his reputation, and that even beyond the border of Greece. The great physician's return from Athens was speedily followed by **an** invitation from Artaxerxes, **King of Persia.*** The plague that had devastated **Greece had passed eastward, and was** committing destructive ravages throughout the **Persian** Empire. Artaxerxes implored Hippocrates to give him and his subjects the benefit of his advice. He **offered at the** same time the magnificent *honorarium* of **two** talents **of** gold yearly.† The patriotism or the prudence of Hippocrates led him to refuse this offer, tempting as it was. He would not, he said, and doubtless **with** sincerity, give the benefit of his advice to the hereditary enemy of his country. **At** the same time, we may suppose, he reflected to himself that he would be putting himself, without any possibility of appeal, at the mercy **of a** tyrannical and unscrupulous master. But one of **the Persian envoys succeeded in doing a little** business of the same **kind on his own account. He found** the pupil less resolute against **the temptations of a great** bribe than the master had been. Accordingly he engaged Demoleon to come in the capacity **of physician to himself**

---

* Artaxerxes Longimanus, so called from the circumstance of his right hand being longer than his left. He reigned from 465 to 425.

† About £5,200, ($25,000), if gold is to be reckoned at thirteen times the value of silver. This is Herodotus' calculation, and it probably held good in Greece for a century or more from his time, until, in fact, the enormous influx of gold from the Asiatic conquests of Alexander altered the proportion.

and his household.   The King would have the opportunity of availing himself of his advice if he pleased.   Artaxerxes was disappointed at the refusal of Hippocrates, but he did not disdain the help of a man who had shared his practice, and was probably acquainted with his system.   Demoleon prescribed at Susa and Persepolis the remedies which his master had employed at Athens, the burning of huge fires in the street and squares, and the use of an antidote.   The pestilence either yielded to these influences, or, as is more probable, had exhausted its force.   At any rate Demoleon got the credit of having vanquished the enemy, and was rewarded by a munificent present from the King and by an enormous practice.

He might have accumulated great wealth but for an unlucky complication for which he can scarcely be considered to have been to blame.   Necessity sometimes compelled a departure, in the case of the physician, from the strict rules of seclusion with which the Persian women were surrounded.   Demoleon was called in to visit the daughter of a Persian noble.   She was a beautiful girl, or rather would have been beautiful but for the fact that she was blind.   It was a case of cataract, and the Greek physician, who was as bold as he was skillful, ventured on an operation which at that time had scarcely been attempted, or even thought of.   It proved entirely successful.   The gratitude of the father was shown by a munificent present of gold and jewels ; that of the daughter by the gift of her heart.   One of the very first objects on which her eyes rested when the bandage was permitted to be removed was the form of the young physician who had restored to her one of the greatest **joys of life.** Under any circumstances it was likely to please **her ; and** Demoleon was in the bloom **of early manhood,** and **his fair** complexion and golden hair showed in attractive contrast to the swarthy hues of her countrymen. The result was that she fell deeply in love. Demoleon was **not** without prudence, and would have hesitated to listen to any promptings of his own heart, for he too had been greatly impressed by the beauty and grace as well as by the pathetic patience of the sufferer. Amestris —that was the young lady's name — guessed readily enough that the physician would not venture to speak, and she took the matter into her own hands. She did not speak herself ; for that, passionate as was her affection, would have **been** impossible ; but she got some one to speak for her. Her nurse—the nurse **was** generally the *confidante* of antiquity—undertook the task of communicating with the young man. One day she gave him a pomegranate, saying at the same time that he would find the fruit especially sweet. Her words would have seemed ordinary enough to any one that might have happened to hear them ; but the young physician, whose feelings made him susceptible, suspected, he could not say why, **a particular** meaning. Opening the fruit he found a ring engraved with **a** single Greek word—*Be Bold.* The next day he thanked the giver of the fruit with **emphasis.** "**It** was sweet to the core," he **said.**

After that the affair proceeded rapidly. The young man, **who, as** may be guessed, did not hurry the case of his patient, found an opportunity of declaring his love, and in the following summer the two lovers fled together. All the arrangements had been carefully made. The girl feigned sickness, and the physician prescribed a residence among the hills and a simpler life **and** plainer diet than the patient was likely to get in her father's house. Her foster-mother was the wife of a sheep master who rented some extensive pasture on the hills of Southern Armenia, and it was settled that Amestris should pay her a visit. The lady was sent off under a small escort, no one dreaming that the family of an influential noble would be molested on **its** journey. Yet, curiously enough, a band of brigands was bold enough to enter the caravanserai where the party was lodging on the fourth night after their departure from Susa. Certainly the keeper of the inn, and, possibly, the commander of the escort, had been bribed—Demoleon's successful practice had put him in the command of as much money as he wanted. For **a long time** Amestris absolutely disappeared. Her father searched everywhere and offered munificent rewards for information, but he could find and hear nothing. No one knew that a couple of travellers, who might have been two brothers journeying in company and followed by three well armed servants, were in fact Demoleon, Amestris, and the pretended robbers. The party followed much the same route as was afterwards taken by the Ten Thousand, and, after not a few hair-breadth escapes, arrived in safety at the same destination,—the city of Trapezus.

Three years of happiness followed. Then the beautiful Persian died. She never repented of **having** given **her** heart to the young physician, who was the best and most affectionate of husbands. But she missed her family and all the associations **of** her **early** life, and pined **away under the loss. Return was** impossible ; she could not go back without her **husband, and to** return with him would have been to expose him, if not herself, to the certainty of death. The hopelessness of the situation broke her heart ; and **all her** husband's skill, even the more potent influence of her husband's love, failed to work a cure.

The widower could **not prevail upon** himself to leave the place where he had enjoyed his short-lived happiness. He might have gained wealth and fame in larger cities, but he preferred to spend the rest of his **days at Trapezus.** There, indeed, he was almost worshipped. He had a singularly light and skillful hand ; his experience, **though, of course,** not so large as he might have collected elsewhere, was always ready for use ; and he had the **rare,** the incommunicable gift of felicitous guessing—guessing **we call it,** but it is really the power of forming rapid conclusions from a number of trifling, **often** half discerned indications. **Anyhow he** achieved some very marvellous cures ; performed with success operations **which** others did not venture to attempt ; diagnosed diseases with remarkable skill, and was extraordinarily fertile in his expedients. **It was** specially characteristic of him that while he was never satisfied till he had thoroughly enquired into **the** causes of disease, **he was unwearied in his** efforts to relieve the inconvenience **and painfulness** of a patient's symptoms.

So alarming did the condition **of** Callias become after **his** return from the banquet, that Demoleon was called in without loss of time. All that he could do at the moment was to give a sleeping draught, intending to make a thorough examination of the **case next morning.**

Shortly after sunrise he was by the bedside. Callias was conscious enough to be able to describe his feelings; what he said indicated plainly enough that his illness had been developing for some days past, and had been postponed by sheer courage and determination. It was in fact something like what we call gastric fever; and the experienced physician saw enough to convince him that he should have a hard battle to fight. The patient was young, vigorous, apparently sound of constitution, and, as far as he could learn, of temperate habits. All this was in favor of recovery; but it was not more than was needed to give a glimpse of hope.

Demochares, who had a strong regard for the young man, as indeed every one had that had been brought into contact with him, intercepted the physician as he was leaving the house after a prolonged examination of the patient.

"How do you find him?" he asked.

Demoleon shook his head. The gesture was not exactly despairing, but it indicated plainly enough that the situation was serious.

"You will put him all right before long?" returned the merchant, alarmed at the gravity of the physician's manner.

"All these things lie on the knees of the gods," said Demoleon, quoting from his favorite Homer. (It was a maxim of his that a man who did not know his Homer was little better than a fool.) It may be said that the physician was more than a little brusque in manner and speech. Twenty years of solitary life had made him so, for since his wife's death he had held aloof from all the social life of the place.

"What ails him?" enquired the merchant.

"A fever," was the brief reply.

"Does it run high?"

"Very high indeed."

"You have bled him, of course."

The physician's answers to enquiries were generally as short as the rules of politeness permitted; occasionally, some of his questioners were disposed to think, even shorter; but there were remarks that always made him fluent of speech, though the fluency was not always agreeable to his audience.

"Bleed him, sir," he cried, "why don't you say at once stab him, poison him? No, sir, I have not bled him, and do not intend to."

"I thought that it was usual in such cases," said the merchant timidly.

"Very likely you did," answered Demoleon, "and there are persons, I do not doubt, who would have done it, persons, too, who ought to know better." This was levelled at a rival practitioner in the town for whom he entertained a most thorough contempt. "Do you know, sir," he went on, "where men learnt the practice of bleeding?"

"No, I do not," said Demochares.

"It was from the hippopotamus. That animal has been observed to bleed himself. Doubtless the operation does him good. But it does not follow that what is good for an animal as big as a cottage is good also for a man. Doubtless there *are* men for whom it is good. When I have to deal with a mountain of a man, one of your city dignitaries bloated by rich feeding, by chines of beef and pork and flagons of rich wine, I don't hesitate to bleed him. His thick skin, his rolls of fat flesh, seem to require it. In fact he is a human hippopotamus. But to bleed a spare young fellow, who has been going through months of labor and hard living would be to kill him. I wonder that you can suggest such a thing."

"I am sure I am very sorry," said the merchant humbly.

"Happily no harm is done," replied the physician, cooling down a little. "And, after all, this is not your business, and you may be excused for your ignorance, but there are others," he went off muttering in a low voice, "who ought to know better, and ought to be punished for such folly. It is sheer murder."

I do not intend to describe the course of the long illness of which this was the beginning. There were times when even the hopefulness of the physician—and his hopefulness was one of his strongest and most helpful qualities—failed him. Relapse after relapse, coming with disheartening frequency, just when he had seemed to have gathered a little strength, brought him close to the gates of death.

"I have done all that I can," said Demoleon one evening to Epicharis the nurse. "If any one is to save him, it must be you. If you want me, send for me, of course. Otherwise I shall not come. It breaks my heart to see this fine young fellow dying, when there are hundreds of worthless brutes whom the earth would be better without."

Epicharis never lost heart; for a nurse to lose heart is more fatal than the physician's despair. For nearly a week she scarcely slept. Not a single opportunity of administering some strengthening food did she lose—for now the fever had passed, and the danger lay in the excessive exhaustion. At last her patience was rewarded. The sick man turned the corner, and Demoleon, summoned at last, to alleviate, he feared, the last agony, found, to his inexpressible delight, that the cure was really begun.

"You are the physician," he cried, as he seized the nurse's hand and kissed it ; "I am only a fool."

Winter had passed into spring, and spring into summer, before Callias could be pronounced out of danger. Even then his recovery was slow. Some months were spent in a mountain village where the bracing air worked wonders in giving him back his strength. As the cold weather came on he returned to his comfortable home in Trapezus. Though scarcely an invalid, he was still a little short of perfect recovery. Besides it was not the time for travelling. Anyhow it was the spring of the following year, and now more than twelve months from the time of his first illness, when he was pronounced fit to travel. Even then it was only something like flat rebellion on the part of his patient that induced Demoleon to give way. The young man was wearying for home and friends. He had heard nothing of them for several months, for communication was always stopped during the winter between Athens and the ports of the Euxine, while the eastward bound ships that always started after the dangerous season of the equinox had passed, had not yet arrived.

CHAPTER XXVII.

CALLIAS started about the middle of April, **according to** our reckoning. His journey **to the** Bosphorus was much retarded by contrary winds. For some days no progress could be made, and **it** was well into May before he reached Byzantium. There he was fortunate enough to get a passage in a Spartan despatch boat, which took him as far as the **port of Corinth,** thus carrying him, of course, beyond his destination, but to **a** point from which it was easy for him **to find his** way to Athens. **It was** about the beginning **of** June when he landed at the Piraeus. He did not doubt for a moment about the place where his first visit was due. The fact was that he had no near relations. **The kinsman who was his legal** guardian had always given up the business of looking after **his** ward's property to Hippocles; and now that Callias was his own master, **there** was little more than **a** friendly **acquaintance between** the two cousins. **The** alien's house **was, he** felt, **his real** home, nor **had he given** up the hope that in spite of Hermione's strongly expressed determination, he might some day become **a member of his** family.

Hippocles happened to have just returned from his business at **the** shipyard, **when the young** Athenian presented

THE ACROPOLIS AT THE PRESENT DAY.

himself at the gate. Nothing could be warmer than the welcome he gave his visitor.

"Now Zeus and Athene be thanked for this," he cried as he wrung the young man's hand. "That you had come back safely from the country of the Great King I heard. Your friend Xenophon told me so much in a letter that I had from him about a year ago. Then I heard from him that you were dangerously ill. After that all was a blank, and I feared the worst. But why not a word all this time?"

"Pardon me, my dear friend, I think I may say that it was not my fault. For months I was simply too ill to write. When I came back to Trapezus, the winter had begun, and there were no more ships sailing westward. I should have written when communications were opened again, but I was always in hopes of being allowed by the physician to start, and I had a fancy for bringing my own news. And how are you?"

"I am well enough," replied Hippocles, "but we have been passing through times bad enough to shorten any man's life. I don't speak of trade. There have been troubles there, but when one has ventures all over the world, it does not matter very much as far as profits are concerned, if things do not go right at one place or another. It has been the state of home affairs that has been the heaviest burden to bear. I thought we had touched the bottom when the city had to surrender to Lysander. But it was not so, and I might have known better. The Spartans, of course, upset the democracy."

"Well," interrupted Callias, "I should have thought that

that would not have been by any means **an** altogether un-
mixed evil."

"Yes," said Hippocles, "and there have been times when
I have been ready to think the same. But wait till you see
an oligarchy in power, **really in** power, **I mean, not** with **a**
possible appeal to the people, and so a chance of having to
answer for themselves before them, but with a strong
foreign garrison behind them. We had that state of things
in Athens for more than half **a year. One** might almost
say that it was like a city taken **by storm. No** man's life
was safe unless he was willing to do the bidding of the Tyrants—the "Thirty Tyrants" was the nickname of the men
that were in power in those days. Who would have thought
that Theramenes would ever have been regretted by honest
men? Yet it was so. **He** thought his colleagues were going
too far, and opposed them. **He** was carrying the Senate
with him, for many besides him were beginning to feel uncomfortable; so they **murdered** him. The Thirty had, **you**
must know, a sort of sham general assembly—three thousand
citizens picked out of the whole number **as** holding strong
oligarchical opinions. Amongst the laws that they had made
one was that none of these Three Thousand were to be condemned without a vote of the Senate. The name of Theramenes was, of course, on the list, and, **as he** had a majority
of the Senate with him, **he** seemed safe. Well what did
Critias, who was the leader of the **violent** party, do? He
filled the outer circle of the Senate house with armed men,
the Senate, you must understand, sitting in the middle surrounded **by** them. Then he got up and said, 'A good
president, when he sees the **body over** which he presides

about to be duped, does not suffer them to follow their own counsel. Theramenes has duped you, and I and these men here will not suffer one who is the enemy of his country to do so any longer. I have therefore struck his name off the **list** of the Three Thousand. This leaves me and my colleagues free to deal with him without your assent.' The Senate murmured, but dared do nothing more. The **officers** came and dragged the man from the altar to which he was clinging. An hour afterwards he had drunk the **hemlock.** The gods below be propitious to him, for great **as were his** misdeeds he died in a good cause and as a brave man should die.* Things have not been so bad since the 'Thirty' **were** upset, but there is a sad story to tell you."

Callias paused awhile. At last he screwed up his courage to put a question which he had both longed and feared to put ever since he had set foot in the house.

" And your daughter, is she well? "

" **Yes,** she is well."

" And still with you? "

" Yes, she is at home," briefly answered the father.

Hermione had **in fact, refused several offers which every** one else had thought highly eligible. Hippocles, though by **no means anxious to lose a daughter who was not only a**

---

* The last scene of his life is described by Xenophon. I give the passage with some explanation. When he drank the fatal cup he threw the dregs on the floor with the peculiar jerk given in playing the game of Cottabos. This game had several forms; but the feature common to them all was the heaving of wine out of a cup. Sometimes the object seems to have been a kind of fortune telling. A guest when he had finished his cup would jerk out any dregs that might be left. At the same time he named the guest who was to drink next, and the sound made by the drops falling was supposed to give some omen good or bad. "To the gracious Critias," said Theramenes. It was to be a prophecy of his fate. As a matter of fact Critias fell a few weeks afterward in a battle with Thrasybulus and the exiles of the democratic party.

companion but a counsellor, was growing anxious at what
appeared her manifest determination to remain single. He
would have dearly liked to have a son-in-law who would be
able to take up in **time the** burden of his huge business, a
burden which he began to **feel** already somewhat heavy for
his strength. Callias would have been entirely to his heart,
but he had accepted, though not without great reluctance,
his daughter's views on this subject. That she should deny
the young Athenian's **suit, and yet** for **his sake** dismiss all
other suitors—and this he began to suspect to be the fact—
seemed to his practical mind a quite unreasonable course of
action. When a distant kinsman **from Italy, a handsome**
youth of gracious manners and of unexceptionable character,
with even a tincture of **culture, was** emphatically refused,
Hippocles ventured a remonstrance. Its reception was such
that he resolved never under any circumstances to repeat it.
Hermione had **been always** the most obedient of daughters,
but this roused her to open rebellion. "Father," she said,
"in this matter **I am and** must be a freeborn Italian. A
Greek father can arrange a marriage **for** his daughter, but
you must not think of it. I shall give myself as my mother
gave herself before me—if I could **find one as** worthy as she
did," and she caught her father's hand and kissed it, breaking at the same time into a passion **of tears.** "Forgive me,"
she went on in a broken **voice,** "for setting up myself
against you ; but if you love me, never speak on this subject
again." **And** her father resolved that he never would.

The young Athenian felt a glow of renewed hope pass
through him at the father's reply, studiously brief and **cold**
as it was. Anyhow Hermione **was** not married. **What**

could ever occur to change her purpose he did not care to speculate. Nevertheless, as long as she did not belong to another, he need not despair.

"You will **dine with me of course,**" said Hippocles to his visitor, "by good luck I have invited Xenophon. Doubtless that is he," **he went on, as** a kick was heard at the door.†

A few moments afterwards a slave introduced Xenophon ; **and** before the two friends had finished their greetings it was announced that dinner **had been served.**

Hermione was not present at the meal, nor did her father make any excuse for her absence. The presence of any guest not belonging to the regular family **circle, was sufficient** to account for it ; and Callias, **though** he hoped against hope **to see her, could not** but acknowledge to himself **that a** meeting would **have been** highly **embarrassing.**

Conversation did not flag during the meal. **When it was** finished, the **host excused** himself on **the score of** having some business matters on **hand which did not brook** delay ; and Xenophon and Callias **were left to talk over each other's** adventures.

When Callias had told **the story with which my readers** are already acquainted, Xenophon proceeded **to give him a** brief outline of his fortunes **since they had** parted.

"**Well, my dear** Callias," he said, "**you did not lose much** by not being **with us.** While we **were in danger, we stuck** fairly together, though there **were always cowardly and** selfish fellows who thought, not of the general welfare, **but** only of **their** own skins **or their own** pockets. **But when** we were safe at the coast and among friends, **then there**

† It was usual to **kick not** to knock with the hand.

arose endless **division.** And, indeed, I must allow that the situation of the **army** was very trying. Here were thousands of men who lived by their pay, and there was no paymaster. I had a scheme of my own which would really have kept us together. If it could have been carried out, the gathering of the Ten Thousand, even though it had failed of its first object, would not have been altogether in vain. **I wanted** to found **a new** Greek colony. We might have taken **Pharis or** some other city of the barbarians; and if only half of my comrades had been willing to stay, we might have made a rich and powerful place of it before long. But it was not to be. Perhaps I was not worthy of being the founder of such a colony; anyhow the scheme came to nothing. I will tell you how it was. You remember Silanus, the sooth-**sayer. I** never trusted the man. He was quite capable of **garbling** signs **to suit his own** advantage. However **I** could **not** help going to him on this occasion, as he was the chief of his craft. **So** I said, 'Offer sacrifices and determine the omens concerning this scheme of a new colony.' **Now** Silanus was about the only man who had any money in his pocket. Cyrus had given him three thousand daries * for a prophecy that had come true, and he wanted to get home with the spoil. So he was altogether against the idea of a **colony.** When he had sacrificed he could not say that the omens were altogether against the scheme; for I knew nearly as much about the matter as he did. What he did **say** was that there were indications of a conspiracy against me. And he took good care to make them true, for he **spread** about reports **of** what I was going to do **that**

---

* About $15,000.

turned the army against me. So the scheme came to nothing.

"This did one good thing, however, for it helped us on our way home. Trapezus and the other colonies in the east of the Euxine did not relish the idea of a new Greek city which might turn out to be a formidable rival. So they offered to transport the army to the Hellespont and to furnish pay from the first new moon after the departure. This seemed a good offer, and I recommended the soldiers to close with it, and said that I gave up my scheme. 'Only,' I said, 'let us all keep together and let any one who leaves us be counted a malefactor.' For I did not choose that my friend the soothsayer should get the better of it.

"Well, we set sail; our first halt was at Sinope, which is roughly speaking, about halfway between Trapezus and Byzantium. Then the army wanted to make me commander-in-chief. Happily the omen was against it, and I was able to decline. We started again, and got to Heraclea. The people were very hospitable; but some scoundrels in the army wanted to lay a contribution upon the city. Chiriso-phus, the Spartan—I should have told you that on my re-fusal the army gave him the chief command—refused to have anything to do with such an abominable business, and I backed him up. Of course the city shut its gates against us, and we got nothing at all. After this the army broke up into three. One of the divisions, made up of Arcadians and Achaeans, the most unscrupulous and greedy of the whole number, got into serious trouble when they were trying to plunder the country, and I had to rescue them, for two thousand men had stuck to me when the army was thus broken up. Then **the** other division under Chirisophus **were** nearly as badly off, **and I** had to get them out of a **scrape.** After this they came together again, and it was made a matter of death for anyone to propose a separation.

" It was well we did, for everyone seemed bent on treating us as villanously as possible. Would you believe that the Spartan governor of Byzantium actually sold as slaves four hundred soldiers who had found their way into the city? It is true that they were stragglers and had no business there ; but it was an abominable act. **At** last, one Seuthes, who had been chief of the Odrysians, **and deposed by** a usurper, **offered to take the whole army into his pay, if** we would help him to recover his dominions. Every **man** was to receive a stater * per month, **the** captains twice, and the generals four times as much. Also he offered lands, oxen to plough it **with, and a city with** walls. In fact the colony scheme seemed likely to be carried out after all. To me he **was** very munificent in his promises. **I was to** have one of his daughters to wife and a city of my **own."**

" **What** did you say to that? " said Callias.

" Well, the only one of these things that Seuthes really had in his possession was the daughter. **I saw** the young **lady,** handsome I will allow, **and tall ;** but, oh, **such a** savage ! As for the money, and **the land, and** the oxen, and the towns, walled and unwalled, we had to get them for him and then have our portion back. However, it seemed to me the best thing for the army to do, and I advised the men to that effect, and they **agreed,** only it was provided that we **were never to march more than** seven days' journey from

* Something less than $6.

the seacoast.   We had all had enough of marches up the country.   Then Seuthes gave us a feast by way of striking the bargain.

"It was a wonderful scene, and some day I must tell you all about it.   But I must own that for a time I felt as uncomfortable as ever I did in my life.   After dinner when the bowl had passed round two or three times, in came a Thracian leading a white horse.   He took the bowl from the cup-bearer, and said, 'Here is a health to thee, King Seuthes. Let me give you this horse.   Mounted on him thou shalt take whom thou wilt, and when thou retirest from the battle thou shalt dread no pursuer.'   Then another gave a slave, and another some robes for the Queen, and a fourth a silver saucer and a finely embroidered carpet.   All the while I was sitting in an agony, for I was in the place of honor, and had nothing to offer.   However 'our lady of Athens,' who is the inspirer of clever devices, and, it may be Father Bacchus also, for I had drained two or three cups, helped me out of my difficulty.   When the cup-bearer handed me the goblet, I rose and said, 'King Seuthes, I present you with myself and these my trusty comrades.   With their help you will recover the lands that were your forefathers' and gain many new lands with them.   Nor shall you win lands only, but horses many, and men many, and fair women also.' Up got the King, at this, and we drained the cup together.

"Seuthes was not going to let the grass grow under his feet. When we left the banqueting tent—this was at sunset because we wanted to set the guards about our camp—the King, who, for all his potations, was as sober as a water-drinker, sent for the generals and said, 'My neighbors have not yet heard of this alliance of ours. Let us go and take them by surprise.' And so we did. We went that night and brought back booty enough to pay for our day's pay, I warrant you.

"Well, we went on fighting for Seuthes for two months till we had conquered the whole countryside for him. Then the conquered tribes flocked to him—give a Thracian plenty to eat and drink and good pay and he will fight in any quarrel—till he did not want any more. That perhaps was not to be wondered at, but, like the mean hound that he was, he tried to get out of paying us.

"Just at this moment when I thought that we should have to settle with the sword for judge, Sparta declared war against the Persians and wanted all the men she could get. So Thuisbron, their commander-in-chief, came over and engaged the men at the same rate of pay that Seuthes was giving or rather promising. We never got anything but a wretched fragment from the King.

"By this time I had had about enough of campaigning of this fashion. Not a drachma had I made. In fact I was poorer than when I set out. I had even to sell my favorite horse, but Thuisbron bought it back for me.

"Just at the last I had a stroke of luck. That is another story I must tell you some day. But fortunately we took prisoners a Persian noble with his wife and children, his horses and cattle and all that he had. The next day I left the army, but before I went they gave me the pick of the beasts of all kinds. It was a handsome present, I can tell you."

"So, on the whole," said Callias, "you came pretty well out of the business. You returned at least not poorer than you went, you have won for yourself a name which those who **come after us will** not, I take it, forget, and you helped, **at least, to** save the lives of many Greeks from perishing shamefully by the hands of the barbarians. **Are you** not content?"

"Yes," replied Xenophon, "**all** the **more content** on account of one thing you have not mentioned. **For this indeed** pleases me in the matter that **we Greeks have now** found a way **by which we may** both go to the capital of the Persians and return therefrom. Verily, I sometimes wish we had not been so eager to retreat, but had stopped and made ourselves masters **of** the country of our enemies. Per**haps** we were not strong enough ; but, if I can see so far into the future, some one will **do** this hereafter, **and** Greece will be avenged of all **that she has suffered at** the hands of the barbarians."

"**The Master will be glad,**" Callias went on after a pause.

The "Master" **of course was** Socrates. **Xenophon looked at** the young man with some surprise.

"You seem very confident on this point. He indeed was always somewhat doubtful, and certainly there are **great** difficulties when **you** come **to look into it a little more closely.**"

" I really do not know what you mean," **answered Callias ;** "**you have seen him I suppose, for** you have been in Athens several days and know what he **thinks.**"

For a few moments Xenophon stared at the speaker in utter perplexity. Then a light broke in upon **him.** "What," he cried, " you do not know? You have not heard?"

"Know **what? Have heard what? You speak in riddles.**"

"That he is dead."

The young man covered his face with his hands. After a few minutes he recovered calmness enough to speak. "No, indeed, I did not know it. I never thought of such a **thing**. He seemed so full of life **and** vigor. Yet he must have been an old man, **not** far from seventy I suppose, **for** he **was** more than forty at Delium.*　Tell me of what did he die?"

"They killed him."

"Killed him! Who killed him?"

"The people of Athens."

* The battle of Delium (between the Bœotians and the Athenians) was fought in 424. The precise age of Socrates at the time of his death was seventy.

CHAPTER XXVIII.

THE STORY OF THE TRIAL.

IT is not too much to say that the young man was prostrated by the news which he had just heard, for the blow fell upon him with a suddenness that seemed to increase the pain tenfold. He had not been indeed on the same intimate terms of friendship with the great philosopher as the older disciples, Crito, Simmias, Cebes, Phaedo and others had been. But he had regarded him with an affection and admiration that was nothing less than enthusiastic; and he had looked forward to getting his advice about the future conduct of his life with a hopeful eagerness that made disappointment very bitter. To find himself in Athens after all the vicissitudes of fortune through which he had passed, and to learn that the man without whom Athens scarcely seemed itself, was lost to him forever, was a terrible shock. Xenophon's sorrow had not been less keen, but he had been prepared for his loss by at least a few days' previous knowledge. The news had reached him while he was on his way, and the first shock was over when he landed. But there had been nothing to break the news to Callias. He felt as a son might feel who returns home after a long absence in full expectation of a father's greeting, and finds himself an orphan.

So overpowered was the young man that he felt solitude to be absolutely necessary for a time.

"Let me talk to you about it another day," he said to Xenophon, "at present I am not master of myself."

Xenophon clasped his friend's hand with a warm and sympathetic pressure. "I understand," he said. "Yet, I think it will comfort you when you hear how he bore himself at the last and what he said. Come to me to-morrow; Hippocles will tell you where I live."

Early the next morning, Callias presented himself at Xenophon's house, a modest little dwelling, not far from the garden of Academus. He found him in the company of some friends, most of whom were more or less known to the young man as having been members of the circle which had been accustomed to listen to the teaching of the great master. Crito, Menexenus and Æschines, and the two Thebans, Cebes and Simmias, were among the number; and there were others whom he did not recognize. He was greeted with kindness and even distinction. His host had evidently been giving a favorable account of him to the company.

"I thought it best," Xenophon went on to explain, "to ask some of those who were actually present when these things happened, to meet you. I myself, as you know, was not here; and it is well that you should hear a story so important from eye-witnesses, men who saw his demeanor with their own eyes, and heard his words with their own ears."

"I thank you," said Callias. "But tell me first how it was that such things came to pass. It seems incredible to me. I have heard that here and there a man has been found so monstrously wicked that he could kill his own father, though Solon thought it so impossible a crime that he would impose no penalty on it. But that a whole people should be stricken with such madness of wickedness seems to pass all imagination or belief."

"Ah! you do not understand," said Simmias; "I am a foreigner you know; and those who look at things from outside often see more of them than they who are within. I had long thought that Socrates was making many enemies in Athens. And verily if he had said such things in my own city, as he said here, I doubt whether he had been suffered to live so long."

"But he always spoke true things," said the young man, "and things that were to the real profit of his hearers."

"Just so," replied Simmias, "but that they were true and profitable did not make them pleasant, or the speaker of them welcome. What think you would happen to a school-master if his pupils whom he daily corrects and disciplines, sometimes with hard tasks and sometimes with blows, were permitted to judge him, or to a physician if the children whom he seeks to cure of their ailments with nauseous drugs, or, it may be, with the knife or cautery, had him in their power?"

"Truly, it might fare ill with him," Callias confessed, thinking to himself of certain angry thoughts that in his own boyhood he had cherished against his own teacher and doctor.

"Yes," said Crito, "Simmias is right, nor did this matter escape the notice of us Athenians, though we did not perceive it so plainly. **You,** I know, have been much absent from Athens since you grew to manhood, yet you must have **seen** something of this. You were here, for example, when the admirals were condemned after the battle at Arginusæ. Is it not so?"

"I **was** here," said **Callias.**

"And you know how Socrates **set** himself against the will of the people, refusing to put to the vote **a** proposal which he believed to be unconstitutional. **Well,** he suffered nothing at that time, because their will prevailed in spite of him. Yet we saw that there were many who remembered **this against** him, and only waited for the opportunity of avenging themselves upon **him.** Nor was he less constant in opposing the few, **when** he believed them to be acting wrongfully, than in opposing **the many.** Listen now, to **what** he did and said **in the days of** the Thirty. Were you in Athens at that time?"

"No," replied Callias, "I left the city, or rather was carried away from it—" **at** this there was a general laugh, most of the company having heard of the curious story of his abduction—"after the murder **of the** Generals, and did not set foot in it till the other day."

"But you know what manner of men these Thirty were."

" Yes, **I know.**"

"Well, **among other vile things** that they did was this, that they put to death many excellent men whom **they conceived to be** enemies to themselves. Then Socrates, **in that free way of his, said, 'If a** herdsman were so to manage **his** herd that the cattle became fewer and not more, men would consider him a **bad** herdsman. **Still** more would they consider him to be a bad ruler of a city who should so manage it that the citizens became not more but less numerous.' This being reported to Critias, who was a chief among the Thirty, he sent for Socrates, and said to him, 'There is a law that no man shall teach or use the art of words.' Socrates said, 'Mean you by this, the art of words rightly spoken or the art of words wrongly spoken?' On this, one Charicles, who was a colleague of Critias, and was standing by him, broke in violently: 'Since, Socrates, you find it so hard to understand an altogether easy thing, take this as a plain rule, that you are not to talk with young men at all.' 'Truly I desire to obey the law,' said Socrates; 'tell me then what you mean by young men. How young? Up to what age?' Charicles said, 'Up to thirty, at which age men are able to take part in affairs of the State.' 'But,' said Socrates, 'if I desire to buy a thing of a man who is under thirty, is it permitted me to ask what it costs?' 'Yes,' said Charicles, 'you may say so much.' 'And if a man under thirty asks me where Critias lives or Charicles lives, may I answer him?' 'Yes, you may answer such questions,' said Charicles. Then Critias broke in, 'But you must not talk about blacksmiths and coppersmiths and tanners; and indeed you have worn these themes pretty well threadbare by this time.' 'Nor about righteousness and wickedness and such things, I suppose,' said Socrates. 'No, indeed, nor about herdsmen. If you speak of herdsmen and of the herd being diminished, take care that it be not diminished by one more, even by you.'"

Callias listened with delight. "Oh, how like him!" he cried.

"Yes,"replied **Crito,** "like him indeed, and truly **admira-ble.** But such things do not please those to whom they are **spoken,** especially do not please men in power. Then consider the number of empty-headed, ignorant fellows whose vanity and conceit he exposed every **day** by his pitiless questioning. **There** was not a pretentious fool in Athens whom he had not at some time or other held up to ridicule."

"And they deserved it richly," said Callias.

"Yes," replied the other, "but I have never found that a **man liked** punishment more because he knew that he **deserved it.** So you **see that** the city was full of his enemies. And there were some **honest** men who really believed that he did harm by his teaching. What with knaves whom he opposed with all his might, and fools whom he exposed, and right-minded, wrong-headed men whom he could not help offending, there was **a very** formidable host arrayed against him."

"I see," said Callias. "But they must have had some pretext, they could not put any of the things you have been speaking about into a formal charge. Tell me, what did they accuse him of?"

"**Oh, it was** the old story, treason and blasphemy. Men **who would** have sold their country for a quarter of a talent, **men who** believe in **no other gods than** their own lusts, were loud in proclaiming that Socrates had ruined the State, and was teaching the young not to worship the gods."

"Good heavens!" cried Callias, "how dared they utter **such lies?** A better patriot, a truer worshipper of the gods **never lived.**"

"**You** are right ; **yet,** these were the charges against him, these and other things equally absurd, as that he taught the young to despise their fathers and to think meanly of all their relatives and friends, as if he himself were the only friend that was worth having ; that he perverted words from Homer and the old poets to a bad sense, making them mean that no work was disgraceful so that it brought in gain, and that it was lawful for kings and nobles to beat the common people *—these were the charges that they brought against him. And then they added the accusation that Critias and Alcibiades who had done great harm to Athens had both been disciples of his."

"But tell me," said Callias, "how did these liars and villains proceed? And first, who were they? Who took the lead?"

"One Meletus was the chief."

"What! The foolish poet whom every one laughs at?"

"Yes, the very same. He represented the poets. There was one Lycon, of whom, I suppose, you never heard, who represented the public speakers, and Anytus, one of those who came back with Thrasybulus. He had been badly treated, it is true, banished without any good reason, but only a madman could have supposed that Socrates had had anything to do with it. These three brought the indictment. It was in these words :—

---

* The lines from Hesiod :
  " No labor mars an honest name ;
   'Tis only idleness is shame,"
was one instance (quoted by Xenophon in the Recollections of Socrates). Another (from the same source) is the story of how Ulysses stayed the Greeks from hurrying to their ships and leaving the siege of Troy. The common men he struck, but if he found a chief in the crowd he only remonstrated with him,
  " But if he saw perchance, some common man
  Blinded with panic, clamorous of tongue,
  With staff he smote him, adding blow to blame."

" 'Socrates is guilty of a crime. He does not acknowledge the gods whom the State acknowledges, and he introduces other and new gods. He is also guilty of corrupting the youth. The penalty—death.' "

"But such charges hardly needed a defence. Is it possible that a number of Athenian judges found a verdict of guilty?"

"It was so indeed," said Crito, "and I am not sure that you will be altogether surprised when you hear what the accused said in his own defence. I am an old man now, and have watched the courts now for many years; and I have seen not a few men who might have escaped but for what they said in their own behalf. Now I can't tell you all that Socrates said, or even the greater part of it. Our friend Plato is going to set it forth regularly in a book that he is writing. But I can tell you enough to make you see what I mean.

"After he had dealt with various other matters—those calumnies for instance, that Aristophanes set afloat about him now more than thirty years ago—he went on: 'Some years ago, men of Athens, a certain Chaerephon—you know him; some of you went into exile along with him—having been my companion from my youth up, ventured to go to Delphi, and to propose this question to the god: "Is there any man wiser than Socrates?" The Pythia † made reply, "There is none wiser than he." When I heard this I said to myself, what can the god mean? He cannot tell a lie, yet I am not conscious to myself of possessing any kind of wisdom. So at last I devised this plan. I went to one of the men who are reckoned wise, thinking thus to test the

† The priestess of Apollo at Delphi.

oracle, so that I might say, here at least is one that is wiser than I. Now when I came to examine this man—he was one of our statesmen, men of Athens,—I found that though he was accounted wise by many and especially by himself, he was not wise in reality. But in vain I tried to convince him, and I even became odious to him and to many others who were present and admired him. Then I thought to myself, I am at least wiser than this man, for he not knowing, thinks that he knows, while I at least know that I do not know. After this, I went to the poets, tragic, lyrical, and others, and taking to them poems which they had written, asked of them what they meant thereby. And I found that almost always those that had not written these things knew better what they meant than the authors. So I concluded that these also were not wise. And at last I went to the artisans, knowing that they were acquainted with many things of which I knew nothing. And this, indeed, I found to be the case. But I also found that, because they had mastered their own art, each thought himself very wise in other things, things, too, of the greatest importance, and that this self-conceit spoilt their wisdom. These also seemed to be less wise than myself. But all the time that I was doing this I knew that I was making myself hateful to many, yet, because I was bound to obey the god as best I could, I did not desist.

" 'It is true also that many young men hearing me thus questioning others have found delight in this employment and have learnt to imitate me. And they have obtained this result : they have found many persons who think that they know much but in reality know nothing. But

they who are thus discovered are irritated, not so much against their questioners, but against me whom they suppose to have taught them this habit. Hence comes this fable of a certain wicked Socrates who is said to corrupt the young **men.**

"'Nevertheless, O men of Athens, if you this day release **me, I shall not therefore cease** to do that which, as **I con-**ceive, the god commands. **I** shall go about the city seeking wisdom ; nor shall I cease to say to such **as** come in **my way, My friend, can you, being a citizen of** Athens, the most famous city of Greece, help being ashamed if you make riches or rank your highest aim, and care not for that which is indeed the greatest good? This shall I still do to young **or old,** for it is this that the god orders me to do!'"

Crito paused **in his story.**

"Magnificent!" **cried Callias,** "but how **did** the judges take it? It was a downright defiance of them."

"Certainly it **was, and** so they thought it. There was a tremendous uproar. When the noise had ceased, he began again :—'Do not clamor against me, men of Athens, but hear me patiently ; 'tis indeed for **your own** good that you should. For be assured that putting me to death, you will harm yourselves rather than **me.** For, having rid your-**selves** of me, you will **not easily find** any one who will do **for you the office that** I have done, which has been, I take it, that **of a rider upon a** horse of good breed, indeed, **and** strong, but needing the spur. Such a rider have I been to **the city,** sitting close **and** exciting you continually by per-**suasion and reproach.** You will not easily find another like **me ; and** if you **are** angry with me, yet remember that

persons awakened out of sleep are angry with the man who
rouses them, though it may be to the saving of their lives.
And remember this too: what I have done, I have done
without pay; no one can bring up this against me that I
have done anything for gain. If you ask a proof, look at
my poverty—that is proof enough.

"'And if any one ask me why I go about meddling
with every body and giving them advice, and yet never
come forward and give any advice about matters of state, I
make him this answer: There is a voice within me, of
which Meletus idly speaks as if it were another god, which
never indeed urges me to do anything, but often warns me
against doing this or that. This same voice has often
warned me against taking part in public affairs, and rightly
so indeed, for be assured that if I had so taken part, I should
long ago have perished. And do not be offended if I tell you
the truth. No man can be safe who opposes things wrong
and illegal that are done by the people. If he would live,
even but for a short time, he must keep to a private station.

"'Do you not remember, men of Athens, how when you
had to judge the admirals that did not save the shipwrecked
men at Arginusæ, I would not put the motion to the vote?
For though I had never held any public office I was in the
Senate, and it so chanced that my tribe that day had the
presidency. You chose to judge all the men together, acting wrongfully, as you afterward acknowledged. And I
alone of all the presidents opposed this thing, and would
not yield, no not when the orators denounced me, and
would have joined me with the accused. This was in the
time of the democracy.

"'**And** afterwards when the democracy was overthrown, and the oligarchy was in power, what happened? Did not the Thirty send for me along with four others to their council-chamber, and bid us fetch Leon of Salamis, that he might be put to death. This they did, after their habit, seeking **to** involve **as** many as possible in their wicked deeds. Then also I showed not in words only, but in deeds that I cared not one jot for death. For in the chamber I declared **that I** would not do this thing, and when we had gone out, the other four indeed went to Salamis, and fetched Leon, but I went to my own home. Doubtless I should **have died** for this act, but that the Thirty were overthrown **soon** afterward.

"'And what I have done publicly that I have privately also. Never have I conceded anything that was wrong to **any man.** But if any man would hear what I said I never grudged him the opportunity. I have offered myself **to** rich and poor, whether they would question me themselves **or** answer my questions, nor have I spoken for pay, **nor been** silent because I was not paid, nor have I ever said aught to any man that I have not said to all.

"'So much, men of Athens, might suffice for my defence, but if any of you, remembering that other men when accused have brought their children before you seeking to rouse compassion, are angry with me because I have not so done, let him listen to me. I, too, have family ties.

"'From no gnarled oak **I** sprang, or flinty rock, as Homer has it, but am born of man. Three sons I have; two of them are children, one an infant. Should I then bring them before you, and seek to move your pity by the sight of them? Not so. I have seen many thus demeaning themselves, as if, forsooth, you acquitting them, they would escape death altogether ; but such behavior would ill befit those who seek to follow after virtue and honor. Nor is such behavior only unseemly ; it is wrong. For we are bound to convince a judge, not to persuade him, and he is set in his place not to give justice as a favor, but because it is justice. Verily, if I should have to persuade you to act against your oaths I should be condemning myself of the very charge that Meletus has brought against me, for I should act as if I did not believe that the gods by whom ye have sworn to do right are gods at all. Far be it from me so to act. I believe in the gods more than my accusers believe ; and I leave it to these gods and to you to judge concerning me as it may be best for you and for me.' "

" No man," said Cebes, " could have spoken better ; but it was not the speech that would please or conciliate."

" And what was the result?" asked Callias.

" After all there was only a majority of *six* against him ; two hundred and eighty-one against two hundred and seventy-five were the numbers. Then came the question of the sentence. The prosecutor had demanded the penalty of death. 'Socrates,' said the president of the court, 'what penalty do you yourself propose?' * 'You ask me,' said Socrates, ' what penalty I myself propose. What then do I deserve, I who have not sought to make money, or to hold

---

* It was the curious custom in the Athenian courts of criminal justice that the accused, if found guilty, was required to name a counter penalty to that proposed by the prosecutor. The prosecutor, as has been seen, had proposed death. Socrates, under the circumstances, could hardly have proposed anything less than banishment, if he had any wish that it should be accepted by the court.

office in the state, **or to** command soldiers and ships, who have not even attended to my own affairs, but have sought to do to others what I thought to be their highest good? What should be done to me for being such a man? Surely something good, something suitable to one who is **your** benefactor, and who requires leisure that he may spend it **in** giving you good advice. There is nothing, I conceive, more suitable than that I should be maintained at the public expense in the Town Hall, with those **who have done great** services to the State. Surely I deserve such a reward far **more than** he who has won a chariot **race at** the Olympic **games;** for he only makes you think yourselves fortunate, whereas I teach you to be happy.'

" Of course there was a loud murmur of disapprobation at this. Even some of those who had voted for acquittal were vexed at language so bold.

" Socrates began again : ' You think that I show too much **pride when I** talk in this fashion. But it is not so. Let me show **you what** I mean. As to the penalty which the accuser demands, I cannot say whether **it** be good or evil; but the other things which I might **propose in** its stead I **know** to be evils—imprisonment, **or a fine** with imprisonment till it be paid, or exile, which **last,** indeed, you might accept. But **if you cannot endure my** ways, O men of **Athens, think you that** others **would** endure them? And **what a** life for a **man of my** age to lead, this wandering **from city to city !** But if anyone should say, Why, O Socrates, will **you** not depart **to** some other city, and there live quietly, **and hold your tongue?** I answer, To do this would **be** to disobey **the god, and I cannot do it.** And indeed to

live without talking and questioning **about** such matters **is**
not to live at all.   **But I have** not yet named the penalty.
If I had money I should propose some fine which I could
pay ; but I have none, except indeed you are willing to impose upon me some small fine, for I think that I could
raise a pound of silver.   At this there was another growl
from the judges ; and some of us who were standing by
Socrates caught him by the robe, **and** whispered to him.
After a pause, he said, 'Some **of** my friends, **Crito and**
Plato and Apollodorus, advise me to propose a fine of thirty
minas † and offer to be security.   So I propose that sum.'

"Of course **the result** was certain. **A** majority much
larger than before voted for the death penalty. Then the
condemned man spoke for the last time. You will be able
to read for yourself the very words that he said. **I** can now
give you only **an idea** of the end of his **speech.** He had
told the judges, speaking especially to those who had voted
for his acquittal, that the voice that was wont to warn him
had never hindered him in the course of his speech, though
it was **not** the speech that he should have made if he had
wanted to save his **life.** From this he argued that he and
they had reason **to** believe that death was **a good** thing.
' Either,' he said, ' the dead are nothing and feel nothing, or
they remove hence to some other place. What can be better
than to feel nothing ? **What days or** nights in all our lives
are better than those nights in which we sleep soundly
without even a dream? But if the common belief is true,
and we pass in death **to that** place wherein are all who have
ever died, what greater good can there be than this ? If one

† Rather more than $600.

passes from those who are called judges here to those who really judge and administer true justice, **to** Æacus and Minos and Rhadamanthus, is this a change to be lamented? What would not any one of you give to join the company of Homer and Orpheus and Hesiod? or talk with those who led that great army of Greeks to Troy, or with any of the many thousands of good men and women that have lived upon the earth? **Verily, I** would die many times if I could **only** hope to **do this. And** now it is time'—for these were his **very** last words of all—'that we should separate. I go to **die, you** remain to live; but which of **us is** going the better **way,** only the gods know.'"

There was a deep silence in **the room** after **Crito had** finished speaking. It was broken **at last** by Callias, who asked, "How long since was that?"

"Nearly two months," said Simmias, "but by a strange chance Socrates was not put **to** death for nearly **a month** after his condemnation. It so happened that **the Sacred** Ship started **for** Delos just at the time, and during its voyage —in fact from the moment that **the priest** fastens the chaplet on the stern—no man can **be put to death.** For thirty days then he was kept **in prison. There we** were permitted to visit **him, and there we heard** many things **that are** well worth being remembered."

"**I want to hear** everything," cried Callias.

"**You shall in good time,**" said **Crito.** "**Come to my house** to-morrow and I will put **you in the way of your** getting what you want."

"**But** you **ought to hear,**" cried Apollodorus, who had hitherto taken **no part** in the **conversation,** "what the teacher said to me, though, indeed, it shows no great wisdom in me that he had occasion to say it. ' O Socrates,' I said, when I saw him turning away from the place where he had stood before his judges—and nothing could be more cheerful than his look—' O Socrates, this indeed is the hardest thing to bear that you should have been condemned unjustly.' 'Nay, not so, my friend,' he answered, 'would the matter have been more tolerable if I had been condemned justly?' "

There was a general laugh. "That is true," said Crito, "but certainly as far as Athens is concerned, it was a more shameful thing."

CHAPTER XXIX.

CALLIAS, as may be supposed, did not fail to keep his appointment with the utmost punctuality. He found at Crito's house very nearly the same company that had been assembled the day before at Xenophon's. After the usual greetings had been interchanged, the host said, "I propose, if it is agreeable to you all, to hold the conversation which we are to have to-day at the house of our friend Plato. He has written to invite us, not because he can himself see us, for he is not sufficiently recovered from his late illness, but because we shall thus be able to talk with his friend Phaedo; for as all know there is no more fitting person than Phaedo to tell our young friend Callias the things that he desires to hear. For though we were all present, Xenophon only excepted, on that day when the Master left us, having given us his last instructions, yet there is no one who so well remembers and is so well able to describe all that was then said or done. I propose, therefore, that we transfer ourselves to his house."

The proposition met with general assent and the party set out.

Crito naturally took charge of Callias as being his special

guest. As the two were walking, the young man said, "Tell me, Crito, if it is not unpleasing to you, whether in the thirty days during which the Master was held in prison, any efforts were made to **save his life?**"

"I am glad," said Crito, "that you have asked me that question privately and not before others, for, indeed, this is a matter which has caused me no little amount of trouble and shame. Some people blame me **because, they** say, though a rich man I did not bribe the jailer of the prison in which Socrates was confined, and thus enable him to escape. I am blameable, indeed, but for an exactly opposite reason. I did bribe the man—this **of course is in** absolute confidence between you and me—and in this, as the Master showed me, I was wrong. Indeed I never received from him **so severe** a rebuke as I did concerning this matter. But let me tell **you** what happened. I had arranged everything. The jailer was to let him escape. **There** were people ready **to** carry him out of the country. **I** went to him early in the morning of the **day** when the ship was expected to **return.** I told him what I had done. **I made light of the money** that the affair was to cost. I **could well afford it, I said,** and if I could not there were others **ready to** contribute. And then I attacked him, **it was** an impudent thing **to do, but I** felt as if I could do anything that we **should not lose** him. I told him that it was wrong of him to do his best to let his enemies get their way. **I said to** him, 'Thus acting **you** desert your children, **whom you** might bring up and educate. But if you die you **will leave them** orphans and friendless. Either you ought not to have children or you ought to take some trouble **about them.** Surely this does not become one who has made virtue his study throughout his life. And remember what a disgrace will fall upon us, for it will certainly be said that we did not do our best to save your life.'

"**Well, I** cannot tell you now a tenth part of what he said. I have it all written down at home, but I may say what you will easily believe that I was as helpless in his hands as the veriest pretender whom he has ever cross-examined. **I** know that he ended by making me thoroughly ashamed **of** myself. One of his chief arguments was this :

" 'Suppose, Crito, that as I was in the act of escaping, the State itself were to say to me : Are you not seeking to destroy **by** so acting the laws of the State itself? Is not that State already dissolved wherein public sentences are set aside by private persons? What should I answer to such questions? And if the laws were to say, What complaint have you got to make against us that you seek to destroy us? Do you not owe your being to us, seeing that your father and mother married according to our ordering? Have we not given you nurture, education, all the good things that **you** possess as being an Athenian? **Have you** not acknowledged us by living in the city, by having children in it? **And** if they were further to say, Verily, he who acts in this **way in** which you are about to act is **a** corrupter of youth— what could I answer?

" ' And tell me, Crito,' **he went** on, ' whither would you have me betake myself? Not surely to any well-ordered city seeing that I had shown myself the enemy of such order, but rather to some abode of riot, which would indeed ill become one who had professed to be a lover of virtue and righteousnesss.   And as for my children, how shall I benefit them?   By taking them elsewhere and bringing them up not as citizens of Athens, but as citizens of some other State which **I** myself here have judged inferior, seeing that all my life long I have deliberately preferred Athens to it?' Verily, Callias, when he said this, I had no answer.   **But** here **we** are at Phaedo's house.''

Callias was not a little surprised when he was introduced to the man whom he had been brought to see.   Phaedo was **a man much** younger than himself; indeed he had scarcely completed his eighteenth year.   His appearance was singularly attractive, and his manners had all the grace and ease of a well-born and well-bred **man.**   That he was not an Athenian was evident from his speech, which was somewhat tinged with a Doric accent.   Altogether Callias was at a loss to think who or what he could be, and how he came to be regarded as the best interpreter of the Master's last words.   An opportunity, however, arrived for enlightening him. After a few minutes' conversation, a slave appeared with a message for the master of the **house.**   Plato who had been compelled to absent **himself from the** last interview **with** Socrates, as **has been said, was** still so unwell **that his** physician forbade **the excitement of** seeing visitors.   **He** now sent for Phaedo to **entrust him with a** message **of** apology for his fellow disciples whom **he was** unable **to** entertain, and partly to set him free **to act the part of host** in his stead.

Crito seized **the** opportunity **of** his temporary absence from the room to give some particulars about him. ''He comes of a very good family in Elis, and was taken prisoner about this time last year when Athens and Sparta were allies and acting against that country. He was sold in the slave market here, and I cannot tell the cruelties that he endured from the wretch who bought him. Somehow he heard of Socrates, ran away from his owner and begged for the Master's protection. Of course, the only thing was to buy him, and equally of course, Socrates was wholly unable to do this. But the Master, if he had no wealth of his own, happily had wealthy friends. He went to Plato and, by great good luck, Plato had a very powerful hold over the poor fellow's owner; the man owed him a large sum of money, the interest of which was overdue. He was purchased, and at once set free. Plato found that he had been remarkably well educated and that he showed an extraordinary aptitude for philosophy. The lad's devotion to Socrates was unbounded. He never lost a chance of being near him; he was present of course at the last day, and he watched and listened with an intense earnestness that seemed to engrave everything on his mind as one engraves letters upon marble or bronze. But, see, he is coming back. Now you will understand why I have brought you to see him."

The young man, at this moment, returned to the room.

"Tell me, Phaedo," said Crito, "what you saw and heard on the last day of the Master's life. My friend Callias here, who has just come back from campaigning against the Great King, desires to hear it from you, and, indeed, though we all were present on that day, you seem to remember it more accurately than any."

"I will do my best," said the youth modestly. "I do not

know," he went on, addressing himself especially to Callias, "whether you will wholly understand me when I say that I did not feel compassion as one might feel for one who was dying—he was so calm and so happy. Neither, on the other hand, did I feel the pleasure that commonly followed from his discourses, for I knew that he would soon cease to be."

"It was just so with all of us," said Crito, "but go on."

"We had been to visit Socrates daily through the time of his imprisonment, assembling very early in the morning, and waiting till the doors of the prison were opened, and so we did on this day, only earlier than usual, because we knew that the Sacred Ship had arrived the evening before. The jailer came out. 'You must wait, gentlemen,' he said, 'the Eleven * are with him. They are taking off his chains, and are telling him that he must die to-day.' After a little while the man came out again, and said that we might go in. When we went in, we found Socrates sitting on the side of his bed, and his wife, Xanthippe, near him, holding one of his children in her arms. As soon as she saw us, she began to lament and say, 'O Socrates, here are your friends come to see you for the last time.' Then Socrates, looking at her, said to Crito, 'Let some one take her home.' So one of Crito's servants led her away. After a while, for of course I must leave out many things, the Master said, "I have a message for Evenus, who seeks to know, I am told, why I have taken to writing verses in prison. Tell him that a god appeared to me in a dream and told me to cultivate the

* The Eleven were the executioners of the law rather taking the place of the sheriff and the under-sheriff than that of the hangman. The vagueness of its name is an interesting example of the Greek distaste for naming anything terrible.

muses. Tell him also that if he is wise he will follow me as speedily as possible, for it seems that the Athenians **command** that I depart to-day.'

"'But, Socrates,' said Simmias, 'this is a strange piece of advice, and one which Evenus is not likely to take.'

"'Why so,' said Socrates, 'is he not a philosopher? Surely he should be ready to go the road which I am going. **Only** he must not kill himself.' **'Why** do you **say this?' said** Cebes.

"You will correct me," said **Phaedo, turning to the company,** "if I misrepresent anything that you said."

"Speak on without fear," said Simmias, **"you** seem to have the memory of all the muses."

Phaedo resumed, "Socrates said, 'You ask me why a man may not kill himself? Well, **there is** first this reason that we are as sentinels set at a post, which we must not leave until we are bidden; then **again if** men be servants of the gods, as seems likely, how can they withdraw from this service without leave? Would you not be angry if one of your servants were to do it?'

"'True,' said Cebes, "but if we are **the** servants **of** the gods, and therefore in the best guardianship, should we not be sorry to quit it? If so, is it not for **the foolish to** desire death and for the wise to regret it?' **'You** are right,' replied the Master, 'and if I did not expect when I depart hence to go to the realms of **the** wise and good gods and to the company of righteous men, I should indeed grieve at death. And that I am right **in so** expecting let me now seek to prove to you, for what better could I do on this the last day of my life? But stay; Crito wishes **to say** something. What is it?' **Crito said, 'He who** has to give **the** poison says that you must talk as little **as possible, for that** if a man so excites **himself he** has to drink sometimes two **potions or even** three.' 'Let him take **his course,'** said the master, 'and prepare what he thinks **needful. And now to the** matter in hand. Death, then, is nothing **but** a separation of the soul from the body. **That you** concede. And you concede further that a philosopher should care little for the things of **the body,** and that when he is most free from the body, then he sees most clearly the highest and best things, **perceiving,** for instance, right and justice **and honor and goodness,** veritable things all of them, but **such as cannot be discerned with the eyes or** handled with the hands. **For** the body with its **desires** and **wants** hinders us, and makes us waste our time on the things that it covets, so that we have neither time nor **temper for** wisdom. If then we **are ever to** reach **absolute Truth we must get rid of** the hindrance. While we live we do this to the best of our ability, and he is the **wisest** man **and best philosopher** who does **it** most completely; **but wholly we cannot do** it, till the **god** shall liberate **us from the control of** this companion. And this is done **by Death, which is the** complete **separa**tion of soul and body. Shall then the philosopher, **who has** all his life been striving for such **partial separation as may** be possible, complain when the gods send him this separation that is complete? And this is my defence, my friends, for **holding it to be** a good thing to die.' 'Yes,' replied Cebes, **'but many fear that when** the **soul** is thus parted from the body, it may **be now**here, being dissipated like a breath or a puff of smoke when the body with which it has been united dies.' 'You desire, then,' said Socrates, 'that I should prove to you that the soul does not perish when it is thus separated from the body?' 'Yes,' we all said, 'that is what we all wish.' 'First then,' he went on, 'is it not true that every thing implies that which is opposite to it, as Right implies Wrong, and Fair implies Foul, and *to sleep* is the opposite of *to wake?* If so does not *to die* imply its opposite *to live again?*

"'Secondly, is it not true that the highest part of our knowledge is a remembering again? For there are things which we know not through our senses. How then do we know them? Surely because we had this knowledge of them at some previous time.'

"'But,' said Cebes, 'may it not be true that the soul has been made beforehand to enter the body; and having entered it lives therein, and yet perishes when its dwelling is dissolved?'

"'Being of a frail nature, I suppose,' said the Master, 'it's all to be blown away by the wind, so that a man should be especially afraid to die on a stormy day.'

"At this we all laughed, for we did laugh many times and heartily that day, though now this may seem to others and indeed to ourselves almost incredible, seeing what we were about to lose.

"'Well,' the Master went on, 'I will seek to relieve you of this fear. Is it not true that things that are made up of parts are liable to be separated? And is it not also true that the soul is not made up of parts, but is simple and not compounded? Also it is visible things that perish; but the soul is not visible. Again the soul is the ruler, and the body the servant. Is it not true that the divine and immortal rule the human and mortal senses?'

"To this we all agreed.

"The Master began again, for he now, as I may say, had to put before us the conclusion of the whole matter. 'We may think thus, then, may we not? If the soul depart from the body in a state of purity, not taking with it any of the uncleannesses of the body, from which indeed it has kept itself free during life as far as was possible—for this is true philosophy—then it departs into that invisible region which is of its own nature, and being freed from all fears and desires and other evils of mortality, spends the rest of its existence with the gods and the spirits of the good that are like unto itself. But if it depart, polluted and impure, having served the body, and suffered itself to be bewitched by its pleasures and desires, then it cannot attain to this pure and heavenly region, but must abide in some place that is more fitted for it.'

"Much else he said on this point to which we listened as though it were another Orpheus that was singing to us. And when he had ended and sat wrapt in thought, we were silent, fearing to disturb him. And so we remained for no little space of time in silence, he sitting on the bed, as if he neither saw nor heeded any of the things that were about him, and we regarded him most earnestly.

"After a while he woke up, as it were, from his reverie and said, ' You have agreed with me so far ; yet it may be that you have yet fears and doubts in your minds which I have not yet dispersed. If so let me hear them, that I may, if it be possible, rid you of them, for indeed I cannot, as I conceive,

leave behind me a greater gift for you than such a riddance. **Speak** then, if there is anything that you would say.'

"Simmias said—I put, you will perceive, his argument in a **few words:** 'May it not be that the soul is in the body **as a** harmony **is in a** harp? For the harmony is invisible and beautiful and divine, and the harp is visible and material and mortal. Yet when the harp perishes, then the harmony also, of necessity, ceases to be.'

"When Simmias had ended, Cebes began: 'I do indeed believe that the soul is more durable **than** the body. Just so; the wearer is more durable than the thing which he **wears.** Yet at the last, one thing that he weaves proves to be more durable than he. **So** may the soul outlast many bodies, and yet perish finally, worn out, so to speak, by having gone through so many births.'

"Have I put these things rightly, O Simmias and Cebes?" said the young philosopher, addressing them, "though indeed **I** have made them very brief."

"You have put them rightly," the two agreed.

"When we heard these things," Phaedo went on, "we were also greatly disturbed; for we desired to believe that which the Master was seeking to prove, and seemed to have attained certainly, and now we were **thrown** back again into confusion and doubt."

"And how did the Master take it, O Phaedo?" said Callias; **"for indeed** I feel much as you describe yourselves as having **felt.** Having reached a certain hope, not to say conviction, **I am now** disturbed by **fears."**

"Nothing could **be** more admirable than his behavior. That he should be able to answer, was to be expected; but that he should receive these objections so sweetly, so **gently,** and perceiving our **dismay,** quickly encourage us, and, so to **speak,** reform our broken ranks—this indeed was beyond all praise.

"I myself **was** sitting **on a low seat by the side of his** bed. He dropped his hand, and stroked my **head and** the hair which lay upon my neck, I wore it long in those days,* for he was often wont to play with **my hair.   Then** he said, 'I suppose, Phaedo, that you intend **to cut off these** beautiful locks to-morrow, as mourners are wont to do.'

" 'I suppose so,' **I said.**

" 'But you must cut them off to-day and not to-morrow **if** our doctrine be stricken to death, and we cannot bring **it to** life again.' Then he turned to Simmias and Cebes, **and** said, 'Hear **now what I have to say,** but while you hear, think much of the truth but little **of Socrates ; and be on** your guard lest in my eagerness I deceive not myself only but you also, and leave **my sting** behind **me** when **I die** even as does **a bee.** You, Simmias, think that the **soul may** be but as a harmony in the body.   But do you not remember what we said about all knowledge being a remembering, and that what the soul knows it has before learnt?   It existed then before **the** body ; but a harmony cannot exist before the things are put together of which it **proceeds.   Then** again harmony may be more or **less ; but one soul cannot be** more a soul than another.   And **if, as the wise men say,** virtue is harmony and vice **discord, we have a harmony of** a discord, **which cannot be ; finally one part of the soul**

* A young Greek wore his hair long till he reached the age of eighteen. This little detail is a proof of Phaedo's extreme youth at this time.

often opposes another, as reason opposes appetite ; how then is the soul a harmony? You, Cebes, hold, indeed, that **the soul is durable, but may not be immortal.** Hear then my answer. You **believe** that there are ideas or principles **of** things, and that these ideas, being invisible, are **the real** causes of things that are visible.' Cebes acknowledged that he did so believe. 'Is not now the soul the principle of life, and is not this principle the opposite of death? **In** its essence, therefore, it is immortal ; but that which is immortal cannot be destroyed, no, even though there are things **which seem to threaten** its existence.'

"**In this we all agreed.** After this Socrates discoursed in **many words about** the abodes and dwelling-places of the **dead** both **good and bad, and** of the manner in which they **are** dealt with by the **powers** thereunto appointed. But of this I **will speak on some other** occasion, if you will. At **present time is** short, for **I** must not leave the sick man any longer, only I will relate the very end of the Master's discourse and the things that happened after.

"'To affirm positively about such matters,' he said, '**is not the part** of a wise man. Yet what I have said seems reasonable. And anyhow he who has scorned **the** body and **its** pleasures during life, and has adorned **the soul** with **her** proper virtues, justice and courage **and** truth, may **surely** await his passage **to the other world** with a good hope. But **now** destiny calls me, and I must obey. But I will bathe before I take the **poison, that** the women may not have the trouble of washing **my body.**

"Then Crito **asked :** ' Have you any directions to give us?'

"' Nothing now ; **if** you rightly order your own lives. you will do the best for me and my children ; but if you do not, then whatever you may promise, you will fail.'

" ' But,' Crito asked, ' how shall we bury you ? '

" ' As you will,' said he, ' provided only you can catch me and that I do not slip out of your hands.' Then he smiled, and said, ' Crito here will not be persuaded that I am saying the truth.   He thinks that *I* am the dead body that he will soon see here, and asks how he shall bury me.   Assure him then that when this dead body is laid in the grave or put upon the pyre to be burnt it is not Socrates that he sees. For to speak in this way, O Crito, is not only absurd but harmful.'

" After this he bathed, remaining in the bath-chamber for some time. This being ended, his children were brought to him, and the women of his family also. With these he talked awhile in the presence of Crito, and afterward commanded that some one should take the women and children away. And it was now near sunset. Hereupon the servant of the Eleven came in, and said, ' O Socrates, you will not be angry with me and curse me when I tell you, as the magistrates constrained me to do, that you must drink the poison. I have always found you most gentle and generous, the best by far of all that have come into this place. You will be angry, not with me, for you know that I am blameless, but with those whom you know to be in fault. And now, for you know what I am come to tell you, bear what must be borne as cheerfully as may be.' And saying this the man turned away his face and wept.

" ' Farewell !' said Socrates, ' I will do as you bid,' and looking to us he said, ' How courteous he is ! All the time

he has been so, sometimes talking to me, and showing him-
self the best of fellows. And now see how generously he
weeps for me ! But we must do what he says. Let some
one bring the poison, if it has been pounded; **if** not, let the
man pound it.'

"'But,' said Crito, **'the sun is still** upon the mountains. I have known some who would prolong the **day**
eating and drinking till it was quite late before they drank.
Anyhow do not be in **a hurry. There is** still plenty of
time.'

"'Ah!' said **Socrates,** 'these men **were** quite consistent.
They thought that they were gaining so **much** time. But I
too must be consistent. I believe that I shall gain nothing
by dying an hour or two later, except indeed the making of
myself a laughing stock by clinging to life when there is
really nothing left of it to cling to.'

"Then Crito made a sign **to** the slave that was standing
by; he went out, and after some time had passed brought
in the man whose duty it was to give the poison, and who
brought it in ready mixed in a cup. When Socrates caught
sight of him, he said:

"'Well, my friend, you know all **about** these matters.
What must I do?'

"'You will only have to **walk** about after you have drunk
the poison, till **you** feel a sort of weight in your legs. Then
you should lie down, and the poison will do the rest.'

"So saying, he reached the cup to the Master, who took
it. His hand did not shake; there was not the least change
in his color or his look. Only he put his head forward in
the way he had, and said to **the man:**

"'How about making a libation from the cup? May we do it?'

"'Socrates,' said the man, 'we pound just so much as we think sufficient.'

"'I understand,' said the Master. 'Still we may, nay we must, pray to the gods that my removal hence to that place may be fortunate. The gods grant this! Amen!' And as he said this he put the cup to his lips and drank it off in the easiest, quietest way possible.

"Up to that time we had all been fairly well able to keep from tears. But when we saw him drinking the poison, when we knew that he had finished it, we could restrain them no longer. As for myself I covered my face with my mantle, and wept to myself. Not for him did I weep, but for myself, thinking what a friend I had lost. And others were still more overcome than I was. Only Socrates was quite unmoved.

"'Why all this,' he said, 'my dear friends? I sent the women away for this very reason, that they might not vex us in this fashion. I have heard it said that a man ought to die with good words in his ears. Be quiet, I beseech, and bear yourselves like men.'

"When we heard this we were not a little ashamed of ourselves, and kept back our tears. He walked about till he felt the weight in his legs, and then lay down on his back —this was what the man bade him do. Then the man who administered the poison squeezed his foot pretty strongly, and asked him whether he felt anything. He said no. Then the man showed us how the numbness was going higher and higher.

"'When it reaches his heart,' he said, 'he will die.'

"When the groin was cold the Master uncovered his face —for he had covered it before—and said, 'Crito, we owe a cock to Æsculapius ; pay it, do not forget.'

"These were the last words he said.

"'I will,' said Crito, 'is there anything more?'

"But he made no answer. A little time after, we saw him move. Then the man uncovered the face, and we saw that his eyes were set. Then Crito closed his mouth and his eyes."

Phaedo left the room hastily when he had finished his narrative. For some time there was silence. Then Apollodorus spoke.

"You know, my friends," he said, "that I am not very wise nor at all learned ; but he bore with me and my foolishness, and you will also because you know I loved him. Let me say then one thing. Much that Socrates said that day I did not understand, nor do I understand it now when I hear it again. Yet no one could be more fully persuaded than I was that he spoke the truth. And what persuaded me was the sight of the man. So brave was he, so cheerful, so wholly convinced in his own mind, that no one could doubt that he was indeed about to depart to a better place."

CHAPTER XXX.

THE CONDITION OF EXILE.

THE story that Callias had heard of the last days of his
Master, and heard, of course, with many details which it is
now impossible to reproduce, made, it need hardly be said,
a profound impression on him. First and foremost—and
this was what the dead man himself would have been most
rejoiced to see—was the profound conviction that this
teaching, inspired, as it was, with a faith which the immediate prospect of death had not been able to shake, was absolutely true. The young man can hardly be said to have
had any feeling of religion in the sense in which we understand that word. To believe in the fables, grotesque or even
immoral, which made up the popular theology, in gods who
were only exaggerated men, stronger, indeed, but more
cruel, treacherous, and lustful, was an impossibility. The
poets' tales of the Elysian plain and of the abyss of Tartarus
had in no wise helped towards producing any emotions of
the spiritual kind, any wish to dwell in an invisible world.
The most sacred of these poets in his description of that
world as another earth in which everything was feebler, paler,
less satisfying than it is here, had certainly repelled rather
than attracted him. Now this want had been supplied; the
lofty teaching of duty, duty owed to country, kinsfolk,

friends, fellow-citizens, fellow-men, that he had heard from the Master was now supplemented and sanctioned by this clear enunciation of a doctrine of immortality. The young man felt that he could face **the world,** whether **it** brought him prosperity or adversity, **joy** or sorrow, **life** or death, with a more equable soul or more assured spirit than he had ever dreamed could be possible.

His immediate duty, however, was less clear. When his country lay under the heel of the Spartan conqueror, Hermione had pointed out to him—not without sacrifice of herself, as he sometimes could not help feeling, what he owed to the city that had given him **birth. But** now, how did **the case stand?** Athens had suffered a second, a more fatal fall. She might repair her losses; **she** might retrieve **defeat.** But when she had definitely broken with right **and** truth, had deliberately **chosen the** worse rather than **the better, w**hat **hope,** what remedy **was** there? And **what** was the obligation on himself? Could he aspire to a career in a State which **was** so false to all the principles of life and government?

The two or three days that followed **the conversation re**lated in my last chapter were spent **by the young Athenian** in debating with himself the question : **What am I to do?** But the more he thought over the problem, **the more com**plex **and intricate** did it **seem** to **become.** Just when he was beginning **to despair, a** solution, rude and peremptory, but satisfactory in so **far as it** admitted of no questioning, was forced upon him.

He had just risen **on** the morning **of the fourth** day, when **a** visitor **was** announced. It **was Xenophon,**

looking, as Callias thought, serious, **but not depressed.**

"And what have you been doing these three **days?"** cried the newcomer.

"Thinking," replied **Callias.**

"That is exactly what **I** have **been** doing myself, **and I** would wager my chance of being **Archon** next year, **a very** serious stake indeed, **that** we **have** had the same subject for our thoughts. **You have** been debating with yourself what you are to do?"

"Exactly **so; and I am** no nearer a conclusion than I was when I began."

"Well, some one else has been good enough to save us the trouble of deciding. Listen to this. I have a friend in **office, I should tell you,** and **he has given me** an early copy of **what will be soon** known all **over** Athens. 'It is proposed **by Erasinides, son of Lysias, of the** township of Colonus, that Xenophon, **son** of Grythus, of the township **of Orchia,** and Callias, **son of Hipponicus,** of the township **of Eleusis,'** and **some twenty others, whose names** I need not trouble **you** with, 'be **banished from Athens** for unpatriotic con- duct, especially in **aiding and abetting the** designs of Cyrus, **who** was a notorious enemy **of the Athenian people.' Well; that** is going to be proposed **to the Senate to-day. My friend,** who knows all about the strings, and how they are pulled, tells me that it **is certain to** be carried. **In the course of a few days it** will be brought **before the Assembly,** and **I have no doubt whatever that it will be accepted."**

"**But** what have the Athenian people got to do with Cyrus, **who is** dead and gone, and can **neither help nor** hurt?"

"**Ah!** you **don't understand.** The Lacedaemonians, you

know, have declared war against the Persian King. Of course that gives the Athenians a chance of becoming his friends. It is true that things are not ripe just yet for anything decisive or public. We are allies with the Lacedaemonians, and can't venture to quarrel with them. But this is a matter at which they cannot take offence, but which will most certainly please the Great King. He has not forgotten the Cyrus business, you may depend upon it, and it will delight him to hear of any who had a part in it suffering for their act. That is why we are to be banished. It is disgraceful, I allow, to find a great city banishing its citizens in order to curry favor with the barbarians; but it is a fact, and we must take it into account."

"And what shall you do?"

"I shall go to Asia. I had intended to go in any case, for I have private affairs there, nothing less important, I may tell you in confidence, than marrying a wife. Then I shall find something to do with the Spartans, among whom I have some very good friends. Come with me. You too, might find a wife; that will be as you please; but anyhow I can guarantee you employment."

"I confess," said Callias, after meditating awhile, "that I do not feel greatly drawn by what you suggest. As for the wife, that prospect does not please me at all; and, as you know, I am not so much of a Spartan-lover* as you.

---

* The Greek *philo-lacon.* The word had been applied to Cimon, son of Miltiades, who had always been a popular statesman and so might be used in a friendly way. If Callias had spoken of Xenophon as disposed to *laconismus* it would have been almost an affront, this word meaning not so much admiration of Spartan ways of life as devotion to Spartan interests.

You must let me think about it; you shall have a final answer to-morrow."

When Xenophon had taken leave, Callias went straight to Hippocles, and happened to arrive just as a messenger was leaving the house with a note addressed to himself, and asking for an early visit. Callias related what he had just heard from Xenophon.

"You do not surprise me. In fact I also have had a private intimation from a member of the Senate that this is going to be done, and it is exactly the matter about which I wished to see you. But tell me, what does Xenophon advise?"

Callias told him.

"And you hesitate about accepting his offer?"

"Yes; I do more than hesitate; I feel more and more averse to it the more I think of it."

"You are right; to take service with the Spartans must, almost of necessity, mean, sooner or later, some collision with your own country. It was this that ruined Alcibiades. If he could only have had patience, he could have saved himself and the Athenians too, but that visit to Sparta ruined both. No; I should advise you against Xenophon's suggestion."

"But where am I to go? I have thought of Syracuse. But I do not care to go back to Dionysius. He was all courtesy and kindness; but I felt suffocated in the air of his court. And we never feel quite safe with a tyrant."

"I have thought of something else that might suit you. I am going to start in a few days' time on a visit to my own native country, not to Poseidonia—I could not bear to see the barbarians masters there—but to **Italy.** There are other Greek cities which still hold their **own,** and **they are well** worth seeing. You might, too, if you choose, pay another visit to Rome. You will **at** least have the advantage of being out of this dismal round **of** strife **to** which **Greece** itself seems doomed. Our countrymen there have, I know, faults of their own ; but they do contrive to live on tolerably good terms with each other."

The plan proposed seemed to **Callias** to promise **better than** any that he could think of and he accepted the offer with thankfulness. **A** few days afterwards he was gazing for what he felt might well be the last **time** at the city **of** his birth. Bathed in the sunshine **of a summer morning** stood the Acropolis, crowned with its marble temples, and, **towering** above all, the gigantic statue of Athene the **Champion,** her **outstretched spear-point** flashing in the light. What glories he was leaving behind him ! What lost hopes, what unfulfilled aspirations of his own ! The tears of no unmanly emotion were in his eyes as he turned away, but not before he had caught sight of a well-known house by **the** harbor **of** Piraeus. This seemed to be the **last** drop of bitterness in his cup. She had lost **him for his** country's sake, and now he had lost her, **too.** He turned and found himself face to face with Hermione ! **There** was something in **her look** which **made his heart thrill;** but she did not give him time to speak.

"Callias," she said, "you gave up what you said **was** dear to **me,**" and her blush deepened as she spoke, "for Athens' sake. **But now—if** you have not forgotten—"

He needed to hear no **more. The** next moment, careless of the eyes of the old helmsman, he had clasped her in his arms.

"I can allow myself to love the exile," she whispered in his ear.

Author's Postscript.

It is impossible for the writer of historical fiction, especially if he wishes to suggest to his readers as many subjects of interest as possible, to adapt the literary necessities of his work to fit in with the actual course of events. But he is bound to point out such departures from historical accuracy as he feels constrained to make. It is quite possible that a correction may serve to impress the real facts upon his readers more deeply than an originally accurate statement would have done. I therefore append to my tale a list of

CORRIGENDA.

1. I was anxious to include the Battle of Arginusæ in my story. It was the first scene in the last act of the great drama of the Peloponnesian war. At the same time I felt bound, having made up my mind to give a description of a Greek comedy, to choose the *Frogs*. It has a literary interest such as no other Aristophanic play possesses, and it is at once more important and more intelligible to a modern reader. But to bring the two things together it was necessary to ante-date the representation of the play. I have put it in the year 406 B. C. It really took place in 405. I have also made the battle happen somewhat earlier than in all probability it really did. The festival of the Great Dionysia, at which new plays were produced, was celebrated in March. We do not know precisely the date of Arginusæ, but it is

likely that it was later **in the year.** **A** similar correction must be made about **the** embassy **of** Dionysius. **It may** have taken place when the **play** was really produced, but in 406 Dionysius **was too busy** with **his** war with Carthage **to** think of such things.

2. I have ante-dated, **this time by** several **years, the capture** of Poseidonia by the native **Italians. Here again we** have no record of the precise **time ; but it probably happened** somewhat later in the century.

3. **I do not** know whether **I am wrong in** making **Alcibi**ades escape **from his castle in Thrace immediately after the** battle **Ægos Potami. Plutarch** would **give one** rather **to understand that he fled after the capture of** Athens. **It is quite** possible, **however, that he** recognized the defeat as fatal to Athenian **influence of the** Thracian coast, and that **feeling his own position to be no longer** tenable, **he retired** from it at once.

4. I have taken some liberties with the text of Xenophon's **narrative.** The trial of the generals **by their own soldiers,** the athletic **sports,** and **the** entertainment described **in my** story are all **taken from the** *Anabasis,* but they do **not come** so close together **as I have found it** convenient to put them.

5. It is a moot point among historians **whether Xeno**phon returned to **Athens after he had quitted the Ten** Thousand. **Mr. Grote thinks that he did ; and his authority** is perhaps **sufficient** to shelter **such a humble person as my**self. It has **also been debated whether he was banished in** 399 or some **years later. I am inclined to think that here I am accurate.**

6. **I need** hardly say that the **Thracian** national song is

of my **own** invention. Xenophon simply says that the Thracian performers went off the stage singing the "Sitalces." **That** this was a song celebrating the achievement of the king of that name (for which see a classical dictionary) cannot be doubted.   But we know nothing more about **it,** and I have supplied the words.

7.   It is not necessary to say that the "diary" of Callias is an invention.   To be quite candid I do not **think it was** at all likely that a **young soldier** would have kept one, or even been able to write it up daily.   **But** I wanted to **give some** prominent incidents from Xenophon's story, and had not space for **the whole,** while a mere epitome would have been tedious.

8.   I must caution my readers against supposing my hero **to be historical.**   There was a Callias, son of Hipponicus, at this time, a very different man.

9. **I have** taken the defence **of** Socrates from Plato's *Apology*, not from Xenophon.   **The** former is immeasurably superior.

INDEX.